Praise for

JASMINE CRESSWELL

and

B.J. DANIELS

"Cresswell delivers a sexy, romantic suspense story with a subtle sense of humor, a pace that doesn't let up, and characters who make you care."
—*Library Journal*

"...the talented B.J. Daniels does a great job blending past and present storytelling, which results in an exciting read."
—*Romantic Times*

"[Cresswell's books are] romantic suspense at its finest."
—*Affaire de Coeur*

"B.J. Daniels sets a truly intriguing scene."
—*Romantic Times*

"Ms. Cresswell masterfully creates a full, rich story with characters who will touch your heart. She drops clues skillfully, unwinding the tale piece by piece in such a way as to capture readers from the very first."
—*Romantic Times*

VEILS OF DECEIT

JASMINE CRESSWELL

is the multitalented author of over forty novels. She has won numerous awards, including the RWA's Golden Rose Award and the Colorado Author's League award for best original paperback novel. Born in Wales and educated in England, Jasmine has lived in Australia, Canada and six cities in the United States. The parents of four grown children, she and her husband now make their home in Sarasota, Florida.

B.J. DANIELS

A former award-winning journalist, B.J. Daniels is the author of thirty-seven short stories and fourteen novels. Many of her books are set in Montana, where she lives with her husband; two springer spaniels, Zoey and Scout; and a temperamental tomcat named Jeff. When not writing, she enjoys reading, camping and fishing, and snowboarding.

VEILS OF DECEIT

JASMINE CRESSWELL

B.J. DANIELS

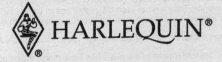

HARLEQUIN®

TORONTO • NEW YORK • LONDON
AMSTERDAM • PARIS • SYDNEY • HAMBURG
STOCKHOLM • ATHENS • TOKYO • MILAN • MADRID
PRAGUE • WARSAW • BUDAPEST • AUCKLAND

ISBN 0-373-83550-7

VEILS OF DECEIT

Copyright © 2003 by Harlequin Books S.A.

The publisher acknowledges the copyright holders
of the individual works as follows:

FREE FALL
Copyright © 1989 by Jasmine Cresswell.

KEEPING SECRETS
Copyright © 2003 by B.J. Daniels.

Visit us at www.eHarlequin.com

Printed in U.S.A.

CONTENTS

FREE FALL

Jasmine Cresswell

CHAPTER ONE

LIZ SAW THE CROWD outside her apartment building as soon as she turned the corner from the bus stop. Her mouth went dry and her stomach lurched in horrified recognition. Her hands cradled her waist.

"Oh no! Please, no!"

She wasn't sure if she spoke aloud. Blood drummed in her ears, cutting off sound. Inside her silent world, the lights of the squad cars flashed with hypnotic brilliance, glazing the falling snow with orange glitter. One, two, three. Three whirling lights. Three blue-and-white Denver police cars.

Last time, in Seattle, they'd only sent two.

Liz read the neat copperplate inscription on the door of the car nearest her: To Serve and Protect. A great motto, much favored by police departments. It looked so much better than To Harass and Intimidate.

Her gaze raced feverishly over the neon-lit scene. Two dozen spectators, three squad cars, a half-dozen cops—but no ambulance.

No ambulance, and no paramedics. Hope flared briefly. Maybe this time there never had been an ambulance. Maybe the police were here to investigate a burglary. Liz started running.

She saw the chalk outline on the pavement as soon as she'd elbowed her way through the crowd. The spring snow wasn't settling, and the chalk shone white and clean in the evening darkness, a wet gingerbread figure sketched on asphalt. A child's drawing, except for the blood.

Fear clawed at her throat. Liz swayed, grasping the police barricade for support. Dear God, it had happened again.

"You sure missed a horrible sight," commented the woman next to her. "They only moved the body ten minutes ago. The side of her face was smashed right in from where she fell. Terrible tragedy." The conventional words of grief didn't succeed in masking the relish in the woman's voice.

Liz fought to control the sickness welling up inside her. "Was it a young wo—? Do they know who it was?"

"A girl from one of the apartments. Look, you can see the open window up there on the top floor. That's where she fell from. Or jumped."

Liz didn't look up; she didn't need to. Her stomach gave another warning heave, and she pushed through the barricade, barely making it to the corner of her apartment building before she vomited.

When she finally stopped retching, she straightened to discover herself surrounded by three uniformed police officers. One of them—a sergeant—held out a wad of tissues. She wiped her mouth. The policemen watched, their eyes hard.

"The victim a friend of yours, Miss?" The inquiry was polite but cold.

"Maybe.... I think so.... I don't know.... I live here."

"Terrible for you to come home to all this." The sergeant's voice had warmed, now that he knew she wasn't just an overcurious bystander with a weak stomach. "Which apartment is yours? I'll see that the officer guarding the entrance lets you in."

She glanced up, finally allowing herself to look at the open window, a big bay in the center of the sixth floor. It was hers, of course. Hers and Karen Zeit's. She had known all along that it would be.

"I live in 6B," she said flatly, returning her gaze to the ball of soiled tissues.

She felt the policemen exchange glances. She closed her eyes, shoving the tissues into the pocket of her jacket and wrapping her arms more tightly around her body. She was shivering, she realized, and the little clicking noise resonating inside her head had to be the chattering of her teeth.

"You'd better come along inside and get warm."

She forced herself to look at the sergeant. "What's happened to Karen?"

"There's been an accident," he replied, his voice gruff. His two younger colleagues shuffled their feet and stared over her shoulder. They were worried, poor things. Worried about how a law-abiding citizen was going to take this shocking intrusion of violence into her life. It wasn't true that cops had no emotions. Liz had found that out in Seattle. The first time, when Brian died, they'd all been very sympathetic.

This time, once they knew the truth, they weren't likely to waste much time on sympathy. Some bright-eyed cop, eager for promotion, would check with the authorities in Seattle, and Liz would instantaneously be transformed from victim into suspect. Being a suspect was no fun at all. She'd found that out when Jill killed herself, only four short weeks after Brian.

She needed to know the worst about Karen, to have the horror confirmed. "Is my roommate dead?" she asked brusquely.

The sergeant made soothing noises, avoiding her eyes. He put a hand beneath her elbow, guiding her toward the rear entrance of the apartment building. "I think we should talk about this inside, where it's a bit warmer. Lousy weather for May, isn't it? But that's Denver for you. Swimsuit temperatures one day and a blizzard the next. If you'll follow me, I'll ask the apartment manager to make you a cup of coffee."

Liz allowed herself to be led in through the service lobby and down to the basement where the superintendent had his apartment. She sat meekly at the appointed table and waited in silence while one of the policemen brought her a cup of coffee.

Dear God, Karen is dead. Dead. The awful word echoed in a bleak rhythm with her chattering teeth.

The policemen didn't ask how she wanted her coffee served, and presented it already laced with milk and sugar. The oily liquid tasted revolting enough to jerk her into renewed awareness of her surroundings. The sergeant had disappeared, to be replaced by a tall man, wearing a raincoat that was a fraction too tight. A homicide detective: she'd learned to recognize the breed. She wondered how long he'd been standing on the other side of the Formica-topped table, staring at her.

"I'm Lieutenant Rodriguez," he said, flashing a badge and a small smile. Three months ago, she would have found the smile reassuring. Now she knew better. She blinked her eyelids, the only part of her that seemed capable of movement.

"I'm sorry you had to find out about your roommate this way."

"She's dead," Liz said flatly. "Isn't she?"

"I'm afraid so. If it's any consolation, Miss Meacham, I'm sure your roommate died instantly."

Instantly. Ten seconds after she hit the ground? Twenty? A minute? Liz blinked again, then glanced at the lieutenant. He doesn't look Hispanic, she thought. She stirred her mud-gray coffee, wondering how he knew her name. Perhaps the superintendent had told him. She could have asked, but it was too difficult to form the question. Shock always seemed to reduce her brain to a scattershot incoherence of half thoughts. Maybe she should carry a sign: Sharing an Apartment with Liz Meacham is Terminally Hazardous to Your Health. Horrifyingly, she found that she wanted to laugh.

She took another sip of coffee, swallowing the

laughter along with the disgusting brew. The lieutenant's chair scraped over the thin carpet as he sat
down. Gradually she became aware of the acrid
smell of stale cigarette smoke. Her senses, numb
ever since she turned the corner from the bus stop,
were beginning to function once again. The cigarette
smoke, now that she could smell it, made her stomach roil. All in all, it might have been better if her
body had stayed numb.

"There's a few questions I need to ask you, Miss
Meacham. I'm sorry, but there's nobody else we can
ask."

Liz avoided the lieutenant's eyes. She stared into
the kitchen, where she could see the police sergeant
talking on the phone. The apartment manager was
at the sink, filling his percolator. She shuddered,
then dragged her gaze back to the lieutenant.

"Have you told Karen's parents yet? They live
somewhere near Detroit, in one of the suburbs. I
guess their phone number is on the bulletin board in
Karen's bedroom."

"We found it, and we're working on notifying
the parents. Have you shared an apartment with the
deceased for long, Miss Meacham?"

The deceased. Karen probably hadn't been dead
more than a couple of hours, and already she had
been transformed from a human being to an item of
official jargon. Liz wished she could switch off her
awareness of Karen's humanity as easily as the detective. She ran her index finger around the rim of
her mug. "I moved in with Karen six weeks ago."

"I see. And did you know her before that, Miss Meacham?"

"No. I only moved to Denver recently." Liz spoke rapidly, giving the lieutenant no time to interject awkward questions. "I met Karen at a party a couple of days after I arrived in town. She was looking for a roommate, and I was looking for somewhere to live. We were glad to find each other."

The lieutenant wrote painstakingly in his notebook. Unlike TV cops, who never seemed to take notes about anything, Liz had learned that real-life policemen wrote everything down. The lieutenant turned the page. Did it take that long to write "Deceased met roommate at a party"?

"Just for the record, Miss Meacham, would you tell us where you lived before you moved in with the deceased?"

Liz's fingers closed around her mug. So there it was, the question she had been dreading. The innocuous-sounding question she had known would come up sooner or later. She wished it hadn't come up quite so soon.

She cleared her throat. "I lived in Seattle."

Lieutenant Rodriguez was not a fool. He obviously heard the tension in her voice, although she'd tried hard to smooth it out. Damn it, she wasn't responsible for Karen's decision to jump out of their apartment window. She wasn't some freakish, latter-day version of Typhoid Mary. Despite what had happened to Brian and then to Jill, the rational part of Liz's brain still insisted that suicide was one of the few deadly diseases you couldn't catch from your roommate.

"Seattle is a big city, Miss Meacham. Could we have an address, please? Just for the record, of course."

Of course, she thought with silent irony. Nevertheless, she gave him what he was asking for. "755 West Arbor Avenue. Apartment 14D."

Jill's address. No point in saying she'd lived there less than a month before Jill had been found splattered on the pavement outside their living-room window. No point in explaining that Brian had committed suicide a month before Liz moved in with Jill. On the other hand, there was no point in lying. Her name alone would be enough to pull up all the facts on the Seattle police computers.

"Do you know where the deceased was employed, Miss Meacham?"

She should have been more alert to Karen's moods, Liz berated herself. Karen had seemed uptight these past few days, ever since Liz had returned from Mexico. But Liz had deliberately refrained from inquiring, deliberately kept her distance. Since Brian died, she hadn't wanted too much emotional closeness—

"Miss Meacham?"

With considerable effort, Liz focused her attention on the detective. "I'm sorry, I didn't hear your question."

"The deceased, Karen Zeit. Do you know where she was employed?"

"She worked for Dexter Rand. She was the senior secretary in his Denver office."

Lieutenant Rodriguez finally showed a degree of surprise. "Dexter Rand? You mean the senator?"

"Yes." Liz didn't—couldn't—elaborate on the stark response.

"Oh, brother, the media are going to love this," the lieutenant muttered under his breath, scribbling in his notebook. "Was the deceased interested in politics?"

"Not that I know of. I think she just enjoyed the hectic pace of Dexter's office."

Something in her voice must have betrayed her. Or perhaps it was her slip in using Dexter's first name. The lieutenant looked up quickly. "Nothing personal in their relationship?"

"Not that I know of."

"Would you have known?"

The look Liz gave him was cool. "Probably not."

The lieutenant changed the subject. "And you, Miss Meacham? Where do you work?"

"I'm in charge of market research at Peperito's. You probably know them. They're headquartered near the airport."

"Peperito's? The Mexican-food company?"

"Yes."

The lieutenant smiled, a genuine smile this time. "My wife always buys their *salsa*. She says it's the best."

"Thanks. We really work hard to keep up the quality. We import all the spices from Mexico."

"Is that so?" The lieutenant flipped through his notes, his moment of informality over. "Well, back to the matter at hand. Did the deceased give any indication that she was depressed, Miss Meacham? Did she have any reason to take her own life? Any arguments with men friends...colleagues...the senator...that sort of thing?"

"I don't know much about Karen's personal life," Liz said. "I travel a lot with my job and I don't suppose Karen and I spent ten evenings together in six weeks. I just came back from an extended business trip to Mexico."

"Is that why you shared an apartment, because of the travel? You and Miss Zeit could both have afforded your own place, I guess. Rents in Denver aren't that high."

"It was one of the reasons. I need to keep expenses down. My mother's in a private nursing home." Liz clasped her hands on the table and stared at her thumbs. Her nail polish was chipped, she realized. Karen would never have left the office with chipped nail polish. Karen had been the most immaculately groomed woman Liz had ever met.

Too immaculate to contemplate ending her life smashed to smithereens on a driveway overlooked by two large trash Dumpsters.

The thought sprang unbidden to the forefront of Liz's mind, then lodged there, obstinately refusing to go away. "Are you sure it was suicide?" she asked the lieutenant. "Couldn't it have been an accident or—or something?"

Why in the world had she said that? Good God, was she actually trying to suggest to the police that Karen's death might not be suicide? Hadn't she had enough trouble as a murder suspect in Seattle? Liz clamped her lips tightly shut, before she could make any more disastrous suggestions.

Rodriguez, thank heaven, didn't pick up on any undertones to her question. He shrugged. "An accident's not likely. There's a kitchen chair pulled up to the living-room window and an open bottle of Scotch standing next to the chair. The bathroom sink has aspirin spilled into it. I guess she might have taken aspirin for a headache, then decided to clean the windows and drink neat Scotch at the same time." The lieutenant's tone suggested that after several years on the city police force, he'd learned to accept any act of human folly as possible. "I'd say everything points to a straightforward suicide, except she didn't leave a note, and suicides usually do. The autopsy will tell us more."

Brian and Jill hadn't left notes, either. Brian had shot himself in front of an open window. Then, four scant weeks later, Jill had filled herself with prescription tranquilizers and pushed herself out head-first from the fourteenth floor of their Seattle apartment. How many more variations could be worked on the theme of suicide victims spread-eagled on the sidewalk?

Three bloody, crumpled blobs, waiting to greet Liz, waiting to torment her with the knowledge that she had been totally insensitive to their problems, totally insensitive to the edge of desperation that must have crept into their lives.

Unless they hadn't committed suicide.

Brian's suicide had seemed tragic but within the bounds of possibility, given his recurring black moods. Jill's suicide a few weeks later had seemed a terrible, malignant coincidence. But Karen's suicide strained the limits of Liz's credulity. Three roommates tumbling to their deaths within three months just didn't make any kind of sense.

Unless they had been murdered.

Liz sprang up from the table, hearing her chair crash behind her as she groped blindly toward the bathroom. She stumbled into a closet and a bedroom before she found the right door. The light was on. The room was empty. She leaned over the sink and turned on the hot water full force. She heaved for a few seconds but, thank God, she didn't throw up. Her stomach had nothing left to vomit except two sips of coffee.

She was still sluicing her cheeks in zombielike repetition when the lieutenant appeared in the doorway.

"Feeling better?" he asked.

Liz raised her head from the sink. "I feel one hundred percent lousy."

"We'd like to ask a few more questions."

"No." She shook her head. The police were going to find out about her past sooner or later, but tonight she was too tired and too scared to face up to any more of Lieutenant Rodriguez. "I want to go to a hotel," she said abruptly.

"If you wait another half hour until the technicians have finished upstairs, you can go into your apartment and pack a suitcase."

"I don't want to go into my apartment." Liz fought to keep her voice calm. "I can't hang around any longer. I'll buy a toothbrush at the drugstore. I want to get out of here, Lieutenant. Now."

Surprisingly, he didn't protest. Perhaps he was afraid she might faint, bang her head on the tile floor and then sue the city for harassment. God knows, and she knew, having glimpsed herself in the bathroom mirror, she looked rotten enough to give anybody cause for alarm. She'd lost weight steadily since Brian died, and she'd begun to appear skeletal even with makeup on and her clothes in order. Tonight, with every trace of color drained from her face, she looked like a death's-head.

Liz pushed her way out of the bathroom, ignoring a final question from the lieutenant. She grabbed her purse from the table as she passed by. "I'll be in the airport Hilton," she said tersely, knowing Rodriguez had no grounds to detain her. Not yet. Not until he contacted his counterparts in Seattle. Then Lieutenant Rodriguez was going to start asking himself how many coincidences he wanted to believe. How many dead roommates could a law-abiding citizen explain away?

"Do you need a ride, Miss Meacham?"

"No thanks. My car's right in the parking lot. I

took the bus this morning because the roads were so icy, but it's not freezing anymore.''

"Still, you want to drive carefully, Miss Meacham. We don't need any more accidents tonight.''

Liz smiled bitterly. "I don't seem accident-prone, Lieutenant. At least not personally.''

"You're lucky,'' Rodriguez said, but she felt his gaze follow her as she left the room.

CHAPTER TWO

THE TRAFFIC LIGHT flicked from amber to red and Liz drew her Honda to an obedient halt. When the light turned green thirty seconds later, she gazed at it blankly until the irate honking of several horns reminded her that green meant Go.

But go where? She drove across the intersection and stared into the darkness, trying to discover where she was. Alameda Avenue, according to the signpost. Alameda, heading west toward the mountains.

How did I end up here? she wondered. Her mind felt thick and slow-moving, and her hands sat clumsily on the steering wheel, alien attachments at the end of her arms. The simple act of guiding the car through traffic demanded intense concentration. She'd intended to drive straight to the airport Hilton. Instead, here she was on the fringe of some of Denver's most prestigious real estate. The Denver Country Club was only a few blocks away. The Polo Club was even closer.

So was Dexter Rand's Denver home.

The thought came and went without making any particular impact. Liz waited at another traffic light, then turned left. Dexter's house loomed ahead of her at the end of the cul-de-sac. With a shiver of anticipation, she recognized that she'd intended to drive here all along.

She parked the car against the only free stretch of sidewalk and stared at the high brick wall surrounding Dexter's home. As if offering her a welcome, the lights from the upper windows gleamed through the dark evergreens that lined the driveway. Liz grimaced. A false impression, if ever she'd seen one.

The house was a handsome brick-and-timber affair, vaguely Tudor in style, with a spectacular yard designed for summer entertaining. Liz knew all this because she'd tempted fate once before, dropping Karen off for work one morning. But she wasn't sure why she had come here, tonight of all nights, or what she expected to accomplish. Dexter Rand was the last man in the world she wanted to ask for help or comfort.

I'll tell him about Karen before the police get to him. Maybe I owe him that much.

That simple decision exhausted Liz's mental capabilities. She got out of the car, locked it and pocketed the keys, feeling vaguely pleased that she hadn't done something dumb like leaving them in the ignition.

She wrapped her woolly scarf around her chin to shut out the biting wind, and walked up the driveway. *I'll just tell him about Karen, nothing more,* she reassured herself, listening to her boots crunch on the icy path. *I won't mention Seattle, or murder,* or anything like that. She needed to formulate her thoughts into simple instructions, or she knew her control would vanish into a shapeless fog of fear.

She rang the bell. A maid opened the door, and a muted babble of voices and laughter greeted Liz as soon as she stepped inside. Her heart sank. Of course! Dexter was giving a party. That was the reason for the welcoming lights and for all the cars parked along Pinewood Road. She should have recognized the signs. Dexter Rand, national hero, U.S. senator, former Air Force test pilot, and all-around important person, never came home from Washington without entertaining. His house was probably crammed with local VIPs, not to mention aspiring VIPs and the inevitable hangers-on who came for the free cocktails. It had been crazy to drive over here. It had been even crazier to imagine she'd actually get to talk privately with Dexter.

"Good evening, ma'am. May I take your coat?"

Liz blinked and stared at the maid. Her coat. The maid expected her to stay and socialize. It was really funny, if you stopped to think about it.

"Er...no, thanks," Liz mumbled. "I don't think I'm staying." She attempted a smile. "I'm sorry. Wrong party."

Her smile was not much of a success. The maid's welcoming glance faded into a look of downright suspicion, and she glanced over her shoulder, obviously searching for a security guard, or at least a hefty male waiter. Liz didn't want to be thrown out.

She turned to go, fumbling for the handle of the front door.

A sudden tension at the base of her spine caused her to look over her shoulder, so that she and the maid saw Dexter at almost the same moment. The maid greeted him with evident relief. Liz stared at him in numb silence. All she could think of was that he looked even better in real life than he did on television. His six-feet-two-inch body was still perfectly proportioned, and his dark, coarse hair remained indecently thick, with no more than the occasional thread of gray to mark the passing of the last nine years. On him, even the crow's-feet around his eyes looked good. She wished he'd gone bald or developed a beer belly. Except, of course, that Dexter Rand never drank anything as plebeian as beer.

"This young lady was just leaving," the maid said.

"But not before I've had a chance to say hello, I hope...." Dexter's professionally warm voice trailed away into stunned silence. "Liz?" he asked hoarsely. "Liz, what in the world are you doing here?"

"Karen's dead."

She hadn't meant to drop the news with such a devastating lack of finesse. If she had been in full control of her actions, she would never have come near Dexter Rand. They had successfully avoided each other for nine years, and this was hardly the ideal time to choose for a reunion.

"Karen? You mean Karen Zeit, my secretary?

What in the world happened?'' For a moment, but only for a moment, Dexter looked blank. Then his usual capacity for quick thinking under pressure reasserted itself. It was a skill that had made him invaluable as a test pilot. Liz had seen him use it to even greater effect when facing inquisitive reporters on the Hill. Whatever he was feeling, Liz knew he would reveal none of it.

"This is terrible news," he said, his voice tinged with just the right amount of sorrow. "A terrible shock, too. Karen seemed so healthy when she left here this afternoon. Was it…? It must have been a car accident?"

The old, destructive desire to prick Dexter's damnable self-control stirred among the debris of Liz's emotions. She spoke without giving herself time for second thoughts. "No, not a car accident. They found her dead on the sidewalk outside her apartment building. The police think she jumped."

"She killed herself? Oh, my God!" For an instant Liz saw stark horror in Dexter's eyes, then he reached out and drew her farther into the foyer, away from the front door. Control once again masked his expression.

"Poor Karen," Dexter said. "I'm sorry, so very sorry. I knew something was on her mind, and now I'm kicking myself for missing the signs that things were getting desperate." His gaze flicked over the name printed on the maid's fancy apron. "Gwen, could you help us out by finding Evan Howard, and asking him to come to my study as soon as possible?''

"I would, sir, but I don't know what Mr. Howard looks like."

"Blond, short, thirtyish. Slender build. Anybody on my staff can point him out to you."

"Certainly, sir. I'll find him right away. You want him in your study, you said?''

Dexter nodded, and Gwen, seeming reassured by Dexter's calm, take-charge tone of voice, walked off briskly in the direction of the main reception rooms. Liz wanted to mock the maid for being so gullible, so susceptible to Dexter's aura of control, but she couldn't. Why had she herself come here, if not to let Dexter take charge? In the last resort, wasn't that what she'd always wanted Dexter to do? Hadn't she always expected him to walk behind her, picking up the disorganized pieces of her life and rearranging them into some neat new pattern?

The thought was shocking in its novel perception of their relationship, and she shoved it angrily aside. Good grief, she must be closer to the edge than she'd realized if she was actually finding excuses for Dexter. Dexter, the inhuman superachiever. The man had exploited her from the day they first met.

"Let go of my arm," she said through her teeth. The anger felt good. Much better than the numb fear that had preceded it. "I'm leaving, Dexter."

"No, you're not. We need to talk." He gave a passing guest one of his patented thousand-watt smiles, slipped his arm around Liz's waist, and propelled her with iron force through the foyer, skillfully eluding the half-dozen people who tried to engage him in conversation. He finally stopped at a heavy oaken door and punched an electronic key code into the pad above the lock. He opened the door and stood back to let Liz pass. His manners always had been impeccable, she thought with a twist of irony. That was only one of the reasons she had found their constant fights so unendurable. She had screamed and yelled like a demented banshee, while Dexter politely—condescendingly—explained the error of her ways.

Even the distant memory of those painful times was enough to make Liz boil inside, a vulnerable nineteen-year-old again instead of a mature woman approaching thirty. She glanced around the room in an effort to calm her unruly emotions.

For anybody who knew Dexter well, the study contained few surprises. The room looked almost the same as the study Dexter had furnished in their Frankfurt apartment: comfortable and efficient, without any particular hint of luxury. The money in Dexter's family had been rattling around so long, he never felt any need to remind people that he had it. Nothing of the nouveau riche about good old Dex. Liz watched, fighting an unwelcome sensation of being transported back in time, as he opened a concealed cupboard in the paneling and revealed a small bar. He poured two brandies.

"Here," he said, offering one to Liz. "I need this, even if you don't."

"I don't drink in a crisis," she said, finally managing to look straight at him. "I learned not to."

He grinned, damn him, his gray eyes cruelly mocking. "Good lesson," he said, downing his own brandy in a single swallow. "You must've had a smart teacher."

"Experience. The best one of all."

For a split second, she felt the tension arc between them, and she knew her words had gotten to him. But when he turned around from the bar he displayed no emotion other than polite concern. He wasn't about to rehash old arguments, a fact for which she ought to be grateful.

"Let's sit down," he said, gesturing toward the sofa. "Damn it, I still can't believe she's dead! We spent two hours together this afternoon going over a speech, and she didn't give a hint of being desperate enough to walk out of here and kill herself. What happened?"

"The police think she threw herself out of the living-room window. I guess she must have...done it...right after she got home from work."

Dexter's eyes were shadowed with pain and a hint of some other emotion Liz couldn't identify. "That's terrible, almost unbelievable." He frowned. "Maybe I just don't want to believe it because I feel so guilty. How could she sit and chat about her plans for the weekend, when she intended to do this to herself a couple of hours later? How could I have missed all her signals of despair? Hell, she must have given me a dozen of them, if I'd been looking."

"Maybe not. Maybe something happened after she got home. A devastating phone call or something."

"I sure would like to think so." Dexter looked up, a new question obviously occurring to him. "How do you know all this, Liz? Come to think of that, how did you know Karen? She never mentioned your name to me."

Liz avoided his eyes. "She was—my roommate."

"You were sharing an apartment with my personal secretary?"

"Yes. Is that illegal or something?"

The pause before he replied was almost undetectable. "Not illegal. Surprising. Did she know about—us?"

"No."

"Odd that she never spoke about you."

"We'd been sharing the apartment less than two months. She probably had no reason to mention me. Why would she?"

He shrugged. "Things like that usually come up in conversation, although Karen never did talk much about her friends."

"I wasn't a friend, only a roommate. We didn't know each other at all well."

She spoke with more vehemence than the subject demanded, and Dexter scrutinized her intently for a moment before taking another sip of brandy. From his perspective, it must be hard to believe that Liz hadn't anticipated a meeting between the two of them from the moment she moved in with Karen. With an unwelcome flash of self-knowledge, Liz realized he was right to be suspicious. At some deeply buried level of her subconscious she had known that living with Karen would eventually bring her smack into the middle of Dexter's orbit. Thankfully, he asked her another question before she had time to pursue this uncomfortable new insight.

"What are you doing here in Denver, Liz? When we parted company, I didn't think anything would tear you away from life in the Big Apple."

If only he knew, Liz thought ruefully. If only he knew how grateful she'd been five years ago to find an obscure job in an obscure corner of southern Ohio. Better that he should never know. Pride made a great substitute for other emotions. She smiled brightly.

"It was tough leaving New York, but you know what companies are like these days. If you want a promotion, you have to be prepared to relocate, and I was tired of the entertainment industry."

"Why didn't you go back to skating, not even to teach?"

She pushed her fingers through her hair, her smile brighter than ever. "I doubt if anyone on the Olympic team would have me, and I'm not interested in anything else. There's nothing more pathetic than a second-rate athlete trying to eke out a living on the fringes of the sports world."

"You aren't a second-rate athlete, Liz, and we

both know it. You went to pieces during that last championship, although God knows why. No skater spends years in training and then walks out onto the ice for an Olympic contest with her mind obviously elsewhere. I've always suspected your sister had something to do with it.''

"Alison?" He was so far off the mark that it was almost funny. "Poor Alison. You never did like her, did you?"

"The fact that she was your twin didn't make her your friend, Liz. You never would understand that simple fact."

Liz laughed harshly. "Funny thing," she said. "Nine years and nothing changes. Isn't this about where our last conversation ended?"

Dexter stared into his empty glass. "You're right, and this isn't the moment for hashing over the past. We should be thinking about Karen. Did you discover…? Are you the one who discovered her?"

"No." Liz drew in a deep breath. "When I came home tonight, she was already dead. They'd already moved her. All I saw was the outline of her body on the pavement…."

Dexter put a hand over hers. "I'm sorry, Liz. Really sorry. That must have been a hellish sight to come home to."

She stared at his hand, fighting a ridiculous urge to give way to tears. The strength of his fingers had always fascinated her, especially the way he used that strength so considerately when he made love. In bed, Dexter had not been the cool, self-possessed man of his public facade. In bed, she had always been able to make him lose control. When they made love, she had glimpsed facets of another, more vulnerable man. In bed, she had sometimes thought that Dexter loved her.

He continued to cradle her hand in his clasp. "Why don't you think Karen committed suicide?" he asked softly. "Why do you think the police have got it all wrong?"

Liz jerked up her head and tugged her hand away, anger and a strange relief combining in an explosive mixture. "Damn you, Dexter! Why don't you ever ask the same questions anybody else would ask?"

"Because you don't want me to ask the standard questions. You came here for a reason, Liz, and that must be connected with Karen's death. If you believed she'd committed suicide, you wouldn't have come. Only something really important would reconcile you to seeing me again. We didn't exactly part friends, and I imagine my marriage to Susan only made things worse."

She sprang up from the sofa, turning her back on him. "I'm sorry about your wife," she said abruptly. "Nowadays you don't expect a woman as young as Susan to die of heart disease."

"Statistically it happens, but I guess we never anticipate people we love becoming part of the statistics." There was a tiny pause, and Dexter's voice roughened. "Amanda has found it really difficult to accept her mother's death."

Liz swallowed hard. "How old is Amanda now?"

"She's almost eight, and in my totally unprejudiced opinion, she's gorgeous." Liz could almost hear Dexter smiling. "She was born exactly a year after Susan and I got married. A great anniversary gift for both of us."

Nothing he said was news to Liz, but she'd felt obligated to get the topic of his wife and daughter out of the way. She heard the warmth, the gentle caring that crept into his voice when he spoke their names. Now she knew exactly how he sounded when he loved someone without reservation—and she wished she didn't.

"But you aren't here to discuss Amanda," Dexter said. "Why did you come, Liz? What's bothering you so much about Karen Zeit's death that you were prepared to talk to me face-to-face?"

As soon as he asked the question, Liz realized that she planned to tell him the whole truth, at least insofar as she could call her pathetic smattering of suspicions *truth*. She wasn't entirely comfortable with her decision, and walked over to the windows, keeping her back toward him when she finally spoke.

"I think Karen was murdered."

Silence. She was grateful that he didn't protest, or tell her in polite euphemisms that she was crazy. After a second or two, he simply walked over to where she was standing, turned her around and looked at her assessingly with those cool gray eyes of his. He asked only one question. "Why?"

"Karen isn't my first roommate to die. I was

working in Seattle until I moved to Denver at the beginning of March. I shared apartments with two other people there, and both of them died almost the same way as Karen. Either a few weeks of living with me is enough to drive sane people crazy, or somebody is systematically killing off my room-mates." She tried a smile, without much success. "Nice alternatives, huh? Liz the Witch, or Liz the Intended Victim."

"Not nice alternatives at all, and both of them hard to believe. First question, if you're the intended victim of a plot, why is somebody killing off your roommates? Why not murder you directly?"

"Maybe the killer makes mistakes?"

"You mean he's murdering by remote control, and the wrong person keeps ending up dead?"

"Something like that."

"Three times? Come on, Liz, even a psychopath would do a better job of fine-tuning his methods than that."

"Then how can it be murder, Dex?" The old nickname slipped out almost unnoticed. "Three un-connected suicides may be hard to believe, but three unconnected murders belong to the land of paranoid fantasy."

He put an arm around her and drew her back to the sofa. "We reach an obvious conclusion: the deaths aren't unconnected."

She held her body very straight against the cush-ions. "You mean I'm the connecting link?"

"You have to be. That's the only logical explanation."

"But, Dex, I'd never even met Karen Zeit until two days before I moved in with her! And she had no links to either Brian or Jill. She came from a different part of the country, her work was different. All their work was different—"

"What did your other roommates do?"

"Brian was a university professor, and Jill was a social worker. Jill was in her twenties, Brian was forty-five and Karen was thirty-something. Dex, they have nothing in common."

"But they do. We just established that. They all shared an apartment with you."

"Which brings us right back to where we started. It makes no sense, Dex. Nobody has a reason to kill off my roommates."

"On the contrary," he said neutrally. "If you're the person doing the killing, everything makes perfectly good sense."

Liz felt herself turn cold with horror. "You think...you believe I murdered my roommates?"

"It seems—unlikely."

"Thanks for the ringing vote of confidence." Liz dug her fingers into the cushion. "Dex, for God's sake, I didn't murder those people. Don't you know me well enough to realize I could never kill anybody? Particularly not by pushing them out of a window."

"I don't think we know each other at all," Dexter said. "Not nine years ago and certainly not now.

But that's beside the point, I guess. I was simply suggesting that there must be logical explanations for three roommates of yours getting themselves murdered. I pointed out the most obvious one.''

The chilling fear that had been clawing at Liz for hours began to take on a sharper reality. ''The police are going to arrest me,'' she said, her voice shaking. ''Somebody's going to contact the police in Seattle and then it will all be over. I'm going to be arrested, Dex.''

His grasp on her hands tightened reassuringly. ''Not if I can avoid it.''

''How can you keep me out of jail when you don't even believe I'm innocent?''

''I didn't say that, Liz. I simply suggested that we don't know each other very well.'' His gaze became unexpectedly sympathetic. ''You're freezing, Liz. Let me pour you another brandy, strictly for medicinal purposes.''

He was right about one thing: she was freezing, inside and out. And if she was headed for a jail cell, she might as well make the most of her remaining few hours of freedom. ''All right, thanks. I think I could use some of your vintage cognac.''

Dexter walked to the bar and reached for clean glasses. ''Aside from the fact that you can't believe the coincidence of three roommates committing suicide within three months, do you have any other reason for thinking Karen and the others might have been murdered?''

She shook her head. ''Not a thing, unless you

count my feeling that they weren't suicidal sorts of people.''

"Did you know them well enough to judge?"

"Not Karen, maybe. But the other two. Jill and I had been acquainted with each other for a couple of years. We belonged to the same health club. And Brian…I guess you could say we knew each other pretty well.''

Carefully, Dexter returned the stopper to the brandy bottle. "Were you and Brian lovers?" he asked.

"We'd talked about getting engaged. We were living together.''

"That doesn't answer my question, Liz.''

"I think it does. If it's any of your business.''

Before Dexter could say anything more, a perfunctory knock at the door was followed by the sound of the lock clicking open. A slender man with pale blond hair and a perspiring forehead erupted into the room, trailing an aura of generalized disaster.

"Dexter! Thank God you're here!''

"Hello, Evan. I'm glad Gwen managed to find you.''

"Gwen? Who's she?'' Without waiting for an answer, Evan rushed on. "Dexter, what in blazes are you doing hiding away in here? Holy hell's breaking loose out there, and nobody can find you. I just had a call from the police. Karen's been found dead outside her apartment, and the reporters are already swarming—'' Evan broke off abruptly, as he suddenly realized Dexter wasn't alone. He drew himself up, mopping his forehead with a silk handkerchief pulled from his breast pocket. In the blink of an eye he transformed himself into a dapper, deferential assistant.

"Oh, I'm sorry, Senator. I didn't know you were entertaining. When you've given your guest her drink, perhaps you could spare me a moment? In private? There are a couple of administrative matters that need your attention. When you've finished with your guest, of course."

"Let me introduce you two to each other," Dexter said, a definite note of wry humor in his voice. "Liz, this is my public-relations aide, Evan Howard. Evan, this is my former wife—Liz Meacham."

"Your ex-wife?" Evan looked as if he might faint. "How do you do, Ms. Meacham. I thought you lived in New York."

"Somebody hasn't been keeping your files up-to-date, Mr. Howard. I haven't lived in New York for more than five years."

"Liz lives in Denver," Dexter supplied. "She shared an apartment with Karen Zeit."

Evan dropped his handkerchief. "Holy hell," he said.

Dexter smiled. "Now that you've mentioned it, Evan, I guess that's pretty much what I was thinking."

Evan bent to pick up his handkerchief, and Dexter turned to hand Liz her brandy. For a split second their gazes locked in rueful, shared amusement. The unexpected moment of intimacy made Liz profoundly uncomfortable. She and Dexter Rand did not operate on the same mental wavelength. She didn't want to operate on the same mental wavelength as Dexter Rand. That was one of the illusions that had led her into trouble before.

Taking things calmly was obviously not one of the skills Evan had been hired for. "The media are gonna crucify you, Dex. Holy moly, what have I ever done to deserve this?"

"Signed on to my staff?" Dexter suggested mildly.

Evan ignored this remark. His eyes narrowed in acute concentration. "There's no way we can keep her name out of the paper," he muttered, staring at Liz without really seeing her. "They're bound to find out she was married to you—she's listed on all your official bios. World Champion Figure Skater, Liz Meacham." He nibbled his lower lip. "There must be some angle we could come up with. How about you approached Liz to teach the orphans in that school you sponsor? We'll tie it into the Olympic program somehow. Make it sound patriotic. Overcoming personal differences for the good of your country."

"Why in the world would I approach Liz? There are a dozen world-class skaters active in Colorado, and everybody in the skating business knows Liz hasn't been near an ice rink since she left Germany."

"You're right. Skating stinks." A gleam lighted

Evan's eyes. "How about a reconciliation? Now there's an idea. You and Liz are getting together again. Remarriage in the air, and all that good stuff."

"No," Liz said flatly. "No. We'd never be able to pull it off. And how would a story like that help? It would just fan the gossip flames."

"How about telling the truth?" Dexter suggested. "There's a radical new approach for you to consider, Evan. You could tell the reporters that I had no idea Liz was living in the same apartment as my personal secretary, and that until tonight we hadn't spoken to each other in nine years."

Evan's expression turned sour. "Damn it, Dexter, nobody's gonna believe a dumb story like that! Your ex-wife lives with your personal secretary, who commits suicide for no apparent reason. Even you must see the scandal sheets will have the three of you locked up in some sort of bizarre triangular love nest before the first edition hits the streets."

Liz stood up. "I'm sorry, Dexter. I've really done you a bad turn by coming here. I've only been in Denver a few weeks, and half that time I've been out of the country on business trips. If I'd stayed away, we could have played down our past connection. After all, we both know it has absolutely nothing to do with this case. Isn't there some back way I could get out of here and avoid all the reporters who are probably lying in wait out front?"

Evan beamed his approval. "An excellent suggestion, Ms. Meacham. I'll let you out through the kitchen and arrange for one of the catering people to drive you home.''

"But my own car's parked out front on Pinewood Road. How will I get it back?''

"Don't give your car another moment's thought, Ms. Meacham. If you'll let me have the keys, I'll see that somebody gets it home to you tomorrow, inconspicuously. What sort of car do you drive?''

"A Hond—''

"It doesn't matter what she drives," Dexter said. "You surely don't think we're going to smuggle her out of this house without causing comment, after at least twenty guests saw me walk down the hallway with her? I'll bet there are already at least a half-dozen rumors making the rounds about the 'mystery woman' I escorted into my study."

"Then what do you suggest? That we take her out front and introduce her as your ex-wife? Just when the story about Karen is breaking? Damn it, Dexter, you can't afford a breath of scandal with the crucial hearings before the Armed Services Committee about to resume. And this sure ain't a breath, it's a gale!''

"I suggest that we don't have much choice except to ride it out. My feeling is that Liz should spend the night here, so that we can work on our stories while you hold the reporters at bay. Then Liz and I'll meet the press together, tomorrow morning. Is that okay with you, Liz?''

It seemed slightly less okay than spending the night in a cage with a hungry tiger. The only thing that might possibly be worse was the prospect of driving to a hotel room and spending the night alone with her imagination and her suddenly overactive memories. She looked at Evan Howard. "Dexter's right," she said quietly. "I think maybe it would be best if I stayed here."

Evan's horrified gasp gave Liz a perverse twinge of satisfaction. She had met dozens of men like Evan during her skating career, and despised most of them. There was some consolation in the knowledge that if Evan Howard didn't like the idea of her spending the night in Dexter's house, then her decision to stay couldn't be all bad.

She thought she detected the merest flicker of surprise in Dexter's expression when he heard her response, but all he said was, "Handle the press for me, will you, Evan? Liz and I are going to put our heads together and see if we can come up with a few reasons why Karen Zeit might have been murdered."

"Murdered!" Evan's already pale complexion turned faintly green. Then he swung quickly on his heel. "Don't tell me," he said, "I don't want to know what you're talking about a minute before I have to. I'll do the best job I can with those reporters, but I'm warning both of you. You'd better come up with a damn good story."

"Don't worry." For the first time, Liz could hear a note of bitterness in Dexter's voice. "We're experts. We've done all this before."

CHAPTER THREE

FOR ONCE, AMANDA'S antics were not absorbing all of Dexter's attentions. He held her hand, relishing the contact of baby-soft skin against his palm, but answered her nonstop barrage of questions with only half his attention.

He had suspected a leakage of classified information from his Washington office for at least six months. An undercover FBI operative had been working secretly on Dexter's staff for the last two. So far, the investigation had been spectacular for its lack of success. As far as Dexter was concerned, Karen's death threw a whole new light on the situation. Was it possible that the leaks had originated in Denver, rather than Washington? Was that why none of the carefully planted red herrings were turning up anywhere?

Guiltily, Dexter acknowledged he was worried less about Karen's death than the part his ex-wife might have played in it. If Karen had been something more than the dedicated office worker she seemed, could Liz possibly be as bewildered and innocent as she had sounded the previous night? He didn't think so. There were limits as to how far he was prepared to stretch the long arm of coincidence.

One fact was irritatingly clear. Liz's unexpected arrival on his doorstep had thrown him for a loop, not least because of the impact her physical presence had upon him. Until last night, Dexter had assumed that his old, tumultuous feelings about Liz had all been resolved. It was a shock, and not a pleasant one, to discover she still exerted the same sexual fascination that had almost destroyed him the first time around.

The sun cast brilliant light but little heat and Dexter scowled, feeling the chill of the morning air now that he had finished his daily three-mile run. "What's the matter, Dad?" Amanda demanded, seeing his frown.

He heard the anxiety in her voice and quickly smoothed his expression. "Nothing's wrong," he said, squeezing her hand. "How could anything be wrong when you're out here playing with me?"

"We're not playing, just walking. I wish the snow hadn't gone away. We could've built a fort."

"We did that already this year. May is too late for snow. In a couple of weeks you'll be asking to go swimming."

"I like swimming. So does Spot." Amanda patted the Labrador who trotted patiently at her side.

"I know Spot likes swimming—he likes it too well! This year we're going to train him not to jump into the pool when we have guests."

She giggled. "Maybe. Spot likes swimming with lots of people, though."

"Unfortunately, most of my guests don't return

the compliment.'' Dexter glanced at his watch. ''We have five more minutes, honey, and then we have to go inside. What game do you want to play?''

''Catch.''

''Okay.'' Dexter took a chewed-up tennis ball from his daughter and threw it toward a far corner of the backyard. Amanda and the dog bounded after it in hot competition. Spot—his daughter had insisted on the name, despite the fact that the Labrador's sleek black body bore not a single mark—was the inevitable winner. He obligingly fell over his front paws and allowed the ball to trickle out of his mouth into Amanda's waiting hands.

''I got it, Dad! I won!'' She buried her nose between the Labrador's ears, hugging him tight before throwing the ball back toward her father. This time Spot wasn't prepared to be generous. Outstripping his mistress, he snatched the ball with all the skill of his retriever heritage and bounded off toward his favorite hidey-hole in the bushes. Panting, Amanda ran up and skidded to a halt alongside her father.

''He won't come back for ages. Play baseball with me?'' She reached into the pocket of her oversize sweater. ''I've got another ball.''

''I wish we could, sweetheart,'' Dexter said regretfully. ''But I have a meeting early this morning, and I need to change my clothes. There's no time for baseball.''

''You always have meetings.''

''I guess it seems that way sometimes.'' He rumpled her hair, loving the feel of curls tickling his fingers. "But the work I do is important, honey. Unfortunately, there just aren't enough people in Congress who really understand military technology, and I do. There are some decisions our government has to take where my opinion can really make a difference."

"'Cos you were a pilot?"

"Mmm, sort of. And because I'm an engineer."

"If it's so important, why can't I come to your meeting? Maybe I oughta learn about airplanes and things instead of dumb old math at school."

Dexter grinned. "Good try, honey, but you know the answer. The meeting's important for me, school's important for you. And if we don't hurry and get back inside, you won't have time to wash the dirt off your hands before your ride gets here. Then I'll be in trouble with Mrs. Morton again."

She gave one of the gurgles of laughter that always made his heart ache. "Don't be silly, Dad. Mrs. Morton can't be mad at you. You're a grown-up and she works for you."

"And you think that makes me safe from Mrs. Morton's wrath? Young lady, you have a lot to learn!"

Amanda chuckled again, understanding the teasing tone of his voice, if nothing else. "Do you have to go back to Washington next week, Dad? I wish you didn't."

"I'm afraid I do, honey." They had reached the kitchen door and he gave her a quick hug, trying not to let her wistful look get to him. Most of his colleagues in the senate couldn't understand why he spent every spare minute that wasn't devoted to the defense budget campaigning for adequate, federally funded day-care centers. But then, most of his colleagues weren't single parents and didn't understand the burden of guilt mothers and fathers felt when forced to spend long hours away from their children. He gave Amanda another kiss. "Have a good day in school and I'll see you tonight. That's a promise."

Dexter left his daughter washing her hands under Mrs. Morton's eagle-eyed inspection. He crossed the hallway at a brisk pace, wondering just how rational his plans for the upcoming press conference actually were. In the cool light of morning, he was beginning to see a dozen problems that hadn't been apparent the night before.

Face it, he told himself wryly. You were functioning strictly on the no-brain, multihormone level last night. You were so busy feeling furious about the past and horny about the present that you'd have agreed the moon was made of green cheese, if she'd suggested it.

The realization that Liz still retained the power to make him act like an idiot wasn't calculated to sweeten Dexter's mood. Once this press conference was over, he'd make damn sure he didn't see her again. If she needed help, he'd pass her over to Evan. Evan would have no trouble finding her a good private investigator or a first-class lawyer, and that was about all the personal attention he owed her.

Dexter took the stairs two at a time, stopping with great reluctance when he heard Evan's voice. "Senator, I'm so glad you're back from your morning walk with your daughter. You have somebody waiting to see you, Senator."

Not only did Evan sound twice as pompous as usual, he also wore one of his gloomiest and most official faces. Dexter's spirits sank a notch. "If it's a reporter, Evan, you know I don't have time for any personal interviews this morning."

"It's not a reporter, it's the police. A Detective Rodriguez. He wants to see you right now, Senator. He says it's urgent."

Dexter glanced down at his watch. When Evan called him "Senator" three times in as many sentences, it meant big trouble. "I have twenty minutes to shower, shave and change for the press conference we called. That means I can give your detective five minutes—unless he cares to wait until after the press conference."

A tall, slightly overweight figure in a raincoat appeared in the foyer behind Evan. "Five minutes would make a good start, Senator. There are a couple of facts in connection with Karen Zeit's death that I need to go over with you. I'm Lieutenant Rodriguez, by the way, with the Denver Police Department."

Dexter concealed his racing thoughts beneath a polite smile. "Good to meet you, Lieutenant, although the circumstances certainly aren't very pleasant. Why don't we go into my study? That seems as good a place as any for us to talk.''

''I'll see that we have coffee and rolls set out for the press conference,'' Evan said. ''Unless you need me to stay with you, Senator?''

''At this hour of the morning, if we want the reporters to act like human beings, coffee should definitely be your first priority.'' Dexter kept his response light, although he had already picked up the tension—hostility?—emanating from the lieutenant. ''And check that Amanda gets off to school okay, will you, Evan?''

''Certainly, Senator. I'll be expecting you in five minutes. I'm sure Lieutenant Rodriguez understands how busy your schedule is this morning and will limit himself accordingly.''

What the devil had the detective been saying to Evan? Dexter wondered. His aide rarely kept up the ''deferential servant'' act for more than a few minutes at a time, but this morning he was behaving like a bad imitation of Jeeves.

''You have news about Karen's death?'' he said to the lieutenant, shutting the study door. ''Have you discovered something that sheds light on why she committed suicide?''

The detective didn't answer directly. ''That's a fancy lock you have there, Senator.''

''I frequently have confidential papers in here,'' Dexter replied shortly. ''We had a burglary some six months ago, and the security company suggested electronic locks. What was it you wanted to tell me about Karen?''

''Well, Senator, we've discovered several rather interesting things. First of all, I think you should know that we don't believe Karen Zeit committed suicide.''

''You mean her death was accidental?'' Dexter asked, knowing damn well that the lieutenant meant nothing of the sort.

Rodriguez looked at him without expression. ''Karen Zeit contacted an agent with the Colorado Bureau of Investigations last week. She insisted that her life was in danger. She said somebody was planning to murder her.''

''What?'' Dexter made no effort to conceal his shock. He ran his hands through his sweat-stiffened hair, his mind racing. What in God's name had his seemingly quiet and unassuming secretary been involved with after hours? ''I guess it's absurd to say that the idea of anybody wanting to kill Karen strikes me as ridiculous.''

''Hardly ridiculous, considering that she *is* dead. I'm sure you realize, Senator, that the Bureau gets crazies coming in every day, telling us their life is in danger. Half of them think they're in communication with aliens from another planet, and most of the rest are borderline psychotics. Karen Zeit didn't quite fit the pattern, although she was too frightened to tell the agent exactly why her life was at risk. She wanted police protection, but wasn't prepared to say more than that somebody in a position of power was out to kill her.''

"So did you give her protection?"

There was a tiny pause. "No, we didn't," Rodriguez admitted. "CBI funding doesn't stretch to looking after citizens who won't say who's threatening them, or why their lives might be in danger. It's all they can do to take care of the people who are obviously at risk."

"I think at the minimum I should have been notified of her concerns."

"Yes, that was an oversight."

"I have a suspicion, Lieutenant, that the people at the Bureau are taking Karen's worries much more seriously this week than they were last."

"Death does have an amazing tendency to concentrate the mind," the lieutenant agreed mildly. "Particularly when the death is murder."

"And you're sure Karen was murdered?"

"Our preliminary investigations have disclosed some interesting facts about Ms. Zeit's death. The pathologist has found evidence of bruising around her mouth and wrists. This bruising occurred some time before death, and not when she fell out of her apartment window. The pathologist suggests that the marks are consistent with the deceased being forcibly restrained and compelled to swallow something—sleeping pills and whiskey, perhaps? With the combination of drugs and alcohol found in her system, she would have been unconscious within ten minutes. Think how easy it would have been for a murderer to push her from the window of her apartment and quietly disappear into the shadows.''

"But God in heaven, man, what reason would anybody have for killing Karen? She was a pleasant, efficient secretary, but she always struck me as completely—ordinary.''

"In some lines of work, Senator, the ordinary sort of person is the most dangerous.''

"If that's what you're thinking, Lieutenant, I recommend that you speak with Agent Waterman at the FBI. He's been rerunning some of the background checks on members of my staff.''

"Has he indeed?" Lieutenant Rodriguez scribbled furiously in his notebook. "There is one other point, Senator. Did the deceased have any men friends that you're aware of?''

"She had one or two friends who were male. No steady boyfriend, as far as I know.''

"No boyfriend, eh? Interesting you should say that, Senator, because Karen Zeit was nine weeks pregnant when she died.''

Dexter felt a fresh surge of astonishment. "But how in the world could she have gotten herself pregnant?''

Rodriguez actually smiled. "The same way as any other woman, Senator. She was sexually intimate with a man.''

"I understand the biology,'' Dexter responded impatiently. "But Karen was thirty-three years old and reasonably sophisticated. Why would she make a mistake like that? We're not talking about some high-school kid who's never heard of birth control.''

"Why do you assume Ms. Zeit made a mistake? Perhaps she was in love with the father. Maybe she wanted to get pregnant, to force his hand in some way."

"But who was the father, for heaven's sake? Who could he have been? One way and another, Karen spent nearly sixty hours a week with me. That doesn't leave much time for an outside social life, especially one she's keeping secret."

The lieutenant's voice was very dry. "An excellent point, Senator."

Dexter's head shot up. "Oh no, Rodriguez. You're barking up the wrong tree. Karen Zeit was my secretary, and that's all she was. Quite apart from the fact that I would never have an affair with a member of my staff, Karen just wasn't my type."

"Strange you should say that, Senator. The first thing that struck me was how much she looked like your wife."

"Like Liz?" Dexter shoved his hands into the pockets of his sweats. "Oh, I see. You mean like Susan."

"You seem confused, Senator. What's so confusing about Karen Zeit's appearance? Either she looked like your wife or she didn't."

"I've been married twice," Dexter said curtly. "I suppose Karen looked a bit like my second wife, although their personalities were very different."

"I didn't know you'd been divorced, Senator."

"Then you must be one of the few people in the United States who doesn't know all the gory details, Lieutenant. My first wife and I practically got divorced on television."

"And your first wife's name was?"

"Elizabeth Meacham."

"Elizabeth Meacham!"

Dexter felt obscurely satisfied in having finally shaken Rodriguez's cast-iron calm. "Before you say anything more, Lieutenant, I know that my former wife was sharing an apartment with Karen Zeit. I also know that I have to be at a press conference in precisely eight minutes. Regretfully, our time together has just run out." Dexter walked over to the desk and pressed a button on the intercom system. Evan responded instantly.

"Yes, Senator?"

"I have to shower and dress. Maybe you could answer any other questions Lieutenant Rodriguez might have."

"I'll be right there, Senator."

Dexter turned to the detective. "If there's anything else you feel we ought to discuss, perhaps you could phone me some time this afternoon."

"A phone call won't be necessary, Senator. You've given me several useful leads to work on, and I'm sure if I have any more questions, we'll be able to fit a face-to-face meeting somewhere into your busy schedule."

The look Dexter gave the detective was hard with

challenge. "I'm not planning to leave town, Lieutenant, at least for the next couple of days."

"That's very cooperative of you, Senator."

"No. I merely have several important meetings scheduled in Colorado. Good morning to you, Lieutenant."

Evan appeared in the doorway and Dexter turned abruptly on his heel, leaving the study without saying another word.

LIZ GLANCED AT HER WATCH. The press conference was scheduled to begin in five minutes, and Dexter hadn't been anywhere near her since he said a courteous good-night at ten o'clock the previous evening.

She certainly couldn't complain that her comfort had been ignored. Her bathroom was stocked with every toiletry she might need, including a new toothbrush. Her clothes had been whisked away last night and returned early this morning, cleaned and pressed by an expert hand. Promptly at eight, a delicious breakfast had been brought to her bedroom, and Evan Howard had stopped by no less than three times, ostensibly to ensure that she was keeping to schedule, but in reality to make sure she had the details of the agreed story fixed firmly in her mind. Evan didn't like wild cards in his neatly ordered system, and had made it abundantly clear that he considered Liz the wildest of the wildest. Considering her decorous lifestyle over the past few years, she found his opinion of her almost funny. Almost, but not quite. Today nothing seemed really funny.

Liz coiled her hair into a smooth knot and pinned it swiftly in place. She peered at her reflection in the brightly lighted bathroom mirror, grimacing at what she saw. Years of appearing before the public had left her an expert with makeup, and she had managed to transform her unkempt appearance of the night before into a neat, expressionless mask. Understated pink lips, understated pink cheeks, discreetly darkened lashes. Evan and Dexter would both be thrilled, she thought cynically. The doll-like woman in the mirror looked like the perfect appendage for a politician.

Only her eyes betrayed her. Blue and turbulent, they revealed far too much of what she was feeling. They stared back at her from the mirror, disturbing reminders of a passionate child-woman who no longer existed, except in dreams. Liz closed her eyes. When she opened them again, the blue-gray depths were wiped satisfyingly clean of expression. Now her lifeless eyes matched the porcelain texture of the rest of her face.

When Dexter came to the door two minutes later, she was able to greet him with a polite detachment that would have been impossible during their marriage. She inquired if he'd slept well, if Amanda had gotten off to school on time, if all the arrangements for the press conference had gone smoothly. Meaningless conversation that covered over the horrors of silence. Some things, she discovered, did get better with the passage of time.

Dexter waited for her to finish spouting conversational gambits, then assessed her appearance with the faintest of smiles. "You look well armored against the fiends of the press."

"I figured I might need to be."

"With luck, you'll be able to get away with saying no more than how sorry you are that Karen's dead."

"That's the plan," she agreed.

"Liz, there's no time to talk now, and we need to. Can you spare fifteen minutes after the conference?"

"If you think it's necessary. My office isn't expecting me until lunchtime." She looked at the stairs, which provided a convenient excuse for not looking at him. "Dexter, I owe you an apology. I shouldn't have come here last night. The last thing I want is for you to feel obliged to help me. In fact, there's nothing for you to help me with. Three of my roommates have committed suicide. It's a terrible coincidence, but one I'll have to learn to live with."

"There've been some developments you should know about—oh hell, there's Evan, and he's got the *Boulder Post* editor with him. Smile, Liz. We're on."

She had to admire the way Dexter handled the editor, with just the right mix of friendliness and reserve. He introduced Liz by name, without mentioning their previous relationship. The editor showed not a flicker of recognition.

All four of them walked into the main reception room together, and the buzz of voices from the assembled journalists faded into immediate silence.

Evan had been much too smart to set up anything as formal as a podium and microphone. Dexter walked to the center of the small space that had been left at one end of the room and faced the dozen or so reporters and three TV camera crews. Liz was surprised that so many media people had turned out on what surely must be a fairly routine sort of story. Unfortunately, this was a situation in which Dexter's unusually high profile didn't work well for him.

"I'm sorry that the occasion for our get-together this morning is such a sad one," Dexter said without preamble. "Karen Zeit had been my personal secretary for the past year. She worked long hours with tireless efficiency, and kept my personal and business schedules untangled with almost magical skill. She will be sorely missed in my office, and by her colleagues. I like to think that we had become friends, as well as employer and employee, so that her loss is a double blow for me. I think most of your questions can be answered far better by the police department than they can by me, but I'll do my best to respond to anything relevant."

Six reporters were on their feet. Dexter nodded to one of them. "Joan."

"You say Karen was your personal secretary,

Senator. What exactly were her duties, and did you often work out of your home?''

Dexter accepted the question with a bland smile, far too old a hand to allow the sleazy subtext of her question to bother him. Liz almost felt sorry for the reporter when Dexter launched into a long, dry explanation of how his office was organized. Karen's duties, it seemed, had consisted chiefly of coordinating his schedule, serving as liaison with his office in Washington, and helping him with fund-raisers and charitable events. "She was kept very busy, but she had nothing to do with any of my Senate committee work," Dexter concluded. "We try to channel most of that through my Washington office. Since I'm on the Armed Services Committee, a lot of my work is classified and therefore off-limits for Karen. She'd never received official security clearance, which all of my staff in D.C. has."

That's one in the eye for you, Joan. Liz watched the disgruntled reporter sit down, and allowed herself to relax very marginally. With luck and a bit more of Dexter's skill, they were going to get through this conference with flying colors. Perhaps she wouldn't even have to speak.

She had allowed herself to relax too soon. A reporter from one of the TV stations spoke up next. "I was talking to the superintendent at Karen Zeit's apartment building this morning, and it turns out that she was sharing her apartment with a young woman called Elizabeth Meacham. It's not such a unique name, of course, but you were once married to a member of our U.S. Olympic figure skating team, and her name was also Elizabeth Meacham. Is this just a strange coincidence, Senator, or is it possible that your secretary was sharing an apartment with your ex-wife?''

Dexter's grin was a masterpiece of rueful, good-natured resignation. ''It's no coincidence, Harry, as I'm sure you realized.'' Dexter turned and smiled toward Liz. ''We anticipated that this item of news would set all your journalistic noses twitching, so my former wife very kindly volunteered to join us here this morning. Liz.''

Dexter held out his hand in a casual, welcoming gesture. Liz rose to her feet, stretched her neat pink-glossed lips into a smile and walked across the room to Dexter's side. The ten feet of padded carpet seemed to take so long to cross that they might as well have been ten miles of icy tundra. It had been a while since she last faced a roomful of journalists, but not long enough to forget how easily they could savage you.

''Karen and I met at a party a couple of months ago,'' she said. Her voice sounded husky and she cleared her throat, angry at the appearance of nervousness. Behind her, the silent strength of Dexter's presence gave her a burst of confidence. ''We talked about sharing an apartment. When I found out who Karen worked for, I explained that Dexter and I had once been married. Neither Karen nor I thought that had any bearing on our decision to share an apartment, so I moved in.''

The faces of the journalists blurred into a single, avid mob, all shouting questions at her. Deafened by the bombardment, she forced herself to maintain her inner calm. A question from one of the TV journalists caught her attention.

"Hard feelings toward the senator?" she said with a casual smile. "Oh, no. Dexter and I reconciled our differences a long time ago. We're both ten years older now, and events have taken on a whole different perspective." If she'd been a kid, she'd have had her hands behind her back crossing her fingers when she uttered that whopper.

The editor from the *Boulder Post* was on his feet. "Senator, I understand from sources inside the police department that the CBI is working on this case. I also understand that the autopsy results suggest that Karen Zeit didn't commit suicide. As of now, the police are treating this as a case of homicide. Do you have any comment on that?"

Liz plastered the noncommittal look onto her face so firmly that she was afraid it might never come off. Dear heaven, how long had the police suspected Karen had been murdered? She looked up at Dexter, marveling that he could appear so calm. At nineteen, she had never bothered to look below that surface calm. Now—instinctively—she recognized how much effort it was costing him to appear unconcerned.

"If the police autopsy suggests that Karen Zeit was murdered, then I certainly would have no grounds or expertise for disputing their verdict,"

Dexter said. "If it does turn out that she was murdered, I hope very much that her killer is found quickly and brought to justice."

Some sixth sense retained from her years under a constant publicity spotlight alerted Liz to the fact that the *Post* editor was disappointed with Dexter's reply. Her intuition warned her that the man had come here meaning to make a killing. In the split second pause as the reporter formulated his next question, she saw him coil for attack. "So you have no fears, Senator, that this investigation is going to touch close to home?"

"Karen was my personal secretary. Obviously I'm extremely interested in finding out how she died."

"And how about the note she left, Senator?"

"What note?"

"The one claiming you're the father of her baby and that you refused to marry her."

CHAPTER FOUR

DEXTER NEVER LOST his cool amid the hubbub of the aggressive questions that followed. But despite his most skillful efforts, it took him almost half an hour to get rid of the clamoring journalists. Only the promise that he would issue another statement within forty-eight hours finally persuaded the reporters to sheath their pencils, pack up their equipment and leave.

From the evidence of their avid expressions as they rushed herdlike for the doors, Liz had no problem inferring that the phone wire would soon be vibrating with not-quite-libelous accounts of the thrilling story. She could already visualize the headlines. "Senator's Triangular Love Nest Explodes" would be one of the milder versions.

Evan turned out to be almost more difficult to pacify than the journalists. He paced up and down the study, his self-control obviously shot, trying—with a singular lack of success—to invent some way to put an acceptable public relations gloss on the sordid facts.

Liz watched Dexter soothe his aide, and reflected how much her ex-husband must have changed to employ someone like Evan. In the old days, Dexter's indifference to the press had been monumental, and he'd often been impatient with Liz's efforts to placate the powerful TV sportscasters. She was surprised to discover that she hoped he hadn't changed too much. Oddly enough, Dexter the Arrogant was far more acceptable to her than Dexter the Media Manipulator.

He finally handed the sweating and swearing Evan a glass of club soda. "Look, Evan," he said, putting his arm around the distraught publicist's shoulder. "We have to face reality, tell the truth, and move on from there."

"Truth and reality never won any election I heard about."

"I'm still fighting you on that," Dexter said wryly. "In the meantime, you have to accept there's no way to turn Karen's death into a public relations coup for me. All we can do is control the worst of the damage by saying as little as possible and making damn sure that everything we say is true. Stop trying to achieve anything more, or you'll give yourself an ulcer."

"I already have an ulcer. I shouldn't be drinking this carbonated junk. Gas bubbles are murder on my stomach."

"Then let's work on saving you from ulcer number two." Dexter's jaw tensed slightly. It was the only sign of impatience he allowed himself. "We're all agreed that being suspected of murder makes lousy publicity for a U.S. senator, so stop sweating it."

"Why did she have to leave a note, for God's sake?"

"You heard what Rodriguez said. He thinks the note was part of an unmailed letter to me."

"Why did she need to write, for heaven's sake? She saw you every day!"

Dexter's smile was hard. "You didn't ask the more important question, Evan. Why did she write something that wasn't true?"

Evan remained silent, and Liz thought she detected a brief flash of hurt in Dexter's gaze. When he spoke, however, his voice was crisp and businesslike. "For what it's worth," he said, "I would like you to know there isn't a word of truth in Karen's note. If it isn't a forgery, she was fantasizing."

Evan's head shot up, and Liz thought she saw genuine astonishment in his eyes. "You're sure of that? You didn't get her pregnant? You're saying you two weren't—you know—intimate?"

There was a hint of weariness in Dexter's reply. "No, we weren't intimate. You're taking Lieutenant Rodriguez too seriously, Evan."

"No." Evan's voice was quiet now. "The truth is, Dexter, Karen told me in confidence that the two of you were lovers. You know, after that weekend you went up to Aspen together. She was...um... hoping to marry you. I told her not to count on it." He cast a worried glance in Liz's direction, then plunged ahead. "I warned her that you hadn't been taking your women...um...seriously since Susan...."

When had Dexter ever taken his women seriously? Liz thought cynically. Certainly not during his marriage to her.

"You repeated all this to Lieutenant Rodriguez?" Dexter asked.

Evan hung his head. "I had to. He kept on asking all these questions about Karen and you. I had to tell the truth, Dexter, you can see that."

Liz could barely refrain from asking why truth suddenly ranked so high on Evan's list of priorities. Dexter merely shrugged. "Whatever Karen may have said to you, I wasn't her lover and I didn't get her pregnant. Damn it, I never even kissed the woman, much less had sex with her! We had rooms on separate floors of the hotel, and worked on the final draft of a speech to the League of Women Voters that weekend in Aspen."

"Sure, Dexter, if you say so, but remember the police'll probably be able to run paternity tests on the fetus—"

Dexter cast a single, hard glance at his publicist. "That's good news."

Evan reddened. "Yeah, I guess it is. I'm sure their tests will prove the baby couldn't have been yours, of course."

"Of course." Dexter didn't bother to disguise the heavy irony in his reply. "If the lieutenant asks, tell him I'd be delighted to give a blood sample for comparative testing. Think positively, Evan. Count your blessings that it's two years until I'm up for reelection.''

Evan visibly brightened. It was becoming clear to Liz that facts as concrete entities scarcely existed for him—how things would appear in the media made up his personal version of reality. ''That's true. Two and a half years, actually. Hell, we have plenty of time to come up with a convincing explanation for everything.''

Liz spoke for the first time. For some reason, she found Evan's lack of faith in his employer distinctly annoying. ''There's even the faint hope that the police might have discovered what truly happened by then. In which case, you might not need to invent any stories about anything.''

''I guess.'' Evan clearly placed about as much hope in the possibility of the police solving the mystery as he had faith in his employer's innocence. ''What do you want me to do, Dexter? Should I work on a statement for you to make to the press tomorrow?''

''Right now we don't seem to have any clear ideas about what I should say, so that seems like an exercise in futility. Why don't you make an appointment to consult with Needinger?''

''Your lawyer? That's a great idea.'' Evan cheered up again. ''Needinger has lots of clout at the police department. He can talk to Lieutenant Rodriguez and make sure we get all the up-to-date information. We don't want reporters springing any more surprises on us. That clunker from the *Boulder Post* this morning was enough for a lifetime. What are you going to do for the rest of the day, Senator? Do you plan to stick to your original timetable? You have a dinner scheduled with the governor, remember?''

"You might cancel that, with my profound apologies. I'm sure he'll be relieved not to have to make polite conversation while we both sit and wonder how likely I am to be arrested before dessert is served.''

Evan winced. "Bite your tongue, Senator. How about the rest of your schedule?''

Dexter glanced at the calendar spread open on his desk. "I'm planning to spend the next hour or so talking to Liz. Seems to me we have some useful information to share, she and I.''

Evan viewed Liz with distinct lack of favor. "If you really think that's wise, Senator—''

"I think it's very wise," Dexter said firmly. "I'll keep the afternoon appointments. And could you call the agency for a temporary secretary? Bonnie's never going to cope on her own.''

"Very well, Senator." From the number of times he'd said "Senator" in the past two minutes, Liz decided Evan once again felt in control of the situation. He gave a smooth smile. "I'll see you after lunch, when I've had a chance to check things out with Needinger.''

"If he needs to see you, you know my schedule.''

"Yes, Senator." Evan nodded his head toward

Liz. "Goodbye, Ms. Meacham. It's been a...um... pleasure meeting you."

She actually felt her mouth twist into a small smile. "I hope your pleasures aren't always so traumatic, Mr. Howard."

Her reply seemed to disconcert him. He smiled nervously, then hurried from the room with a final word of acknowledgment to his employer. Liz waited until the door closed. "For your sake, I hope he's better at his job than he seems," she said dryly. She flushed. "I'm sorry. That remark was uncalled-for."

Dexter seemed amused rather than offended. "He's actually damn good at his job. He has a knack for turning complex policy positions into easy-to-grasp, easy-to-read statements, and he can charm a mob of hungry journalists better than anybody I know."

Liz thought back and realized Dexter was right. Evan Howard had shown no sign of being traumatized until they'd been alone in the study. "Nursing him through a nervous breakdown every time there's a crisis seems like a stiff price to pay."

"He's not usually this upset. He's always a worrier, but I must say Karen's death seems to have thrown him for a total loop. He normally panics for ten minutes, then has the whole situation under control ten minutes later."

"Maybe he's thrown because he thinks you killed her."

Her words fell into a little pool of silence. Dexter

stopped riffling through the pages of his calendar and looked up at her. "What about you, Liz? Do you think I killed Karen?"

She gave an odd little laugh. "I wish I could say yes. After the debacle of our marriage, I rather like the idea of you groveling in the courts over a messy crime of passion. It would make you seem semihuman."

"Translated, does that mean you don't believe I murdered my secretary?"

She smiled wryly. "Crazy, isn't it? The evidence all points to you, but somehow I don't believe you did it."

"Why not?"

"Maybe because I can't imagine you ever feeling passionate enough about a woman to kill her."

He looked away. "You're wrong," he said quietly. "I've felt that passionate—and that desperate. But not over Karen."

Susan, Liz thought, and was aware of a sharp little twist of pain in her stomach. Why had he felt so desperate about Susan? Was he implying that his second wife had been unfaithful to him? Surely not, although Liz considered it a splendid irony of fate if she had. The adulterer finally stung by his wife's adultery.

"You're very quiet," he said. "Does that mean you're wondering if I'm guilty, after all?"

"No, I guess I'm quite sure you didn't kill her."

"Should I be flattered?"

"Maybe. Or perhaps I can't believe you're guilty because the evidence is too convincing."

"When there's a bullet-ridden body on the floor and the only other person in the room holds a smoking gun, it's reasonable to conclude that the person holding the gun had something to do with the bullet-ridden body."

"Are you trying to convince me you killed her, Dexter?"

"I'm trying to discover why on earth you believe I didn't. Knowing your opinion of my character, I can't believe it's a burning faith in my integrity."

"Let's just say I have a perverse intuition that this time the guy with the smoking gun didn't pull the trigger."

"You know who the police are going to suspect if they ever give up on me, don't you?"

"Yes. I know I ought to run to Rodriguez screaming that you did it. Because if you didn't kill Karen, that surely puts me right at the top of the police list of likely murderers. Except I know I didn't kill her, or my other two roommates. So maybe you didn't kill her either, despite all the evidence."

"Or get her pregnant?"

She glanced down at her hands. "I—don't know about that."

His voice sounded harsh. "I suppose I should be grateful for small mercies. I guess it's better to have your ex-wife consider you a lecher who's fooling around with the office staff than to have her think you might be a murderer."

Liz dug her nails into her palms. "You...were unfaithful while we were married. How do I know what your sexual morals might be nowadays?"

"I was never unfaithful to you," Dexter said, sounding suddenly tired. "But let's not open that old can of worms. I don't think we can have a single thing left to say on the subject of our marriage. God knows, we said it all nine years ago, and most of it in front of a TV camera."

"I still have nightmares about that night." Liz had no idea why she suddenly made the admission that pride had kept inside for so many years.

"Which part of the night?" Dexter asked quietly. "The medal you'd just lost, or the public disintegration of our marriage?"

She hesitated before admitting the truth. "Both."

Dexter was silent even longer than she had been. "With the proper training, you could have come back in time for the world championship," he said finally. "You were a brilliant skater."

"The psychological moment had passed, I guess." Liz shrugged off the lingering regret that could still grab her by the throat when she gave it the chance. "At least the tabloids aren't interested in me anymore. That must be one of the few compensations for getting old and out of shape!"

Dexter's gaze flicked over her. "You don't look out of shape to me," he commented. "Your body's as spectacular as ever." He continued without giving her a chance to respond. "Look, Liz, why don't we make a deal? I'll agree that you're an innocent victim in the deaths of all three of your roommates, if you'll agree to give me the benefit of the doubt about Karen and her pregnancy.''

''Does it matter if we believe each other?''

''I think maybe it does. The police aren't going to look very far for their murderer when they have you and me as such convenient suspects, and I'd like to find out what I'm being set up for. Because I sure as hell don't think it's coincidence that my secretary got herself murdered while she just happened to be living with my ex-wife.''

''You think I'm setting you up?''

''No, but it's a possibility. A remote one, but I've learned not to discount possibilities. Shall we talk about it?''

''For heaven's sake, why in the world would I bother to set you up?''

''Revenge?''

''Good grief, Dexter! Quite apart from the fact that killing three people seems a somewhat excessive revenge, I'm not neurotic enough or obsessed enough to have spent nine years waiting to get back at you because you're a terminal louse and we had a rotten divorce.''

''I see.'' He grinned faintly. ''You mean, a plot to castrate me would meet with your approval, but setting me up for murder goes too far?''

To her surprise, she found herself answering his grin. ''Something like that,'' she agreed. ''Although now that you mention it, I can't think why I didn't come up with the castration idea years ago.''

"No creative imagination," he said promptly. "Your creativity all goes into your skating."

She smiled, then sighed, feeling a sudden sadness. "Nine years later, and we still come around to the same old topics, don't we? Dexter, I haven't skated in nine years. Wherever my creativity is going these days, it's not into the ice."

He closed the desk calendar with a snap. "You're right. We should stick to Karen's murder and not waste time rehashing the past. Would you be willing to help me come up with some ideas as to who might have killed her?"

"Surely that's something we should leave to the police."

"Unfortunately, I think the police will soon decide that they have all the ideas they need."

"You think they'll arrest you? Or me?"

"How about both of us?"

It was at moments such as these that Liz understood why people smoked. Her hands desperately needed something to do before the rest of her exploded. Dexter seemed to sense her panic. He emerged from behind the desk and crossed the room to sit beside her on the sofa.

"Liz, if we put our heads together, I think we can come up with several insights the police won't have. You see, we know quite a lot that they don't. For example, I know that Karen wasn't pregnant with my baby and that we didn't have an affair. You know that you didn't kill her or your other two roommates."

"Okay, but where do we go from there?"

"At a minimum, it gives us a couple of avenues to explore. Who was the father of Karen's baby, and why were your roommates killed? Those aren't going to be burning questions on the police investigation."

"But, Dexter, that brings us back to where we started out last night. I haven't the faintest, remotest idea why my roommates were killed. I've spent the past day and a half trying to imagine any possible connecting link between the three of them. Believe me, there isn't one."

"Were they friends? Acquaintances?"

"Of course they weren't!"

"How do you know?"

"Because they never mentioned each other! Because they moved in completely different circles! Because there's no *reason* for them to have been friends!"

"We don't know of any reason for them to have been murdered, but they were. Okay, maybe they weren't bosom buddies, but are you sure that they'd never met?"

She stared at him, eyes wide with the shock of realization. "No, I don't know that they'd never met," she murmured. "Not for sure. But when I moved in with Karen I told her that I'd been living with a woman called Jill Skinner, who'd died. If Karen knew Jill, why wouldn't she have said so?"

"Liz, stop reacting and start thinking. If Karen and Brian and Jill shared some secret that got all three of them murdered, do you think any of them were going to worry about a little secret like not telling you that they knew one another?''

''Are you saying that they conspired to trick me into moving in with them for some deep, dark purpose we know nothing about?'' Even to her own ears, her voice sounded distinctly breathless.

''I'm saying you should consider the possibility. And they didn't have to share a deep, dark purpose. People conceal information for all sorts of reasons. After all, you never told Karen that you'd been married to me.''

''That was different. There was no reason to mention a relationship that didn't—doesn't—exist anymore.''

''How do you know your roommates didn't have a similar sort of reason? Maybe Brian had been married to Jill. Or Karen.''

''No! He'd been single for years. He told me his marriage ended right after grad school....'' Her passionate denial trailed away into unconvincing silence.

''You see?'' Dexter said softly. ''You never checked up on Brian's story, did you?''

''People usually tell each other the truth—''

''But not always.'' Dexter got up and walked over to his desk. Depressing a button, he spoke into the intercom. ''Mrs. Morton, could you please make us a pot of coffee and a couple of sandwiches? Thanks.'' Turning back to Liz, he looked at her thoughtfully. "Who first suggested that you should move into Karen's apartment?"

Liz cast her mind back, trying to visualize the crowded room at the party where she had first met Karen. "I did," she said. "I'm almost sure of it. Karen asked me all the usual questions, like how long I had been in Denver, where I was working, that sort of thing. I told her I'd just started a new job at Peperito's, and that I was looking for a room-mate. She told me that by coincidence her roommate had just moved out—"

"As far as I know, Karen never had a roommate. The subject came up once, and she specifically told me she lived alone." Dexter must have caught some fleeting change in Liz's expression because his eyes flashed dark with irritation. "We were talking about a spate of burglaries in her neighborhood, Liz, not a prospective seduction."

"Maybe it was the burglaries that changed her mind."

"Could be. Who was giving this party? Whoever it was, must be a friend of Karen's."

"Pieter Ullmann."

"The skater?"

"Yes, he won the gold at the last Olympics."

"I detect a tinge of acid in your voice. Didn't he deserve his gold?"

"Sure he did. He's probably the best male skater since Scott Hamilton. I'm just tired of athletes who think an Olympic gold is the master key to unlock every woman's bedroom door. Pieter skates like an angel and has a mind like a sewer. Unfortunately, when I'm around him, I keep forgetting the angelic part and smelling the sewer.''

Dexter laughed. ''So why did you go to his party?''

''Mikhail invited me to go with him. Pieter was—is—his star pupil at the moment.''

''Of course, I should've remembered. There was enough press coverage of them both during the winter games.'' Dexter's voice was carefully neutral. ''How is Mikhail these days? I haven't seen him since he first arrived in the States after his defection, but I heard lots of good things about his teaching program, even before Pieter carried off the gold.''

''Mikhail's the best figure-skating coach in the United States,'' Liz said, smiling affectionately as she thought of her brother-in-law. Now that Alison was dead, and their mother barely aware of her surroundings, Mikhail was Liz's closest substitute for a family.

''He's never tried to persuade you back onto the ice?''

''We don't have any sort of professional relationship. Mikhail always admired Alison's skating style much more than mine. That's what first attracted him to her.''

''Technical perfection over fire and heart?''

''Alison was a magnificent skater!''

''You always said so,'' Dexter agreed. An odd note of hesitancy crept into his voice. ''Are you thinking of marrying him, Liz?''

She could justifiably have told Dexter it was none of his business, that he'd lost the right to pry into her affairs years ago, but somehow she found herself confiding the truth. "No, never," she said. "He was Alison's husband. Alison was my twin, and the two of us had always been so close, at least until you and I got married. I could never think of Mikhail as anything except a brother."

A light tap at the door heralded the arrival of Mrs. Morton with a carafe of steaming coffee and a plate of smoked-salmon-and-cucumber sandwiches. As soon as the housekeeper left the room, Liz took a generous bite of sandwich and grinned across at Dexter.

"There are a few advantages to being filthy rich," she said, leaning back against the sofa pillows. "In my next life I'm going to reincarnate as somebody who presses buttons and makes sandwiches appear."

"Take care that the masters of the universe aren't listening, or you may come back as a music-hall conjurer."

She laughed, then sobered abruptly, the sandwich losing its appeal. "Smoked salmon was Karen's favorite, too. Oh God, Dexter, she didn't deserve to end up splattered on a parking-lot pavement."

"No, she didn't. Nobody deserves to die that way. But at this point, we can't do anything to help her except try to find her killer. Which I guess brings us right back to your decision to move in with Karen. With all the advantage of hindsight, would you say that it's possible you were maneuvered into sharing an apartment with her?''

''Of course it's possible—''

''But not probable, you think?''

''I don't know!'' Liz's voice faded into silence while she tried to remember the exact chain of events. ''I don't know about Karen,'' she said finally. ''But if it'll make you feel better, I can be more positive about my decision to move in with Jill Skinner. That wasn't my decision, it was Jill's. I was numb after Brian died, and she virtually made the move for me. At that point, I was so shattered I'd have moved in with Dracula if he'd been prepared to pack my suitcases and hire the U-Haul. So if you want to suspect some vast conspiracy with me as the helpless pawn, the person to start with is Jill Skinner.''

''Tell me about her,'' Dexter suggested. ''And about Brian.''

It was easier to discuss Jill, so she did that first. ''Like I told you last night, Jill and I knew each other for at least two years, but we weren't close friends. We went to the same health club and sweated through the advanced aerobics class, then commiserated about our aching muscles over fruit juice in the locker room. We saw each other three times a week, but until we shared an apartment, I don't think I knew anything more about her than that she had a terrific body, she was around my age, and had a job as a social worker.''

''And once you moved in with her?''

"I found out that she was neat, a vegetarian, a sympathetic listener, and that she took care never to intrude into my space. She had a lot of friends, but she socialized with them in restaurants, not in the apartment. Dex, what can I say? She was a great roommate, but we weren't bosom buddies."

"What about her friends?"

"As I said, she had lots of them. Male and female. She was out most nights."

"Did you like her friends?"

Once again, Liz fell silent. "I don't think I ever met any of them," she admitted finally. "Except maybe to say hi at the door."

"In fact, if you added up everything you know about Jill, you just might be able to fill two sides of a small piece of paper."

Liz felt a chill ripple down her spine. "That's an underestimation, but not by much."

"What about Brian? Did you know him any better?"

"Of course I did! I was living with him, for heaven's sake!"

"You were living with Jill and Karen, too."

"No, I was sharing an apartment. It's different."

"Is it? Aside from what he was like in bed, do you know any more about Brian than you do about Jill and Karen?"

"Yes," she said, through gritted teeth. "Unlike some people, I don't hop into bed with anybody who looks good in a pair of pants."

"Well, bully for you." Dexter's smile was lethal.

"So what intimate details do you know about our friend Brian?"

"He was a professor at the university," she replied. "He had a doctoral degree in electrical engineering. He was forty-five, and a wonderfully calm, considerate human being. He'd been married once when he was a student, but the marriage only lasted a few months before his wife left him for another man." She smiled grimly. "As you can see, we had a lot in common."

"Failed marriages, or chips on your shoulders?" Dexter inquired with excessive politeness.

She wished she could think of some brilliant, scathing retort that would reduce him to dust. Of course, she couldn't. "Brian had a very well-balanced personality," was the best she could come up with.

"I'm so sorry," Dexter pretended sympathy. "Was he boring in bed, too?"

He had been incredibly boring in bed, but Liz had no intention of stepping into that particular nest of vipers. Not with Dexter, of all people. She got to her feet, carrying her plate and cup over to the heavy silver tray Mrs. Morton had left on a side table. She smiled with freezing politeness.

"I've just noticed it's noon already. I have to get to work. My boss isn't too understanding when it comes to taking time off to cope with personal crises. Murder or no murder, he's going to want my latest market-research figures charted and on his desk."

Dexter reached out and captured her hand. He exerted almost no pressure, but somehow she felt incapable of walking away. "Liz, I'm sorry. I owe you an apology. We left a lot of things unresolved between us when we split up, and I think we've both been carrying around some excess emotional baggage, but that's no excuse for what I just said."

"It's been a tough morning," she said, not looking at him.

"Things are likely to get tougher, not easier. This isn't the moment for me to start hurling insults."

"No, I guess it's not. Maybe we should both try to count to ten before we speak to each other."

He broke a moment of silence. "Where are you going to stay tonight?"

She blinked, dismayed by the question. Where was she going to stay? Dear God, she hadn't given that problem a moment's thought. One thing was for sure: she couldn't go back to her apartment, wherever else she went. At the moment, she felt she would never be able to live in an apartment—any apartment—again.

"I hadn't thought about it," she admitted. "But it should be easy enough to find a room near the office. There are dozens of motels around the airport."

"You could stay here," he said. "We have plenty of room."

"Thank you very much for the offer, but I don't think—"

"Liz, we could help each other, if you'd only

spend some time with me. We haven't even started to work out a list of Karen's friends—"

"Dexter, we already agreed that I know almost nothing about Karen, and even less about her friends."

He put a finger against her lips, gently silencing her. "I'll bet you don't know half of what you know," he said lightly. "Liz, please consider it. For both our sakes."

She closed her eyes, cursing silently. She never had been able to resist Dexter when he gave her one of his tender, sincere looks. She'd grown up a lot in the last nine years, but the extra maturity didn't seem to have done a darn thing for her susceptibility to Dexter. She had more self-control these days than she'd had when she was nineteen, but his offer was still incredibly tempting—partly because she didn't want to spend the next few nights pacing up and down a lonely motel room with the specters of Karen and Lieutenant Rodriguez looming over her shoulder.

"All right," she said, drawing in a deep breath. "If you really think it would be helpful, I'll pack a suitcase after work and join you later on this evening."

"Wonderful." Dexter's smile was warm, happy, intimate—and made her want to scream in protest at its devastating effect on her hormones. Why couldn't he have developed sagging jowls and a belly to match? She held her body stiff as he gave her a quick, friendly hug.

"See you tonight, Liz. I'll be waiting for you."

CHAPTER FIVE

LIZ BARELY SURVIVED her afternoon at the office. The combination of an overloaded desk and colleagues consumed by curiosity proved as exhausting as the morning's press conference. Since she'd only recently started work at Peperito's, her colleagues had not yet become friends, and their fascination with her sudden notoriety inevitably came across as prying. Even her boss, a middle-aged workaholic, took ten minutes off from studying his sales charts to bludgeon her with questions. He seemed to have a tough time deciding which part of the breaking news story was most deplorable: Liz's past career as a—failed—skater; her short-lived marriage to the famous Senator Rand; or her involvement in a juicy murder that was clearly destined to remain on the front pages of Colorado's newspapers for several weeks.

Liz was literally shaking with fatigue by the time she turned the key in the lock of her apartment door and pushed it open. The sight of Pieter Ullmann lounging in Karen's favorite armchair proved the final straw to her self-control.

"What the blazes are you doing here?" she demanded. "Who let you in?"

"And I'm thrilled to see you, too, darling." Pieter switched off the television set, jumped gracefully to his feet and bounded across the room to drop a kiss on her cheek. She turned her head just in time, and his kiss landed on her ear.

"Knock it off," she said wearily. "Who let you in, Pieter?"

"Your superintendent's wife," he said cheerily. "I gave her my autograph, and she was thrilled. Her granddaughter sleeps with my picture under her pillow."

"How touching. However, I don't sleep with your picture under my pillow and I already have your autograph, so I'd be grateful if you'd leave. I have a bunch of things to do tonight."

"I came to offer you my sympathy," he said, sounding mortally wounded by her curt rejection. "And my help."

"Thanks. The sympathy's accepted, the help isn't needed. Goodbye."

He winced. "Liz, darling, try to show a few social graces."

She threw her coat onto the nearest available chair. "I'm too tired to be socially gracious. Go home, Pieter."

"Being the generous person that I am, I'll ignore your hostility and invite you to come back to my apartment. What do you say, Liz? I'll call the caterers and we can have a quiet dinner, just the two of us. Champagne. Lobster. Whatever you want."

"And then a quiet little night in bed? Just the two of us?"

Pieter smiled. "Darling, my bedmates are much too ecstatic to be quiet. If you'd only allow yourself to let go now and again, you'd know that my performance in the bedroom is even more spectacular than on the ice. So you know how wonderful that must be."

Liz freed herself from his arms and made her way to the kitchen. "The trouble is, Pieter, I'm old-fashioned enough to think the bedroom is a place to make love, not take part in a performance."

"Darling Liz, you can't be that old!"

Against her will she laughed, and the laughter turned into a yawn. "Believe me, I'm that old. And tired, as well." She opened the fridge, realizing as she peered inside that she was almost grateful to Pieter. Finding him in the apartment had taken some of the sting out of her return.

"If you don't want to go and pursue more promising quarry, you could stay and have a drink. It looks like you can have white wine, soda or orange juice."

He sighed. "I'd better say orange juice, since Mikhail is your brother-in-law and you'll probably report back to him. You two are like Siamese twins."

"Good grief, Pieter, I'm not that much of a witch! Besides, despite all your weary man-of-the-world act, I know damn well that you keep to your training program, whether Mikhail's on your back or not.

You can't fool me. I know what it takes to reach Olympic standard as a figure skater.''

He took a swallow of orange juice and grimaced. ''Liz, darling, I can see that this is one of your nights for being a bore.''

''I agree, so why are you staying? Pieter, I mean it when I say I'm not coming back to your apartment.''

''Dearest Liz, if you don't want to have the best night of your life, that's your business. My sole purpose at this moment is to make you happy. If you want me to hang around drinking orange juice, that's what I'll do. It's creepy to think of you being here alone. Karen was really inconsiderate to get herself murdered in your apartment.''

''Gee, you're right!'' Liz loaded her words with sarcasm. ''If she'd had a smidgen of good taste, she'd surely have asked her murderer to search around and find some other window to push her out of. Murderers are always so cooperative about that sort of thing.''

Pieter stirred an ice cube into his juice with a finger. ''You're not going to spend the night here alone, are you, Liz?''

''No,'' she said, a little surprised by his sudden seriousness. ''I'm not staying here. I'm going to a friend's house.''

''Whose?''

''Nobody you know. We…um…work together.'' She silently apologized for the lie, but had no intention of telling gossipy Pieter where she was really going. "I just stopped by to pack a suitcase. In fact, I have to get started on my packing right now." She picked up her diet soda and walked toward the narrow hallway of the apartment.

Pieter followed her into her bedroom without bothering to ask permission. Bedrooms and the ice rink were his natural habitat, and he obviously felt equally at home in both. He kicked off his shoes and stretched out comfortably on her bed.

"Am I in the way, Liz darling?"

"No more than usual." She opened a drawer and dumped a pile of sweaters onto his stomach. "Here, choose me a couple, would you?"

Pieter obligingly began sorting through sweaters. "Liz," he said with determined casualness. "Did you see much of Karen over the past few weeks?"

"Not much. I was in Mexico City meeting with Peperito's suppliers until Friday."

"Oh. Did she say anything to you about—um—anything?"

Liz belatedly remembered it was at one of Pieter's parties that she had first met Karen. She straightened from her search through the bottom of the closet for a missing sneaker, and turned around to face Pieter.

"How well did you know Karen Zeit?" she asked quietly.

He stared at one of her turquoise sweaters as if he'd never seen such a mesmerizing garment. "Not well. I scarcely knew her at all, in fact."

"Well enough to take her to bed?"

A flash of Pieter's usual brittle manner reappeared

momentarily. "Dearest Liz, even you should realize it's the people you don't know that you go to bed with. With someone you know, you might have to talk afterward."

Liz's gaze remained cool. "I take it that means you and Karen were bedmates?"

"Then you take it wrong." Pieter got off the bed and handed Liz two pink sweaters. "Here, pack these. You look like death warmed over. You could use some color in your clothes, because you sure as hell don't have any in your cheeks."

"Thank you." Liz took the sweaters, her voice softening. "Pieter, are you sure you're not the father of Karen's baby?"

"Yes, damn it, I'm sure! The baby wasn't mine! It couldn't have been, because we never slept together."

"Then why are you yelling?"

"Because she came on to me like gangbusters, and a whole bunch of my friends know that."

"I didn't know you ever turned down a willing female, Pieter."

"You don't know a hell of a lot," Pieter said tightly. "About me, or about your roommate. From the way Karen approached me, I'd guess half the men in Denver could have been the father of her baby. But whoever the father was, it wasn't me." Pieter swallowed the last of his orange juice, muttered an obscene epithet and pushed himself off the bed. "Damn Mikhail and his training schedule. I'm planning to go out and party."

"Pieter, don't go for a minute! Have you told the police what you know about Karen?"

"I don't know anything about Karen."

"You know she came on to you."

He laughed harshly. "Are you crazy? In the first place, I don't know a thing about her general behavior. All I know is how she behaved with me. And in the second place, don't you think I have enough problems with the media without asking for trouble? I've already got two teenagers suing me in paternity suits, and I swear to God I've never set eyes on either of them."

"The police think Dex—Senator Rand is the father of Karen's child."

"That's their problem. Or his. Anyway, it sure isn't mine." Pieter zipped up his jacket and strode out of the bedroom. Liz hurried after him.

"Pieter!"

He stopped but didn't turn. "Yeah?"

She swallowed, surprised at the words that came out. "Take a cab home from the party if you drink too much."

"I could do that." He swung around and looked at her, his eyes shadowed. "Have you thought about taking a vacation, Liz? Somewhere a long way away from Denver?"

"I only just moved here, for heaven's sake!"

"Looks like now would be a real good time to move on."

"Pieter, what are you trying to tell me?"

He shrugged, reaching for the door. Liz had the

feeling he was regretting having come, regretting even more having spoken so freely. "Nothing, babe. I guess I'm just running off at the mouth. See you around, huh?" He left the apartment, slamming the door loudly behind him.

LIZ'S PACKING still didn't go as quickly as she'd hoped, even after Pieter left. She was interrupted by two phone calls. One came from the nursing home in Durango where her mother was being cared for. The ostensible purpose of the call was for the head nurse to reassure Liz that Mrs. Meacham remained unaware of her surroundings and was therefore not at all worried by the news stories that had been blasting forth all day on the lounge TV. But Liz couldn't help suspecting that the real purpose of the call was to find out if she'd been arrested.

The second call came from a journalist offering Liz five thousand dollars for "the inside story on your affair with Senator Rand."

It had been so long since she'd needed to field this sort of call that Liz let the journalist rattle on while she stared at the receiver, literally bereft of words. Finally she gathered her wits together sufficiently to respond.

"The senator and I are not currently having an affair. We did not have an affair in the past, nor do we plan to have an affair in the future. That's my exclusive inside story and you're welcome to it. For free." She banged down the receiver. "I hope that broke your eardrum," she muttered.

Her suitcase finally packed, she was almost at the front door of the apartment when the phone rang again. She hesitated, not wanting to confront another journalist—or Lieutenant Rodriguez, for that matter. When the phone continued to ring, the conviction grew that it was Dexter, calling to say he'd changed his mind about having her stay with him. Reluctantly she snatched the receiver from the cradle and barked, "Hello!"

"You sound horribly fierce, Lizushka. What is all this that I hear is going on up there in Denver?"

"Mikhail!" With a sigh of relief, she sank into the chair alongside the phone. Mikhail had married Alison just as Liz's own marriage to Dexter was going down in flames. He had defected from the Soviet Union during the world figure-skating championships five years ago, shortly after Alison had died in an Aeroflot plane crash. Drawn together by shared grief, he had been Liz's closest friend and confidant ever since his arrival in America. The warm sound of his accented voice made her smile, and she felt herself relax for the first time in hours.

"I'm sorry I sounded so aggressive. I expected you to be a reporter."

"Ah! That explains everything," he said with a laugh. "You and the reporters are never friends, yes?"

"No, we sure aren't. This morning's session with the wolf pack reminded me how much I love obscurity."

"I was at the rink all day and I didn't hear the

news until I came home and turned on the TV while I cooked supper. Lizushka, this is terrible. Another of your roommates is dead, and you have been seeing Dexter Rand? What in the world have you gotten yourself into?''

"I don't know, Mikhail. I just absolutely and completely have no idea.''

"But how did you get mixed up again with that monster Dexter? I know how bitter you felt after your divorce, and rightly so.''

"Karen Zeit worked for him.''

"And you never knew this? In all the weeks you shared an apartment with her, you never discussed her job?''

Liz felt herself blush. "I knew Karen worked for Dexter,'' she admitted.

Mikhail said nothing, but she could feel the silence gradually fill with his concern. "I thought we were friends,'' he said at last. "Good friends. Why didn't you tell me about Karen's job?''

"It...there was nothing to tell.''

"Are you sure, *dorogoya?*'' He spoke the Russian endearment softly. "I don't want you to get hurt again. Are you quite certain that the smiles you exchanged with the senator on the TV were just for the reporters?''

"I'm a hundred percent positive! That news conference didn't mean a thing in terms of our personal relationship. We just decided that it would look better for both of us if we joined forces to meet the press, that's all.''

"With you and Dexter, things are not likely to be so simple, Lizzie. I hoped you'd finally gotten over your hang-ups for this ex-husband of yours."

"I have!" she declared vehemently. "Don't you see, Mikhail, it's because he means nothing to me that I was determined not to move out of Karen's apartment. I never planned to see Dexter, or speak to him, so what difference did it make who she worked for?"

A rueful note crept into Mikhail's voice. "As it turned out, *dorogoya*, rather a lot."

"But I had no way of knowing Karen would be killed. No way of knowing that I'd be thrust into Dexter's orbit again. Besides, this will all blow over. Believe me, I have no intention of staying within his striking range."

There was another worried silence before Mikhail spoke again. "Liz, do you not think it is time to tell the police about what has happened to your last two roommates? They already believe Karen was murdered. How is it going to look when they find out you were living with two other people who both died by falling out of windows?"

"Brian shot himself first," she said, as if that made the situation somehow less suspicious.

"Shot himself—or was shot? Do you not realize that the police will soon ask you this very question?"

"But I haven't done anything," she protested. "Eventually they'll find the people who are responsible, and in the meantime, I refuse to worry. In this country people are innocent until they're proven guilty.''

"The United States is a wonderful place, Lizushka, the best in the world. But in this country the police want to write SOLVED across their file covers, just like in Russia.'' His voice was husky, his accent strong enough to add a beguiling touch of emphasis to his vowels. Liz felt a familiar rush of affection.

"Mikhail, you worry far too much about me. I'm not nearly as vulnerable as you think.''

"I do not think you are vulnerable. But you are my sister, the twin of my Alison. Of course I must worry. How can I remain calm while the police bumble around, searching for a solution? How do we know that the murderer will not turn his attention to you while the police plod through their 'routine investigations'?''

She shivered, then said staunchly, "If somebody wanted to kill me, Mikhail, they would surely have done it by now.''

"Who knows what this crazy murderer's motivations might be?''

Her control wavered, perilously close to breaking. "Oh God, Mikhail, don't you realize it's the pointlessness of all this that's driving me crazy?''

Mikhail backtracked immediately, obviously upset that his concern for Liz's welfare had made him add to her worries. "I am a fool,'' he said softly. "You are right not to concern yourself about a problem that cannot have anything to do with you. There is no reason for anybody to wish to kill you.''

She made an effort to laugh. "It's not as if I'm going to leave somebody a trillion dollars when I die.''

"And you live like a nun, so it cannot be a crime of passion. *Dorogoya*, let us stop talking about this horrible situation and turn to more pleasant subjects. I did not call to alarm you, but to issue an invitation. You will not want to be alone tonight, so I will drive up to Denver and bring you home to my house. You can spend the night with me in Colorado Springs and take my car into work tomorrow. The drive will be a little long for you, but we shall have dinner together tonight and enjoy each other's company over a glass of wine, so that you will say the long commute was worth it. You know you can stay with me for as many days as you wish. Forever, if you would only agree to it.''

His generous offer produced an immediate wave of guilt in Liz. During the past twenty-four hours she had scarcely given Mikhail a thought, so exclusively had her attention been focused on Karen's death and her own meeting with Dexter. The obsession with Karen's death might be understandable, but the obsession with her ex-husband was not. Why in the world hadn't she remembered Mikhail when she'd been trying to come up with an alternative to checking into a hotel? Why had she so meekly agreed to spend another night with Dexter?

"Mikhail, I would love to come to Colorado

Springs," she apologized. "But I've already agreed to go to…" She let her words trail off, as reluctant as she had been with Pieter to admit where she was going. Mikhail wouldn't gossip, but he would call her a fool—which she probably was—and right now she didn't feel strong enough to face another brotherly lecture.

"I've already promised to spend the night somewhere else," she amended. "With a friend from work." She blushed at the lie.

"Well, I'm glad you've found a place to stay. Is this new friend male or female?"

She could hear the hurt behind the cheerful words and felt like a worm. It seemed more important than ever not to let Mikhail find out where she was going. He simply wouldn't understand that her decision to spend the night at Dexter's house was entirely practical, based on her need to find an answer to the mystery of Karen's death. Mikhail had known her well at the time of her marriage breakup, and would never accept that she was cured of her infatuation. Knowing that she was spending a second night in her ex-husband's house, he would read all sorts of false significance into the arrangement.

"A married man with a child," she said finally, sticking as closely to the truth as she could. "Pieter Ullmann was pestering me to spend the night at his apartment, and since I didn't feel in the mood to become his bedtime bunny of the week, I accepted an invitation from a…from a colleague."

"Has Pieter been bothering you?" Mikhail's

voice was sharp. "That boy is a great skater, but he's about as mature emotionally as a two-year-old."

"The poor guy's only twenty, isn't he?"

"Twenty-one, going on fifteen."

Liz laughed, chiefly from relief that her brother-in-law wasn't pursuing the question of precisely where she planned to spend the night. "I learned to handle the Pieters of this world a long time ago," she said. "You forget how many young men I met who were dazzled by their own Olympic medals and thought I ought to be dazzled, too."

He joined in her laughter. "You're right. You have worked so hard at becoming the efficient woman executive that I forget you were once poetry on ice, and everybody's heartthrob. Well, *dorogoya*, since you are determined to desert me, I shall eat my Stroganoff alone. Think of all that sour cream and fresh paprika and weep."

"I will for sure! It'll probably be hamburgers and French fries for me, if I'm lucky."

"Serves you right for abandoning me. Will you come down to the Springs on Saturday? We will share our favorite meal."

"It's a date," she said, relief flooding her because she had brushed through this difficult conversation without mortally wounding Mikhail's sensitive Russian soul.

"Goodbye, Lizushka."

She was halfway to Dexter's house before it dawned on her that her arrangement to spend the night with her ex-husband had been a somewhat casual thing—scarcely a commitment graven in stone. To avoid hurting Mikhail's feelings, all she had needed to do was call Dexter and explain politely that she no longer wished to accept his invitation.

Liz wondered why this obvious solution had not occurred to her earlier.

It required very few minutes' reflection to decide it would be wiser not to inquire too deeply into the workings of her psyche.

THE MEETING with Igor, his contact from the embassy in Washington, D.C., didn't go as well as he had hoped. He'd noticed that their meetings in Denver nearly always ended on a sour note, and he wondered if Denver's high altitude gave Igor a headache. Certainly, tonight had been one of their less pleasant sessions, despite the fact that Karen had been so successfully taken care of.

Everything had started off well enough, although he'd been too smart to relax and rest on his laurels. Igor was notorious for his habit of lulling his minions into a false sense of security before letting fly with brutal criticisms.

He had set the right tone for the meeting by providing Igor's favorite food. The KGB man had beamed at the generous supply of greasy packages set out on the table, and had selected a jumbo-size box of French fries and a double hamburger.

He himself didn't eat such poisonous foods, of course. He merely watched as Igor squirted ketchup onto the fries, making swirls of bright red sauce. He reflected cynically that Igor couldn't have been allowed to do enough finger painting when he was young. Soviet nursery schools had always been big on patriotic songs and notoriously indifferent to child psychology.

After several minutes of munching, Igor looked up from his earnest consumption of French fries. "So, Karen Zeit is dead. It was time. Past time. She was becoming nervous, I think." Igor had an annoying habit of stating the obvious.

"Yes, Comrade Secretary. As I told you, she feared the FBI investigation authorized by Senator Rand would blow her cover. There is an FBI agent working in the senator's Washington office, and unfortunately, our operatives haven't yet identified him. Karen was very worried. As you know, her past wouldn't stand up to detailed scrutiny."

"I am all too aware of the limitations of the identity we provided. With this murder investigation going ahead full steam, we work under time pressure." Igor munched through a mouthful of burger. "At least the main part of our mission proceeds according to plan. The trap has been satisfactorily set. The senator is already receiving some very unfavorable press."

"Yes, Comrade. And the press conference with his ex-wife can only work to our advantage."

"Ah yes! The former wife of the senator. I am glad that you yourself bring up the subject of Ms. Meacham." Igor licked up a drop of ketchup with a long, pink tongue, closing his eyes in appreciation of the exquisite flavor. "If Congress would only stop trying to sell democracy to the third world and concentrate on hamburgers, the Americans would be invincible."

He smiled, as he was supposed to. Igor liked to be thought of as a humorist. "I expect Congress wishes to export both hamburgers and democracy, Comrade Secretary."

Igor wiped his fingers delicately on a paper napkin. "Hamburgers transplant better than democracy. But, to return to the subject of Ms. Meacham. I hope you have that situation firmly in hand? She is the high-risk element of our operation. She must be seen in public with the senator, but she cannot become too close to him."

"I understand, Comrade Secretary. Ms. Meacham is completely under control."

"Hmm." Igor managed to express a great deal of doubt in a small grunt. "It is one thing for Ms. Meacham to appear at a press conference with her former husband. It would be an entirely different matter if the two of them should start to become—intimate. You have assured me that the hatred between Elizabeth Meacham and Dexter Rand makes any exchange of information extremely unlikely. I trust you have not miscalculated."

He was beginning to sweat, and surreptitiously wiped his palms on the edge of the tablecloth. "Believe me, Comrade Secretary, there is no chance of that. Elizabeth Meacham despises the senator after the way he treated her at the time of their divorce. I have heard this same story repeated on all sides.''

"And your own observation?''

"Agrees completely with what I've heard.''

"I expected her to be with you tonight. Where is she?''

"I invited her to have dinner with me, but she refused. However, there is no cause for alarm. She's spending the night with one of her colleagues.''

"If she is not precisely where we want her to be, then there is cause for alarm. Your much-vaunted success with other women is of no value to us if you cannot attract Ms. Meacham sufficiently to control her movements.''

He couldn't stop his gaze sliding disparagingly over Igor's bulging waistline and clumsy, peasant-like hands, then immediately realized it was a mistake to have allowed his disdain to show.

"Comrade Champion,'' Igor said softly. "My duty to the motherland does not require that I should have a desirable body. My duty requires only that my wits remain sharp and that I possess a profound understanding of the American political system. It is clear that I am fulfilling my duties. Are you fulfilling yours?''

"Yes, yes, of course, Comrade Secretary. Is Karen Zeit not dead? Is Senator Rand not in trouble?'' He decided it might be smart to make no further mention of Liz Meacham.

"Who was the father of Karen Zeit's baby?'' The

question was slashed across the table with the sting of a whip.

He made the fatal mistake of lying. "Senator Rand—"

"Would never take his secretary to bed. He is the model of bourgeois propriety. You are the father of her baby, Comrade. Is that not so?"

Regretfully, he realized he had little choice but to tell the truth. "It isn't certain, Comrade Secretary, but the child could be mine. Karen fell hopelessly in love with me, and her infatuation jeopardized the safety of our operation. I had sex with her only to keep her content. Naturally, I had no idea that she would be so careless as to allow herself to become pregnant."

Igor banged his fist on the table, and the little packets of ketchup jumped with the force of the blow. "You play me for a fool, Comrade Champion. Do you expect me to believe that Karen never told you she carried your child? What reason could she have had to become pregnant, if she did not want you to marry her?"

Thank God, he had murdered Karen. Now she would never be able to contradict his story. He lifted wide, innocent eyes to meet Igor's accusing gaze. It was a blessing that he had always had such marvelously honest eyes. "Comrade Secretary, I swear to you that Karen never once mentioned to me the fact that she was pregnant. Perhaps she knew the child wasn't mine."

Igor grunted. He was a past master of the expressive grunt. This one conveyed scorn, disbelief and indifference in almost equal measure. "We have more important problems to worry about at this moment, I suppose. Our government is running out of time. Our secret lobbying against the new F-19B fighter jet has not been as successful as we hoped. This is an effective weapon, Comrade, and by some miracle, many U.S. senators on the Defense Appropriations Committee understand that fact."

"The new president isn't much in favor of expensive weapons development."

"But on this occasion, there is rare bipartisan support for the project. Except for one or two die-hard pacifists, the F-19B has met with nothing but approval. It is undetectable by radar. It is faster than any other plane now flying. It can carry conventional arms as well as nuclear warheads, and it can come in low to pinpoint a target. Possession of such a plane would give the United States an enormous strategic advantage. Therefore we cannot allow it to go into production. And unless we can convince Dexter Rand to campaign actively against it, the Senate Appropriations Committee is likely to vote funds for production of the plane within a few weeks."

"I understand, Comrade Secretary. I realize that Dexter Rand must be made to declare publicly against the plane. We need to control his vote. His chairmanship of this senate committee has already proven disastrous to the interests of the Soviet Union."

Igor gave another of his grunts. "From our point of view, he does far too good a job of separating useful military technology from projects that are never going to work. Who would have thought the senators would be smart enough to select a military expert to chair their armaments committee?"

He didn't bother to answer what was clearly a rhetorical question. Senator Rand's appointment to the Appropriations Committee had been causing gray hairs in Moscow ever since it was first announced. He spoke reassuringly. "The details of our plan to control the senator have been meticulously worked out, Comrade. With luck, Dexter Rand will soon be a useful tool in our hands instead of a thorn in our sides."

"Luck doesn't factor in our government's planning, Comrade. I trust that you have left no part of this operation to luck."

Inwardly he cursed the aggravating old buzzard. Outwardly he smiled. "The plans have been perfected to the last tiny detail, Comrade Secretary. We will deal with the senator and with Elizabeth Meacham before the end of the week." He paused for a moment, then pressed ahead with the question that was at the forefront of his mind. "Have the necessary personnel arrived from Moscow?"

Igor's response was curt. "She is already in the embassy."

"There is—a message for me?"

"She looks forward to seeing you soon."

He would have liked to ask more questions, but

knew that Igor would delight in withholding information. "Do you want me to review the details of our plan for the abduction, and for Elizabeth Meacham's murder?"

"No." Igor rose to his feet. "I am well aware of your plans. Have you forgotten that I approved them in the first place? I am spending the next few days collating the evidence that will prove that Senator Rand murdered Ms. Meacham. Just be sure that your own part of the operation is carried out with similar efficiency."

"It is all taken care of, Comrade Secretary. We shall need the photographs when the senator goes to Washington."

The damned old buzzard grunted again. "A word of warning, Comrade Champion. Neither the senator nor Elizabeth Meacham is a fool. Each of them knows that they did not commit murder. Take care that their efforts to save themselves do not unravel our plans."

"Their efforts to extricate themselves from the trap cannot succeed," he said, with a touch more confidence than he actually felt. "There are no trails for them to follow. We've made sure that whatever line of investigation anybody pursues, they will find only dead ends."

"Very dead, I trust." Igor put on his jacket. "Dead is highly desirable."

He wasn't sure he'd understood. "I'm sorry, Comrade Secretary? If you would be so good as to clarify..."

"One of your collaborators is no longer useful to us, and unfortunately he knows too much. Take care of him, Comrade. Take care of him soon, before his nerves get us all into trouble."

He rose to his feet, relieved that the interview had ended on a relatively positive note. Killing was easy. "I understand, Comrade Secretary. The matter will be taken care of expertly. I will kill him myself."

"No more windows, Comrade. I'm getting tired of windows."

"Certainly, Comrade. There are many other ways. I think perhaps a knife."

Igor grunted.

CHAPTER SIX

DINNER WAS LONG OVER by the time Liz finally returned to Dexter's house. The housekeeper answered the door and directed her to a family room overlooking the backyard, where Dexter and his daughter were engaged in a game of dominoes. From the fierce frown of concentration wrinkling Amanda's forehead, Liz concluded that the game was being taken very seriously by at least one of the participants.

"Your visitor, Senator Rand. Miss Meacham's here."

"Thanks, Mrs. Morton." Dexter stood up and came across the room to greet Liz, and the housekeeper left, insisting on carrying Liz's case up to the guest room.

"Glad you made it back. Amanda and I were beginning to wonder what had happened to you."

"I'm sorry. I was delayed at the office and then I couldn't decide what I needed to pack. But I should have phoned."

"Don't worry about it. You had other things on your mind. Do you need dinner?"

"No, thanks. I stopped at Burger King on the way over."

He grinned. "Shush, don't let Amanda hear those magic words. She had to suffer through chicken breasts, mushrooms and fresh fruit salad. She tells me I'm the meanest dad in the world to keep ordering such yucky meals."

Liz's smile was only a touch strained. "Sounds like you're bringing up a deprived child, Dex. Don't you know that too much nutritious food damages the psyche?"

His eyes softened as he glanced over at the table, where his daughter was occupied in building a long, low wall of dominoes. "She's gorgeous," he said simply. "Not a hint of damage so far. Come and meet her."

Liz gripped her purse a little tighter. "Does she...um...does she know we were married?" she asked, trying to think up some reasonable excuse for hanging back. She couldn't very well say *I hated her mother so much, I don't want to meet her.*

"I told her, but she doesn't seem to find the information relevant. As soon as she realized you weren't about to become her stepmother, she lost interest in our relationship."

Liz followed Dexter across the room, curiosity to meet Susan's child still mixed with a confused grab bag of other emotions. Her stomach knotted painfully when Dexter rumpled Amanda's hair in a casual gesture that spoke volumes about his love.

"Hey, honey, I'm sorry about our game. This is Elizabeth Meacham. She's the friend of mine I told you about, and she'll be staying with us for a few days.''

Somebody had obviously taught Amanda very good manners. Or maybe, Liz thought with a touch of bitterness, courtesy to inferiors was bred into the genes of people like Dexter and Susan—part of their birthright, along with their infuriating self-possession. Amanda hopped off her chair, dark curls bouncing. *Susan's curls. Susan's green eyes. But Dexter's arrogant, stubborn chin.* Amanda held out her hand. "Hello, Mrs. Meacham. It's nice to have you here.''

Liz took the tiny hand into her own. It felt warm, a little bit sticky and oddly trusting. She swallowed hard, resisting the craziest impulse to reach down and sweep the child into her arms. Surely she was imagining the vulnerability she saw in those stunning green eyes? "Hello, Amanda." She sought for something to say that was both suitable and honest. Her gaze fell on the dominoes. "Who's winning?"

"It's kind of a draw at the moment." Amanda squinted up at her father. "Will you have time to finish the game, Dad?"

He glanced down at his watch. "It's past your bedtime already, young lady."

"But it's Friday. So there's no school tomorrow."

Dexter sat down at the table with a mock sigh. "I guess we'll have to finish, then, or you'll claim you won."

She giggled. "No, I wouldn't. I have to let you

win at dominoes, 'cos I always beat you so bad at Nintendo.''

Dexter shot a rueful glance in Liz's direction. ''Don't let this child get you in front of a TV set with a joystick. Believe me, it's a totally humiliating experience.''

The jealousy Liz felt as she watched Dexter joke with his daughter was intense and shocking. She realized that she resented Susan's success in carrying Dexter's child to term more than anything else. Nowadays she almost never thought about the possibility of becoming a mother herself, and yet for a moment, she felt a pang of loss so sharp that her miscarriage might have occurred nine days instead of nine years ago.

Dexter glanced up, his eyes darkening with sudden concern. ''Liz, are you sure you're okay? You look awfully pale.''

''I'll be fine.'' She flashed a determined smile, something she seemed to be doing a lot lately. ''But I might go and beg a cup of tea from Mrs. Morton, if she's still in the kitchen.''

''She's probably gone to her room. If so, help yourself to whatever you want.''

''Thanks.'' Liz's main purpose wasn't to drink or to eat; it was to escape from the unbearably cozy scene of domestic intimacy. ''Good night, Amanda, I'm glad to have met you. See you tomorrow, Dexter.''

''Night, Mrs. Meacham.''

"I'll join you in the kitchen as soon as we've finished our game."

"There's no need—"

"We have things to talk about," Dexter said quietly. "For one thing, we need to decide what we should do tomorrow. Also, Lieutenant Rodriguez came to see me again this afternoon."

She swung around, looking at him inquiringly. "He's been checking our alibis," he said. Glancing at his daughter, he added, "I'll talk to you later."

"You need a six, Dad," Amanda interjected.

Dexter laid down a domino with a triumphant flourish. "Ha-ha! Now you need a six, too, and I don't think you have one."

Liz left the room. She doubted if either Dexter or his daughter noticed her departure.

THE DOMINO GAME lasted less time than she would have expected. Dexter came into the kitchen just as she finished pouring out her cup of orange-and-cinnamon tea.

"Would you like some?" She gestured to the pot.

"Thanks, but you sit down. I'll get it." He searched in a couple of cupboards until he found a cup and saucer—he evidently didn't spend much time in the kitchen—then sat next to her at the polished wooden table. "Rough day?" he asked softly. "You look beat."

She stirred her tea with great concentration, although she never took sugar. "No worse than yours, I expect."

He smiled grimly. "That leaves plenty of scope for rough. How were things at the office?"

"Busy. Awful."

His smile relaxed slightly. "Rarely have two small words conveyed such a wealth of information. That sums up my day perfectly." He took a sip of tea. "As far as I can tell, the police have moved us up from being run-of-the-mill suspicious characters into being prime suspects. The preliminary pathology results show that Karen died around four-thirty. The highly efficient Lieutenant Rodriguez has checked our schedules and determined that neither of us have alibis. He clearly suspects us of working in collusion to do away with poor Karen."

"He thinks we were working together?"

"He's convinced of it. We were planning to marry again, you see, only Karen inconveniently became pregnant and wouldn't have an abortion. Since U.S. senators from Colorado can't hope to get elected with sex scandals featuring prominently in their résumés, you and I hatched this plan to toss Karen from a window and make it look like suicide."

The scenario was so preposterous that she would have laughed if she hadn't been so scared. "That's pretty far-fetched as a motive for you to commit murder. It's flat out ridiculous for me. What in the world am I supposed to get out of all this?"

"Me. And my money." He caught her look and his mouth twisted into a wry grimace. "My dear Liz, the lieutenant can't be expected to understand that you wouldn't take me if I came gift-wrapped in million-dollar bills.''

She had the oddest impression that she could hear pain beneath his flippant words. ''For a double layer of packaging I might consider it,'' she said.

He looked at her long and hard. ''That's a considerable improvement over the situation nine years ago. My lawyer said the sound of my name was enough to make you turn green by the time our divorce case hit the courts.''

She looked away. ''I was very young then.''

''Yes.'' He hesitated. ''So was I, you know. Not in years, perhaps, but in experience.''

Liz turned around and stared at him in astonishment. ''How can you say that? You were the most sophisticated man I'd ever met! You'd already traveled half across the world. You were the Air Force's ace test pilot. You were a millionaire—''

''And I knew no more about falling in love and being married than you did,'' he interjected quietly. ''Aside from acute hormonal spasms when I was in my teens, I'd never been in love until I met you. A lot of the time we were together, my emotions were…''

He didn't finish his sentence and she prompted him. ''Yes?''

''Out of control is the best way to describe it, I guess.''

She twirled her teacup on its saucer. It was Dresden porcelain, she noticed, antique and beautiful. Probably imported into the States by Dexter's grandfather, who had once been America's ambassador to Germany. It was Germany where Liz had competed in her last, disastrous skating championship. She cradled the delicate china in her hands, as if by doing so she could contain her memories of that awful time.

"What are you thinking about?"

"The Olympics," she replied honestly.

He didn't have to ask which Olympics. They both knew. "That was a bad night for you," he said. "For both of us."

"I was six weeks pregnant," she said suddenly. "I'd torn a ligament in my ankle and I felt so sick I thought I was going to throw up every time I turned my head."

His body stiffened with shock. "Pregnant! Liz, my God! Why didn't you tell me?"

She traced the thin gold rim of the cup with her thumb. "I was...afraid you'd be mad at me. Because you said you didn't want children and you thought I was taking birth-control pills."

"And you weren't taking pills?"

She shook her head, then laughed, mocking her younger self. "I wanted to trap you into staying married," she admitted. "So I used the oldest trick in the world. And then, when I found out I really was expecting a baby, I was too scared to tell you. Not to mention telling my coach, who'd have thrown a fit at the prospect of his star athlete going on maternity leave." Her mouth twisted into a painful smile. "I'd worked out the perfect trap, except I was afraid to spring it."

"What happened to the baby, Liz?"

"I miscarried a couple of months later."

"And you still didn't tell me? Good God, was I really such a monster?"

She finally looked up at him. "I don't know. By that time, I couldn't see you clearly anymore. Susan was always in the way, blocking my view."

He stretched out a hand, then allowed it to fall back into his lap without touching her. She realized now—as she never would have nine years earlier—that he was afraid of offending her, afraid of her rejection. His voice when he spoke was tight, not with impatience as she would once have thought, but with regret. "I never was unfaithful to you during our marriage, Liz. Whatever Ali... Whatever anyone may have told you, Susan and I never made love until after you'd divorced me."

"Alison never suggested you and Susan were lovers," she said. "Susan told me herself."

Silence descended, thick, heavy and fraught with tension. "If Susan told you we were lovers during the time you and I were married, then she lied," Dexter said at last. "I'm sorry, Liz. I must have been doing a lousy job of handling my relationships for them to have gotten so screwed up."

"It was a long time ago," she said, and suddenly the trite words were true. She pushed the cup of tea away, leaning back in the chair to ease cramped muscles. "A long time ago, in a faraway place, with people who've changed so much they're hardly the same.''

''You've changed,'' he agreed. ''You're softer. More beautiful.''

''Thank you.'' She was shocked by the intensity of pleasure his comment provoked. She got up from the table, carrying the teapot over to the sink so that she could hide the sudden color staining her cheeks. ''We'd better get this conversation back to the present, Dexter, or the lieutenant will be pounding on the door to arrest us and we'll have done nothing except trade compliments about how mature we've gotten since we savaged each other in the divorce courts.''

''I wish that sounded funny. The bit about the lieutenant coming to arrest us, I mean. But the fact is, I have no alibi. I left a meeting with the manager of Stapleton Airport at three forty-five. I should have arrived here about twenty minutes later. I actually arrived home at five o'clock.''

''What happened?'' she asked, returning to her chair.

''I went to the library,'' he said wryly. ''The main one, downtown. The meeting with the airport manager had finished a half hour earlier than we expected, and I've been wanting to double-check some facts in a book on Denver's old, ethnic neighborhoods. Nobody was waiting for me, so I grabbed the chance.''

''Did you check the book out? There might be a time on the computer.''

"No, the book's for reference only. And before you ask, no, I didn't speak to any of the librarians. I knew where the book was shelved and I went straight there."

"It's a lousy alibi, Dex. Don't you have a research staff to double-check facts for you? Important senators don't visit the library unless it's an official visit."

"Liz, honey, you're singing the lieutenant's song. But you're no better off than I am. Rodriguez claims you left your office at the crucial time without telling anybody where you were going."

"Of course I didn't say where I was going!" Liz protested. "That was the whole point of the exercise. The darn phone hadn't stopped ringing all day, so I hid in one of the typists' offices, trying to catch up on my paperwork."

"Where was the typist?"

"Out sick with the flu."

"Well, good luck telling that one to the lieutenant."

Liz laughed, then sobered abruptly. "When I'm with you, I forget to take the situation seriously. Then, as soon as I'm alone, all the reasons why I should be panic-stricken come rushing back. I mean, we could end up in the electric chair, Dex."

"In Colorado they use the gas chamber."

"Gosh and golly, now I feel much better!"

He smiled, reaching out to clasp her hand. Her stomach danced a little jig. "We're going to find out what's behind this, long before things reach that stage, Liz.''

Several seconds passed before she gathered her wits sufficiently to move her hand. "Pieter Ullmann was at my apartment tonight," she said, breaking the momentary silence. "From the remarks he dropped about Karen, I guess several people could have been the father of her baby."

"He'd had an affair with her?"

"He said not. But he also claimed she came on to him in a big way."

Dexter frowned. "Odd, isn't it, how we get to know people in such a one-dimensional fashion? I can't even picture Karen as a sexually active woman, let alone a sexually aggressive one. Now that it's too late, I'm feeling guilty because I spent so little time thinking about her as a person. Maybe if I'd been more attentive to her needs, none of this would have happened."

"You're being too hard on yourself. She was an employee, Dexter, not a close friend."

"She was a damn good administrative assistant, that's for sure. We always seemed to exchange the usual chitchat about our personal lives, and yet once the lieutenant started questioning me, I realized I knew almost nothing about her. Not even trivial things like whether she preferred Beethoven or Bruce Springsteen."

"Rodriguez thinks you're concealing information."

"Of course he does. Unfortunately I'm not. In

fact, I wish I knew something—anything—that would give us a starting point to unravel what was going on in Karen's life. I suppose you haven't come up with any wonderful new insights since this morning?"

"Nothing wonderful. But I've been thinking a lot about what you said last night. About how my room-mates must have had something in common, something that linked them."

"And you thought of a link?"

"I'm not sure. It's so tenuous, you may think it's silly to mention it."

"At this point, nothing's too silly to mention."

"Well, like I told you, Brian was an engineer and Jill was a social worker, and Karen's basic training was secretarial. But in a weird sort of way, all three of them worked for the government, although their jobs were so different it almost doesn't coun—"

"Explain their connection to the government," Dexter interrupted, his body radiating a sudden tension.

She was startled by his intensity. "Karen's link is obvious. She was your personal assistant, and you're a U.S. senator."

"Go on. What about Jill?"

"She worked as a civilian employee for the Navy. The naval shipyards in Bremerton are so huge, they basically employ the whole town, so I never gave her employer a second thought when you asked me last night. She worked in the personnel-management division."

"And Brian?"

"He was a professor of electrical engineering at the university, but he didn't do much teaching, and I think his recent research was in the field of electronics. Almost all his income came from projects funded by the government, and a lot of his work was secret, I do know that."

"Have you any idea what he was working on when he died?"

"Not specifically. Even if it hadn't been secret, I wouldn't have understood what he was doing. Electronic microcircuitry isn't exactly my area of expertise. He mentioned once that he was part of the design team for a new fighter jet that was on order for the Air Force. He was brilliant at his work, everybody agreed on that."

"A new fighter jet," Dexter muttered. He stared abstractedly into the middle distance, then finally rose to his feet. "I need to make a phone call to Washington," he said. "Come into the study, will you? Liz, I think—just possibly—you may be onto something."

"Mind telling me what? You think it's significant that all my roommates worked for the government?"

"Yes, I do, although at the moment I don't see precisely how. What we need is information, and I should get that from my phone call."

Dexter opened the door to his study, shut it behind them, then pressed a section of wall paneling next to the bar. A small, concealed door sprang open to reveal a scarlet telephone. Dexter punched in a long series of numbers, gestured to indicate that Liz should take a seat on the sofa, and waited in patient silence for about thirty seconds.

"This is Senator Rand," he said finally. "I want to speak with Agent Harry Cooper. Patch me through, please."

Liz glanced at her watch. It was ten o'clock in Denver, midnight already in Washington, D.C. Agent Cooper either kept late office hours or slept with his scarlet phone next to the pillow. She leaned back against the cushions of the sofa, listening to Dexter identify himself again, first by name and then by a series of numbers.

She wondered why she felt so little surprise at Dexter's active response to her suggestion of a job link among her dead roommates. Perhaps the unreality of her situation was beginning to affect her. From the day Brian died, she had felt distanced from her everyday life, as if she could only react to events, not take charge of them. Three days earlier, for example, she would have said that being alone with Dexter was as unlikely as the possibility that Karen Zeit would be murdered. Now Karen was incontrovertibly dead, and she was spending the second night in a row with her ex-husband. Her world had lost it familiar boundaries.

"Professor Brian Jensen," she heard Dexter say. "An electrical engineer. Full professor. Possibly working on the F-19B fighter jet project. The control panel for all the F-19s came out of Seattle. I want you to find out anything and everything you can about him. He supposedly committed suicide four months ago.''

There was a short silence, followed by Dexter's reply. ''In Seattle. He shot himself, then fell out of his apartment window. There must have been a police investigation.''

Another pause, much longer this time, then Dexter's reply. ''I need this information, Cooper. I need it soon. I'm asking as a personal favor. I'll beg, if you want me to.''

Silence. ''Thanks, Cooper. I owe you one. By the way, I'm beginning to wonder if the leak is from Denver, and not from D.C. You might want to talk to your chief about that. Maybe we have the undercover operative in the wrong place, which would explain our lack of progress. If we do, Karen's death gives us the perfect excuse to introduce somebody at this end. I'm going to need a new assistant.''

Another pause. ''Fine. But please, just make sure she can type and knows something about party politics.'' A final brief moment of silence, and then Dexter said good-night, hanging up the phone and closing the wall cabinet.

''Is that a secret phone?'' Liz asked, not sure whether to be impressed or amused.

''Not very secret. Everybody who has access to this room knows about it. But it's supposedly 'safe.' The signal's scrambled, so it's protected against wiretaps.''

''Do all senators get a safe red phone?''

"Not all of them. A lot depends on their committee assignments. I chair the Senate Committee on Defense Appropriations, so a great deal of top-secret material comes into my hands. Not only secret because of policy decisions, but because the technology is new."

"And that's why you got the phone?"

"Part of the reason." Dexter came and sat beside her on the sofa. Their knees touched, and she carefully moved away.

"I feel like I'm dragging out your teeth without benefit of anesthesia," she said. "Can you tell me what that phone call was all about?"

"There have been leaks of classified information from my Washington office," Dexter said slowly. "Nothing too important until a couple of months ago, when the specifications for a section of the new F-19B fighter jet turned up for sale on the international black market."

"But how do you know all this? Presumably black-market arms dealers don't go around shouting to the world about their sale item of the week."

"I can't answer your question, Liz. I've already revealed far more than I officially should. Let's just say certain government agencies manage to keep effective tabs on who's selling what to whom."

"Are you allowed to tell me why those government agencies decided the black-market specifications came from your office?"

"Top-secret documents have an extremely limited distribution, and each copy is marked with identifying data. The specifications that turned up on the black market were obviously photocopies of material that had come from my office.''

"If you haven't found out who was responsible for the original leak, how do you stop future ones?''

"Liz, I know I sound like a bad actor in a thirties movie, but the answer is: *We have our ways*.''

"Do your ways work?''

"Hopefully. So far they seem to be working.''

"It's certainly a strange coincidence that Brian should have been working on the F-19 plane when he died.''

"Very strange. Which is why I've asked my contact at the FBI to run a comprehensive check on Brian Jensen's background.''

"Couldn't you ask the FBI to run checks on Karen Zeit, as well?''

"You heard my conversation with Harry Cooper. The FBI is short of money and staff, and they're already expending too much of both on my office. I had to beg to get anything done on Brian Jensen. Unless the Colorado law-enforcement authorities ask for FBI assistance, we haven't a hope of persuading the Bureau to run two background checks simultaneously. Besides, Karen lived with you and worked with me. Between the two of us, surely we ought to be able to come up with some information about her, once we start digging.''

"I brought her address book with me.'' Liz searched in her purse, then produced the slender maroon notebook with a flourish. "There aren't too many names in it, which should make it easier to track people down.''

Dexter took the book and quickly thumbed through the pages. ''The lieutenant slipped up, didn't he? Why didn't he take this away with him?''

''Karen kept it with her recipe books in the kitchen. I guess the police passed right over it.''

''Hmm. Your name's here with a work phone number, so is mine with a D.C. address and number. Here's Evan Howard's home address and phone number.'' Dexter flicked over the pages. ''Home addresses and numbers for all the people in my Colorado office. Phone numbers for the hairdresser, the doctor and the dentist. An address for Pieter Ullmann. No phone number. And there are a dozen names I don't recognize. How about you?''

Liz leaned over so that she could see the pages as Dexter turned them. Her body was pressed against his from shoulder to thigh, and suddenly, over the chasm of nine years' separation, she felt the achingly familiar rush of sexual awareness. She couldn't move away without drawing attention to her reaction—which Dexter had given no sign of sharing—so she drew in a deep breath and reminded herself that she was a mature woman of twenty-eight, not a hormone-flooded teenager of nineteen.

''Rachel Landers is a woman Karen took gourmet cooking lessons with each Saturday. They went somewhere in Colorado Springs.'' Liz was delighted to hear that her voice sounded cool, crisp and businesslike. Unfortunately, the rest of her wasn't doing so well. She drew in another deep breath. "Bev Dixon and Rita Kominsky are tennis partners. I don't know any of the others. They all seem to be men."

"Did you notice something odd, though?" Dexter's voice was a little husky and he coughed to clear it.

"They're all Denver or Colorado Springs addresses," Liz said, wondering why he didn't move away, now that they'd finished looking at the address book. "Is that what you mean?"

"Yes." Dexter's voice was still husky. "Karen only came to Colorado from Kansas City two years ago. You'd think she'd have one or two friends from Kansas that she kept in touch with."

"Maybe she filed those addresses somewhere else."

"Maybe." Dexter closed the notebook with a snap and got purposefully to his feet. Liz tried hard not to feel bereft.

"Anyway," he said, "it seems to me our Saturday morning is mapped out for us. We have to try to talk to everybody on this list, starting with the people whose names neither of us recognize."

"Sounds good. What about Amanda, though? Won't she resent it if we leave her alone all day?"

"Mrs. Morton takes her to karate class in the morning—"

"Karate! I thought little girls were supposed to dream about ballet and pink tutus."

He grinned. "Amanda seems to prefer white trousers and stinging chops to the head. Anyway, she always brings a couple of friends over for lunch afterward, so she won't miss me. But I have promised to spend the evening with her.''

"That works out well, because I've agreed to have dinner with Mikhail.''

"Are you planning to spend the night with him?" Dexter's question was a miracle of neutrality. ''Just so as I know whether to lock up the house or not,'' he added.

Liz looked at him steadily. "No," she said. "I'm not planning to spend the night with Mikhail tomorrow, although I often do.''

Dexter turned away, his movement abrupt. "Would you like a nightcap? A brandy? A diet soda?"

"No thanks. But you're right, we should get to bed.''

Her words fell like stones into the sudden silence, weighted with a meaning she had never intended to give them. Dexter shoved his hands into the pockets of his pants, as if he didn't know what else to do with them.

"It's still there, isn't it?" he said quietly. "For both of us.''

"I don't know what you me..." The lie died away, unfinished. "Yes," she admitted, meeting Dexter's gaze. "It's still there. But I realize now that people don't have to...to get involved just because they're attracted to each other.''

Dexter came and stood in front of her. His dark

brows lifted, giving him a sardonic, almost derisive air. "You think now we've talked about it, we'll be able to ignore the tension between us and get on with more important things?"

"We should be able to. We're mature adults."

"How adult?" he murmured, pulling her into his arms and holding her lightly against his lean, hard strength. Liz tried to ignore the shiver of delight that coursed through her, but she didn't move away.

His head bent slowly toward her, his breath warm against her skin. Against her will, her eyes drifted closed, so she didn't see the moment when his mouth covered hers, but she felt his touch with every fiber of her being.

With a quiver almost of despair, Liz melted into his arms. Why did Dexter's kiss turn her to fire, where other men's attempts at lovemaking left her cool and faintly bored? The years of separation hadn't dulled her memory of what it was like to share Dexter's bed, and when he trailed tiny, seeking kisses around the edge of her mouth, she had a brief moment of madness when she wondered what depth of pleasure would be in store, if she allowed herself to follow him up the stairs into the welcome darkness of his room.

His hands left her shoulders and slid into the tight knot of her hair, pulling out the pins so that he could run his hands through the silken strands. For a single insane minute she allowed herself to be drawn unreservedly into the kiss, until the heat flooding her body triggered some primitive warning that soon she would leave herself with no choice but to surrender.

Panting, shaking, she drew herself away. ''No!'' she whispered. ''Please, Dex, don't make me feel this way....''

As soon as she had spoken, she realized just how much those few words revealed. Dexter, thank God, didn't challenge her. Instead, he lightly touched a forefinger to her lips.

''You taste even better now you've grown up,'' he said.

CHAPTER SEVEN

THE FIRST PART of Saturday morning taught Liz how frustrating—not to mention exhausting—a supposedly simple investigation could be. She and Dexter called first on Karen's tennis partners, who agreed that Karen played tennis regularly and well. None of them had any idea who her other friends might be, or what she did when she wasn't playing tennis.

Dexter suggested that their next move should be to check out the men on the list. Six of the dozen men listed in Karen's notebook weren't home. Another had moved out of state, leaving no forwarding address. Four were at home and willing to answer questions, but had nothing more to say than that they'd met Karen only recently and didn't know her very well.

The last person on their Most Wanted list turned out to be an airline steward, who'd just flown back to Denver from Hong Kong. The news of Karen's death clearly came as an unpleasant shock to him, since he hadn't read any American newspapers for a couple of days. His surprise might have contributed to his willingness to talk but he—like all the others—denied being a close friend of the dead woman.

"Karen was just somebody I met at a party, if you know what I mean."

"Yes, I know what you mean," Dexter responded neutrally. "Did she spend more than one night with you?"

"How d'you know she spent the night?" The steward's voice contained a heavy touch of belligerence. "I never said anything about taking her home, and I sure didn't get her pregnant."

"Karen mentioned something once...." Liz carefully didn't specify what her roommate had mentioned, and the steward jumped in.

"Hey, whatever she said, it wasn't any great love affair between us, you know. She was feeling lonely and upset about some guy or other who'd dumped on her, and I offered her a few hours of fun. To take her mind off things, you know? We only met a couple of times after that first night."

Dexter spoke quickly. "Did she tell you anything about the man who'd been treating her so badly? His name, perhaps, or where he lived?"

The steward gave a reminiscent smile and winked. "Hey, she might have done, if you know what I mean. I guess I never paid too much attention to what Karen said. That little lady was some bundle of fire, a regular crackerjack in bed. We were really something together." He caught Liz's eye and saw that his kiss-and-tell boasting wasn't going over too well.

"Maybe I do remember one thing," he amended. "This guy who'd dumped on her—she mentioned once that she worked for him. Like he was her boss, if you know what I mean, and he was taking advantage.''

Dexter's face revealed nothing of what he was thinking. ''Yes,'' he said. ''We know exactly what you mean.''

Liz quickly asked another question, but the rest of their conversation revealed little more than that the steward remained very impressed with his own skill in the bedroom.

''He and Pieter Ullmann sound like soul mates,'' Liz commented as they returned to the car. ''We should introduce them to each other.''

''He certainly seems like a bad choice of companion, if Karen was feeling unsure of herself,'' Dexter agreed. He clicked the seat belt closed, not looking at Liz when he spoke again. ''Feel free to report what we just learned to Lieutenant Rodriguez. In fact, it's probably your civic duty to report everything the man said.''

Liz stared out of the window, although she didn't really see either the budding trees or the sunny stretch of suburban road. Despite the steward's damning words, she had the strongest conviction that Dexter wasn't the father of Karen's baby. She wondered if she was a complete fool to continue believing in his innocence. Nine years ago, she had allowed sexual attraction to overcome her common sense and even her own self-interest. Was she doing the same thing again?

Dexter's voice broke into her reverie. ''For what

it's worth, Liz, I'll repeat that Karen and I were never lovers, so I can't be the father of the child she was carrying. Although, God knows, after what that steward said, there's no reason for you to believe me.''

"Actually there is.'' Liz's thoughts became clearer in her own mind as she spoke. "In the first place, I don't think you'd ever get involved with somebody working in your office. Why would you bother when you have so many other choices? Washington is full of eligible women who'd love to be the mistress of a young, powerful senator, and you like being a senator too much to risk your job over a love affair with one of your staff.''

He smiled ruefully. "I'm not sure if that's a flattering assessment of my character or not. Anyway, it's something of a moot point, because I don't think most people would buy your reasoning. Elected officials have affairs all the time with partners who are flagrantly unsuitable. Despite all the aggressive journalists dogging their footsteps, they always assume they'll be able to keep the details of their personal lives hidden.''

"You may be right. But there's a more important reason why I don't believe you killed Karen. I've seen you with Amanda and I'm sure you'd never murder a woman who was carrying your baby. If Karen had been pregnant with your child, you'd have married her—even if only to have a fighting chance of claiming custody.''

"Rodriguez would say Karen might not have told me she was pregnant."

"He can't have it both ways. If you didn't know she was pregnant, you had no reason to kill her."

Dexter sent her one of the smiles that always made her heart turn over. Damn him. "Thanks, Liz," he said simply. "I appreciate the vote of confidence." He turned on the ignition. "Well, if you're not bound and determined to head for the nearest police station, we have an interesting question to resolve. If Karen didn't mean me when she referred to her boss, who did she mean?"

"An old boss from Kansas City?"

"Could be."

"Why did she leave her last job?"

He frowned in concentration. "She'd worked on somebody's political campaign, and they'd lost, if I'm remembering correctly."

"Who checked her references?"

"Evan Howard does all the screening of candidates for my Colorado offices. I'll ask him to check the personnel files and get back to me with some names and addresses." He gestured to the notebook lying on Liz's lap. "Do we have any other hot leads in Denver?"

"Except for the people who are out of town, there are no more men left on our list."

"Then let's go visit one of the women. Unless you're hungry?"

She shook her head. "Not at all."

"Then how about visiting some of the people

from my office? Maybe she indulged in heart-to-hearts over the watercooler.''

"We could try them. But Rachel Landers's home is much closer than anybody who works for you. She has an apartment on Havana, and that's only ten minutes from here."

"Okay." Dexter headed the car west. "Rachel Landers? Wasn't she the woman Karen took cooking classes with?"

"Yes. They went to some retired master chef in Colorado Springs. If Karen ever mentioned the chef's name, I've forgotten it, but he's obviously darn good. Karen always came back to Denver with the most delicious food. I never accepted invitations to eat out on Saturday nights."

"She never invited you to go with her to cooking class?"

"She was too smart for that. You know me and kitchens."

"Still?"

"Still." She smiled. "Not many people have my astonishing level of skill, you know. There can't be many adult females in the world routinely able to scorch water."

Dexter's grin changed to a frown. "You know, I could have sworn Karen didn't enjoy cooking, although I can't remember why I have that impression."

"You must be mistaken. Nobody could prepare food like we ate on Saturdays, unless they enjoyed cooking. Karen was a real expert, Dex." She peered out of the window. "Here's Rachel's building. Her apartment number's 304."

Rachel Landers, a plain woman of about thirty-five, eyes almost invisible behind pebble-lensed glasses, was at home and more than willing to co-operate. Delighted to be entertaining a United States senator and a former world figure-skating champion—even if the morning newspaper had implied they might well be guilty of murder—she insisted on serving them freshly brewed coffee and home-made pastries.

"I can see you put your gourmet cookery classes to wonderful use," Liz said, finishing a mouthful of flaky, raspberry-filled turnover.

Rachel blushed with pleasure. "When you punch numbers in a bank all day, it's nice to do something creative on the weekend. I made those pastries last night. They're quite simple, once you learn how to manipulate the Greek phyllo dough."

Liz suddenly realized how surprising it was that they had found Rachel at home. "Has your class been canceled for this morning?" she asked.

"Oh no, but it'll take me a while to find another ride." She pointed to her glasses. "I see quite well close up, but I'm not safe behind the wheel of a car. Chef Robert is the best teacher in the Rocky Mountain region, and Karen made his class possible for me. I was very grateful to her. I shall miss her a lot. For the ride and for the company."

Liz savored her last bite of pastry. "That was

wonderful, Rachel. You're an even better cook than Karen was.''

"Thank you." A hot red blush crept up Rachel's neck. Not a flush of pleasure, Liz realized, but of acute embarrassment.

"Did you and Karen meet at a cooking class?" she asked, wondering what could possibly have upset Rachel in such an innocuous compliment.

"No." The blush receded. "I do a little bit of catering on the side, and a customer recommended me to that nice young man who won the Olympic medal for figure skating. Oh, you probably know him, since you're in that line of work yourself. Pieter Ullmann. He was so young to be hosting a party, but he'd just won his gold medal and he was celebrating.''

Liz felt a little leap of excitement. "You met Karen at Pieter's house? That must have been over a year ago.''

"Yes, like I said, it was just after Pieter had come back from the Winter Olympics.''

Liz wasn't sure whether to be excited or disappointed. On the one hand, it was interesting to learn that Karen's acquaintance with Pieter stretched much farther back than he'd been willing to admit. On the other hand, she'd been half hoping that Rachel would reveal some entirely new name and set of relationships. She smothered a small sigh of frustration, recognizing that she and Dexter were clutching at straws. There was no good reason for a casual acquaintance like Rachel to have any deep insight into Karen's personality and friends.

Dexter returned his coffee cup to the tray. "How many of Chef Robert's classes had Karen actually attended with you, Miss Landers?"

Again the ugly red flush stained Rachel's neck and pushed into her cheeks. She sat down hard on a nearby chair. "I don't know what to say, Senator," she mumbled, flashing a wary glance from Dexter to Liz. "You see, I read in the papers that she was pregnant."

"What has Karen's pregnancy got to do with her cooking lessons?" Dexter asked. "Was she having an affair with the chef?"

Rachel stared fixedly at her sensible, low-heeled shoes. The flush had now crept up to the tips of her ears. "The cookery classes were just a cover," she whispered. "Karen never attended them."

Liz stared in surprise. "Never attended? But who cooked all that wonderful food she brought home?"

Rachel hung her head even lower. "I did. Karen paid me for everything she took home. There's only me, you see, and I can't eat everything I prepare."

Dexter leaned forward, and although his voice remained calm and soothing, Liz could see tension in every line of his body. She reflected that nine years earlier she would have heard the calm and totally missed the inner tension. Odd how she had been married to Dexter and perceived him less clearly than she did now, when they were mere acquaintances.

"Why did Karen bother to set up such an elaborate pretense?" Dexter asked. "Do you know why she wanted everyone to think she was attending cookery school, when she wasn't?"

Rachel looked away, blinking rapidly behind her pebble glasses. "Yes, I know. She was—having an affair."

"With a married man, you mean?"

"That's what I assumed. Why else would she have to sneak around and hide what she was doing? I sometimes wondered if her lover was in an important public position, as well as being married, you know?" Rachel threw an embarrassed, inquiring look in Dexter's direction.

"I'm not married," he said quietly. "I admired Karen as an employee, but that was the extent of our relationship, and we never had an affair."

"Oh, of course not! I never meant...I don't want you to think, Senator...I'm sure you wouldn't dream..."

Liz took pity on Rachel's floundering efforts at a disclaimer. "Karen never mentioned the name of her lover to you, Miss Landers?"

"Oh no, she never said anything specific about him. Just how much she loved him and then, toward the end, how he wouldn't treat their relationship seriously. How he'd taken advantage of her loyalty." She looked up, her expression apologetic and more than a little guilty. "I know I shouldn't have covered up for Karen. Some poor wife probably spent her Saturday mornings wondering what her husband was up to. But Chef Robert is such a wonderful instructor, and he teaches the business side of catering as well as the food presentation. It's my dream to set up a full-time catering service...." Once again her voice trailed away.

"I doubt if Karen would have ended her affair, even if you'd refused to cover for her, Miss Landers. She'd have found another alibi. I don't think you need carry around too big a burden of guilty conscience."

Dexter's words seemed to cheer Rachel, and she perked up enough to insist on pouring them another cup of coffee and boxing a chocolate torte for them to take home.

"I'll call on you when my daughter needs her next birthday cake," Dexter promised, and Rachel's answering smile was so gratified that her plain face became almost attractive.

"Do you want to chat with some of your employees now?" Liz asked when they had said their farewells and returned to the car.

"You don't sound thrilled at the prospect."

"I just think we're going to hear more of the same stuff we've been hearing all day. You might as well save yourself the hassle of driving all over Denver, and talk with them on Monday." Liz got into the car and waited while Dexter filtered into the stream of traffic. "Surely if one of your employees knew anything really startling about Karen, they'd have told you by now."

"I'm sure they would. It's getting late anyway, so we may as well head for home."

Liz muttered in exasperation. "Dex, have you noticed that Karen never said a word about her love life to you or to me, but she seemed willing to reveal her deepest emotional problems to virtually everyone else? People who were barely acquaintances."

"I did notice. I also noticed that she may have talked a lot, but she never seemed to give people any practical details about her lover. Was he old or young? Handsome or ugly? Rich or poor? Where did he work? Where did he live?"

"Presumably he lived in Colorado Springs. That's where she went every Saturday."

"Maybe. Or maybe not. It's only a forty-five-minute drive from the southern suburbs of Denver to the Springs, and there are a dozen motels along the highway."

"We know that he was married, and that Karen claimed he was her boss," Liz pointed out.

"Do we? I'd say those are conclusions people drew, which might tell us more about the people drawing the conclusions than they do about Karen. The fact is, we've spoken to eight people this morning, and not one of them really knew anything about her or her lover. In fact, nobody seems to know anything more about her than you and I."

"But why would she be so secretive?"

Dexter shrugged. "The obvious answer is that she had something to hide."

"You mean she was scared to reveal the name of her lover?"

"Something like that. It seems to me that either Karen or her lover stood to lose a lot if their affair became public knowledge."

"Nowadays, it's difficult to imagine how any affair could be that threatening."

"I may have become paranoid in the last two days," Dexter remarked, "but I keep thinking that if Karen had wanted to set me up as her murderer, she couldn't have done a better job. All this rushing around town, muttering dire things about her cruel boss and her broken heart. Naturally everyone concluded she was talking about me."

"I agree, but she couldn't have known she would be murdered, so she couldn't have been setting you up, even if she had some obscure motive for revenge."

"She couldn't have been setting me up for murder," Dexter agreed, "but how about for a paternity suit?"

"And the murderer just took advantage of the groundwork Karen had laid, so to speak?"

"It sounds possible, don't you think?"

"Except that Karen was an intelligent, educated woman. She must have known that blood tests today can determine paternity with ninety-nine percent accuracy. And if you weren't the father, how could she set you up?"

Dexter frowned as he turned the car off Alameda and headed toward his home. "Maybe she was just going to *threaten* me with a paternity suit, unless I paid her and her lover lots of money.''

''That's it!'' Liz squirmed around inside her seat belt so that she could look at Dexter. ''Of course, that's it, Dex! She hoped you would pay up to avoid the bad publicity. She knew all the voters would say 'there's no smoke without a fire,' and that half of them would read about the lawsuit but never get around to reading the verdict, when you were proven not to be the father. Sometimes an accusation doesn't have to be true for it to cause a heck of a lot of damage.''

''I guess that's possible,'' Dexter agreed slowly. ''Except that sort of scheming doesn't fit the efficient, bland Karen I knew.''

''But then it seems you didn't know her very well. Neither did I.''

''True. She's the last woman I'd ever have suspected of being promiscuous. I feel like I'm watching a character in a play, who's repressed Miss Prim-and-Proper in Act One. Then in Act Two she fixes her hair, rips off her glasses and bingo!—she's a sultry bombshell.''

''I guess this morning's investigations have taught us something,'' Liz said. ''For whatever reason, Karen was playing a part with both of us. And she lied a lot.''

He grimaced. ''Great return for seven hours of running around town. Damn, but I wish we could come up with a few more names to check out. At least then I'd have the illusion we were achieving something.''

"Remember five or six of the men listed in Karen's address book weren't home.''

"I'll try to reach some of them by phone early this evening, or first thing tomorrow.'' He glanced at his watch. "Probably tomorrow. Today's pretty well shot. Normally I'd ask Evan, but he's worked two eighteen-hour stints back-to-back. He deserves the rest of the weekend to himself.''

Liz glanced at her own watch. "I hadn't realized how late it is. I'll have to hurry if I'm going to be in Colorado Springs by six-thirty.''

Dexter made a smooth turn into the long driveway leading to his house. "I have a dinner meeting tonight with a dozen or so suburban mayors, and it would be wonderful if you could join me.''

"I'm sorry,'' she said. "I've already accepted another invitation. Didn't I mention that I was having dinner with Mikhail?''

"Possibly. I don't remember.'' Dexter's voice was cool. "Are you sure I can't persuade you to change your plans? Take pity on the poor journalists. Think how exciting they could make their Sunday editions, if we turned up together at the same function.''

Liz felt a wave of frustrated irritation, an unpleasant reminder of feelings that had been all too common in the days of her marriage. "No, you can't persuade me to change my mind,'' she said, her voice as cool as his. "Offering myself up as journalistic fodder isn't my idea of Saturday-night fun. Besides, I've not seen Mikhail since Karen died, and I'm looking forward to relaxing with him for a couple of hours.''

''He's done some outstanding work for the Special Olympics Committee,'' Dexter said. The praise seemed torn from him, as if it hurt to admit any good points about Liz's brother-in-law. For some reason, Mikhail—along with Alison—had always been high on Dexter's list of nonapproved persons. For the first time, Liz thought to question why.

''What in the world has Mikhail done to make you despise him, Dexter?''

''Nothing,'' he said curtly. He punched the button on the remote-controlled garage-door opener, then broke a momentary silence by turning to her and giving a rueful smile.

''Sorry,'' he said. ''I'm being a pain in the neck. The fact is that I don't like Mikhail, and I've no reason to dislike him. It makes me feel guilty, which is why I snap every time someone mentions his name.''

Liz didn't reply for several seconds, then she turned and met Dexter's gaze with a dawning sense of wonderment. ''Do you know, Dex, that's the first time in our entire relationship that you've ever admitted to possessing a single irrational feeling?''

''You sound as if you think that's good.''

''It's more than good. It's marvelous! I feel like breaking into a rousing rendition of the 'Hallelujah' chorus.''

His eyes gleamed. "Feel free," he said, drawing the car to a halt inside the garage. "As I remember, you have a lovely voice. Although I never recall hearing you sing *The Messiah*."

Against her will, Liz felt her cheeks flame with heat. She had a tuneful but oddly throaty voice, which imparted a sensual promise to even the most innocuous of tunes. Dexter had once told her that she could make "Yankee Doodle Dandy" sound like a love song. Liz had only ever sung for him in the privacy of their bedroom, and her songs had almost never reached the end. They would both be lying on the bed, tugging at each other's zippers and buttons, long before the final verse.

"Dexter, we don't have time for chitchat," she said, avoiding his gaze. "It's over an hour's drive from here to Mikhail's house, and I still have to shower and change."

Dexter wasn't to be deterred from his line of questioning, although he led the way out of the garage into the rear hallway. "Do you still play the guitar?" he asked.

"Not in the past few months," she said. "I haven't felt much like playing since Brian died."

Dexter halted his swift progress along the corridor and turned to face her. His hands lightly touched her shoulders. "I'm sorry, Liz," he said softly. "I have this urge to catch up on what's been happening in your life, and I keep forgetting this is the third time within a few months that you've lost a friend."

The warmth of his hands felt almost like a caress.

The sensation was strangely comforting. "The odd thing is," she admitted, "now that I know there's a chance my roommates were all murdered, I actually feel better. I've felt so unbearably guilty from the moment Brian died. You know, going over and over in my mind if there had been any clues that should have warned me he was in trouble."

"And were there?" Somehow she found herself held in a loose embrace, while one of Dexter's hands stroked gently up and down her back.

"He'd been irritable on occasion and he apologized by saying his research wasn't going well. But if he didn't commit suicide, then his mood can't be important, can it?"

Dexter's arms tightened around her. "Probably not, but—"

"Senator!" Evan Howard appeared at the end of the corridor, noticed that his boss was not alone, and gave Liz a halfhearted nod. Without haste, Dexter released Liz from his grasp and returned Evan's frazzled greeting with a friendly smile.

"You look as if this hasn't been a good day, Evan."

"It's been an awful day. Karen's file is missing from our personnel records, and some squirt of a police sergeant virtually accused me of destroying it to protect you. Then Lieutenant Rodriguez came around and when he found out you weren't home, he acted like you'd caught the first available flight to South America."

"He must have been reassured when you told him we'd only gone to Aurora."

"Hell, Dexter, how can you joke at a time like this? Do you know what the lieutenant has discovered? There are no records for Karen prior to the time she arrived in Denver. Her name and social-security number were fakes. Or at least they were stolen. They belonged to some baby who died in a car accident."

"Fakes!" Liz exclaimed. "So we don't even know Karen's real name?"

"Nothing. We don't know anything about her."

Liz subsided into stunned silence, while Dexter stared abstractedly into the distance, his expression unreadable. Evan began to look calmer, now that his revelations had produced a suitably amazed response. He shepherded the unresisting Liz and Dexter into the living room.

"What about our reference checks?" Dexter queried. "We always run a routine credit check, and call at least two work references. How can we have done that for someone who has no past?"

"Of course she had a past when I checked on her!" Evan almost exploded. "Damn it, I spoke to Harry Spinkoff's campaign manager. A guy called John Booth. I even remember the name, because I thought how odd it was for parents to inflict the same name as Lincoln's assassin on their kids."

Dexter cut into what was obviously becoming an endless flow of aggrieved reminiscence. "And you gave all this information to the police?"

"I told them she passed our investigation with flying colors. Banks, doctors, credit bureau, security—the whole caboodle. Everything checked out. Except they don't seem to believe I did any of it, because I can't find the darn file. How could it possibly go missing right at this crucial point? We never lose paperwork."

"Of course it isn't missing," Dexter said with a touch of impatience. "It's been stolen." He got up and walked to the door, seeming to remember Liz's and Evan's presence only at the last minute.

"I have to make a couple of phone calls," he said, and left the room without any further attempt at an explanation.

Evan pulled out his handkerchief and patted his forehead. "Why doesn't he just admit the darn baby was his and have done with it?" he muttered.

Liz looked at him coldly. "Possibly because it wasn't."

"Then who took the file? He's the only person with access to those cabinets apart from me."

Her temper flared, chiefly because she was furious with herself for defending Dexter. Why was it that after only a couple of sweet smiles, she was ready to jump through the hoop for the darn man?

"He's the only person with legitimate access, Mr. Howard. Hasn't it occurred to you yet that somebody is trying very hard to set Dexter Rand up for murder?"

CHAPTER EIGHT

AFTER COPING WITH Evan Howard, not to mention all the other frustrations of the day, it was a relief to turn into Mikhail's neat, flower-bordered driveway. Over the past few years, since his escape from Soviet Russia, Mikhail had become more than a brother-in-law to Liz; he had become her closest friend. She had moved to Colorado at his urging, and even before her move, when she had been living in Ohio and then in Seattle, they had seen each other frequently. Their shared interest in skating and their mutual love of Alison gave strong roots to their friendship.

Mikhail already had the door open by the time she parked the car. "The caviar's on ice!" he called out. "So's the vodka."

She grinned, appreciating the familiar routine in a world suddenly adrift. "Those slimy fish eggs are all yours, Mikhail, and you know it. Where's my fried chicken?"

He made a comical face of disgust, tossing his brown, windblown hair out of his eyes. "Your grease-and-cholesterol snack is warming in the oven. You can smell it right out here."

"Mmm-mmm. Yummy. Thank heaven you're not my trainer, you old grouch." She brushed her cheek against his in greeting. "Pieter is welcome to you, slave driver, gold medal and all."

"Pieter never breaks his training," Mikhail responded tranquilly. "That's part of the reason he won at the Olympics. Your trainer wasn't strict enough with you."

"So you keep telling me." Liz walked into the family room that led off the kitchen and curled up in her favorite armchair. "Ease up, old codger! I'm not in training for anything anymore."

"Except a heart attack," he muttered in mock disapproval. "And old codger, what means this?"

"A term of affection," she said, her eyes bright as she glanced up at him. "Oh, Mikhail, I'm glad to be here. These past few days have been hell."

"Now you are here you can relax." He poured her a vodka and tonic, adding a slice of fresh lime before handing her the glass. He took his own vodka neat, Russian-style, without ice. That, apparently, didn't offend his health consciousness. He put a platter of dip and raw vegetables on a coffee table comfortably within reach of Liz's chair, then took his own seat nearby. "Do you want to talk about things, Lizushka?"

She was surprised to find that she did. She launched into a detailed account of finding Karen's body, trying her best to share with Mikhail the horror she had felt in experiencing the same terrible trauma three times within four months. She described as honestly as she could the strain of the press conference and the frustration of her unproductive investigations with Dexter. The only element missing from her story was the unexpected ambivalence of her personal feelings toward her ex-husband. Since she wasn't ready to admit those feelings even to herself, she saw no reason to expose her idiocy to Mikhail's brotherly scorn.

When she finally ran out of steam, he took her glass and insisted on refilling it. "Your first drink barely smelled the vodka bottle," he said, when she reminded him that she had to drive back to town. "Besides, what is this nonsense, *dorogoya*? You don't have to drive anywhere, you can stay here. You should stay here. Why must you rush back to Denver?"

She blushed, knowing that Mikhail didn't approve of Dexter any more than Dexter liked Mikhail. "I need to look in at the office tomorrow and clear up my mountain of paperwork." It wasn't precisely a lie. She had every intention of spending the morning in the office.

Mikhail frowned, and she tried to gloss over a tight little silence. "How a company as small as Peperito's can generate so many internal memos, I'll never know."

"Too many desktop computers," Mikhail said, banishing his scowl. "Once everybody finds out how to make columns on their screens, they feel compelled to invent figures to go inside their columns." He tossed off his glass of vodka in a single swallow. "You haven't told me the whole story, have you, Liz? You're not just going back to Denver. You're staying with that monster of an ex-husband, aren't you?"

She swished the lime around in her drink. "Yes. How did you know?"

His smile was rueful. "Lizushka, you are the world's worst liar. Your nose turns pink with embarrassment if you try to tell the smallest fib."

"Right at the moment, he isn't being much of a monster, Mikhail. He's too busy trying to find out what was going on in Karen's life."

"*Dorogoya*, you are not only the world's worst liar, you are also the world's most softhearted fool. Your miserable ex-husband knows exactly what was going on with Karen. He was having an affair with her and got her pregnant. Can you not read the newspapers, Liz? Have you not heard the police detective interviewed on TV? What is his name, this lieutenant?"

"Rodriguez," she said absently. "Mikhail, I know the evidence looks damning. But when the lieutenant finds out about my other two roommates, he's going to think I'm involved in something, too. And Lord knows, nobody could understand less about what's going on than me."

"And because you are guilty of nothing, you assume Dexter is equally innocent? *Dorogoya*, you should move to the Soviet Union. My former government needs citizens like you."

She laughed, more than a little embarrassed by

her apparent gullibility. "Most people would say you're right, Mikhail, I'm sure. But in my heart of hearts, I know Dexter isn't any more guilty than I am. Dexter is too smart to plan a crime and leave himself such an obvious suspect. Someone is setting him up."

The oven pinged and Mikhail rose to his feet. "And just who do you think is setting up the great Senator Rand? Who could possibly plan such a thing? They would need to know that Karen was pregnant, for one thing—"

"Half the town seems to have known that," Liz said. "In fact, I had moments today when I wondered if Dexter and I were the only people in Denver who didn't know Karen was having an affair with a married man."

Mikhail smiled sympathetically, wrinkling his nose as he handed Liz her plate of reheated chicken and biscuits. "Well, perhaps you are right, and anyway, it is not of great importance to us whether or not your ex-husband seduced his secretary. While we eat, let us talk of more cheerful subjects. I have happy news to report to you, Lizushka."

A tiny break in his voice caused Liz to look up. "Mikhail?" she asked. "It isn't—is it your mother?"

He nodded, stretching his mouth into a huge grin as he reached behind the cushion to produce a letter written on heavy, embossed paper. "You have guessed it," he said. "Read what I have received from the embassy."

Liz laughed, sharing his happiness. "Mikhail, I don't read Russian."

"I forgot. Alison, you know, had begun to learn." For once, the mention of his dead wife brought no sadness to Mikhail's eyes. "In brief, the letter says that my mother has completed all the necessary paperwork, and that regional approval has been given to her request for an exit visa."

"Thank God for *glasnost*," Liz breathed. "Oh, Mikhail, what wonderful news!"

"I do not become too excited," he cautioned. "But my mother requires only one more step, this one from the ministry in Moscow."

Liz had spent five years following Mikhail's tortured efforts to secure an exit visa for his elderly mother. Their hopes had been high on several occasions in the past, so she knew better than to assume "one more stamp" would be a trivial detail in the endless progression of setbacks and false hopes. "How long do you think the final approval might take?" she asked cautiously.

"One day is sufficient for my mother to travel to Moscow, if she receives permission to buy an airline ticket." He shrugged with Slavic resignation. "If the authorities decide to be difficult, then we may still be talking of years."

Liz sought for something comforting to say, and found little. Her faith in Soviet officialdom was no deeper than Mikhail's. "Surely the embassy wouldn't have written the letter unless things were looking good?"

Mikhail smiled sadly. "Lizushka, you know better than that. But I allow myself a little bit of hope and today—yes, today I am truly optimistic. I do not allow myself to think that tomorrow I may again be in the depths of despair. Now eat up. Your chicken gets cold, and I have more good news. I spoke yesterday on the phone with my mother."

"But that's great! The authorities allowed your call to go through without any hassle?"

"They did. And she sounds in excellent health, most cheerful. She has been receiving the money I send, and has bought a new cooking stove." Mikhail chuckled. "She is the envy of the neighborhood, and very pleased with herself."

Liz swallowed hard over the sudden lump in her throat. "Mikhail, you know I'm counting the days for you."

He gave her hand a grateful squeeze. "I know, *dorogoya*. And since we are talking of mothers, what is the latest news from Durango?"

"The head nurse called the other day, and I visited with Mom two weeks ago. Nothing much seemed to have changed."

"She doesn't recognize you at all?"

Liz shook her head. "Nothing. The doctor commented recently that her type of memory loss is very rare. She can remember the names of public figures, like the president, for example, but she has to keep being reminded of the names of her nurses."

"It's as if her personal life doesn't exist."

"Exactly, and of course that's the most painful

thing of all. When I call her Mom, she looks right through me. At least she doesn't have to mourn Alison, although I often wonder if there's a psychological component to her memory loss."

"The doctors insist that her symptoms are entirely physical, don't they?"

"Of course. They can see the brain damage on their machines. Why would they bother considering that the machines don't tell the whole story?"

Mikhail patted her gently on the arm. "You hope for miracles, Lizushka. Could you not try to remember only the good times before your mother's stroke, and forget about yearning for the impossible?"

"Most of the time, that's what I do. The rational part of me has accepted that she's never going to be cured. The stroke after Alison's death destroyed the part of her brain that stores family memories."

"Certainly she is content with the life she leads, and her physical problems do not become worse. I was down south to judge a skating contest last month, you know, and I paid a quick visit to the nursing home. Really quick, though. It was little more than in the front door and out the back, with just time to say hello as I walked through her room."

"You're too good to us, Mikhail," Liz said impulsively. "Most sons-in-law have to be nagged into tolerating the occasional family get-together. You pay half my mother's nursing home expenses, and then visit her as well, even though she doesn't recognize you. You know how much I appreciate your caring, don't you?''

He grinned. ''*Dorogoya*, you thank me a minimum of three times per visit. How could I not know? But your thanks are unnecessary. Your mother is also the mother of Alison, who was my wife, and in Russia we hold such relationships close to our hearts. The great American capitalist system has made me rich, simply because I can teach people how to skate and win competitions. How else should I spend my money, if not on the mother of my wife?''

Liz pushed away the remainder of her chicken, assailed by a sudden memory. ''The anniversary of Alison's death was last week. With everything that happened, I'd forgotten. I'm sorry, Mikhail.''

''After five years, I have discovered that the pain fades, and all that is left are happy memories. Now when I think of Alison, I recall her beauty on the ice and her warmth in my arms. Believe me, I do not dwell in my thoughts on the crash that took her from me.''

''If the grief is finally fading, maybe it's time for you to think of marrying again.''

He put his hand to his heart, rolling his eyes in pretended passion. ''Liz, my love, you wound me with your careless words. I think of marriage all the time, but you will not have me, so what am I to do?''

She smiled. ''I was serious, Mikhail. Don't you

want to find yourself some nice American girl and produce dozens of little Olympic champions?''

"One day," he said, sobering. "But the right woman has not yet appeared. Alison is not an easy woman to replace, as you will realize. In the meantime, I hope it won't offend your sisterly ears if I confess that even though I have not yet found the mother of my children, I do not spend every night alone in an empty bed."

Liz just managed to conceal her start of surprise. Intellectually she had never expected Mikhail to remain celibate. In addition to being one of the best-looking men she knew, he had a tempting athletic body and an appealing gleam in his dark gray eyes. Moreover he worked in a glamorous job that kept him surrounded by beautiful, lissome females. Emotionally, however, she was shocked by his admission, mostly because Mikhail had always kept his sexual activities screened from her view.

"You are blushing again, Lizushka." Mikhail's voice was warm and faintly quizzical. "I did not think American women knew how."

She laughed. "I've been cursing my pale skin since high school. You know I turn scarlet for every reason under the sun—and sometimes for no reason at all."

"I know," he said softly. "And you know that my love for Alison will always be buried deep in my heart—"

"But you can't love only a memory," Liz interjected. "You can't and you shouldn't. There's no reason in the world to apologize because you enjoy feminine company, Mikhail.''

The doorbell rang, breaking the slight tension between the two of them. ''One of your luscious lovelies?'' Liz queried lightly.

He pulled a face as he walked to the door. ''More likely an angry mother whose child I refused to take on as a student. I think sometimes to buy a guard dog.'' He opened the door. ''Pieter! I wasn't expecting you tonight. Nothing's wrong, I hope? No pulled muscles or sprained wrists?''

Pieter's voice came low and urgent. ''Mikhail, I'm in big trouble. The police came to see me. They found a letter in Karen's papers—''

''You'd better come in and calm down, Pieter. Liz is here.''

''Hell, Mikhail, you don't understand. The police have found this letter, and it looks like my writing. The police expert swears it is my writing. Hell, man, that letter is big trouble for both of us.''

Mikhail's voice took on the cool authority of trainer to athlete. ''Pieter, come inside and sit down. We'll talk about this when you stop pacing on my doorstep like a caged tiger. This is America, not Russia. The police do not jump to conclusions without proof.''

''This letter is proof, man.'' But Pieter sounded calmer, and he greeted Liz with some of his usual cockiness. ''Hello, beautiful.''

''Hello, Pieter. Forgotten my name?'' she queried dryly.

He looked at her blankly, and Mikhail thrust a small shot glass into his hand. "Here, drink this. Trainer's orders."

Pieter took a tiny sip of the vodka, then put the glass aside, glancing at Liz almost defiantly. "I'm okay now," he said to Mikhail, holding out his hands. "See, steady as a rock and I'm sitting down like a good boy."

He's embarrassed, Liz thought, finding this sudden reminder of Pieter's youth almost endearing. *He's still young enough to be embarrassed because he doesn't like hard liquor.*

"So tell us what caused this visit from the police," Mikhail said, settling into his own chair.

"They found a letter, shoved inside one of Karen's journals. Man, it's trouble. It reads like I'd been involved in blood doping before the last Olympics, and Karen was trying to blackmail me."

Liz gave an exclamation of concern. "But, Pieter, didn't you explain to the police that blood doping's only useful to endurance athletes? There would be no point in you trying to boost your blood supply for a figure-skating competition."

"That is irrelevant," Mikhail said impatiently. "Pieter claims he didn't write the letter, so what we must do is contact our lawyer and insist on having a copy submitted to an independent graphologist." He banged his fist on the counter and muttered some obscure Russian curse. "This whole stupid mess over Karen is becoming ridiculous. She was a boring woman, who could not remain alone in her own bed for fear of what she would discover about herself. And now Liz and Pieter are drawn into her silly problems.''

''You think the...um...what's-it—what you said...'' Pieter's vocabulary ran to nine different translations of *Let's make love, beautiful woman,* but few English words longer than two syllables, Liz reflected.

''You mean the graphologist.''

''Yeah. Will he be able to prove I didn't write the letter?'' Pieter asked hopefully.

''I am sure. Come, we will phone the lawyer right away and you will find there is no problem.''

Liz admired the ring of confidence Mikhail was able to inject into his voice. She didn't know all that much about graphology, but she had the impression it was an inexact science and that handwriting experts often showed an alarming tendency to disagree on whether or not documents had been forged. Mikhail, however, obviously knew his student well. Under his trainer's calming influence, Pieter looked a different man from the frightened young person who had appeared on the doorstep ten minutes earlier.

''I'll clear up in here while you phone,'' Liz offered, carrying the debris of her chicken into the kitchen.

''Thanks,'' Mikhail responded, his mind clearly with the lawyer.

Liz covered the remains of the caviar with plastic wrap, returning it and the vodka to the fridge. She had stacked the plates in the dishwasher, wiped down the counters and plumped up all the cushions before Mikhail and Pieter reappeared.

"The lawyer's coming right over," Mikhail said briefly.

"Great. In that case, I'm going to leave you guys to it," she said. "I've been a bit short on sleep these past few days, and an early night would be welcome."

Both Mikhail and Pieter protested that there was no reason for her to go, but she felt their secret relief when she insisted that she needed to get back to Denver. She knew Mikhail well enough to guess that he was a great deal more worried than he cared to admit. Quite apart from any problems Pieter might face, Mikhail could not possibly afford to have the rumor getting around that his athletes indulged in illicit practices in order to win.

She gave Mikhail a hug as he walked her to her car. "Don't worry," she said. "The letter's obviously ridiculous, and anybody who knows anything about figure skating will be able to tell the police that. It must be a forgery."

"You are so swift to rush to everyone's defense," Mikhail said, his smile wistful. "Even Pieter, whom you do not like. *Dorogoya*, did it never cross your mind even for an instant that Pieter is so nervous because the letter is his?"

"And true, you mean?" Liz couldn't disguise her bewilderment. "Are you saying that you suspect Pieter did infuse himself with extra blood?"

Mikhail hesitated. "I...shall be very careful not to ask," he replied slowly.

Liz drew in a deep breath. "I'm not naive," she insisted. "But why would he do such a dangerous thing for such a minuscule advantage?"

"You were once in the finals of the Olympics, Lizushka. If you had thought that an extra dose of your own blood might—just might—give you the chance to win, can you swear you would not have taken the chance?"

"Yes, I can swear," she said. "Oh, don't get me wrong. Not because I'm so superethical, although I like to think I am. But I'd have been in such dread of discovery by the Olympic Committee that any possible edge I might have gained by injecting the blood would have been wiped out by nerves."

"Pieter, I think, does not share your sensitivities. If he wished to deceive the Olympic Committee, he would believe he could do so, and get away unpunished. I do not say that he blood-doped. I say only that it is possible. And to anybody except you, of course, I will swear that the very idea is nonsense. We are so free with our discussions, Lizushka, that sometimes I forget that I should not burden you with the truth of my thoughts. I have, perhaps, given Pieter's career into your hands. I ask that you do not voice my doubts to the police, although I shall understand if you feel you must speak."

"The police already know about the letter," Liz said. "They have graphologists they can consult.

My opinion as to whether or not Pieter might have blood-doped is irrelevant.''

"Thank you," Mikhail said. "I had better not leave Pieter alone any longer, or his nerve may once again fail him. Drive safely, Liz."

"I'll call you tomorrow to find out what the lawyer said."

"Fine. And by next weekend, let us hope the police have made an arrest, so that we can put all this nonsense behind us."

LIZ WAS BONE-WEARY by the time she pulled the car into the garage at Dexter's house. The fatigue, she realized, was mental far more than physical, the result of too many questions chasing too few answers around and around her brain.

Dexter had given her a set of house keys, and she opened the door leading from the garage to the kitchen, stopping abruptly when she realized she wasn't alone. Dexter sat at the table, his face lined with a weariness that matched her own. The stubble of the day's beard made a dark shadow across his face. His tie hung loose, and his shirt buttons were unfastened. Perversely, he didn't look rumpled, merely devastatingly sexy and more than a touch vulnerable, she had to admit. Liz mentally armored herself. Dexter was at his most dangerous on those rare occasions when he allowed himself to appear vulnerable.

"You're home early," he said. "I'm surprised

Mikhail didn't barricade you in his spare bedroom, rather than let you come back to my house.''

''It's been a long day,'' she said, ignoring his taunt. ''Several long days, in fact. I wanted an early night. How was your dinner?''

He rattled the ice cubes in his glass. ''The dinner was murder, if you must know.'' He laughed harshly. ''No pun intended.''

''The suburban mayors insisted on talking about Karen?''

''No.'' He looked up, his eyes veiled and hard to read. ''They wanted to talk about us. About you and me.''

''There is no *us*, for heaven's sake!''

''Try telling that to the suburban mayors. I ought never to have suggested you should stay with me, Liz. Evan was right when he said the reporters would find out you were here and put their own construction on the facts.''

''You're not responsible for my choices, Dex. You didn't bind and gag me.''

''But I've exposed you to the worst sort of media gossip, and I know how much you hate that.''

''I'm older now, and not at all famous. Journalists bother me less.'' She walked over to the fridge and poured herself a glass of chilled water. ''What precisely were the suburban mayors accusing us of?''

''Precisely isn't quite the word. 'Vague but all-encompassing' would be more appropriate. They seemed to have two main schools of thought. Most of them believe that you and I are passionately in love and killed Karen because we found out she was pregnant with my child.''

"Didn't it occur to them that it would have been simpler for us to pay Karen to keep quiet?''

"*Simple* isn't a favorite mayoral concept,'' he replied dryly. "If you'd ever read an official town-zoning plan, you'd know that mayors aren't noted for their commonsense approach to life's everyday problems.''

"And most of the mayors believe you and I were dumb enough to commit a murder where we were the most likely suspects?''

"Seems so. Or else they believe—''

"Am I going to like this theory any better?''

"I doubt it.''

She sighed. "I may as well hear the worst. Tell me anyway.''

"You and I are passionately in love, and Karen committed suicide when she found out about our relationship.''

She frowned in exasperation. "This is crazy, Dexter! Why would you have been impregnating Karen, if the two of us are passionately in love?''

"That interesting question doesn't seem to have occurred to the mayors. Or their spouses.''

She sipped her water, avoiding his eyes. "Why are they so set on the passionately-in-love part of the story?''

He shrugged. "We were married once before. Now you've reappeared in my life, they refuse to believe we're just good friends.''

"Would they believe wary acquaintances?"

"Is that what we are?" he asked quietly.

"I don't know." That was true. "I haven't thought about it." That was a lie.

It was his turn to stare with great concentration into his glass of melting ice cubes. "I had a phone call this evening from the chairman of the Reelect Dexter Rand Committee."

"Let me guess," Liz said flippantly, wanting to move the conversation from ground that seemed suddenly treacherous to her emotions. "He asked you please not to murder any more secretaries before next November. Right?"

"No. He asked me to get married. To you."

All at once, Liz's hands were ice-cold. "I see," she said carefully. "Did you tell him we already tried that once? With spectacularly disastrous results?"

"He knew already. He'd like us to try again."

"What did you say?"

"No comment."

"A political career sure does demand sacrifices," she said, determined to keep her tone light. "Are you thinking that you might be willing to get remarried to me, simply to keep your voters happy?"

"I would never marry anyone, least of all you, for such an inadequate reason."

She lifted her head and met his gaze head-on. "You still hate me that much, huh?"

"I don't hate you, Liz. I never did."

"Gee!" she said with heavy sarcasm. "At last I

understand. You've been suffering from unrequited love. All those months when you damn near froze me to death with your icy looks and frosty behavior were because you needed to mask the real you, and your burning fire of uncontrollable passion.''

''Yes,'' he said simply. ''That's exactly what happened.''

Inwardly she was shaking, but all she said was a flippant. ''Give me a break, Dexter.''

''I'm telling you the truth. Finally.''

''Your love for me was so overwhelming it left you tongue-tied? Come on, Dexter. Are you forgetting about the pilots who elected you Stud Supreme of the Frankfurt military base?''

''For heaven's sake, Liz, there's a difference between acquiring an asinine reputation as a stud, and being a man who's mature enough to handle a complex relationship with a woman.''

''And when you married Susan you were suddenly mature?''

He was silent for a long time. Eventually he pushed his chair away from the table and stood up, turning his back on her. ''I never loved Susan,'' he said. ''That made a big difference.''

''It's easier to be married to someone you don't love?''

''Maybe.'' Slowly he turned around to face her again. ''Susan was a wonderful mother and the perfect political hostess. We were good friends, who respected each other's lifestyles. I would say our marriage was as happy as most others.''

Dex was describing the sort of marriage she might have had with Brian, Liz realized. In retrospect, she could scarcely believe she had almost let herself be sucked into such a cold, bloodless relationship.

"Would you want another marriage like that?" she asked.

His eyes strayed to her mouth and remained there, causing her entire body to flood with heat. "Last week I would have said yes."

She could guess—perhaps—what had caused him to change his mind, but didn't ask for confirmation. She didn't want to hear again that he shared her own unwilling sexual awareness. Dexter was a perfectionist, and given the mess they had made of their marriage, she understood how he might feel the need to rewrite their joint past by entering into a new, more mature relationship in the present. Unfortunately, she also knew—God, how she knew!—that she couldn't afford to risk getting too close to Dexter. While he might end up feeling more comfortable, she would end up badly burned.

His gaze lingered on her mouth, causing her tongue to thicken and her planned answer to die unspoken somewhere deep in her throat. Her instinct for self-preservation seemed to have taken a holiday, because she didn't run screaming for safety when he closed the small gap between their bodies and wrapped her in his arms.

"God, I missed you, Liz," he murmured, and the hesitancy in his voice touched off a response that no amount of aggressive male confidence could have provoked. Her knees felt shaky, blood pumped thickly through her veins, and her body ached with a sweet, familiar pain. She closed her eyes, knowing what would inevitably follow, but wanting him too much to care.

Their kiss was like every other kiss they had ever shared, and yet it was utterly different. Her body still ignited with the same, immediate force. Her veins still ran hot with fire, and her stomach still knotted tight with desire. But something in his touch was different, just as her response was different from everything that had gone between them in the past. This time, his lips moved over hers with supplication as well as expertise, and her response lacked the old humiliating element of helplessness. Her body's reaction was primitive, fierce, elemental, but it was a reaction given of her own free will.

They couldn't continue a kiss of such intensity for long without progressing to a stage of lovemaking Liz wasn't ready to contemplate. Reluctantly she pulled her mouth away, turning her head to one side. His body pulsed against hers, and for a moment his lips hardened demandingly. Then she felt him relax, and he rested his forehead against hers for a fleeting moment before stepping away.

"Maybe you should go upstairs first," he said. "And you might want to consider locking your door."

She tried to laugh, but it came out as a breathy, husky sound, not at all what she had intended.

"Dex, you're long past the stage of finding yourself swept away by overmastering passion."

"Am I?" he asked. "Funny, I was just thinking that I hadn't felt such a strong urge to push a woman to the floor and fall on top of her since..."

"Since?" she prompted, knowing that if she'd been smart, she'd have remained silent.

"Since the only time I ever did it before," he said. "In Frankfurt. With you."

Liz wondered how many fingers she would need to burn before she finally realized she was too close to the fire. She drew in a deep breath and from some hidden corner of her soul extracted a remaining shred or two of willpower.

"Good night, Dexter," she said with convincing firmness, then spoiled the whole effect by turning tail and running from the kitchen as if her life depended on it.

CHAPTER NINE

THE OFFICE WAS blissfully empty on Sunday morning. Liz worked assiduously on her paper mountain and succeeded in reducing it to a modest-sized hill. Wanting a break before tackling the fine print of the latest market-research report, she contemplated the rival merits of McDonald's and the local health-food bar. She had just reluctantly decided that the health-food bar was the winner, when the phone rang.

"Elizabeth Meacham," she said absently, wondering if there was any way to convince her taste buds that bean sprouts were more enjoyable than French fries.

"Liz, this is Evan Howard."

The PR man's voice came low and urgent over the phone, and Liz's attention snapped back with a jerk.

"Evan? Is something wrong? What's happened?"

"I need to see you urgently. At my house. We'll be safe there. I have something important to tell you."

The muted roar on the line was pierced by the distinctive beep of a car horn. "Are you calling from a phone booth?" she asked. "I can scarcely hear you."

"Yes, but I'm going home right now. Liz, you have to come and see me." His voice sounded frankly desperate, although she knew enough to take his desperation with a grain of salt. Evan was not a man notable for his calm disposition.

"I don't know where you live," she said. "And what about calling Dexter—?"

"No!" His command was sharp, instantaneous. "No! Don't say a word about this meeting to Dexter. It would be dangerous for both of us."

"Evan, you have to tell me what this melodrama is all about. If it's connected with Karen's death—"

"My address is 244 South Clark," he interrupted. "Clark intersects with University. Be there as soon as you can." The hum of an empty wire warned Liz that Evan had hung up.

She grabbed her purse and dashed for the parking lot. Despite Evan's penchant for self-dramatization, she had detected a note of true fear in his voice, and she had an uncomfortable conviction that what he was about to tell her was something important—and quite possibly something she didn't want to hear. About Dexter? As far as she knew, she and Evan had no other mutual friends.

She drove too far south, and it took her longer than it should have done to find Clark. The street, part of a pleasant residential neighborhood, was Sunday-morning quiet, but the sunshine and peace didn't reassure her. Oppressed by a sudden sense of urgency, Liz parked the car haphazardly against the sidewalk and dashed up the steps leading to number 244.

The house was a typical Denver bungalow, recently restored. The door had been carved into the sort of artsy-craftsy look Liz would have expected from Evan, and she had to search to find the doorbell, which was nestled against the stem of an opulent bunch of cast-iron grapes. An electric buzzer sounded loudly within the house when she pressed the bell, but elicited no response. For a man who had been so insistent in his request that Liz come calling, Evan didn't exactly seem to be panting by the front door for her arrival.

She pressed the button a second time, her sense of urgency dissipating into the more familiar irritation Evan usually provoked. The buzzer once again faded into silence. The street remained empty and somnolent. Infuriated by her wasted trip, she searched around for a note or some other sign that Evan had been expecting her. Again nothing.

"Next time I'll know better than to come tearing out to meet you," she muttered, straightening from her foray into the flowerpots. She blew a stray strand of hair off her forehead, gave the bell another half-hearted push and surveyed the door one final time.

She had no idea what impelled her to test the handle, except maybe a generalized feeling of frustration. To her astonishment, it gave under her fingers, and when she pushed, the door swung open.

Feeling a bit like Goldilocks, Liz stepped into the

narrow hall. "Evan?" she called. "Are you home? Is everything okay?"

She took two or three cautious steps into the hallway, and then two or three more. Nothing greeted her save the echo of her own footsteps. Staring around, she saw a series of half-open doors leading into silent rooms.

Belatedly it dawned on Liz that she was not terribly smart to be walking into an unknown house in response to a phone call from a man she scarcely knew. In fact, in retrospect she realized she couldn't even be entirely sure that it was Evan who had called her. The connection crackled, the caller had spoken softly, and the noise of passing traffic had drowned many subtleties of inflection.

With the sudden conviction that at any moment Karen's murderer was going to burst out of the hall closet and bop her on the head, she swung around and ran back down the hallway.

She had almost covered the short distance to the front door, when a slight, almost inaudible sound caused her to glance to her left. Coming back along the hall, her angle of sight into each of the rooms was different. For the first time, she noticed a foot, encased in a black leather loafer, poking around the edge of the living-room door.

Liz stopped, her breathing shallow and her stomach churning with dread. Instinctively tiptoeing, she crept into the living room.

Evan lay on his back, his face drained of color,

his eyes closed, one hand resting limply around the knife handle protruding from his rib cage.

"Oh God! Dear God, no!" Liz whispered in agonized supplication. She fell on her knees alongside Evan's body, ripping open the neckline of his shirt, desperately seeking the pulse she was certain she wouldn't feel.

When he groaned, she jumped with shock, her hand slipping into the patch of blood that was congealing around the knife. His eyes flickered briefly open, then closed.

"A doctor," she instructed herself, wiping her hand on her skirt. "I must call the doctor." She half rose to her feet, pausing when Evan opened his eyes again.

"Liz..." Her name was no more than a breath of sound, and she leaned over him in order to hear, bracing herself on the floor above his shoulder to prevent her weight from resting on his blood-seeping wound.

"It's all right," she murmured. "Everything's going to be okay, Evan, I'm here."

"Liz?"

"Yes, I'm Liz. I'm here, and I'm going to get a doctor."

His eyes blurred, and although he stared straight at her, she wasn't sure he knew to whom he spoke. "They will have to kill you...." he said. He made a horrible gurgling sound, which Liz realized was meant to be a laugh. "I didn't know.... I was a fool.... I loved her so much. I did it for her."

"Who did you love?" she asked urgently. "Was it Karen?"

He didn't answer. "Evan," she said. "Oh God, Evan, who did this to you?"

His thoughts seemed to follow their own track, or perhaps he hadn't even heard Liz's question. "He is...so beautiful...and so danger—" His eyes rolled upward and he fell silent.

"No!" she protested. "No, damn it, you're not going to die!" She cupped his lips under her mouth, trying to force air into his lungs. Only when she was panting and dizzy with exhaustion did she stop the hopeless task.

She leaned back, pushing her sweat-soaked hair away from her forehead, and in that moment became aware of the dried blood coating her hands. She stared hypnotized at the ugly red splotches, her body gripped by an uncontrollable shuddering. A groan of horror pushed its way out of her throat, but she didn't—couldn't—move. She was still kneeling beside Evan's body, bloody hands wavering in front of her eyes, when the door to the living room banged open.

DEXTER HAD A PREMONITION of disaster as soon as he arrived at Evan's house and found the front door unlocked, but no sign of a police squad car. *A setup, then? Maybe. But then again, maybe not.* He had the feeling that whatever was going on, his enemies very much wanted him to remain alive.

Careful not to make any sound that would betray

his presence, he slipped into the narrow hallway. His body tensed reflexively, alert for any hint of danger as he looked around. There was no sign of Evan, and nothing seemed disturbed, but the house was much too quiet. The silence vibrated with a special kind of menace, and the hallway smelled of death.

No sound came from the living room, but he would stake his life on the suspicion that someone was in there. His life, perhaps, was what he would be staking. With infinite care, he edged toward the living-room door. He knew better than to attempt any form of unarmed combat when he was out of training, but his old skill at moving noiselessly hadn't been lost. So far he wasn't taking much of a risk.

He paused before making the final, dangerous move past the half-open door of the living room. If somebody was lying in wait behind that door, he would be virtually without defense. As he paused, he heard someone groan. A woman. He would swear it was a woman. He would swear it was Liz.

Dexter reached out and banged the door open, adrenaline surging as his body fell automatically into the attack mode. The door crashed against the wall, telling him nobody was concealed behind it. He took a single step into the room, then froze.

Liz, her face and hands smeared with blood, was three feet away from him, crouched over Evan's— obviously dead—body.

For a moment she didn't seem aware of his presence, then her head jerked up, and she stared at him from terrified blue-gray eyes. Eyes that had haunted his dreams for the past nine years. Even now, as his pulse calmed and reason took over, he recognized his instinctive, involuntary response to her beauty.

"What happened?" he asked. The question came out brusquely, not only because of Evan's death, but because he was tired of remembering, tired of yearning for the unattainable, tired of wanting a mental rapport with Liz that would match their physical awareness.

She didn't say anything, but her eyes widened in panic. Her mouth opened, then closed again, and he realized that she was literally incapable of speech.

He walked to her side, a brief glance at Evan confirming that there was no need to rush for a doctor. Dexter had seen violent death too often during his years as a fighter pilot, and he felt a wave of bitter anger against the person who had so brutally ended Evan's life. He controlled the anger and the accompanying grief. At this moment he needed facts, not emotion.

"What happened?" he asked Liz again, more gently this time. He knelt down to brush his thumbs swiftly across Evan's eyes, restoring a tiny measure of dignity to the sprawling body. Then he put his arm around Liz and helped her to her feet.

She flinched at his touch, as if she couldn't bear the warmth of human contact so close to violent death, but he was relieved to see some of the wildness leave her eyes. "I didn't do it," she said. "Dexter, I didn't kill him."

"I never thought you did." He spoke the truth. Despite the compromising situation in which he'd found her, he knew Liz hadn't killed Evan. Like many athletes, she was indifferent to her own physical pain, but she'd always been squeamish about other people's. There might be some facets of Liz's character that remained mysterious to him, but he knew she could never have thrust a knife into a man's chest and then knelt beside him to watch him die. He smoothed a hand along her spine, calming her as he would have Amanda. "How did you get in? Was the front door open?"

"Yes. I j-just w-walked in."

"Did you see anything suspicious?"

"No. The house was empty.... Evan was—like that—when I found him."

She had always been a hopeless liar, and he knew at once that she wasn't telling the truth. Evan might have been at the point of death when she entered the living room, but he hadn't been dead. That was why she was covered in blood. She'd tried to save him.

"What did Evan say to you before he died?" Dexter asked quietly.

She looked at him with renewed horror, as if she couldn't bear to hear the question, and he saw full-blown panic return to her face. "The police," she muttered. "Oh God, the police!"

She tore herself out of Dexter's arms and dashed blindly down the hall, bumping into an ornamental stand and sending a china vase crashing to the floor. He doubted if she even heard the vase fall.

He followed her into the kitchen, his most immediate concern to calm her down before he called the police. She rammed the faucet full on and splashed steaming water onto her face, scrubbing with a ferocity that suggested she wanted to wash away not only Evan's blood, but all memory of the scene in the living room.

"Did you call a doctor?" he asked. If she had, they needed to worry about the imminent arrival of somebody who was going to ask a series of very awkward questions.

"No, I didn't call anybody. I've got to get out of here! You should go, too." Liz was clearly hanging on to her self-control by the merest thread. "Did you touch anything?" she demanded. "We have to get rid of our fingerprints." She elbowed past him without waiting for a reply, a roll of paper towels clutched in her hand.

"Liz, stop! Talk to me for God's sake! You can't dash around wiping off fingerprints!"

"Watch me!"

He caught hold of her arm. "Sit down, calm down, and tell me what happened."

"Sit down! Calm down!" She laughed, and began rubbing feverishly at the front door handle. "I'm getting out of here, Dexter, just as soon as I've cleaned off my prints. If the police find me anywhere near Evan's body, they're going to have me handcuffed and in a squad car as soon as they can spit out a Miranda warning. I don't blame them, either. If I were in Lieutenant Rodriguez's shoes, I'd arrest the pair of us.''

Despite her panic, Dexter knew she had a point. His lawyers weren't likely to leave him lingering in jail longer than a couple of hours, but did he really want to subject himself to all the publicity an arrest would cause? On the other hand, he and Liz had discovered a crime and had a duty to report it. Sometimes, he thought wryly, duty was a damn nuisance.

''Nothing's going to bring Evan back to life,'' Liz said, almost as if she had read his thoughts. ''And since I can't help him, I don't see any point in getting myself arrested.''

She was right, Dexter conceded. Moreover, he suspected he might be playing straight into the murderer's hands if he and Liz were found here, hovering over Evan's body. Like the audience that is distracted by the conjurer's dazzling display of silk scarves, so that the crucial card can be slipped up his sleeve, Dexter had the feeling that the police and the FBI were having their attention directed to the murders of Evan Howard and Karen Zeit, while some much more complex evil was being plotted elsewhere.

''Where do you plan to go?'' he asked.

''To the airport. To some place faraway.''

''Is Boston far enough?'' he asked, coming to a decision. ''I planned to take Amanda to stay with her grandparents, anyway. If we left this afternoon, I'd just be moving things up a couple of days.''

''I couldn't possibly impose on your parents—''

''Please come,'' he said, not even sure himself why her company seemed so important. ''We have a lot to discuss, a lot of information to share, and there's no time now.''

She was suddenly very still, and he knew that he had touched a sensitive nerve. It occurred to him for the first time that she probably suspected him of being involved in Evan's death. Her question confirmed it.

''Why did you come here?'' she asked. ''I thought you planned to spend the morning with Amanda.''

''I did. But somebody called, claiming to be a police officer, and said Evan had found Karen's missing personnel file. He asked me to come over here right away. Since there's no sign of a policeman or a file, I guess we can safely assume the call was a fake. What brought you?''

''A phone call. Evan insisted he had something very important to tell me.'' She looked away. ''He also told me it would be dangerous to get in touch with you.''

''Dangerous?'' Dexter tried without success to fit this piece of information into the puzzle. ''Who was it dangerous for? Did he say?''

She hesitated for a second or two. ''For me. For Evan. Not for you. At least, I don't think for you.''

''I see.'' In fact, he saw a lot more than he wanted

to. Like the reason for her panic at the sight of him. "Liz, I didn't kill Evan."

The color had once again completely faded from her face. "That's what you said about Karen, too."

"You're right," he replied quietly. "It looks suspicious, doesn't it?"

"Yes." Her reply was no more than a whisper.

"You told me you didn't murder Karen, though she was your third roommate to die. And you told me you didn't kill Evan, though I found you hunched over his body, covered in blood."

"I was trying to give him mouth-to-mouth resuscitation."

"I believe you."

He let the words fall into the sudden silence of the hallway. He thought she was about to speak, when the blare of a police siren shattered the quiet. Liz tensed, her entire body going ramrod stiff.

"Do you think they're coming here?"

"Doesn't sound like it, the direction's wrong. But we'd better leave, just in case. There's a back entrance. Let's take it." He didn't point out that if they'd been set up, somebody would have notified the police, for sure. For once, he was grateful for the fact that response time to emergency calls was less than wonderful.

She hesitated, momentarily irresolute. "Afraid you're aiding and abetting a murderer, Liz?" he queried softly.

"Just—afraid."

He sensed her continuing resistance and her doubt, but there was no time for explanations, even if he could have provided them. He took her hand and pulled her along the hall toward the kitchen. "Liz, we don't have time for any more protestations of innocence. We've got to get out of here."

She obviously agreed with that, if not with his innocence. "My car's in front," she said, as they emerged into Evan's backyard.

He stopped and listened for a moment before taking her hand. "No police around that I can hear," he said, guiding her down the narrow path to the front of the house. "Drive your car to the airport and leave it in long-term parking. That's as good a place to get rid of it as any. Then book us three one-way tickets on the next flight to Boston. Do you have money?"

"A credit card."

"Good. I'll meet you at the departures gate."

"My clothes..." she said. "The blood—"

"Stop off at one of the big discount stores on the way to the airport. Change in their ladies' room and throw away the skirt you're wearing. And I'll pack a suitcase for you at the house."

The sound of another siren sliced through the air, and this time it didn't conveniently fade into the distance. Dexter sprinted toward his car. "I'll pick up Amanda," he said. "Give me one hour. Get moving, Liz! You don't have time to stand around thinking!"

HE WAITED until he was safely home before placing the call to Igor. For some reason, he felt the need for familiar surroundings before he confessed what had happened. Anyway, his home phone was as safe as a phone booth, and a lot quieter. They sent in professionals to sweep the phone line regularly, and he himself was expert at checking for bugs. Not that anybody suspected him, so there was no reason in the world to anticipate a bug. Even Igor—who was paranoid about security—had agreed that he could make sensitive calls from his home in perfect safety.

It wasn't easy to dial the number. His fingers, poised over the buttons, shook. Igor did not tolerate mistakes on the part of his underlings, nor did he believe in effete capitalist notions like forgiveness. Igor eliminated his mistakes, thus preserving his reputation and saving the Soviet state a great deal of money in pension benefits.

He wondered if this was a mistake he could cover up. Damn Elizabeth Meacham to hell! She'd always seemed such an asexual creature, he'd been sure the senator wouldn't have a chance of getting close to her. Particularly since their divorce had been so bitter. But Evan had sworn he'd seen them kissing—in the kitchen, of all places, and it hadn't been a friendly peck on the cheek. Thank God, he'd been instructed to kill Evan Howard. It was one thing to admit that Elizabeth Meacham seemed closer to the senator than was desirable. It was another thing to admit they had been observed locked in a passionate kiss. That was a piece of information he'd make sure never filtered back up to Igor. It was grotesque to think of Liz responding to Dexter Rand, after the number of times she'd turned him down!

He put the receiver back into its cradle and drew in a series of short, deep breaths. An old trick learned in competition, but it calmed him, just as it had done before the Olympics.

No point in delaying this call any longer. He drew in one final, cleansing breath and punched out the numbers quickly, before he could lose his nerve. After all, he had a success to report along with the failure. Evan was dead. Quickly and cleanly dead, although there had been that split second when his hand had wavered. He wasn't quite sure why that had happened. He couldn't possibly be losing his nerve for simple things like killing. Not now. Not when their plans were so close to success. Not when the intolerable wait was almost over.

"Yes." Igor always answered the phone himself on the first ring. It was a small, chilling example of his efficiency.

"Evan Howard has been taken care of in accordance with your instructions," he said. His voice, he was pleased to note, sounded strong and confident. "You were correct, as always, Comrade Secretary. He was no longer reliable. He threatened to tell the police that Elizabeth Meacham was in danger."

"Did he know the Meacham woman is to be killed?"

"I'm sure Evan knew nothing." He hoped to God

that was the truth. "Karen Zeit was immensely effective in bending her lovers to her will, Comrade Secretary, but I'm afraid that—toward the end—she was not always discreet." Because she had developed this insane obsession that they should marry. How many people had she blabbed to before he silenced her? "Evan should never have known my name," he added. "Karen was totally unprofessional in revealing it."

"You chose Zeit. You ran her. You should have controlled her. If you hadn't impregnated her, she might have been more reliable."

"Yes, indeed, Comrade. But no harm has been done. Neither Karen Zeit nor Evan Howard knew why Elizabeth Meacham must be killed. In fact, I doubt if Evan knew much more than the fact that Karen wished very much for a job on the senator's staff. It was the order to destroy Karen's personnel file that disturbed him. As you suspected, he was beginning to think far too much about what was going on."

"Karen Zeit and Evan Howard are now part of the past. We are concerned with the present and the future. Our visitor from Moscow is now fully prepared for her task. The final stage of our plan may be set in motion. I assume Senator Rand is being followed?"

"Yes, Comrade."

"Where is he? Is he implicated as ordered in Evan Howard's death?"

He drew in a deep breath. "The police, unfortunately, did not arrive in time to find him in Evan's house. I have been informed that he is now at home.''

Igor grunted. ''This is your official order to set the next stage of operation in motion.''

''Yes, Comrade Secretary.'' Should he admit that Liz had been at Evan's house? Should he drop a hint that maybe—just maybe—Liz and the senator were becoming more intimate than was desirable? If he spoke up, the plan could be amended, if necessary. If he remained silent, life would be easier now, but might be impossible later. He wiped away the sweat that was beading on his forehead.

''There is one more thing, Comrade.''

''Yes?''

''Elizabeth Meacham and the senator...''

''Yes?''

''They have spent a great deal of time together over the past few days. It seems that our assumption that they would be mutually hostile and avoid each other was not entirely correct.''

''Our assumption?'' Igor asked softly. ''My plan was based on your assessment of Elizabeth Meacham's likely behavior, Comrade Champion. Are you telling me that I must revise my plan?''

''I suggest only that you keep in mind that the senator has seen the Meacham woman quite frequently over the past few days.''

Igor grunted. ''I will ensure that my plans cover all eventualities. Your task is so simple, Comrade

Champion, that I hope sincerely you will not screw up.''

The American slang was so unexpected that for a moment he couldn't reply. He swallowed and said finally, ''The kidnapping will proceed on schedule.''

Igor hung up without speaking again.

CHAPTER TEN

MOST OF THE PASSENGERS had already boarded the plane for Boston when Liz spotted Dexter and Amanda hurrying along the moving walkway to the flight gate. Dexter held an oversize panda, presumably because Amanda's arms were already filled with a scruffy teddy bear and a neon-yellow stuffed rabbit. An Easter gift that had been unexpectedly successful, Liz guessed, eyeing the creature's virulent pink satin ears with disbelief.

Even from a distance of fifty yards or so, she could see that Amanda was hopping with excitement, and that Dexter was smiling down at her, the hard lines of his jaw softened into tenderness, every angle of his body speaking of love and the urge to protect. When they reached the end of the walkway, he clutched the panda in his teeth, freeing a hand to help his daughter onto firm ground.

In that moment, Liz knew—without logic, but with utter, unshakable conviction—that Dexter was no killer. Evan's dying words might mean a multitude of different things, but she would never accept that Evan had intended to accuse his employer of murder. She had decided days ago that Dexter would never kill a woman to rid himself of the threat of a paternity suit. Today, witnessing the agony of Evan's death, she had lost her mental bearings for a while. She had spent the past two hours wondering why she was waiting to board a plane with a man who could well be a murderer. Now she realized that Evan's stumbling words had temporarily distorted her understanding of Dexter's character. Watching him with his daughter, she knew that her instincts were a safer guide to the truth than a dying man's semiconscious ramblings.

"Time to board?" Dexter asked as he approached.

"Yes, it's a DC-10. We're all together. Nonsmoking." She glanced toward the suddenly silent child. "Hi, Amanda. Would you like me to hold one of your animals?"

"No, thank you, Ms. Meacham. I can hold them myself." Her response was exquisitely polite—and totally lacking in warmth.

"Please call me Liz. 'Ms. Meacham' makes me feel like your teacher."

"You're nothing like any of my teachers," Amanda said positively.

Liz decided not to explore the precise meaning of that statement. Dexter, she noted, was looking faintly amused by his daughter's covert hostility. She wondered why. "We'd better get moving," she said brightly. "We don't want the plane to leave without us."

"I like going to Grandma's house." Amanda

threw down the words more as a challenge than as a statement. Eyeing Liz with a hint of speculation, she added, "Grandpa's fun, too. We go fishing. Only him and me."

"How nice for you," Liz said and smiled, somehow refraining from pointing out that "fun" was just about the last word she would have used to describe the dour, fastidious Mr. Rand, Sr. Dexter's prim and proper parents, with their old-fashioned, aristocratic attitudes, had been one of the greater tribulations of her brief marriage.

Amanda took the window seat, Dexter squeezed his long legs into the cramped center position, and Liz took the aisle. "Sorry," she apologized. "None of my credit cards would stand first-class fares. You're flying as *Mr. Meacham*, by the way."

"Good idea. It might throw the journalistic hounds off the scent for a while."

"Not to mention the police."

"I'm not sure that we can avoid the police," Dexter said. "I told my housekeeper where we're going. I didn't want to create the impression that we were running away."

"I thought running away was exactly what we were doing."

He grinned. "Good grief, no! Just beating a strategic retreat."

"Translated into plain English, that sounds to me a heck of a lot like running away."

"Who's running away, Daddy?" Amanda's childish treble floated with appalling clarity across the hum of the engines and the clatter of the meal carts. "Is it Ms. Meacham?"

"Nobody's running away," Dexter replied. "Not literally. Here, have a lollipop." He pulled the candy out of a plastic bag tucked into his briefcase. "My emergency kit," he murmured to Liz. "Before Amanda was born, I wondered why parents ever gave their children candy or cookies. Then I wised up to the real world."

"Why is Ms. Meacham coming to Boston?" Amanda asked, licking her lollipop.

"Because I asked her to. I want her company."

Amanda digested this information in silence. "Is she going with you to Washington?"

This time her comment was overtly unfriendly, and Liz wondered what had prompted the change in Amanda's attitude. When they'd first met a couple of nights ago, the child had been more than ready to be friendly.

"I hope Liz will come with me." Dexter didn't rebuke his daughter for her rudeness, but he gave subtle emphasis to his use of Liz's name. "You know, Liz is a very good friend of mine, and I hope she'll be a friend of yours, too, one day."

Amanda scowled. Without replying, she leaned down and pulled a coloring book out of her carry-on bag. Dexter watched her for a second or two, then turned back to face Liz and spoke softly. "Her best friend at school took her aside yesterday and gave her a long lecture, during which she apparently pointed out that stepmothers are always mean and wicked. Amanda has converted overnight from wanting me to marry again into wanting me to remain single forever.''

Liz spoke quickly. "She certainly has no reason to view me as a threat."

He hesitated for an instant. "We've spent a lot of time together the past few days, you and I. Naturally, she doesn't understand why."

Amanda thrust her picture under Dexter's nose. "Look, Daddy," she said. "What color shall I do the house?"

After that, Dexter devoted most of his attention to entertaining his daughter, and the tedium of the four-hour flight was interrupted only when the flight attendant arrived to serve cocktails and dinner. Liz normally avoided meals on planes, but realizing she had eaten nothing all day, she chose something optimistically called chicken cacciatore. Dexter and Amanda chose beef bourguignonne. The attendant seemed to have considerable difficulty in deciding what each tray contained, which wasn't surprising, since both the beef and the chicken were smothered in an identical dark red sauce. Happily, Liz discovered she was too hungry to care which dinner she got.

Darkness had long since descended when Dexter finally drove the rental car into the maple-lined driveway of the centuries-old Rand family home. Amanda, wedged between Liz and her father on the front seat of the car, fought a valiant battle against dozing off. With a visible effort, she would straighten up and demand attention every time Dexter addressed a remark to Liz.

Strangely enough, Liz found this typical childlike need for attention and reassurance more endearing than the polite self-possession Amanda had displayed on the first occasion they met. A couple of times she had to restrain herself from putting an arm around the child and saying, "It's okay. Relax. I'm not going to take him from you. I couldn't, even if I tried."

Dexter's parents caused an even stranger reaction within Liz. Either time and a grandchild had mellowed them out of all recognition, or her perspective was vastly different from the tension-filled days of her marriage.

They greeted her with the polite, formal reserve she expected. Her reaction to their cool courtesy, however, was neither irritation nor a burning sense of her own inadequacy. It was merely relief. One of the advantages of centuries of selective breeding, she reflected wryly, was that proper Bostonians seemed to have a repertoire of polite conversation for every occasion. Meeting a divorced former daughter-in-law, who had recently shared an apartment with their son's murdered-possible-mistress, seemed to present no special problems.

"How are you, Elizabeth? You look very well. I hope the flight wasn't too tiresome. I asked the housekeeper to put you in the blue bedroom. I'm sure you will find it comfortable."

Liz had nothing to do except mumble platitudes—a soothing end to a traumatic day.

By contrast, their welcome to Amanda showed just how far off the mark Liz had always been in assuming that neither Mr. nor Mrs. Rand was capable of deep emotion. They welcomed their granddaughter with a brief kiss on the cheek rather than the exuberant hugs and kisses traditional in some families, but love shone in their eyes, and their voices were warm with the intensity of their feelings.

What was more, Amanda clearly understood that she was the apple of her grandparents' eyes, and basked in the glow of their devotion. The adults shared coffee and liqueurs, while a maid brought in a tray of hot chocolate and cookies especially for Amanda. Curled up between Mr. and Mrs. Rand on the sofa, she displayed her drawings with the entirely accurate expectation that they would be rapturously received. Leonardo da Vinci could not have had his early sketches examined with more attention or greater enthusiasm, Liz reflected in silent amusement. If only Mr. Rand's colleagues at the bank could see him oohing and aahing over Amanda's purple house, their impression of his personality might undergo a radical change.

Amanda's artistic treasures had finally been laid to one side as she drooped more and more wearily against her grandmother's shoulder. "We'll talk tomorrow," Mr. Rand said to Dexter. "No, my boy, don't hurry your brandy. Stay here with Elizabeth.

I'm sure you need some time to yourselves right now."

"Thanks. I'll just get Amanda to bed—"

"Indeed you won't." Mrs. Rand rose gracefully to her feet, demonstrating that it was possible to interrupt with every appearance of perfect manners. "Amanda and I have a special story to read tonight. We've been saving it since last time she was here, haven't we, dear?"

"Yes. It's called *The Secret Garden*, and now I'm big enough to read it to Grandma."

"If I may, I'll come along and listen, too." Mr. Rand put his brandy snifter on the tray. "I seem to remember that was always one of my favorite stories."

Mrs. Rand looked across at her son. "You'll show Elizabeth where the blue room is, Dexter?"

"Of course. Good night, Mother."

The masculine Rands exchanged handshakes. Mrs. Rand gave her son a brief peck on the cheek, but Liz noticed, as she wouldn't have done nine years earlier, that the older woman's eyes were bright with unshed tears. "I'm glad to have you home, Dexter," she murmured. "If there's any way we can help…"

"You've helped already," he said. "Just being with you and Dad puts things into better perspective." Hunkering down, he held Amanda close. "Sleep tight, poppet. I'll see you in the morning."

She clung to his neck for a few moments, then

turned quite happily to take her grandmother's hand. "Good night, Ms. Meacham," she said pointedly.

There was no doubt about it, Liz thought ruefully. The Rand family genes got to work early, teaching little junior Rands how to annihilate their enemies with politeness. On the brink of returning an equally cool good-night, she astonished herself by bending down and gathering Amanda into a swift hug.

"My name's Liz," she said softly. "It would be awfully nice if you could call me that. Sleep tight, Amanda. Give Rabbit a kiss from me."

Amanda didn't return Liz's hug, but neither did she reject it, which seemed a step in the right direction. Although why she felt this pressing need to be accepted by Dexter's daughter, Liz couldn't quite decide.

When Amanda and her grandparents left the room, a silence descended that was less than comfortable. "What I want more than anything in the world is a shower," Liz said.

"Me, too. I'll show you to your room."

"You don't have to bother. Just give me directions."

"The second door on the right as you go up the staircase. There's a connecting bathroom."

"Fine. Well, thanks for everything, Dexter. I'll see you in the morning."

"I should be thanking you," he said quietly. "But you're right. We'll do better if we talk in the morning. You must be exhausted, and by coming here, we've bought ourselves some time to relax."

"Yes. It was a pretty miserable day." She didn't move, and neither did Dexter. "Well," she said at last. "I guess I'd better be on my way. Second room on the right, wasn't it?"

"Yes." Dexter was noted as a brilliant conversationalist. At the moment, however, he seemed to be having as much difficulty as Liz in finding anything coherent, let alone brilliant, to say.

"Um…good night," she managed finally.

"Er… Sleep well."

His voice sounded as tense as she felt—which was like a tightly tuned guitar string, waiting to be strummed. Unfortunately, this sort of tension had become very familiar to Liz over the past few days. She felt it anytime she was with Dexter, but when they were alone together, it became almost unbearable. Her body screamed out the message that if she stepped forward into Dexter's arms, her tension would be wonderfully, blissfully, released. Her mind, meanwhile, sent out frantic reminders about what had happened the last time she allowed her physical desires to control her response to her former husband.

For once in her life, Liz got smart. Without trying to explain her actions, she turned abruptly on her heel and hurried from the room. Too many more minutes of staring at Dexter, and she might have done something totally crazy. Like telling him what was on her mind. And at that precise moment it surely wasn't murder.

No BATH, not even after a grueling competition, had ever felt so good. Liz shampooed her hair and scrubbed every inch of her body with imported English lavender soap. She couldn't expunge the morning's horrific memories, but the hot water helped to rinse away at least some of her guilt at leaving Denver. Evan had been long past mortal help when she and Dexter abandoned him, and yet she was having difficulty in smothering the sharp prick of her conscience. She had been the last person to see Evan alive. Therefore she felt an obligation to report everything she had heard and seen to the police. Somewhere in her childhood civics classes she had obviously absorbed the lesson that policemen were good guys, and anybody who evaded them was bad. Liz felt bad, as if she deserved to be arrested.

She stepped out of the claw-footed tub, which was no decorator touch but had been there, she was sure, since "modern" plumbing was installed in the Rand mansion at the turn of the century. She wrapped her damp hair in a hand towel and her body in a bath towel, which was fluffy, but not overlarge. Yawning, she pushed open the door and stepped into her bedroom.

Dexter, clad in a T-shirt and faded jeans, sat on the bed. Her bed. "We need to talk," he said. His voice sounded low and oddly thick.

She tightened the towel above her breasts, although it was already so tight that breathing seemed difficult. "Now? This minute? I thought we decided everything could wait until the morning."

"Not this." He stood up and came toward her. "Precisely what happened that day in Frankfurt?" he asked.

"In Frankfurt? At the Olympics?" She was so astonished that she forgot to hold onto her towel. He caught it for her and handed her the ends, but not before his gaze had made a swift, burning assessment of everything the towel was supposed to conceal.

"Thank you," she said, her voice husky.

"You're welcome." His gaze rose slowly from the swell of her breasts to the curve of her lips, and stayed there. Fire exploded in her veins and raced throughout her body.

Don't look at me! she wanted to shout. But another part of her yearned to throw the towel to the floor and yell, *Yes, look at me! Look at what you've been missing for the last nine years!*

In the end, it seemed simplest not to say anything. Besides, she needed all her concentration. Her fingers were trembling so much that she couldn't complete the simple task of tucking one end of the towel into the other.

"Here, let me," he said. His hands, cool against the blazing heat of her skin, traced the swell of her breasts and then slowly, with infinite care, tucked in the ends of the towel together. "What happened that night in Frankfurt?" he asked quietly.

Defiance shaped her reply. "I messed up," she said, the old defensive mechanisms rushing into action. "I threw away a first-place standing and robbed America of its guaranteed gold. Didn't you read the newspapers?''

"I'm all grown-up, Liz, and I've learned not to believe everything I read.''

"You were there. You saw for yourself.''

"I don't think I saw the truth.''

She turned away, shaking with the pain of remembering. "It doesn't matter now. It's a long time ago. I was winning at the end of the short program. I skated terribly in the final segment of the contest. I lost. There's nothing else to say.''

His hands were on her shoulders, his callused thumbs circling in a hypnotic massage. "I always blamed Alison,'' he said. "I assumed that somehow she messed up your concentration. But it wasn't Alison, was it? It was Susan. If it had been Alison, you'd have talked to me afterward.''

She drew in a long, sharp breath. "Yes,'' she agreed, her voice scarcely more than a whisper. "It was Susan.'' Honesty compelled her to add, "And it was me, too. In the last resort, Susan didn't have the power to make me lose. It was entirely my own fault. Champions like Pieter Ullmann can block absolutely everything out of their minds except what they need to do to win. Alison had that same capacity, although her artistic skills were never quite strong enough to take her to the absolute top. My problem was the opposite. Technique and artistry weren't hard for me, but my coach warned me that my mental discipline was never up to scratch. I always allowed my feelings to affect my skating.''

"That's why you were so damn brilliant," Dexter said, an odd hint of anger in his voice. "Your coach was wrong to try to train the emotion out of you. When you had a really good day, you weren't just a superb skater, you were fire and passion captured on ice."

She twisted in his arms, suddenly needing to see his face. "I didn't know you were so impressed by my skating," she said.

He gazed down at her, eyes hooded. "I never once saw the end of your long program, because I couldn't stand the emotional tension you generated. That was why I had to choose my seat so damn carefully, so that you wouldn't notice when I stopped watching."

"Why didn't you ever tell me any of this before?"

His shoulders lifted in a self-mocking shrug. "I was young. I was intimidated by your talent."

"Intimidated! You? Good grief, Dexter, you were the most arrogant, self-assured man I'd ever met—"

"In my own area of expertise, maybe. You showed me that there was a whole creative side to the universe that I'd never even suspected. A lot of the time when I was with you I felt hopelessly…inadequate."

"And I felt inadequate because I couldn't be controlled and efficient like you." She wanted to laugh, or perhaps to cry, with the frustration of so many months when they had totally failed to understand each other. "Why didn't you tell me what you felt?" she asked.

"Because I was a fool. And because I was a combat pilot, working in a brutally masculine environment, testing supersonic jet fighters. I'd spent years being trained not to express my feelings. It needed to be that way, or we'd have gone to pieces every time a test plane showed up with problems. Nerves over my wife's skating performance didn't fit too well with my macho self-image. How the hell could I talk to you about the way I felt, when I couldn't even admit the truth to myself?"

She felt a wave of regret, not for her lost Olympic medal, a loss she'd long since learned to live with, but for the foolishness of two people who'd thrown away a marriage because they were too scared to admit that they were less than totally competent, less than a hundred percent perfect. She smiled sadly. "Wouldn't it be nice if there was some way to prevent people getting married until they're mature enough to handle it?"

His answering smile was wry. "Heck, half of us would never pass the test." He ran his hand slowly down her side, shaping the narrowness of her waist and the delicate flare of her hips. "I wish I'd known you were pregnant," he said.

"Alison was the only person I told. I was so sure you'd be angry. I didn't want you to be tied in to a marriage that you regretted."

He didn't answer her directly. "I saw Alison hand you a glass of something to drink, right before you went out on the ice. You know, all these years I assumed she'd put some sort of drug in it.''

"Dexter, she gave me Gatorade! And I took maybe two sips maximum! Why in the world did you suspect Alison of doing something so horrible?''

"Because she was jealous of you—''

"You mean, you thought she was jealous of me.''

"No, I haven't changed my opinion about Alison. I may not have assessed my other relationships too clearly, but I always understood Alison. She hated the fact that you skated so much better than she did. You were her twin—''

"But not an identical twin,'' Liz protested. "We were no more alike than any other set of sisters who happened to be the same age. It's not surprising our ability levels were different.''

"Believe me, Alison didn't see it that way. She envied your talent.''

Liz looked away. "She's dead now, so we can never resolve this disagreement. Besides, that night in Frankfurt, she had nothing to do with what happened. I'd pulled a tendon in my ankle during practice and I was pumped full of Novocain and pain-killers. That was a big part of the problem. But it was Susan who destroyed my concentration, not Alison. Although in the last resort I don't blame anyone but myself. I should never have let Susan get to me.''

"What did she say, Liz?''

"Does it matter? I accepted a while ago that she

was so far removed from the world of competitive skating that I truly don't think she understood the damage she caused by talking about my failing marriage an hour before I was due to go out on the ice. The whole incident's over, Dexter. We have no reason to discuss it.''

''It's not over,'' Dexter said. ''How can it be over, when what she said affected our lives for the past nine years? Tell me, Liz. I need to know.''

She stared abstractedly into the distance, seeing the cavernous entrance to the ice rink as if it were yesterday. ''Susan told me she was in love with you,'' she replied slowly. ''That was no surprise. Everyone on base knew she'd been in love with you for years.''

''And that threw you enough to destroy your concentration?''

''No. But she pointed out that her father was your commanding officer, and that she was the perfect wife for you.''

''I'd known her for five years,'' Dexter interjected impatiently. ''Didn't it occur to you that if I'd wanted to marry her, I could have done that years before I ever met you?''

Liz lifted her eyes to meet his. ''She told me that you finally realized you should have married her, not me. That you bitterly regretted our marriage, and that our lifestyles were totally incompatible. Given the fact that you and I couldn't be in the same room without starting to fight, what she said seemed to make a lot of sense.''

"Given the fact that we couldn't be in the same room without tearing each other's clothes off and making passionate love, what she said made no sense at all."

Liz's mouth twisted painfully. "I didn't know our sexual relationship was anything special—"

"Dear God, Liz, you can't have been that naive!"

"Whatever you felt for me, it seemed pretty easily transferable. You married Susan a month after our divorce was final."

"Because I was so damn torn apart, I didn't care anymore! I wanted peace and quiet and calm and stability. And..."

"And?"

"I'm ashamed to admit it, but I wanted you to think I didn't give a damn. I didn't want you to know that I was bleeding inside and grieving for what we'd shared. No siree, I wasn't going to have people feeling sorry for me. Hell, if I married Susan fast enough, everybody would think I'd had another woman lined up and waiting all along, and that suited me just fine." He flushed slightly. "You deserved better. For that matter, so did Susan. She wasn't vindictive, you know. Just entirely, totally without imagination. She thought you were an unsuitable wife for me. She saw how tempestuous our marriage was. She concluded that I would be happier married to her. She told you her conclusion. Logically, as far as she was concerned."

"Unfortunately, the rest of the world isn't made up of imitation Mr. Spocks."

"Thank God for that!" His hands skimmed back up her body to rest on her shoulders. "You're shivering," he said.

"This bath towel's damp. It doesn't make the best cover."

"Then take it off."

"No!" Her mouth spoke the word with suitable vehemence, but her treacherous body was already leaning toward him in silent longing. Dear God, but she wanted him to make love to her!

He cupped her face in his hands and brushed a thumb tenderly across her mouth. "I want to love you," he said huskily. "I've been aching to feel myself inside you every minute of the past three days. But I'm not falling into the old, destructive patterns again. If you say no, Liz, I'm going to accept what you say. I had my fill of playing caveman when we were married."

He bent his head and kissed her, a long kiss, full of hunger and adult need. "Come to bed with me, Liz," he said, when the embrace finally ended. "Come willingly. Let me know that for once you want me with your heart and mind, as well as your body."

It was a simple request, but one she wouldn't have been able to fulfill nine years earlier. Now, however, she was many years wiser, as well as older. Her gaze never leaving Dexter's face, she let her arms drop to her sides. The towel slipped down her body and fell into a soft heap at her feet.

"I want you in all the ways there are," she said

huskily. "All the ways a woman can want a man. Make love to me, Dex. Remind me of what I've been missing."

For all the passion they had shared during their brief marriage, it was the first time Liz had ever admitted she wanted Dex before she was so fully aroused that she had no choice but to beg for completion. He had obviously not been prepared for her openness, and for a moment she felt him go still, as if he couldn't quite believe what he had heard. Then, with a small, incredulous sigh, he reached out and pulled her into his arms, crushing her mouth beneath his and holding her tight against his hips.

"You feel so right in my arms," he murmured. "God, how did I ever let you go?" His fingers stroked over her breasts, dancing a trail of fire down to her thighs.

"With difficulty. Like me letting you go." Her hands reached for the zipper of his jeans. With an incoherent groan, he took her fingers and guided them in a swift downward movement, opening her hand over himself as he stepped out of the jeans. His lips reclaimed hers with something akin to desperation, and his tongue thrust into her mouth, sparking a thousand pleasure points deep within her.

She clung to him, her body molten, but her mind sharp and clear with the knowledge that she wanted to be held by this man, that she wanted him to caress her, and that his possession would be total only because she willingly gave herself to him.

Dexter swept her into his arms, carrying her to

the bed in a gesture familiar from a hundred previous occasions. But this time her response was different from everything she had experienced before. This time she was mature enough to recognize that he didn't take her to bed as an act of domination, so she didn't cling to him in anguished resentment that her body had once again taken charge of her will.

Instead she curled against his chest, reveling in the sensation of hard muscles rippling beneath her cheek. As soon as they reached the bed, she pulled his head down to her mouth, actively seeking the pleasures of his kiss. At last, after nine years of growing up, she realized that Dexter was not the conqueror and herself the conquered. They were equal partners, each wholly dependent on the other for fulfillment.

"I want you so much," she whispered, her fingers tangling in his dark, springy hair. The wonderment in his eyes made her realize how rarely in the past she had consciously expressed her needs.

"Show me how you want me," he commanded, his voice hoarse.

"Like this." She arched her hips upward in explicit invitation. His answering penetration was swift, deep and total. She felt his possession in every cell of her body, and his name sprang in a reflexive cry to her lips.

"Liz," he groaned. "Liz, my love, never go away again. Don't leave me."

How could she risk a second relationship with

Dex? On the other hand, how could she ever leave him? For a moment Liz was filled with panic. To stay with Dex opened her to the chance of endless pain, but to leave him again would be to condemn herself to a future of bitter regret. Then the icy coldness of her worry vanished, unable to survive in the burning heat of her passion. Her body shook with the rapturous beginnings of climax, and her thoughts spiraled away into darkness.

Clinging to him, murmuring his name, Liz surrendered herself to the ecstasy of ultimate union with the man she loved.

CHAPTER ELEVEN

IT WAS STILL PITCH-DARK when Liz awoke out of a bone-deep sleep. Fear clutched at her throat and chilled her limbs. She rolled over onto her back, staring up at the ghostly glow of the high ceiling, deriving comfort from the warm feeling of Dexter's legs intertwined with her own. Whatever caused her to wake had been terrifying.

She listened carefully to the late-night sounds of the house. All she heard was the rustle of the May breeze in the bushes, the sigh of Dexter's breathing, and the creak of two-hundred-year-old wood settling a fraction of an inch deeper into the ground. Nothing very scary. Nothing to bring her panting and sweating out of a deep sleep.

Slowly the realization dawned that it had been her own dreams that had jerked her so abruptly into consciousness. Liz closed her eyes, trying to return to the drowsy state in which dreams could be remembered. A memory teased at the corner of her mind, and she frowned in fierce concentration. Evan. It had been something about Evan. Something he had said just before he died.

Suddenly, with the brilliance of a spotlight shining behind a flimsy curtain, she realized precisely what it was that had brought her awake. She leaned over and shook Dexter's shoulder. With the instincts of a longtime combat pilot, he sat up, instantly awake and alert.

"What is it?"

"Evan—when he was dying. He said some things, and I didn't tell you. Dex, I'm scared."

He didn't waste time inquiring why she hadn't told him earlier, or even why Evan's remarks had suddenly become urgent at four in the morning. He folded his pillows into a backrest. "What did Evan say that's worrying you?"

"He said somebody would have to kill me."

"What? And you've only just now decided to mention this? For God's sake, Liz, who's going to kill you? Or didn't Evan mention that trivial detail?"

"He just said *they*. And he said several other things at the same time," Liz added defensively.

"They must have been damned exciting if you forgot you were slated as the next murder victim!"

"Not exciting. Frightening. I guess my brain overloaded and stopped processing information logically. At the time I convinced myself he hadn't recognized me—"

"You think that's possible?" Dexter interjected. "You think somebody else may be at risk rather than you?"

"No, I don't. My subconscious obviously treated his words more seriously than the rest of me. Once

I fell asleep, and my mind had time to sort out its impressions, I guess my subconscious decided that Evan had definitely meant me, and that I was at risk.''

''Did he speak to you by name? Give any sign that he'd recognized you?''

''He called me Liz a couple of times. And remember, he'd phoned my office asking me to come around to the house, so he was expecting to see me. Presumably when he went to the door and let in the murderer, he thought it was me. So all in all, it seems like Evan knew exactly who he was speaking to, and tried to warn me.''

Dexter took her hands and pulled her against his chest, stroking her hair with gentle fingers. ''I won't let it happen, Liz. I swear to you, I won't let it happen. Now we know you're at risk, there are all sorts of things we can do to protect you.''

Rationally she knew that even Dexter couldn't stop a truly determined killer, otherwise presidents and princes would never be assassinated, but the passionate concern in his voice soothed the ache of her fear. Hope replaced the knot of dread that lay coiled in waiting at the pit of her stomach. ''Should we call the police?'' she asked.

''I have a better idea than that; we can contact the FBI. I'll explain more later. First I need to know what else Evan said before he died.''

She looked up at him, without moving from the warm circle of his arms. Even in the darkness, the angles of his face seemed hard, uncompromising—

and starkly honest. Nestled against his chest, her body still soft with the imprint of his lovemaking, it was difficult to remember that yesterday, however briefly, she had suspected him of murder.

"What else did Evan say?" She organized her thoughts. "Well, he admitted that he'd been in love with Karen."

Dexter didn't seem surprised. "I wondered if the baby was his," he said quietly. "Once or twice, Evan let slip remarks that indicated he cared about Karen. I never noticed them at the time, only in retrospect, when my twenty-twenty hindsight vision started to operate."

"Why didn't you say anything to the police?"

He shrugged. "I didn't have anything constructive to say. There were already enough groundless suspicions bubbling in the police cauldron without adding mine to the stew. I pointed out to Rodriguez that Evan was solely responsible for personnel records in my Colorado office, and that was as far as I could go."

"You think Evan deliberately lost Karen's file?"

"I suspected it all along."

"But why?"

"Evan screens every applicant for employment. He checks all the references. He would be the first person to know if Karen's records didn't quite tie together. Either he recommended her for hiring, knowing her references didn't check out. Or, more likely, he became suspicious later on, double-checked and then destroyed the file, knowing her records wouldn't stand up to scrutiny.''

''It fits,'' Liz admitted. ''He said that he'd been a fool, and that he'd done it all for her. The odd thing is, Dex, I still don't believe Evan was the father of Karen's baby.''

This time, Dexter appeared startled. ''Did he actually say that? For a dying man, he seems to have said an awful lot.''

''That's just it. He only mumbled a few half sentences, and all the rest is conjecture on my part. But he did make specific reference to another man. It was almost as if discovering Karen was pregnant had finally made him accept the truth. 'He is so beautiful and so dangerous.' Those were the last words Evan spoke before he died.''

Dexter smiled grimly. ''Well, that takes us a giant step farther forward in unraveling the puzzle. Now we know there was a mystery man in Karen's life who exerted a great deal of influence over her. We knew that four days ago.''

''We also know that somebody must have wanted to introduce Karen onto your staff really badly, to go to all the trouble of compromising Evan Howard.''

''You're right. Which makes me more convinced than ever that those security leaks from my Washington office were somehow engineered from Denver by Karen.''

''But she had no clearance to handle secret documents, did she?''

"None. She didn't need it as my administrative coordinator. She handled party political matters, not government material. But the reality is that people become lax about security, particularly with colleagues they know well. By the time Karen made her sixth or seventh trip to my D.C. office, she might have been able to gain access to a supposedly off-limits area. She was probably trained to find ways of doing just that."

Liz shivered, her fear returning with renewed intensity. "But I don't understand what this has to do with me! Why am I going to be killed? Dexter, for heaven's sake, what connection have I got with secret documents missing from your office? I sell *picante* sauce, for heaven's sake, not missiles!"

"Blueprints for part of a fighter jet," he corrected absently. "That's what went missing." He fell silent for a moment. "I wonder if we've been approaching this whole situation from totally the wrong direction," he said at last. "We've been trying to work out ways your roommates might be connected to each other. We've been trying to find out details about Karen's hidden past. Let's look at the puzzle differently. Let's assume *you* are the center of what's going on, not an inconvenient intruder who keeps bobbing up at the edges."

Liz resisted the urge to break into wild, frustrated laughter. "But, Dexter, I am an intruder! How can I be at the center of something when I've not the faintest idea in the world what's going on?"

He looked at her, his expression coolly assessing,

but his eyes conveying warmth and support. "If you're intended as the next murder victim, you don't need to know what's going on. Maybe your death is the crux of the plot. Whatever that plot is."

She refused to give way to the hysteria that threatened to engulf her. Wrapping her arms around her waist, she fought against a wave of sickness by forcing herself to respond logically. "We already know of four people who've been killed. Three of my roommates and Evan Howard. At the same time, your office has been traced as the source for some top-secret blueprints that have turned up on the international arms market. Do I have it right so far?"

"You're making a link between two separate sets of events, but I think the link's justified. We're also guessing that Karen and Evan were at least marginally involved in the theft of top-secret papers from my office."

"But none of this *leads* anywhere!" Liz exclaimed. "So let's say, for argument's sake, that I'm the next victim on the list. What happens then? Does it become easier to steal more secrets? No! Does it protect the master criminal? No! I've no idea who he is! I couldn't reveal a thing about him, because I don't know anything. So someone who knows nothing about anything at all is going to die. Big deal."

"Perhaps they're afraid you might discover who the murderer is?"

"Then they could as logically kill you or Rodriguez. Why me?" Liz jumped out of bed and began pacing. "Maybe Evan didn't recognize me, after all. Maybe I'm not going to be killed. I think we've got this all wrong, Dex."

"Unless," he commented slowly, "unless they want a specific person to be accused of your murder."

Liz's head jerked up and she stopped her pacing. "You?"

"Don't you get the feeling that somebody out there is working very hard to set me up?"

Liz gave a small, scared laugh. "I'm real anxious to frustrate them, Dex. Tell me how."

Dexter stared silently into the darkness for several seconds. His decision reached, he flung back the bedclothes and reached for his jeans. "We'll do what I suggested in the first place. We'll get the FBI to take you into protective custody."

"They'll agree to do that?"

"If I tell them they must," he said, with unconscious arrogance. "Whether or not I'm being set up, you seem to be on line as the next victim. I'll contact Harry Cooper at the FBI...." His voice died away. "Damn! We're not at home. I can't contact him from here, except by calling the Bureau and leaving a message with the switchboard operator. Maybe I'm becoming paranoid, but I don't want to do that." He pulled on his T-shirt, then resumed. "Would you be willing to come to Washington with me on the early flight? Most of the emergency safe houses are in the D.C. area, so you'd be flying to the right place. If we take the first flight out from Logan, we can be talking to Harry in his office by nine o'clock.''

"If I have to fly to Washington in order to stay alive, I vote in favor,'' Liz said dryly. "I've decided recently that I'm amazingly interested in staying alive.''

He walked around the bed and kissed her hard on the lips. "You'd better believe I'm not going to let you die,'' he said. "We have nine years of catching up to do. Last night just made me hungry for more.''

Hungry for what? Liz wondered. For more sex, or a deeper, more meaningful relationship? From prudence or cowardice, she chose not to inquire.

DEXTER'S PARENTS ACCEPTED their son's departure with the same equanimity with which they had greeted his unexpected arrival the night before. Amanda, however, was hopping mad that her father and Liz were once again taking off together.

"I went into your room this morning and you weren't there,'' she told her father accusingly.

"I expect I was in the shower.''

"You were in *her* room.'' Amanda pointed her finger accusingly. "I saw you come out. You like her better than me.''

Liz felt herself blushing, but felt obligated to make some sort of explanation. "Your daddy doesn't love you less, just because he and I are friends,'' Liz said, bending down so that she was at eye level with Amanda.

The child glared at her. "I hate you!" she said and burst into tears.

With less patience than she had ever seen him demonstrate, Dexter took out his handkerchief and dried his daughter's eyes. "Amanda, you're being silly," he said crisply. "You're also being extremely rude to someone who would like to be your friend."

"I want to come to Washington with you!"

"Honey, you can't. I'm sorry. Grandma and Grandpa have agreed to bring you down at the weekend. I'll look forward to seeing you then. In the meantime, please try not to believe all the stories your friends tell you. Stepmothers are often wonderful people, who make the children in their families very happy."

Amanda buried her nose in her grandmother's skirts, ignoring her father's outstretched hand.

"Don't worry, Dexter," Mrs. Rand said with her usual patrician calm. "Amanda will soon settle down with us, and we'll see you on Saturday morning at National, if you'll come to pick us up. We'll take the usual flight."

"Of course. I'll be there."

Liz was concerned about Amanda's escalating dislike for her, but she had little time to mull over the problem. Dexter plied her with questions all the way to the airport, making her recount Evan's dying words in painstaking detail, and then analyzing every possible meaning that they could come up with for the enigmatic phrases. By the time their plane landed in Washington, Liz felt that her brain had been sucked dry, and the only firm conclusion she and Dexter had reached was that some beautiful and dangerous man, clearly not Evan, must be the father of Karen's baby.

"How do we define beautiful and dangerous?" Dexter queried ruefully. "That airline steward we interviewed was damn good-looking in a meaty kind of way, but do you think he could be termed dangerous?"

"Lethally boring," Liz commented. "And the kind of bedmate who likes to find out if you can do it suspended from the chandelier. But I doubt if that's what Evan meant."

"With all his international travel, an airline steward might be able to set up the contacts to make a sale of stolen documents, though. It's a possibility, however remote."

"He didn't seem bright enough," Liz said.

"How do we know that wasn't a brilliant facade?" Dexter's face showed a hint of weariness. "Damn, but I have the feeling we're running awfully hard just to remain in the same place."

The morning didn't improve. Murphy's Law was in full operation, and when they arrived at the FBI building they learned that Agent Harry Cooper was in Seattle until the next day. "Probably checking on Brian for me," Dexter commented ruefully to Liz.

Drawing on all the clout he could muster as a United States senator, Dexter asked to see the director of the Bureau. The director, he was informed with icy politeness, was giving a briefing at the

White House and then was flying by Air Force One direct to Texas. The receptionist, conveying the impression that she was granting an undeserved audience with a divine being, suggested that a deputy chief would be able to speak with the senator at three-thirty that afternoon. "He will have to cancel another appointment in order to see you, Senator," she added reprovingly. "A very important appointment."

"My business with the director does happen to be a matter of vital national security," Dexter said, his own voice biting.

The receptionist looked offended. "National security is what the Bureau deals in, Senator. All our business is of the highest importance."

"You're losing your touch," Liz said teasingly as they emerged from the FBI building. "A few years ago, she'd have been eating out of your hand."

"A few years ago I wasn't old and impatient— and you weren't in danger of being murdered."

His clipped words caused a chill to ripple along Liz's spine. Her steps faltered and she almost slipped. Dexter reached out, steadying her, and she quickly regained her balance. In an unthinking, reflex reaction, she glanced around to see if anybody had noticed her clumsiness.

A thin, middle-aged man, fifteen yards or so to their rear, was pocketing something that looked suspiciously like a camera. She groaned. "Damn! Dex, I think there's a reporter on our tail."

Dexter swung around in the direction she had indicated, reaching the reporter in a few athletic strides. Liz could see that his body was stiff with frustration. "I don't want anyone to know I'm in Washington," he said to the man, his voice low and hard. "I'd appreciate it if you'd not publish any of those pictures you've just taken."

The reporter's expression was difficult to read, but Liz could have sworn she saw fright, as much as anything else. How strange, she reflected. Fear wasn't an emotion she associated with photojournalists on the prowl.

"I'm freelance," the man jerked out. "I can't afford to waste a morning's work."

Dexter pushed a bundle of notes into the man's hand, his mouth twisting with distaste. "Here. That's enough to buy the whole damn camera. I'd like the film, please."

The reporter stared blankly at Dexter, and Liz gained a fleeting impression that, like a cornered animal, the man was poised between fight and flight. With a sudden nervous gesture, he pulled the camera out of his pocket and flipped open the back. He unrolled the film and waved it back and forth in the weak sunlight.

"There," he said. "Now you know for sure I'm not gonna publish these anywhere." He thrust the ruined film into Dexter's hands, snapped the camera closed, and took off at a brisk walk toward the nearby subway.

"Unpleasant little reptile," Dexter remarked. "What next?"

"Don't you need to go to your office?"

"Would you mind waiting there with me until it's time for our appointment with the deputy director?"

"If you like. Or I could check into a hotel—"

"No hotels," he said flatly. "Look, we've decided there's a good chance that someone's going to try to kill you, and then frame me. The best way to protect both of us is to make sure you're always in a group of at least three people. That way I can't be framed, so presumably you won't be killed."

"I hate to cast doubts on such a comforting theory, but what if we're only half right? What if somebody wants to kill me and doesn't care about setting you up? Then your scenario doesn't work."

"Yes, it does," he said, directing her toward his offices on Capitol Hill. "If you're never without three or four people around you, then you can't get killed."

"Unless the three or four people are all in this crazy plot together."

"Liz, after those blueprints went missing, the employees in my D.C. office were checked out so carefully that we almost know the last time each of them went to the bathroom. I suppose I can just imagine the possibility that one of them might have slipped through the screening net, but three? Take my word for it, the people in my D.C. office are clean."

"Don't you ever go to the movies, Dex? It's always the guy who's Mr. Clean personified that ends up being the villain in chief."

"Liz, honey, this isn't the movies. This is real life."

Liz, honey. The words sounded sweet, and Liz allowed herself to relax. After all, she only had to survive until three-thirty that afternoon, and then her problems would be over. Despite all the horror stories in the press about government incompetence, Liz retained an optimistic faith in the ability of the FBI to protect U.S. citizens. The deputy director would listen to her story, wave his magic wand and whisk her away to a safe house. The very name of the place suggested that once there, the risk of being murdered would vanish. While she stayed safe in her safe house, Dexter and Agent Harry Cooper would then busy themselves with the investigation, and before long, some master criminal would be revealed.

A niggling doubt surfaced as Liz contemplated the fact that she had no idea who the master criminal might be, and even less idea of what he was up to. She banished the doubt to a far corner of her mind. What was the FBI for, if not for flushing out master criminals and uncovering dastardly plots?

Whether Dexter shared her sudden lightheartedness, or whether he disguised his true feelings in order not to depress her, Liz wasn't sure. Superficially, however, their mood as they entered his suite of offices was surprisingly carefree. Dexter made brief introductions, and then took Liz into his private office, asking a secretary and two research assistants to join them.

While Dexter busied himself reviewing a forthcoming speech on Air Force overspending, Liz quietly retreated to a corner of the room and made herself useful by tidying the small library of books and softcover publications dealing with Colorado. She was in the midst of arranging a tasteful display of travel magazines trumpeting the beauties of the Rocky Mountains, when the phone rang. It was the sixth or seventh call put through to Dexter already, and Liz had no idea why she suddenly straightened from her magazines, her mouth dry with irrational fear.

One of the research assistants picked up the phone. "A personal call for you on line three, Senator."

Dexter took the phone and listened in silence for about a minute. Without placing his hand over the mouthpiece, he looked at his three staff members and nodded politely toward the door. "I'm sorry, this call may take a few minutes. Would you mind leaving me?"

Liz stepped forward. "Dexter, no! Remember what we agreed."

He looked in her direction, but Liz had the feeling he scarcely saw her. He turned back toward his assistants without acknowledging her in any way. "Would you start work on those amendments, please? Right away."

The young man and the two women trooped obediently from the room. Liz hurried forward and leaned against the desk. ''Dexter, for God's sake, what is it?''

He spoke into the phone as if he had no awareness of her existence. ''I am alone now.''

The voice at the other end of the line echoed in the sudden, suffocating silence of the office. ''Amanda has a message for you, Senator. She says please cancel your appointment with the deputy director of the FBI.''

A child gave an anguished cry. ''Daddy, where are you?''

''Don't leave your office, Senator, and keep Ms. Meacham with you. We'll be in touch.''

The line went dead.

CHAPTER TWELVE

DEXTER RETURNED THE PHONE to the cradle with infinite care. "I was mad at her," he said. "When we left Boston this morning, Amanda knew I was mad at her."

Liz swallowed hard over the horror that had lodged like a physical object in her throat. She reached out and touched him very gently on the back of his hand. He was ice-cold.

"We have to call your parents, Dex. Maybe... maybe Amanda's at home with them. Maybe the call was just some horrible, sick joke."

"You know it wasn't." He pressed a hand against his eyes, as if willing himself to think rationally. "My parents' number is in the Rolodex," he said, and she realized his mind had temporarily blanked out. He couldn't remember his own parents' phone number.

She searched swiftly through the card index, then dialed with shaking hands. It was a personal line, and Mrs. Rand answered the phone with a bright "Hello."

"This is Liz. Liz Meacham. We've run into a bit of a problem here." She refrained from any further explanation, not wanting to worry Dexter's parents, if by any chance the threatening phone call turned out to be a hoax. "Could you please hold on for a moment while I pass you over to Dex?"

She put the phone into Dexter's hand, and he gripped it so tightly that his entire fist went white.

"Where's Amanda?" he asked without any preliminaries.

"Heaven's, you sound fierce," Mrs. Rand replied cheerily. "Amanda's on her way. Your secretary didn't expect to be in Washington until five at the earliest."

"My secretary? You sent Amanda here, to Washington? With my secretary?"

"Well, that's what you asked us to do! And I must say, Dexter dear, your father and I don't agree with giving in to Amanda like this, just because she had a temper tantrum this morning. With all that journalistic fuss over Evan Howard's death, she'd have been much better off staying with us until the weekend. Have you seen the papers this morning—?"

"My secretary came to your house to collect Amanda? Is that what happened, Mother?"

"But of course it is. You should know, for goodness' sake, she was following your instructions. Judy came, that nice young woman from your Washington office that I always speak to." Mrs. Rand's voice was no longer cheery, but choked with the beginnings of fear. "She gave me your note, Judy I mean, and said that she and Amanda would have to hurry to catch the next flight. I packed her suitcase.... Dexter, dear heaven, has the plane crashed or something?''

''No, Mother. Nothing's crashed.'' Liz could see the monumental effort with which Dexter pulled himself together. The veins stood out on his forehead as he gritted his teeth, using sheer force of will to lower his voice into a semblance of its normal tone. ''I'm glad Judy decided to try for the earlier plane. I'm sorry, Mother, I didn't realize she and Amanda had already left Boston. I didn't mean to alarm you.''

''But, Dexter, you *have* alarmed me! Two minutes ago you didn't seem to know what I was talking about. Are you sure everything's just as it should be?''

''Of course, everything's fine.''

''Dexter, you sound—strange. Promise me nothing's happened to Amanda. Did we do the right thing in allowing her to go with your secretary?''

The vein in Dexter's forehead throbbed, but by some miracle of control he kept his voice steady. ''Yes, Mother, please don't worry. You did exactly what I wanted. Liz and I—'' He swallowed hard. ''Liz and I both felt that Amanda was getting far too upset about our relationship. It seemed better to have her here with us.''

''I've never understood this modern obsession with having one's children approve of one's adult relationships.'' Mrs. Rand spoke with some of her normal tartness, and Dexter's grip on the phone relaxed marginally.

"Mother, I have three separate people making urgent hand signals at me. I must go. Will you and Dad still come down to D.C. this weekend?"

"Probably not. Just make sure you bring Amanda to stay with us as soon as school's finally out. In fact, we were thinking of taking her on vacation to—"

"Mother, I'm now fielding four sets of hand signals. I'll talk to you and Dad later. Bye now."

He hung up the phone, his face drained of every trace of color. "I couldn't tell her," he said. "She and my father wouldn't understand. They'd think it was just a question of paying the ransom, and I don't believe money is what these kidnappers are after. My parents would want to contact the police, and I know Amanda will die as soon as we do that."

It didn't seem like a good idea to allow Dexter to focus his attention on the frightening unknown of what Amanda's kidnappers planned to do. Liz decided to direct his thoughts to the few areas where they might be able to come up with answers. "Is Judy really your secretary?" she asked.

"Yes, one of them."

"Is she in the office today?"

Dexter blinked, focusing his thoughts on the mundane question with obvious difficulty. "I believe I saw her as we came in."

He depressed a button on his intercom and a pleasant voice answered, "Yes, Senator?"

"Judy, have you ever met my mother? In person, I mean?"

"Why no, Senator. Although we've spoken several times over the phone, when she's been trying to track you down."

"Thank you. And I guess you've never met my father, either?"

"No, Senator. He attended a Christmas party once, but I had the flu and didn't get to meet him."

"Thanks, Judy. By the way, screen all my calls, will you? I only want to take personal ones." Dexter flipped off the intercom and leaned back in his chair. "They knew exactly whose name to use," he said bitterly. "I suppose we have Karen to thank for that."

"They took a big risk, though, didn't they? Assuming your mother wouldn't recognize the difference between the impersonator and the real Judy?"

"Not much of a risk. Judy has a pleasant, medium-pitched voice, and as close to a standard American accent as you can get. How distinctive would that be? She introduces herself as my secretary, produces a note from me—"

"And how did they get that, do you suppose?"

He shrugged. "Easily, if they have access to samples of my writing. Not to mention a supply of stationery probably stolen by Karen. Provided the handwriting was close to mine, it would pass muster. My mother isn't likely to submit the damn note to a graphologist before letting Amanda go."

Something prickled at the back of Liz's mind.

Graphologist. Why did that word make her uncomfortable? The connection clicked into place. *Pieter Ullmann.* His defense on the blood-doping charges would rest largely on the evidence of a graphologist. Odd that the irrelevant connection should have flashed into her mind at such a tense time.

Dexter's fist crashed onto the desk, sending papers flying. "Damn it, Liz, I can't just sit here waiting! I'll go mad. Why don't they tell me what they want me to do? God knows, I'm willing!"

"Perhaps we should ask one of your secretaries to cancel our appointment with the deputy director of the FBI? Maybe they're waiting to hear that you've obeyed that instruction before they give you the next one."

Dexter closed his eyes for a second. "Thank God you're here, Liz. At least one of us is thinking like a sane human being." He pressed his intercom again. "Judy, please contact the FBI urgently and tell them that I won't be able to keep my appointment with the deputy director at three-thirty this afternoon. Make all the necessary apologies, won't you?"

"Certainly, Senator. Should I give any special reason?"

Dexter's mouth tightened. "You could say an unexpected emergency."

"I'll call right away, Senator."

Liz walked over to the window and stared down at the crowds hurrying toward the Capitol building. The day was warm, and the men had doffed their jackets, while the women mostly wore bright summer dresses, their arms bare to the sun. The beautiful spring day didn't seem a good moment for contemplating the end of life, either her own or Amanda's, but Liz was very much afraid that her death was the next item on someone's agenda. And by canceling her appointment with the deputy director, she had lost her best chance of safety.

In his inevitable concern for his daughter, Dexter didn't seem to have registered the significance of the demand that Liz should remain in the office. She hoped that the kidnappers simply wanted to prevent her from making contact with law enforcement officials. She feared that they wanted to keep tabs on her for some infinitely more gruesome reason.

Far beneath her, a family grouped itself on a flight of marble steps, posing for a picture. Even at this distance, she could see that the two children were prancing around in excitement, and the parents were attempting to keep them still with fond exasperation. Amanda should be prancing like that, Liz thought. Instead, she was probably bound and gagged in a dark room.... Shuddering, she snapped her mind closed on the unbearable images.

She sensed Dexter come up behind her. "Liz, I'm sorry," he said, putting his arms around her waist. "I went to pieces for a while, but I'm back together again now."

She turned in the circle of his arms, and saw that he spoke the truth. His face was still a stark white, but his eyes were sharply focused and fierce with intelligence. His fear for Amanda had been leashed by his habitual iron control.

"No father could hear that his daughter had been kidnapped and carry on as if nothing had happened," she said. "I understood."

"I've only just realized that it was your safety I put at risk by canceling our appointment with the deputy director. I had absolutely no right to ask you to make that sacrifice."

"You didn't ask," she reminded him. "I suggested that you should make the call."

"And I'm truly grateful, Liz." He drew in a deep breath. "If it'll make you feel any better, I think the kidnappers have already made their first mistake."

She looked up eagerly. "What's that?"

"If they hoped that keeping me in suspense would soften me up, they've miscalculated. Badly. My first reaction to that phone call was as a parent. Whatever they'd asked me to do to get back Amanda, I'd have done it. Now I'm reacting with my head as well as my heart. We may not have much time, Liz, so the first thing I want you to do is memorize a phone number." He picked up a pen and scrawled a series of eleven digits across the back of her hand. "That's what you might call a high-powered emergency number," he said. "Dial it anytime, and you can summon pretty much whatever help you need."

"Why don't you call it now and ask for a commando squad to rescue Amanda?"

"They have some highly trained specialists available at the other end of that number, but they're not miracle workers. We have no idea where Amanda is. Where would a commando squad start looking? It's much better if we wait for the next phone call, so that we at least have a chance to find out what's at stake in this hideous game."

She cleared her throat. "Dexter, in view of your position in the Senate... Have you considered...? I mean, what are you going to do if they ask for another top-secret weapons blueprint in exchange for Amanda?"

He was silent for a while. "I'm going to pray a lot," he said at last. "And then try to fool them. I have convincing fakes—blueprints and specifications—for all the systems currently being considered by our committee. Agent Cooper insisted on getting them when we first tried to track down the source of the leak in my office. All the plans and papers have been produced by government experts and should fool anybody except a top-notch weapons specialist. The errors had to be pointed out to me, and I've had a lot of intensive technical training. With luck, I should be able to get Amanda back before her kidnappers realize they've been cheated."

Liz had no idea how realistic Dexter's hopes were, although she derived some reassurance from the knowledge that he was talking about expert fakes, prepared at leisure, not some botched job rushed through in response to the crisis of Amanda's kidnapping. And it wasn't certain, of course, that the kidnappers wanted blueprints. They might yet astonish both Dexter and Liz by demanding a straightforward cash payment.

The phone rang before she could say anything. "A personal call for you on line three," Judy announced. "Do you want to take it, Senator? The caller wouldn't give her name."

Liz and Dexter exchanged glances. *A woman?* Dexter picked up the phone, his deliberate movements showing the strain placed on his control, she thought. "Put her through, please."

"Dexter, darling, this is Jeanette." He recognized the low, husky and stunningly sexy voice immediately. "I wasn't sure whether you were in Denver or D.C. this weekend. I'm going sailing, and I wondered if you were up for a little rest and recreation."

"I'll have to take a rain check this weekend. But thanks, anyway, Jeanette. I'll look forward to seeing you soon." Dexter hung up the phone.

"I think you just ruined a beautiful friendship," Liz said, trying to lower the level of tension and disappointment. "I'd guess that's the last time Jeanette's going to offer you the full facilities of her boat."

"We're just good friends," Dexter replied impatiently. "Hell, I wish they'd call!"

"Just good friends," Liz repeated, the phrase triggering another memory. This seemed to be her day for making odd connections. "Dexter, do you remember that reporter we met outside the FBI building? In retrospect, does it occur to you that he looked a heck of a lot more like a private detective than an aggressive photojournalist?''

''You may be right, although how a P.I. fits into this—'' The phone rang again and he snatched up the receiver.

''A personal call for you on line three, Senator. The caller preferred not to give her name.''

Dexter's shoulders slumped. ''Put her through,'' he said wearily.

''Good afternoon, Senator.'' The voice was crisp, businesslike, and strangely flattened, as if it echoed through some sort of synthesizer. ''Please depress the red button on the right of your phone, thus scrambling our conversation and making it impossible to trace.''

Dexter pressed the button. ''I have done what you asked.''

''Please wait a moment, Senator, while I check the accuracy of your statement.''

The pause lasted about thirty seconds. ''I am delighted to see that you are prepared to cooperate, Senator. It bodes well for our future negotiations.''

''I want my daughter back. Where is she?''

''Your daughter is well and reasonably happy, although she misses your company. She will continue to be well if you follow some simple instructions. Please listen carefully, Senator, since I don't plan to repeat this information. Within the next half hour, your office will receive a delivery from the Golden Slipper Boutique. The delivery will be made by an employee of the store and will consist of evening clothes and accessories for Elizabeth Meacham. You will pay cash on delivery for these purchases. We know that you, Senator, keep a spare tuxedo in your office. You and Ms. Meacham will dress for the evening in the clothes I have indicated. At six o'clock, having said a cheerful good-night to any of your staffers still lingering in the office, you will summon a cab. You and Ms. Meacham will drive directly to the French Embassy, where a reception for the new ambassador from Chad is being given. Your office, I'm sure, received an invitation. You will be contacted again later this evening.''

The voice stopped abruptly and was followed by an echoing silence.

''Amanda!'' Dexter yelled the name desperately. ''Amanda! Let me talk to my daughter!''

The silence of the phone was absolute. Dexter dropped the receiver into the cradle and turned to look at Liz. ''I wish they'd let Amanda speak to me.'' Despite all his efforts, his voice shook.

''Next time they probably will. Dexter, she'll be all right. They need to keep her well, so that they have something to bargain with. The kidnappers know you aren't going to do a deal unless you have proof that she's alive and unharmed.'' The platitudes seemed unavoidable, even though they were patently false. She wished that Dexter were a little bit less clear-sighted, a little bit better at the art of self-deception. Kneeling beside him, she clasped his hands and pulled them gently against her breasts.

"What in the world do all those bizarre instructions mean, do you think?"

Once again her ploy worked. The practical question brought his emotions back under a semblance of control. "Probably no more than a test to see if we're willing to follow their directions."

"And are we? Is it smart to go partying at the French Embassy because some brutal kidnappers told us to?"

"Yes," he said. "It's smart, because it's the only way we're going to get more instructions." His face became remote, harder than ever. "Liz, I wish I could pretend that I'm offering you a choice, but I'm not. I need you at this reception."

"I'm willing to come with you."

He freed his hands from her clasp, so that he could frame her face. His thumbs stroked a gentle caress across her lips. "Liz, I truly believe that you would be more at risk if you tried to contact the police than if you come with me. But my beliefs may not be a reliable guide at the moment. I have tunnel vision, and Amanda is at the end of the tunnel."

"I wouldn't expect it to be any other way."

His expression didn't soften at all. He bent his head and took her mouth in a quick, hard kiss. "I love you, Liz," he said. "I love you like hell."

A tap at the door was followed by the appearance of a young woman's head, poking uncertainly around the corner. "Sorry to interrupt, Senator, but a delivery boy is here from the Golden Slipper Boutique. He says you're expecting him, and that you owe him six hundred and ninety-three dollars.''

"I'll be right out," Dexter said. "Thanks, Bobbie.''

LIZ EXPERIENCED a definite sense of unreality as she showered in the small bathroom attached to Dexter's office, then dressed herself for the reception. The gown the kidnappers had sent from the Golden Slipper was black, sleek, low cut and elegant. The price tag hanging from the zipper indicated 495 in discreet gold figures. A bargain for some society matrons, perhaps, Liz thought, but for herself, whose clothes usually came from a discount warehouse, there was an undeniable pleasure in the soft swish of heavy silk against the new designer underwear that had come with the gown.

Putting on her makeup, she wondered if French aristocrats on their way to the guillotine had felt something like she did now: a curious mixture of anticipation, defiance and a fear too great to be acknowledged. Why did it seem so important that she should look good for the delectation of a bunch of kidnappers? She could find no answer. But as she twisted the final pin into her long blond hair, she knew that tonight of all nights, she was determined to look her best.

She stepped into high-heeled, diamanté-buckled evening shoes, and pushed her wallet and a few cosmetics into the matching purse also thoughtfully provided by the kidnappers. A final glance into the mirror revealed a sophisticated, attractive woman whom Liz scarcely recognized. With a twinge of sadness, Liz realized that this particular style of dress reminded her of her sister Alison. Alison had loved the dramatic combination of black and silver, choosing the combination for most of her skating outfits.

Liz couldn't allow herself the luxury of such bittersweet, distant memories. At the moment she had more pressing matters to worry about. Like finding Amanda. And keeping herself alive.

THE FRENCH EMBASSY was located opposite Georgetown University Hospital. During the cab ride from his office, Dexter tried to warn Liz of what was in store for her but, lacking any experience of the Washington cocktail party circuit, she was still unprepared for the barrage of attention that was directed toward her.

Washington's inner power elite throve on gossip. A scandal involving one of their own provided meat and drink for the endless round of formal functions that had to be endured. A double murder involving a popular senator rated almost a ten on Washington's ecstasy scale.

"The French ambassador ought to send you a personal thank-you note," Liz muttered after a particularly bruising encounter. "You've obviously made his night. Do you think *anyone* remembers this reception is supposed to be in honor of the ambassador from Chad?"

"Nobody," Dexter replied promptly. "Probably not even the ambassador from Chad."

"When do you think we can leave?"

His expression became momentarily bleak. "I

don't know. Can you hold out for another half hour?''

She took some champagne from the tray of a passing waiter. ''Another glass or two of this, and I might even make forty minutes.''

''Miss Meacham, I believe?'' The voice was soft, insinuating, and Liz felt the blood freeze in her veins. Somehow she forced herself to turn around and face her questioner.

''I'm Elizabeth Meacham, yes.''

The woman was pushing sixty, with teeth and skin yellowed by smoking. ''It's a pleasure to welcome you to our nation's capital, Miss Meacham. I'm sure it was wise of you to take a holiday from Colorado. Do you and the senator have any statement you'd like to make for my column?''

Liz expelled her breath in a rush that left her limp. A journalist. The woman was a darned journalist! Liz wasn't sure whether to scream with frustration or laugh with relief. She was still trying to make up her mind when Dexter intervened.

''If I give you an exclusive, Betty, will you go away and leave us in peace?''

The reporter's eyes gleamed. ''You betcha.''

''Miss Meacham and I recently became engaged and are planning our wedding shortly. There, you owe me one, lady. Coming at this particular time, that announcement is going to make your column the talk of the town tomorrow morning.''

''You and Miss Meacham were married before, and the marriage only lasted nine months. Any reason to expect a longer relationship this time?''

''Don't push your luck, Betty. You can say,

quote: 'The senator commented that this time he was older and wiser. A hell of a lot older and hopefully a hell of a lot wiser.' End quote.'' Dexter turned and looked down at Liz, his eyes darkening as if he meant every word he said. ''Off the record, our marriage is going to work this time, because we're even more in love. At least, I am.''

Although she knew he'd only invented the story in order to get rid of the reporter, Liz's whole body responded to the lie. She felt the heat rise in a deep flush from the pit of her stomach, and her cheeks flamed. With seeming indifference to Betty's avid eyes and flapping ears, Dexter carried Liz's hands to his mouth and dropped the lightest kisses against her knuckles. ''You're always beautiful,'' he said huskily, ''but tonight you're positively stunning. I love you, Liz.''

Her heart hammered wildly in her chest. When he looked at her like that, she couldn't quite convince herself that this was all a charade. She was so lost in the fantasy world Dexter had created that she jumped when Betty's voice intruded. ''Too much sentiment makes me nauseous,'' she said. ''I'll see you two lovebirds later. Like you said, Senator, I owe you one.''

They lingered another half hour at the reception, but no one approached them with cryptic messages or whispered instructions. The crowd had thinned to a mere handful of guests when Liz and Dexter finally took their leave.

''Your limousine, monsieur?'' the doorman asked.

''We'd like a cab, please,'' Dexter responded.

The doorman whistled one up, accepting Dexter's tip with the smoothness of vast experience. "Your destination, monsieur? I will tell the driver."

Dexter and Liz exchanged helpless glances. "To my apartment, I guess," he said. "Tell him The Fountains, in Chevy Chase."

"Certainly, monsieur." The cab door was slammed, and Liz leaned back against the tattered leather of the seat, trying to think of something she could say that might make Dexter feel better.

"Perhaps they couldn't approach us because there were too many people around."

"They could have made the opportunity if they'd wanted to. Betty Stone managed to get us alone, and we weren't even cooperating with her."

Liz developed a sudden fascination with the beading of her purse. "Couldn't you think of any other way to be rid of Betty? Is that why you told her we were getting married again?"

"No. I was a low, underhanded conniving schemer. I told her we were engaged because I hoped it might—" He broke off as the cab swerved violently to the right, cresting the sidewalk but continuing to move.

"What the devil?" Dexter demanded, just as an ambulance with lights flashing and siren howling roared out of the Georgetown hospital driveway and catapulted in front of the cab. The cabdriver braked immediately and swung around in his seat, leveling an extremely menacing gun straight at Liz's head.

"Either of you move and she gets it," he said.

The two doors closest to the sidewalk were

wrenched open. "He has a gun!" Liz screamed in warning.

It was all she said. A leather-gloved hand was clamped over her mouth and she was hauled from the cab. For a crucial second she failed to struggle, thinking that her abductor might be intent upon rescuing her from the gun-toting cabbie. In the two seconds it took to realize her mistake, all chance to scream and attract attention had been lost. With one hand still clapped over her mouth, her captor pulled her arms behind her back with brutal efficiency and bundled her face first onto the floor of the ambulance. The driver didn't even wait for the doors to be slammed behind her before he released the brake and set the ambulance shooting forward into the narrow Georgetown street.

The fist pressing her down to the ground relaxed its pressure. "You can sit up now, *dorogoya*."

She lifted her head, too stunned to move the rest of her body. "Mikhail?" she whispered. *"Mikhail?"*

He smiled the warm, familiar smile she knew so well. "Hello, Lizushka. Welcome to Washington."

CHAPTER THIRTEEN

HE COULDN'T DO A DAMN THING, because they had him covered by two guns: the cabbie's .45 Magnum and the 9-millimeter Soviet Makarov pistol aimed square between his eyes by the squat, balding man who'd just climbed into the front passenger seat.

Dexter silently cursed his helplessness. Dear God! Now they—whoever they were—had not only Amanda, but Liz, as well! He writhed under the knowledge that he had brought Liz into this danger. He was the one who'd insisted they follow instructions and attend the reception at the embassy. He was the one who'd insisted on canceling their appointment at the FBI.

The sick knot of guilt in Dexter's gut hardened into a bitter determination to frustrate his opponents or die trying. And right at this moment, he reflected grimly, it looked as if he was going to die for sure.

The gunman in the passenger seat steadied his aim with brisk professionalism. Not a good sign. "Good evening, Senator Rand. My name is Igor. It is certainly my pleasure to meet you."

Dexter stared ahead in stony silence.

Igor sighed. "It would help your situation, Senator, if you would cooperate. The driver of this cab is about to put his gun away and resume driving. We do not wish to attract the attention of a cruising police vehicle by remaining parked. You will clasp your hands behind your neck, please. If you do not, you will be shot in the knee.''

Igor meant what he said, Dexter was sure of it, and a broken kneecap would make escape virtually impossible. Without breaking his silence, Dexter did as Igor instructed. He stared out of the front window, not deigning to meet the eyes of either of his captors. With a despairing lurch of his stomach, he saw the ambulance containing Liz hurtle off into the darkness, its emergency beacons flashing. An old trick for hurrying from the scene of a crime, but nonetheless damnably effective, he reflected wryly.

Schooling his features into blankness, Dexter held his hands unmoving behind his neck. He carried no concealed weapons, and therefore cherished no hope of outshooting his captors. Any attempt at escape would have to wait.

Igor gave a curt nod to the cabbie, who returned his .45 to the inside pocket of his jacket and immediately set the cab in motion. Dexter had hoped Igor might try to frisk him, but the man was obviously too seasoned a veteran to attempt something so dangerous. Igor knew—unfortunately—that in the close confines of the cab, it would be easy for Dexter to grab Igor's gun and turn the tables on his attackers.

"We are taking you to a house in the country,"

Igor announced. His tone of voice suggested that Dexter should be appreciative of this rare treat. "Miss Meacham will be joining us there."

Dexter tried to show no reaction to this piece of news. He willed himself to remain silent, but lost the battle.

"Where's Amanda?" he asked, the words torn from him. "What have you done with my daughter?" By a superhuman effort, he managed to bite back the need to ask anything more about Liz. It might give him some infinitesimal advantage, if Igor and his crew thought him indifferent to Liz's fate.

"Amanda is already at home with her grandparents, Senator Rand. When we arrive at our destination, I will permit you to make a phone call confirming her safety. You may dial the number yourself, so that you will know there are no tricks, and you may ask any questions that come into your head to ensure that she is indeed at home and unharmed."

"How can I believe you? Why would you—?" Dexter cut off his question. Since he expected nothing but lies in answer, he wouldn't demean himself by asking.

"Ah! You wish, perhaps, to know why we have released your daughter? The answer is simple. We took her to demonstrate our power. We have released her as a gesture of goodwill, Senator Rand. We want you to see that cooperating with us is not a difficult business. It was never part of our plan to harm your daughter. We Russians are sentimental about little children.''

''May I lower my hands?'' Dexter asked curtly. ''My arms ache.''

Igor curled his finger around the trigger of the gun. ''No, Senator Rand. You may not lower your hands.''

Dexter leaned back against the seat and stared out of the cab window. He recognized exactly where they were. Ironically, for all the good it would do him, they were driving past Langley, headquarters of the CIA in suburban Virginia. Now that he had time to reflect on his situation, he found the fact that he wasn't blindfolded deeply depressing. He could think of several reasons why his captors wouldn't have bothered with a blindfold. All of them were unpleasant.

The roads were relatively clear of traffic as they drove through Tyson's Corner, but the cabdriver seemed in no hurry, or perhaps he was avoiding the risk of a ticket for speeding. Their journey continued through Reston until, after about an hour, the cab stopped outside a pleasant-looking house in a semi-rural setting. Dexter recognized the area as one much favored for weekend trysts by Washington's ''in'' crowd.

Igor's method of removing his prisoner from the cab once again demonstrated his experience. At a nod from Igor, the driver, .45 in hand, pulled Dexter from the cab with sufficient force to send him sprawling on the gravel driveway. With a foot in the small of Dexter's back, the driver expertly searched him for weapons.

"He's clean, boss."

Igor exited from the cab and grunted. "Stand up, if you please, Senator Rand. I would remind you that the more quickly you walk into the house and demonstrate some signs of cooperation, the more quickly you will be permitted to telephone your daughter."

They knew precisely which carrot to dangle in front of his nose, Dexter reflected. Unfortunately, the knowledge that he was being manipulated didn't prevent the ploy from working. At this moment, he wanted to hear Amanda's voice with an intensity that overrode all other considerations.

The cabbie dug the .45 into the base of his spine. Unresisting—not that he could have resisted in any way that would have left him alive, he reflected—Dexter allowed himself to be led up to the front door and into the comfortably furnished living room.

"Sit," Igor commanded.

He sat down on the cream leather sofa the man indicated. Later, he cautioned himself. Later you can try the heroics. "I'm ready to phone my daughter," he said, his tone curt.

Igor smiled, displaying a gold tooth. "I see you are a practical man, Senator, who believes in dealing with first things first. I am glad that my superiors, in selecting you for our purposes, did not underestimate your common sense." Igor gestured with his gun to indicate a phone on the glass-topped coffee table. "Please feel free to call your parents' home, Senator."

Dexter picked up the phone and examined it carefully, pulling off the base and unscrewing the mouthpiece. It looked like standard phone-company issue. He could see no sign that it had been tampered with, and Agent Cooper had recently given him a refresher course in methods of bugging and otherwise distorting normal phone service. Dexter screwed the phone together again.

"I want to dial Information," he said curtly.

"Please, Senator, be my guest. You are welcome to test for yourself that this is simply a normal phone. You do realize, of course, what will happen to your daughter, should you attempt to communicate with anybody we deem...undesirable."

"I want to check that the phone isn't rigged to go through to one certain number, manned by your personnel, whatever digits I dial."

"I repeat, Senator. Feel free."

Dexter called Information in New York, and asked for the number of an old friend from his Air Force academy days. The woman responding sounded bored enough to be the genuine phone-company article. He even heard her gum snap as she connected him to the computer, which provided the correct number.

Feeling more confident that the phone hadn't been rigged, he then dialed his parents' home. His father answered with a crisp "Hello."

"Hi, Dad, this is Dex. Sorry to bother you at this hour, but is Amanda there?"

"Yes, she is, but she's on her way to bed. What in the world's gotten into you, Dexter? Dragging her off to Washington, and then turning around and telling your secretary to bring her back again to us! The poor child's exhausted from all that useless flying."

Dexter gripped the phone and willed himself to stay calm. "Let me talk to Amanda, Dad. And could you save the lectures until tomorrow? One way and another, this has been a helluva day."

"Here's Amanda," Mr. Rand said, his tone still disapproving. "It seems she wants to talk to you."

"Hi, Daddy! Why didn't you come to see me when I was in your secretary's apartment? Judy was pretty nice, but I didn't like being there with her. She told me you were too busy to come and see me."

Dexter drew in a long, shaky breath. "Hello, sweetheart, it's great to hear your voice. I'm sorry we missed each other today. Was Judy—? What did Judy give you for lunch?"

"Hot dogs, and she let me have two slices of chocolate cake." Amanda sounded less than interested in Judy. "Why didn't you come to see me, Dad? Why did I have to fly to Washington if you're too busy to come and see me? I felt sick on the plane coming back to Boston, and my ears popped."

"Judy and I had a bit of a mix-up in our communications, sweetheart. I didn't actually know you'd arrived in Washington. I'll explain to you what happened another time. In fact, I didn't really want you to leave Grandma and Grandpa's house, so if anyone else comes to get you, anyone at all, you just stay put with Gran and Gramps, okay?"

"Okay. When are you coming to see me?"

"I don't know exactly, sweetheart, but soon, very soon."

"I miss you, Dad." A small pause. "Is Ms. Meacham with you?"

"Not at the moment." He needed every ounce of discipline he possessed to keep the urgency from his voice and the panic from his expression. "Amanda, promise me you'll stick close to your grandparents, will you? That's very important."

"Okay. Grandpa and I are going fishing tomorrow. And Grandma says I have to go to bed now. It's eleven o'clock and a ridic—ridikolus hour for me to be up."

"Yes, it is late." Dexter's voice thickened. "Good night, Amanda. I love you lots and lots."

"I love you, too." She yawned. "Good night, Dad. Take care."

"I will," Dexter said, holding the receiver long after his daughter had hung up.

"Satisfied, Senator?" Igor asked. "Your daughter, as you heard, is well and happy."

Dexter played back the conversation in his mind. Amanda's chatter had been entirely natural. If there had been kidnappers in the room, coercing her to reply, Dexter knew he would have heard the fear and constraint in her voice. And his father would have been even less capable of pretending cheerfulness than Amanda. There was no way, he decided, that either of them could have been under any sort of duress. Whatever hideous payment Igor might try to exact in exchange for his generosity, Amanda was temporarily safe.

Dexter shifted his position on the sofa and looked straight into Igor's eyes. "Okay," he said. "My daughter's home with her grandparents, and she hasn't been harmed. What do I have to pay to keep her safe?"

AS SHE PULLED HERSELF off the floor of the jolting ambulance, Liz felt no fear. For a crucial few moments, she was aware of nothing save an overwhelming sense of betrayal. "Why, Mikhail?" she asked. "Why are you doing this?"

"Doing what, *dorogoya*?" His warm smile had not changed at all, giving her an unearthly feeling that somehow she must have misunderstood, that somehow she wasn't in danger, that somehow Mikhail was still the same friendly brother-in-law she had known and liked for years.

She shook her head, trying to clear her mind of its dangerous fuzziness. "Mikhail! You've kidnapped me, for God's sake!"

His eyes twinkled in what she now realized was a sickening parody of brotherly teasing. "God, Lizushka, has nothing at all to do with my actions. I follow the orders of my government."

Bile rose in her throat. "Your defection...it wasn't genuine, was it?"

"I am Russian. I will always be Russian. Only you Americans, in your arrogance, would believe that I wished to change my nationality. My defection was a carefully planned move, approved by the leaders of the KGB."

"But why, Mikhail? Why didn't you stay in the Soviet Union? Nobody in America begged you to defect!"

"My government saw an opportunity," Mikhail said. "I willingly took it."

"For your government? The same government that holds your mother hostage—?" Light suddenly dawned in Liz's fuddled brain. "Was that it?" she asked. "Did they promise to get your mother an exit visa if you helped them? Oh, Mikhail, you should have known better. They'll never honor their promises, and you'll be in their service forever."

"My mother," he murmured mockingly. "Ah yes, my dear old mother, pining for her exit visa. You are so easy to deceive, Liz, that it almost becomes boring. There is no mother. I haven't seen the woman who bore me since the day she left me on the orphanage steps in Leningrad. What's more, I have no desire to see the old bag, if she still lives. The staff tell me she was an extremely inefficient whore, who was forever getting pregnant. I was the third bastard of hers that the state had to take care of. And who knows how many abortions the workers of Leningrad paid for on her behalf?"

"I thought that the great and glorious Soviet state had abolished whores," Liz said caustically.

"Only high-paid ones," he said. "And with the current political climate, who knows, even the high-priced ones may soon reappear. We like to feel that our motherland has all the amenities of her capitalist rivals."

Despite the fact that the gun in his hand had never once wavered, Liz couldn't bring herself to believe that her images of Mikhail were so totally false. "What about Karen?" she asked. "Was her baby—? Mikhail, was it yours?"

He shrugged. "Probably."

"Did you—kill her?"

"But of course. It was always our plan to compromise Dexter Rand through Karen. Her death was the catalyst designed to set all the other ingredients of our plan bubbling. My dear Liz, please stop bouncing around. You are making the driver nervous. And you know how sensitive I am to other people's nerves."

"On the contrary. It's obvious I know nothing at all about you."

"*Dorogoya*, you have seen me regularly for the last four years."

"Seen you through blinders, I think."

"Not at all. I am the man who enjoys spending Saturday nights drinking vodka and eating caviar with you."

"But you were living a lie, Mikhail!"

"What is truth? Part of me is that man you spent time with in Colorado Springs."

"It's the other parts of you that I'm worried about. What's going on, Mikhail? Why have I been kidnapped? How are you hoping to set up Dexter?"

"So you did at least work out that much."

"If you're planing to use me as leverage against Dexter, you're wasting your time."

"Lizushka, I never waste my time. That is how I clawed my way out of the orphanage."

"I would say you've been wasting your time for the past four years. How does it help the Soviet Union to have you train Americans like Pieter Ullmann to become Olympic winners? It was a Russian who got beaten into second place."

Mikhail was silent, and enlightenment dawned. "That was a mistake, wasn't it?" Liz breathed. "Pieter was never supposed to win! You assumed you'd be able to psych him out, to tempt him into breaking training at some crucial point. You didn't realize how rock-bottom determined he was to win the gold."

Mikhail's eyes glittered in the dimness of the ambulance interior, but he said nothing.

"That business about blood doping was all nonsense, wasn't it?" Liz persisted. "Were you so angry with Pieter that you and Karen plotted to get his gold taken away from him?"

"Pieter's been a womanizing fool since he was sixteen!" Mikhail burst out. "How was I to know

that where skating is concerned, he is pure dedication and hard work?''

"Two hours watching him on the ice should have
given you a hint," Liz taunted. "Maybe you're not
quite such an expert judge of character as you think,
Mikhail. Your masters can't have been too pleased
with you recently. I doubt if they sprang you from
the Soviet Union so that you could produce winners
for the United States.''

Mikhail leaned forward and backhanded her hard
across the mouth. She tasted blood, but refused to
cry out. He thrust her onto the stretcher bed, prop-
ping her against the wall of the ambulance.

"Whatever my mistakes with Pieter, I have read
your character well, Lizushka. You share in abun-
dance the two fatal flaws of all Americans: you believe your friends tell you the truth, and you have
hope for the future.''

"Those aren't flaws, Mikhail, they're strengths.''

"You are naive, *dorogoya*. Perhaps it is better so.
Perhaps you will be lucky enough to die without
suffering the anguish of knowing your death ap-
proaches. Even now, even at this moment, I can see
that you somehow expect the cavalry to come riding
to your rescue. Isn't that how Hollywood promises
it will be? In the United States, innocent maidens
are never run over by the train.''

"If it's naive to believe that good guys win in the
end, Mikhail, then I'm proud to be naive. Whatever
you're plotting against Dexter Rand, it isn't going
to work out.''

"There is one small flaw in your reasoning, Lizushka. I believe *I* am the good guy and that my cause is just. I also know that the plan we have for subjugating the senator to our will is foolproof. Dexter Rand will be our man by the end of this night, take my word for it."

"You're wrong!"

"We shall see, Lizushka. Now, we are nearly at our destination and I say only this. Prepare yourself for a shock, little sister. I think you will find that we have a most amusing surprise awaiting you."

When they let her out of the ambulance, Liz saw that they were in the driveway of a typical two-story, upper-income suburban house. Whether they had driven into Maryland or Virginia, she had no idea. Of Dexter there was no sign.

Mikhail had bound her wrists together with surgical strapping tape, and he held his hand tightly over her mouth as they walked up the gravel path to the house. His gun poked into the small of her back, so she didn't even consider screaming, but some absurd, lingering hope of rescue caused her to sneak surreptitious glances to the left and right as she was propelled toward the back door.

There were other houses in the neighborhood, she saw, although they were relatively far away and screened behind trees and bushes. But even if she could somehow make a break for it, she knew she couldn't assume those houses represented safety. The chances were good that they contained enemies rather than friends. Mikhail said something in Russian to the ambulance driver, a young man shaped like a gorilla, carrying a submachine gun that seemed to grow like an extension from his right arm.

Sandwiched between the two men, Liz was taken in through a back door and conducted down a brightly lighted staircase to the basement. Liz barely had time to register that it was furnished in typical suburban style—complete with a Ping-Pong table in the center of the large room—before Mikhail bent forward and murmured in her ear.

"The moment has arrived," he said softly. "There is somebody who has been waiting most anxiously to see you, *dorogoya.*"

Liz's heart pounded with sudden, suffocating force and her lungs felt squeezed tight by lack of air. "Who is it?" she asked. "Who wants to see me?"

A rustle of silk whispered behind a Victorian-style screen in the far corner of the room, and Liz's head jerked in that direction, like a puppet's pulled by a string. A slender, fair-haired woman, wearing a scarlet silk robe and a pair of high-heeled black shoes identical to Liz's own, stepped out from behind the screen. Her blue-gray eyes were fringed by long lashes, and her naturally pink lips formed a striking contrast with her pale, almost translucent, complexion.

The pounding of Liz's heart intensified. She felt giddy, nauseous, disoriented. The fear she had held at bay for so long rose up in her throat and emerged in a single giant scream. She gazed at the woman in hypnotized horror. Except for the red silk robe, she was looking at a mirror image of herself.

At the sound of Liz's scream, Mikhail clapped his hand back over her mouth with bruising force, but the woman merely smiled—a cruel, mocking smile that held no hint of sympathy.

"Hello, Lizzie," she said. "It's been a long time, babe."

CHAPTER FOURTEEN

THE NAUSEA WOULDN'T GO AWAY, neither would the dizzying sense of unreality. Liz clutched at her stomach. "Alison?" she whispered. *"Alison?"*

The woman smiled. "That's who I am, sweetie. Although not for long."

"Wh-what have you done to your hair? And your nose is different." Liz realized belatedly that she was hardly addressing the major issue. "I thought… we all thought you were dead."

"You were intended to, sweetie."

"But how could you let us all believe you'd been killed? Good God, Alison, Mom had a stroke when she heard about the plane crash! She's been a helpless invalid ever since, and all over something that never really happened!"

A faint trace of color stained Alison's cheekbones. "Mother had high blood pressure for years, so she was probably headed for a stroke anyway, whatever happened. Besides, she isn't miserable. How can she be, when she doesn't know what's going on? And the Soviet government helps to pay for the best nursing care. I'll bet she's happier than half the people who haven't had a stroke."

Liz stared at her sister in stupefied silence. Alison, she realized in wonderment, truly believed what she was saying. Even as a child, Alison had always been capable of twisting the truth to fit her own personal needs. Apparently that character trait hadn't altered. Liz clenched her fists in an effort to keep herself from screaming.

"What's going on?" she asked tightly. "Why have you suddenly decided to come back from the dead? And why have you changed your hair and your nose to look like me?"

"That, sweetie, should be obvious even to you. Alison Kerachev isn't coming back from the dead. Elizabeth Meacham is merely going to be played by a different person."

"I see." Liz, in fact, saw a hell of a lot more than she wanted to. Like the fact that she was shortly going to be dead. Two Elizabeth Meachams obviously wouldn't fit into anybody's scheme of things. She swung around and sought out Mikhail, who was viewing the encounter from a corner of the room, an amused, proprietary smile flashing occasionally as he looked from one newly identical sister to the other.

"Somebody's gone to a lot of trouble to change Alison's appearance," Liz said. "We both know your government doesn't spend money just to keep its citizens happy, so what's going on, Mikhail?"

"You will know in good time, *dorogoya*."

"Don't call me that!" The endearment lacerated Liz's nerves, and she struggled to regain control of herself. "Something important's at stake here, that much is clear. It must have taken months of surgery and a great deal of money to make so many changes in the way Alison looks."

Alison strolled over to link her arm through Mikhail's. "There wasn't that much to change, sweetie. We weren't identical twins, you and I, but the plastic surgeons tell me our bone structure is remarkably similar. I had to have my nose bobbed, and they did a bit of work on my jaw, which was damn painful and definitely isn't an improvement. I have to tint my hair, because yours has more red in it than mine, but that's easy enough to do, except for the fact that I hate the color. Fortunately our eyes have always been amazingly alike, and they're the most difficult feature to change."

Liz's gaze traveled over her sister's body. "You're thinner. At least in most places."

Alison grinned mockingly, running her hands over her breasts. "You like my new boobs, sweetie? Best quality silicone implants, courtesy of the toiling Soviet masses." She jiggled her bosom with evident satisfaction. "Yes, these almost make up for all the months I spent on a starvation diet, trying to keep pace with your weight loss. Every time Mikhail sent us a new picture and a new set of statistics, you'd lost another couple of pounds and another few inches. What the hell's been going on in your life?"

"My roommates were getting murdered," Liz said dryly. "I have this weird aversion to coming home and finding my friends splattered over the sidewalk. It affects my appetite.''

Alison shrugged. ''They weren't friends, only acquaintances. Besides, you're so damned stars-and-stripes patriotic, you ought to be glad they're dead. They were all spying for the Soviet Union. Karen didn't even exist except as a creation of the KGB. She was smuggled into the country two years ago, direct from her Siberian training camp.''

Liz didn't dispute her sister's statements. There seemed little point. Alison's definitions of patriotism and friendship seemed to have nothing in common with Liz's. ''I'm a market-research specialist with a medium-sized Mexican-food company,'' she said. ''What interest could the Soviet government possibly have in me? Why in the world would they spend all this money to replace a junior manager at Peperito's?''

''Nobody cares about your job at Peperito's,'' Mikhail said curtly. ''We are replacing you in your role as the former wife of Dexter Rand. It is the illustrious senator who interests our government.''

For a few moments, Liz was shocked enough to forget to be frightened. ''You think Dexter won't notice the substitution?'' she asked incredulously. ''He'll know Alison isn't me, the second she walks into the room.''

Alison glanced toward her husband. ''I do hope she isn't correct, sweetie.''

Tight-lipped, Mikhail replied. ''It's unfortunate that your sister has spent so much time with the senator over the past week. Our plans required her to be thrown again into his orbit, which is why she was persuaded to share an apartment with Karen Zeit. However, we didn't anticipate—''

"We?" Alison queried softly..

"I didn't anticipate such an occurrence," Mikhail admitted, scowling at his wife. "Based on your information and the many conversations Liz had with me, it seemed her hatred for Dexter was too great to be overcome, whatever the circumstance. Even so, I am sure he will not detect the substitution."

"And if he does?" Alison persisted.

"In the last resort it doesn't matter—provided the realization doesn't come for a week or two. You know as well as I do that the senator will be forced to comply with our wishes, if he wants to remain alive. Our plan is foolproof."

"But you already kidnapped Amanda!" Liz said. "If the KGB want to force Dexter to do something—anything—you have the perfect method of control!"

"Not at all, sweetie." Alison turned away from a narrow wall mirror where she had been admiring her silhouette. "Kidnapping Amanda gives us only limited control. Either we return her and so lose our hold over Dexter, or we kill her. In which case, once again we have no hold over Dexter. Taking Amanda was nothing more than a device for getting the two of you to the French Embassy, and keeping you away from the FBI."

"You would kidnap a child just to get Dexter and me to the French Embassy?"

"Of course. Why not?"

"Why is Dexter so important to you?" she asked Mikhail. "There must be at least twenty or thirty senators with more political clout than him."

Alison smiled pityingly. "Shall I give her a lesson in world politics, Mikhail?"

"If you wish. Although time marches on, and I see no necessity for explanations."

"That's your Russian background, sweetie. You never think the toiling masses need to know anything. Personally, I'm all in favor of freedom of information."

Mikhail laughed bitterly. "You're not in favor of anything unless it puts power or money into your pocket."

"Are you complaining, sweetie? I've directed quite a lot of those useful commodities your way since we were married, so I suggest you shut up." Alison bestowed a mocking kiss on Mikhail's cheek and walked without haste across the rec room.

She stopped when a few inches still separated her from Liz. For the first time in years, the two sisters were within touching distance. Liz's heart constricted painfully as she looked into her sister's blue-gray eyes and read there the certainty of her own death. The pain wasn't only for her imminent end. She wanted to live—desperately—but at this moment her most profound regret was that Alison could so readily conspire to abet her own sister's murder.

"Why?" Liz asked. "Why are you doing this, Alison? What did I or anyone in our family ever do to make you so full of hate for us?"

Alison gave an odd, defiant little shrug. "How could you understand? You have no idea what it's like to be constantly second best. The apple of Daddy's eye, as long as Lizzie wasn't around to enchant him. Pretty, but not quite as pretty as Lizzie. Smart, but not quite as smart as good old Lizzie. A world-class skater, but not quite as good as the ethereal, passionate Lizzie."

"You're wrong, Alison. Our parents never measured out their love according to how worthy we were. They loved us because we were their children, not because we were pretty or smart, or because we won medals for skating."

Alison totally ignored Liz's remarks. "For a while, I could train harder and win more competitions than you," she said. "But eventually your natural talent showed through. You won the U.S. championship, I bombed out. Then I barely made it into the first round of the Olympics, whereas you were expected to win. And then, to crown it all, there was Dexter—"

"Dexter? What on earth has he got to do with our relationship? You'd fallen in love with Mikhail long before I even knew Dexter."

Alison's mouth twisted into a thin, bitter line. "You never realized how I felt about Dexter, did you? I met him when we first went over to Germany, weeks before you even heard his name. The only snag was, I couldn't get him interested in me, however hard I tried. Finally I persuaded him to come to the rink and watch me skate. Only you were already out on the ice practicing when we arrived. I remember the music that was playing. It was Ravel's *Bolero*, and you were going through a routine that was so erotic that even the cleaners had stopped to watch. So what happened? The same damned thing that always happened to me when you were around. He forgot about me. Dexter saw you and stopped dead in his tracks. The music ended. You looked up. You opened your innocent little eyes wide, smiled your cute, naive little smile, and two minutes later he was at your side, asking you out to dinner.''

''Alison, you know my marriage to Dexter was nothing to envy! It was already broken past repair by the time you married Mikhail and left for Moscow.''

''And I worked damned hard at breaking it, sweetie. With a little help from Susan, who was almost as naive and gullible as you in her own way.''

Liz felt her confused emotions coalesce into a hard ball of pride. She lifted her head. ''No, Alison. You didn't destroy my marriage to Dex. You didn't have that power. Nobody has the power to destroy a marriage except the couple themselves.''

''Well, if you say so, sweetie, but I sure think I helped things along a little. And now I'm going to have the power to do a whole bunch of exciting things where Dexter's concerned. You see, Lizzie, I'm going to make sure that Dexter's votes in the

Senate all go the way the Soviet government wants them to go.''

"You're crazy!" Liz breathed. "Even if Dexter thought you were me, he wouldn't vote according to my instructions. Don't you understand anything at all about his character?"

"Sweetie, I know everything about Dexter Rand. As soon as he became a senator, the KGB started to compile a dossier on him. Right from the first, he was targeted as the senator they most wanted to neutralize.''

"But why?" All Liz's frustration and bewilderment sounded in her question. "I would have thought the KGB had much bigger problems to worry about than the junior senator from an underpopulated state like Colorado."

"You still don't understand, do you, Lizzie? It's Dexter's expertise in weapons technology that's so worrying. Not only is his vote always technically sound, but other senators recognize his mastery of military hardware and follow his lead. Since Dexter took over the Appropriations Committee, Congress hasn't funded a single useless weapons system, and Dexter's managed to swing financial backing for three breakthrough defensive systems that would never have left the drawing board if not for his support.''

So that was it, Liz thought, recognizing the ring of truth in her sister's voice. It was Dexter's years of practical experience in the Air Force, coupled with his outstanding technological training, that made him so dangerous as a senator—and such a valuable target for the KGB. "I still don't see where you come into this, Alison. Do your spy masters plan to have you curl up beside him in bed and seduce him into voting your way? 'Darling Dexter, I love you so much, please vote no on the Phantom X-32 jet fighter aircraft?' Even the KGB can't be dumb enough to think that would work."

Mikhail stepped forward. "Enough," he said. "There is no reason for this conversation to continue. Take off your clothes, Liz. Your sister needs to wear them."

Liz sat down. "Go to hell, Mikhail."

She had known resistance would be useless, but she was tired of surrendering so tamely to her own inevitable destruction. When Mikhail dragged her back onto her feet, she kicked him hard on the shins. His response was a swift, brutal punch to the ribs that knocked the air out of her lungs. As a skater, she had fallen often enough to be quite familiar with physical pain, but she couldn't control her instinctive gag reflex, and for several seconds she fought to draw every breath. When she opened her eyes again, the driver from the ambulance was holding her hands immobile in front of her, and Mikhail was unzipping her gown at the back.

Mikhail gave another Russian command to the driver, who at long last put down his submachine gun. Silently he found the end of the strapping tape and ripped it off Liz's wrist, so that Mikhail could take off the black gown. Once her wrists were free, she struggled to resist being undressed, but achieved nothing except to slow down the process slightly and to receive several stinging slaps from Mikhail and the ambulance driver.

Alison lit a cigarette and puffed on it nervously as Liz's slip was removed and handed to her. Still smoking, she shrugged out of the red silk robe and into the long black slip.

"The damn thing's too tight," she muttered around her cigarette. "Hell, Mikhail, she lost even more weight."

"I think not. Calm down, Allie. You chose the outfit in the first place, remember? You wear the same size as Liz in everything except for the shoes, and you're already wearing the identical pair of shoes." He smoothed the slip over his wife's hips and handed her the dress. "Perfect," he said, closing the zipper.

"She's split the damn seams. Dexter'll notice for sure if he touches me. Why did you let her wriggle around like a stuck pig in a thunderstorm?"

"Split seams are no problem. The senator will expect Liz to have struggled. Here, take her purse. There is makeup inside, and a perfume spray. Do you want me to hold her face still so that you can copy her exact style of makeup?"

Alison grimaced. "Just the eyes. I don't want to go upstairs wearing fresh lipstick and powder."

Liz shivered and bent to pick up her sister's robe. The very thought of being touched by Mikhail—or Alison—made her physically ill. The ambulance driver gestured menacingly with his gun, which he'd picked up again, but he didn't prevent her from slipping into the robe. It smelled of cigarette smoke and Alison's perfume, but Liz felt marginally less vulnerable when Mikhail and his sidekick weren't staring straight at her bra and stockings. Mikhail waited for her to tie the belt, then caught hold of her face and turned it toward Alison. Liz closed her eyes, willing the nausea to go away.

"Very good," Mikhail said softly. "With eyes shut it is easier for Allie to copy your eye shadow."

Liz didn't struggle. When Mikhail finally released her, she turned one final time to look at her sister— the sister who was now a mirror-perfect image of herself. She knew that at any moment she would start to feel fear, but right now, all she felt was anger and sick revulsion, mingled with shame that a member of her own family could contemplate such treachery.

"Alison, don't do this," she pleaded. "Don't betray your own country."

Alison didn't reply at once, and Mikhail jumped in. "Russia is Alison's country now," he said. "Russia has given her power and wealth and a useful task to perform. She owes no loyalty to America, merely because an accident of birth decreed that she would be born here."

"She wasn't just born here. She spent the first nineteen years of her life benefiting from the opportunities that America provid—"

"Try not to sound like such a naive fool, Lizzie

dearest.'' Alison stubbed out her cigarette: "I'll see you around, little sister. Your ex-husband is upstairs, and I don't want to keep him waiting.''

IGOR'S SMILE showed no sign of strain. Positively exuding cordiality, he chuckled at Dexter's grim question. ''You are required to pay nothing, Senator Rand. We ask merely for a little cooperation.''

''Kidnapping Amanda and abducting Elizabeth Meacham at gunpoint isn't likely to inspire me with feelings of goodwill.''

''But, Senator, how can you be so unreasonable? Amanda is safely at home with her grandparents. And, as a further gesture of our extreme benevolence, I have somebody else waiting to see you. She comes now.'' Igor clicked his fingers to the cabdriver, who walked over to the door and pulled it open.

''Dexter!''

At the heartrending cry, he stood up and turned around, just in time to see Liz being half dragged, half carried into the living room. Her arms were held by two men: the cabbie, and another man whom Dexter vaguely recognized but couldn't quite place.

Fighting down his immediate, instinctive impulse to rush to Liz's side, Dexter struggled to remain in control of his reflexes. If he kept his cool, there was a slight chance he might be able to find some weakness in Igor's position that would enable him to bargain for Liz's safety. But if he once allowed himself to start reacting emotionally, it would be all over.

Except in the movies, unarmed combat provided no defense against three expert gunmen. If he gave in to his emotions and started throwing punches, he might—with luck—win Liz twenty seconds of freedom before the bullets exploded in her body.

Liz was obviously not doing too well. *Poor kid,* he thought. He could hear the choked little sounds emerging from her throat as she bravely attempted to silence her sobs, and when her two captors finally released her arms, she ran across the room and collapsed helplessly against his chest, repeating his name in an endless, desperate litany.

Overwhelmed by a primitive masculine urge to hold her tight and pour out meaningless words of love and comfort, Dexter strained to remain alert and rational. He couldn't afford to let Igor guess how desperate he felt about Liz. Dexter knew Igor's type of old, and he had no doubt that the man was capable of ordering Liz's fingernails pulled out one by one if that seemed the quickest or surest way to manipulate him. Willing Liz to understand his coldness, he brushed a hand over her hair in a friendly, but somewhat impersonal gesture of reassurance. He tried to imagine how his father would behave with an overwrought, but distant, relative and modeled his own behavior accordingly.

"Liz, my dear, you must calm down. Hysterics aren't going to help anybody." *That was it,* he told himself on an inner sigh of relief. Just the right mixture of mild affection, tolerance and exasperation.

About a hundred light-years away from what he was really feeling.

"Oh, Dex, I'm so frightened!"

Her words were little more than a squeak of panic, and something deep within him stiffened in surprise. Why was Liz behaving like this? Of all the women in the world, she was surely the one least likely to crumple into his arms and reveal her fears. He would have expected her to come into the room fighting and spitting out defiance to her captors. What the devil had they been doing to her to provoke such an atypical response?

With gentle hands he pried her away from his chest, so that he could look at her more closely. "What's happened?" he asked softly. "Are you hurt?"

"They hit me," she whispered.

Alarm prickled down Dexter's spine. The antennae that had so often warned him of danger in his fighter-pilot days quivered into alertness. Why was Igor allowing Liz to sob out her ill-treatment in his arms? Why did he have this odd sensation of breathless expectancy—as if everybody in the room were waiting for him to show some reaction to this encounter with Liz?

To buy himself some time, he drew her back into his arms and dropped a light kiss on her forehead before reaching up to stroke her hair again. To his surprise, she wriggled within his clasp and turned up her mouth, asking for a kiss.

It was an invitation even Superman could not

have found the strength to refuse. Dexter bent his head and touched his lips to Liz's soft, delicate mouth. She clung to him, her lips parting eagerly, her tongue seeking his. He responded automatically, his mind reeling, waiting for the flame—the inevitable, mind-blowing flame—that always burst into life when he and Liz exchanged kisses. Nothing. His body didn't harden, his pulse didn't quicken. Nothing.

Dexter slowly raised his head from the kiss, breathing deeply, and simultaneously casting a quick, surreptitious glance around the room. He became aware of three things: Liz smelled of cigarette smoke and a heavy, unfamiliar perfume; Igor was looking like a cat who'd swallowed the cream and the canary; and the man who had dragged Liz into the room two minutes earlier was Mikhail Kerachev.

Mikhail Kerachev. Alison's husband. Alison, who was dead. Liz's brother-in-law.

Dexter rapidly concluded that he would stake his life on the fact that the woman in his arms was not Liz.

CHAPTER FIFTEEN

MIKHAIL PULLED ROUGHLY at the woman in Dexter's arms, dragging her away with such force that she tumbled to the floor with a bone-jarring crunch. Dexter had trained enough men in unarmed combat to know that Mikhail's roughness hadn't been faked. Looking down at the whimpering woman, he realized he was in the bizarre position of having to pretend concern for her well-being, when every atom in his body was screaming with concern for the real Liz.

He knelt beside the woman, wondering what subtle signals he had picked up to warn him so quickly that she was a fake. A ringer for Liz, maybe, but definitely not the real thing. He examined her covertly for telltale differences. He'd be damned if he could spot any, except perhaps for the eyes. The blue-gray shade was identical to Liz's. The sweeping lashes had the same upward curve and thickness, the eyebrows the same delicate arch. But the mind and soul looking out from the window of these eyes bore no relationship to Liz's passionate, generous nature. This woman was calculating every tear and every whimper—and as far as Dexter was concerned, her calculation showed.

"Liz, my dear, come and sit on the sofa." Turning to Igor, he spoke stiffly, as he would have done if he'd really felt compelled to ask for a favor on Liz's behalf. "She needs water. And can you instruct your minions to behave with a little less brutality?"

"But certainly. Comrade Mikhail, you have heard the senator. Please refrain from exercising your temper on his ladylove."

"She is not my ladylove," Dexter said swiftly. *Too swiftly?* he wondered. He tried once again to adjust his voice to the controlled, strained tones he would have used if Liz had really been curled at his side, nursing her bruises. "If you think I have any special feelings for Liz, you're wrong. She is merely my former wife. You of all people should know that any relationship between us ceased to exist long ago. We hadn't seen one another in nine years until you precipitated our reunion by killing Karen Zeit."

"The reality of your relationship with Ms. Meacham is of little interest to us, Senator Rand. As is so often the case, truth is irrelevant. The appearance of truth is all that concerns us."

"Is that what this is all about?" Dexter asked. "Is there some specific lie you're expecting me to palm off as truth?"

"Such a quick wit," Igor murmured admiringly. "We shall deal well together, Comrade Senator."

"That seems unlikely. And I am not your comrade."

"Not yet, Senator. But wait. You have not heard

the terms of my proposition. I hope you will agree they are heavily weighted in your favor—given the circumstances in which you find yourself."

"Just state your terms," Dexter said wearily.

"You will change your *Yea* vote on the F-19B fighter aircraft to a *Nay*. Furthermore, you will campaign actively against the plane in the Senate and in the United States as a whole. The vote is already skintight because—fortunately—most people do not have your expertise in military matters. If you switch your vote and speak against the project, the F-19B will not go into production."

"Which will be very convenient for your government," Dexter said softly. "That plane is the best airborne defensive weapon ever to leave the drawing board."

"Indeed. I acknowledge the truth of your statement. In return for this considerable favor, you, Senator, will be allowed to live. In fact, you will be allowed to live precisely as before, with perfect freedom to vote as you please on most other Senate issues."

"Most other issues?" Dexter queried cynically. "Just how many times will I be required to sell my vote in exchange for my so-called freedom?"

Igor smiled tightly. "Only on military matters, Senator. Whenever a vote comes before your Defense Appropriations Committee, you will wait for instructions as to how you are to cast your vote. Otherwise, feel free to follow the dictates of your conscience."

"How generous you and your government are."

"Indeed, I am glad you appreciate our generosity. Do you agree to our terms, Senator Rand?"

"Yes," Dexter said instantly. "I agree."

The woman seated next to him on the sofa drew in a sharp breath, but Igor simply laughed. "Now, now, Senator. We are not fools, and I must tell you that your prompt agreement fails to carry conviction. As a responsible representative of my government, I have to ensure that you do not pretend to agree with us merely to buy your freedom."

Dexter's body tensed. "We should speak bluntly, Igor. I'll tell you frankly that I don't see any way you can force my cooperation, if you allow me to leave here alive."

"You are wrong, Senator. We have a guaranteed method of ensuring your cooperation. Quite simply, Ms. Meacham will die if you do not vote as we have requested. What is more to the point, you will be accused of her murder."

"Dexter, don't let them kill me!" The woman on the sofa clung to his arm, sobbing pitifully.

If anything at all had been needed to clinch Dexter's conviction that this woman was not Liz, her hysterical reaction was it. Careful to conceal his disgust, he bent over her, whispering false words of consolation and encouragement. When he straightened again, he looked at Igor with a scorn he had no need to fake. "If I vote in favor of funding the F-19B, killing Elizabeth Meacham won't change anything. The plane will still go into production, whether or not I'm accused of her murder. True, I'll have to bear the weight of Liz's death on my conscience, but the aims of your government won't be advanced by one millimeter.''

"Alas, Senator, it seems that you gravely underestimate the wisdom of our planning. The circumstances of your trial will seal the fate of the F-19B.''

"Even if I am found guilty, how does that invalidate my vote on a piece of military hardware?''

Igor's laugh was triumphant. "Because the FBI and the CIA in a rare moment of cooperation will uncover documentary evidence proving that Ms. Meacham is a Soviet spy, and that she has been working in collusion for many years with her friend Karen Zeit and her brother-in-law Comrade Mikhail Kerachev. We plan to take a series of most compromising photographs tonight, featuring you and Ms. Meacham. This house is already known to the FBI as a trysting place for personnel of the Soviet Embassy. We will have all the documents we need to make it appear that Ms. Meacham has blackmailed you successfully for some months.''

"How can you hope to prove that, when it's totally untrue?''

Mikhail walked across the room to stand beside Igor. "In several interesting ways, Senator. For example, the military blueprints missing from your office. The FBI has been searching for some weeks without success to find the culprit. We have proof that you yourself were the person responsible for their theft.''

"Karen Zeit stole those documents, I'll stake my life on it."

Mikhail smiled. "The evidence shows otherwise, Senator."

"What's more," Igor interjected smoothly, "the evidence also shows that Elizabeth Meacham coerced your favorable vote on the F-19B and that you then murdered her in desperation to escape from the toils of her blackmail. Tell me, Senator, do you doubt, in such circumstances, that the Senate will reconsider its vote on the new aircraft? I think we can safely guarantee that the Senate will eventually vote against the plane. The only question for you to decide is whether they vote against it before or after Ms. Meacham is killed and you are accused of her murder."

Dexter bought himself time to think by comforting the woman who was once again huddled in his arms. Her capacity for producing crocodile tears was truly remarkable, he reflected. He'd only ever known two women capable of turning on a flood of tears at whim. One was a famous movie actress, now gray-haired and over fifty. The other had been Liz's sister Alison. If Alison hadn't been reported as dead, he would be suspecting... In fact, he was suspecting...

With falsely tender hands, Dexter framed the woman's face and used his thumbs to brush away her tears. The blue-gray eyes stared up at him with barely concealed calculation. *Yes,* he thought grimly. Plane crash or no plane crash, the woman he held in his arms was undoubtedly Alison. Even after nine years, he'd recognize that look of mingled sexual invitation and cold self-interest anywhere.

Igor gave one of his characteristic grunts. "I await your answer with interest, Senator."

Dexter forced himself to stroke his hand soothingly down Alison's back, while his brain raced at a feverish pace, weighing options and calculating odds. "Don't worry, darling, I'll get us out of this mess somehow," he whispered. "You can trust me."

"Oh, Dexter, darling, please save me!"

Her lines had a distinctly hackneyed ring to them, Dexter decided cynically. Obviously exile in Moscow hadn't prevented Alison from watching the current crop of corny American TV shows. He nuzzled her hair. "We'll find some way to escape," he murmured. "You'll see, dearest."

Alison gave a pretty little sigh that ended on a delicate little sob. "Oh, Dexter, you're so brave."

Barely concealing his distaste as she insinuated her fingers between the pearl studs of his evening shirt and stroked his chest, Dexter looked up at Igor. "If I promise to vote as you wish on the F-19B, how do I know Liz will be safe? How do I know you won't kill her as soon as I walk out of here?"

Igor seemed to recognize the first hint of real concession in Dexter's attitude, and couldn't quite conceal the triumphant twitch of muscles in his cheek. The outcome of this elaborate plot had perhaps not been as certain in his own mind as he liked to pretend.

"Senator Rand, how many times do I have to repeat that we are all of us here men of goodwill? Ms. Meacham will be safe, for the simple reason that we wish for your continued cooperation in halting the insane arms race between our two countries. You are a man of peace. My government is a government of peace. In working with us, you will make the world a better place for everybody. Your vote against the F-19B is valuable to us, yes, but it is nowhere near as valuable to us as a continuing voice in the Senate that reliably reflects our views."

That was undoubtedly true, Dexter reflected. A senator whose vote could be counted on in all matters related to the defense and the military would be a tremendous asset to the Soviet government. But he didn't want to seem to compromise too early, even though he was almost eaten up with the desire to get out of the house so that he could initiate a search for Liz. God damn it, he'd call out the whole U.S. Army if need be, but he'd find her!

Dexter removed Alison's straying fingers from inside his shirt, and kissed her knuckles with what he hoped was a reasonable facsimile of tender sorrow. Still holding Alison's hands, he turned again to the Russian. "Somehow, Igor, your goodwill doesn't strike me as a very reliable form of protection for my ex-wife."

"Senator, our government wishes you to be happy. We don't wish to kill Ms. Meacham unless your actions make her death absolutely necessary. Indeed, we hope that one day soon we may read in the newspapers that Washington society has turned out in force to dance at your wedding to Ms. Meacham.''

His wedding to Liz! Like a drumroll underscoring the moment of revelation, Dexter heard the thunderous beat of his heart. Igor, he was sure, had unwittingly revealed the purpose behind the substitution of Alison for Liz. They wanted him to marry her! If Alison became Mrs. Dexter Rand, the KGB would have pulled off the enormous coup of planting one of their agents in the innermost circles of Washington power.

Resisting the impulse to punch her squarely in the jaw, he gazed down at Alison. Soulfully she gazed back up, the picture of suffering womanhood. Her role was obviously to play the terrified victim to the hilt, so that Dexter would be convinced that ''Liz's'' life was in danger and would comply with Igor's demands.

It was symptomatic of the limitations of KGB planning, Dexter thought, that they could seriously believe he wouldn't detect the substitution of Alison for Liz. Although, looking at the perfect duplicate the KGB had created, he was forced to admit that a month earlier he might have been deceived. If Liz hadn't come to him the night of Karen's death…if their old attraction hadn't instantly flared…if they hadn't spent long hours making love until every cell of her body seemed imprinted on his soul…

But none of that helped one goddamned bit with his major problem, which was how to get out of here in time to rescue Liz. If he could convince Igor that he was safely "turned," there was a chance that Liz could be saved. Dexter wouldn't allow himself to calculate just how slim the odds of saving the real Liz actually were. Some calculations were better not made, if he wanted to preserve his sanity.

Why the blazes didn't Alison stop sniffling? Didn't she understand anything about the way her twin would behave? "Hush, sweetheart," he murmured. "We'll find a way to come out of this in one piece, I promise you."

She lifted her face, eyes glistening jewellike with tears. How the hell did she cry so much without smudging her mascara? he wondered.

"Oh, Dexter, how can you save me? You'll never vote against your conscience, I know you won't. You're not that kind of a man, or I wouldn't love you."

The urge to sock her one was getting stronger by the moment. "The F-19B is just a plane," he said, gritting his teeth. "I place more value on human life than on a weapons system. Especially your life, Liz."

Would that do it? he asked himself. Acting wasn't one of his major skills. Did he sound convincingly like a man preparing to compromise his lifelong beliefs to save the woman he loved? He glared at Igor. "But don't think I'm going to vote the way you tell me ever again!'' The last wriggle of a man in a noose. Had he pitched his voice more or less right?

Igor grunted with satisfaction, but Mikhail looked uneasy. He muttered something in Russian to Igor, who dismissed his comment with a curt reply and an impatient wave of the hand. Mikhail was obviously more worried than his boss about Dexter's relatively swift surrender. Dexter decided it might be smart to voice a few more doubts.

''I'm still not sure you'll keep Liz safe,'' he said, draping an arm around Alison's shoulder. ''I think you may be stringing me along. What's going to happen to Mikhail, for example? According to your scheme, he's going to be identified as a spy if I don't vote the way you want. Does that mean Mikhail's volunteering to spend the rest of his life in an American jail? That seems unlikely.''

''Very unlikely,'' Mikhail agreed. ''But it won't happen, Senator. I leave tomorrow—'' He glanced at his watch and corrected himself. ''I leave today for Stockholm, and from there I fly immediately to Moscow. My time of exile in America is over. I shall soon be back among my own people, training Russian skaters for the next Olympics.''

Igor spoke. ''You see, Comrade Senator, we have thought of everything. So may we have your agreement that you will vote *Nay* on the F-19B fighter project?''

Dexter allowed his temper to snap. ''Yes, you have my agreement, damn it! You've left me no choice. And I've told you before, I'm not your blasted comrade!''

Igor smiled. Very gently. ''But, Senator, that is exactly what you have just become.''

He crossed to the sofa and hauled Alison roughly to her feet. ''And now, Comrade Senator, we come to the most interesting part of the evening. The photographs. Would you start undressing your former wife, please?''

THE AMBULANCE DRIVER turned guard looked bored out of his mind but attentive. Gun clasped firmly in hand, he had stationed himself midway between the chair Liz was tied to and the stairs leading out of the basement. Liz had needed about two and a half seconds to decide that appealing to his better nature was unlikely to produce very positive results. Wisely, she had kept silent.

She had reached several other equally gloomy conclusions, among them one that even if she miraculously managed to overpower the guard, she still wouldn't have a snowball's chance in hell of making it out of the house alive. But since she seemed destined to die anyway, she damn well intended to die escaping, not tied to a chair.

A noise overhead—a sound almost like furniture being moved—caught the guard's attention for a couple of minutes. Liz scooted her chair a vital six inches closer to the wall, the carpet muffling the telltale scraping noises. Her goal was the nail head she had seen sticking out of the paneling. If she could just pierce the surgical tape that kept her hands strapped uselessly behind her back, she would be one step closer to a successful escape.

She poked the nail through the tape and began sawing away, keeping her upper body still so that the guard wouldn't realize what she was doing.

She had a couple of advantages, Liz thought, flexing her wrists within the layers of tape. The guard didn't expect her to try to escape, and he didn't know that she was an expert in self-defense—not the stylized self-defense of karate and judo schools, but the real-life self-defense she had been taught by a women's group in New York. Liz had gone to the class after being mugged and almost raped on a New York subway. If she could somehow get the guard to come up close without arousing his suspicion, Liz thought—hoped—prayed—she would have a chance of overpowering him.

From his frequent glances toward the ceiling, it was obvious that the guard's interests lay on the floor above, where the action—whatever that might be—was actually taking place. For a man with a body like King Kong and a trigger-happy finger, playing keeper to a mere woman presumably wasn't much fun.

Her hands were free! A sizable chunk of skin had been left on the nail, but at least she was now potentially mobile. Liz turned an involuntary crow of triumph into a passable imitation of a sob and huddled pathetically in her chair. The guard glanced indifferently toward her, then went back to stroking his gun.

How the devil was she going to get him to come closer? Displaying several inches of thigh wasn't likely to do it. The guy looked as if his bedmate of choice would be a Sherman tank. Liz waited until his gaze wandered toward the door, then toppled her chair with as much of a crash as she could muster on the carpeted floor. For good measure, she added a strangled shriek that she hoped sounded feminine and flustered. She was careful not to scream too loudly. She didn't want to attract the attention of whoever was moving around overhead.

Blood drumming in her skull, she lay on her side, coiled and ready to spring. She watched the guard stride across the room, his body language hinting at irritation rather than suspicion. With a carelessness that Liz prayed might save her life, he allowed the submachine gun to dangle by his side. He came closer. Liz held her breath. His stance suggested he might be in the habit of relying on his size for protection. If so, he might not know it, but he was extremely vulnerable.

Go for his eyes. The instruction from her defense class remained with her, although Liz wasn't sure she'd be able to carry it out.

Your life depends on it, she told herself. *No wimping out, kiddo. This isn't a trial run. This is for real.*

Muttering angrily, the guard bent over her. She launched herself upward from the balls of her feet, butting her head into his stomach with the full force of her weight. Before he could catch his breath, she stomped on his instep with the steel-shafted heel of her shoe, simultaneously sticking her fingers straight into his eyes. He gave a scream of pain even as he raised his gun. He was too late. Liz lowered her fist in a chop that knocked the weapon from his hand. They both dived for it, but she succeeded in grabbing it. She brought the barrel crashing down on his head. It connected with a sickening thud of metal pounding against bone.

The guard keeled over and lay in a crumpled heap on the floor. Liz stuffed a fist into her mouth. She wanted to cry. She wanted to throw up. She wanted to lean against the wall, shaking and shivering.

But she didn't have time for any of that. Tugging the broad silk belt of Alison's robe from her waist, she tied it around the guard's mouth in a makeshift gag. Panting and puffing, she pulled his wrists behind his back and strapped them together as best she could with the tape left over from the roll he and Mikhail had used on her. Right now the guard looked out for the count, but for all she knew, he might revive in five or ten minutes.

"Sleep well, buster," she murmured, wiping her sweaty palms on the sides of Alison's robe.

The stairway was obviously useless as an escape route. Liz had no doubt she would encounter armed opposition long before she reached the upstairs hallway. However, from what little she had been able to see, the house was a typical upper-income suburban home. Which meant that the narrow door in the far corner of the basement was worth exploring. Chances were good that it led into some sort of furnace or utility room.

Tucking the submachine gun under her arm, Liz ran to the corner and pulled open the door. A utility room lay concealed behind the paneling. Never had a bare concrete floor, a dusty furnace and miscellaneous wispy cobwebs looked so attractive. Smiling, she stepped into the little room.

As soon as the door to the rec room closed behind her, darkness descended. Her heart rapidly sliding into her shoes, Liz fumbled for a light switch. Such complete darkness must mean that the room had no windows. *No windows.* And therefore no way out.

When the naked overhead bulb flicked into life, she hesitated, almost afraid to walk around the tiny eight-by-ten space. What would she do if the basement was entirely below ground level? *You'll start digging, that's what,* Liz told herself grimly.

It took her less than a minute to confirm her worst fears: the furnace room lacked any form of window, even a tiny, single pane.

Liz slumped against the plasterboard wall and stared blindly at the furnace. As if to mock her earlier optimistic thoughts, she saw a small gardening trowel, minus its handle, nestled at the base of the hot-water heater. To dig her way out? She gave a bitter laugh. She had no idea where Alison and Mikhail had gone, but she doubted if she had more than thirty minutes before somebody would come back to check on her. Even if she had two hours—an impossible dream—she couldn't dig her way out of the basement in two hours.

But maybe she could find a hiding place and out-wait her captors. Maybe she could squeeze between the furnace and the water heater. Or clamber onto the top of the appliances to reach the ceiling. The acoustical tiles would be easy to remove.

Anything, any hope, was better than surrendering meekly to the fate Mikhail and Alison had in store for her. With renewed energy, she resumed her inspection of the utility room.

She found the grating tucked into an odd position behind the furnace. At this time of year the furnace wasn't operating, so she had only marginal difficulty in squeezing behind the furnace to examine her find more carefully. Clamping down hard on her rising excitement, she peered through the iron latticework at the murky hole behind. She couldn't see all the way to the end, but had the definite impression that there was a faint lessening of the darkness toward the end of the crawl space. A window? *Dear God, let it be a window.*

The grating should have been easy to remove, but rust had welded it stuck and she struggled for almost ten minutes, using the trowel as a lever, before she managed to pry it loose.

Sweating, filthy and triumphant, she rested the grating on top of the furnace, tossed the submachine gun onto the rocky concrete floor of the crawl space, and then heaved herself inside. By lying flat on her stomach and stretching out her hand as far as it would go, she was able to reach the grating and pull it into place behind her.

Surely the crawl space must lead somewhere outside? Wasn't that what they were for—to provide access to water pipes and telephone lines? Liz closed her eyes, willing herself not to hope too fiercely. Squatting, because the rough concrete floor was too painful to crawl on, she waddled and wobbled along the ten feet of dark tunnel. High-heeled evening shoes and a silk robe definitely didn't make the most convenient escape outfit ever invented, she realized.

She was steeling herself for disappointment, so when she found the window she stared at it stupidly, wasting several precious seconds in blank contemplation. It was encrusted with grime and dust, so she scraped at it with the heel of her shoe, trying to detect some sign of an alarm system. As far as she could tell, there wasn't an electronic beam or even an old-fashioned electric wire anywhere in sight.

They can't have been careless enough to leave this entrance to the house unprotected, Liz warned herself. *When you smash this window, all hell's going to break loose.*

But waiting wasn't going to disconnect the alarm system, if there was one. And every minute she delayed made the prospect of pursuit more likely. Drawing in a deep breath, Liz plunged the heel of her sandal through the glass.

Silence. No bells clanged, no sirens hooted, but she knew that meant nothing. Some of the most sophisticated alarm systems flashed silent warnings in every room. In a frenzy of fear, she slashed at the glass with the butt of the gun, indifferent to the shards of glass splattering against her wrists and arms. When the wooden frame was denuded of glass, she pulled herself through, ignoring the ripping of glass fragments on her breast and stomach and legs.

She emerged into a shallow window well, which was slimy with leaf mold and garden debris. Liz peered cautiously over the rim of the well and allowed the night breeze to caress her face with the promise of freedom. She smiled wryly. Cobwebs, crawl spaces, leaf mold, chilly night air. This was her night for finding strange things beautiful.

Body tense, ears straining, she gazed rapidly from one side of the house to the other. She could see most of the front driveway, and it seemed empty. The ambulance must have been driven into the garage, out of sight of any inquisitive neighbors. Abandoning the gun as too heavy to carry, Liz used her upper-body strength to pull herself out of the window well.

She was on her feet, kicking off her high-heeled shoes and running across the damp grass before her conscious mind could scream caution. She ran away from the lighted driveway, away from the front of the house. Like any other frightened night creature, she sought the safety of darkness, and angled through the trees and bushes as she dashed toward the road. At any moment she expected to hear the hue and cry of pursuit. At any moment she expected to hear the hateful softness of Mikhail's laugh. *Dorogoya*. She would never be able to hear that word again without shuddering.

She was on the road now, running along the grass bank at the side. Still no sound of pursuers, only the rasp of her own breath in her lungs and the distant bark of a dog.

The lights of a house loomed ahead. Was it safe to knock on the door and beg for help? Her feet had almost turned into the driveway, when some primitive survival instinct flared to life, reminding her that she had no way of knowing who owned these houses. The owners were as likely to be enemies as friends.

Over the relentless thrumming of blood in her ears, she heard the unmistakable sounds of a car approaching. Instinct once again took over, sending her scurrying for the protection of a clump of shrubbery, thick with spring foliage. Now that she had stopped running, she had time to notice that her teeth were chattering, even though she didn't feel cold. Oh God, she didn't want to die! Not before she had a chance to see Mikhail and Alison in jail. Not before she had a chance to tell Dex how much she loved him.

It wasn't a car she had heard, but a small pizza delivery truck, and it turned into the driveway right next to where Liz was crouching. After her experience with the ambulance, she was no longer trusting enough to believe that a truck saying Poppa Pellini Delivers on its side panels necessarily meant that the truck contained pizzas. Squirming as deeply as she could into the protection of the bushes, she watched the truck draw to a halt.

A young girl in a gingham uniform climbed out of the truck, cardboard carton in hand. If she carried a bomb, Liz could only think it smelled a lot like pepperoni. The girl walked across the grass toward the front door, leaving the engine running and the radio blaring a hit from the top twenty.

Swifter than thought, Liz left the protection of the bushes and ran toward the delivery truck. She threw herself into the driver's seat and let off the hand brake. The truck moved forward. The Fates were on her side, Liz thought, glancing down. It had automatic transmission.

Without a twinge of remorse for having entered the ranks of car thieves and other felons, Liz stepped on the accelerator. Ignoring the anguished shouts of the delivery girl, she gunned the truck out of the driveway.

First she was going to rescue Dexter. Then she was going to eat some stolen pizza.

CHAPTER SIXTEEN

LIZ FOUND THE all-night convenience store about ten minutes down the road at the first intersection she came to. It was obviously a hangout for local teenagers and, despite the fact that it was almost one in the morning, the place was quite crowded.

Liz jumped down from the truck and headed for the phone. A stack of cracker boxes inside one of the windows turned the glass into a shadowy mirror, and for the first time in hours, she became aware of how she looked—and how little she was wearing.

But there was no time to worry about the red silk robe, now tattered, smeared with leaf mold and flapping beltless in the nighttime breeze; no time to worry about the fact that she wore nothing underneath the robe except a lace teddy, a fancy garter belt and shredded stockings. There was certainly no time to worry about what her face and hair must look like, daubed with dust and festooned with cobwebs.

Pulling the robe firmly around her waist, Liz strode into the convenience store with all the dignity a shoeless, mud-spattered woman could hope to muster.

By some miracle, the phone was not only in working order, but nobody was using it. Ignoring the openmouthed stares of two teenagers, who obviously felt somewhat resentful that their dyed-feather mohawks and safety-pinned ears couldn't begin to compete with Liz's bizarre outfit, she picked up the phone and reached for some change—only to realize that she had no money. Her body beaded with cold sweat, she wondered if Dexter and Amanda were about to lose their lives for the sake of a quarter. Shaking, she turned to the teenagers.

"Could you please loan me a quarter?" she asked. "I have a really important call to make. Somebody's life is at stake."

His gaze pitying, one of the youngsters reached into his pocket and flipped her a quarter. "You oughta give him up, lady. Ain't no good thinking he'll stop knocking you around, because he won't."

"Thank you. It's not what you think, but I'm really grateful." She dropped the coin into the slot and dialed the FBI emergency number. Her fingers shook so badly that it was a miracle she managed to dial correctly.

The thirty seconds before an FBI operator came on the line seemed endless. The moment the call connected, Liz started speaking.

"I'm calling on behalf of Senator Dexter Rand of the United States Senate," she said. She knew her voice sounded squeaky and uncertain, but she drew in a steadying breath and continued with all the firmness she could muster. "I have a special emergency number I need to reach, and only the FBI can put the call through.''

''What number's that, Miss?'' The FBI operator sounded bored and irritated, as if she'd already handled more than her share of crank calls that night.

Liz repeated the eleven digits Dexter had compelled her to learn, and sensed an immediate change in the attitude of the woman at the other end of the phone. ''I'm connecting you now,'' the woman said briskly. ''Hold on, please. The connection will take about thirty-five seconds.''

Precisely thirty-two seconds later, Liz was talking to the commander-in-chief of Washington's Special Forces.

ALISON, clad only in a black satin slip, pretended to cringe and sob as Mikhail positioned her in yet another seductive pose on the cream leather sofa. Dexter wondered how many more tears the woman could shed before his temper frayed completely. Not very many, he suspected. He glanced at his watch. One-thirty a.m. Three hours since he and Liz had been captured. Time to get the hell out of here.

''Enough of these damn fool photographs,'' he said, picking up Alison's dress and tossing it to her. For once the role he was playing and the reality of his feelings coincided. ''Igor, you've made your point. These pictures link me to Elizabeth Meacham. They strengthen the circumstantial evidence of the case you're constructing against me. But nothing you photograph here tonight will compel me to vote against the F-19B. You're going to have to trust my word that I'll vote against the plane, just like I'll have to trust you to set Liz free. It's a standoff, Igor. If both of us acknowledge that fact, maybe we can all go home.''

Igor grunted, but whatever reply he might have made was lost as a huge gorilla of a man burst into the room, shielding his bruised and puffy eyes against the overhead lights that had been turned on for the photographs. Waving his arms—seemingly to display a grubby red silk belt—the man burst into a stream of impassioned, apologetic speech in Russian.

Taking advantage of Igor's momentary distraction, Dexter edged toward the arched doorway that connected the living room to the dining room. The overhead light switch was fixed to the connecting wall right by this arch. And the heavy table lamp that provided the only other source of light in the room rested on a nearby coffee table. If he were very lucky he might be able to flip the overhead switch and, in a continuation of the same movement, throw the table lamp at one of his captors. His chosen victim would almost certainly be knocked out, since Dexter's aim was outstanding. And the resulting darkness would provide him with a valuable few moments' head start, if he wanted to make a dash for freedom.

The temptation to go out fighting was great, and yet cool logic warned him that this wasn't a situation that warranted physical action. Pretending to accept

Igor's demands was probably a safer, more certain way to extricate himself from Igor's clutches. Unfortunately, for a man of Dexter's training, pretending meekness required more self-discipline than anything else.

Igor and Mikhail were obviously furious at whatever news the newcomer had brought. Shooting a quick glance at Alison, Dexter saw that she, too, was so perturbed that she had temporarily forgotten her role as Liz. She sat on the edge of the sofa, eyes flashing in cold fury as Igor hurled questions at the gorilla man. There was no doubt in Dexter's mind that she understood every word Igor and Mikhail were saying.

If he was going to make a run for it, the dining room would provide his only possible escape route. Dexter turned unobtrusively to scan the room behind him. A very swift survey was sufficient to tell him that it didn't present a realistic prospect of success. Both doors opened onto the main hallway, and he would undoubtedly be caught long before he reached the front entrance.

Dexter allowed himself one more regretful glance around the shadowy dining room. A slight movement caught his eye, and he froze into absolute stillness. Someone was crouched there, half-hidden by the bulk of the china cabinet. His heart leaped.

A black-clad man, face masked with greasepaint, rose slowly to his feet, fingers pressed against his mouth in an urgent signal for Dexter to keep quiet.

"What is going on over there?" Igor demanded

suddenly. "What are you doing by the door, Senator Rand?"

"Keeping out of your way," Dexter replied easily, shoving his hands into the pockets of his pants and lounging carelessly against the wall. "Seems like you and your friend Mikhail are seriously upset about something."

Igor hesitated. "A minor administrative matter only," he said coldly. "There has been some small mistake in regard to Comrade Mikhail's airplane ticket for Stockholm."

Right, Dexter thought. *That's why gorilla man looks ready to shoot himself, and the rest of you look mad enough to hand him the gun.* Aloud, he merely said, "A mistake in the ticket, eh? It's amazing how no government seems able to get its clerical system working efficiently, isn't it?"

"I admit that our bureaucracy has not yet attained the degree of socialist efficiency we might wish." Igor sounded considerably more mellow. He was too seasoned a campaigner to allow Dexter more than a glimpse of his anger. "Mikhail, why don't you and Yuri go back downstairs to the basement and search for the missing ticket? I'm sure Yuri has simply mislaid it somewhere."

"Very well, if you think it worthwhile. Personally, I think he must have dropped it outside the house." Mikhail took Yuri's arm and propelled him with considerable force toward the basement stairs. Casting a glance toward the sofa, he said, "Lizushka, my sweet, do you not wish to put on your dress? The Comrade Senator will not be able to take advantage of your charming body tonight. That pleasure must await the vote on the F-19B.''

Alison flashed her husband a look of sheer venom, but recalled to a realization of her role, she stood up and struggled into the dress, a fresh set of tears flowing down her cheeks. Dexter thought the woman deserved an entry in the Guinness Book of World Records. Most Crocodile Tears Ever Shed in One Continuous Session.

Mikhail and Yuri disappeared from view. Dexter sincerely hoped they would walk straight into the arms of a pair of waiting commandos. He was becoming more and more optimistic that somehow Liz had managed to escape. How else had the commandos known where to come?

Pretending to refasten the studs on his shirt, he risked another quick look into the dining room. The single black-clad figure had now become four. Dexter let his hand creep up toward the light switch. One of the blackened faces dipped in a brief, authoritative nod of approval.

In a single swift move, Dexter flipped off the overhead switch and leaned forward to grab the table lamp, jerking the cord from the wall socket. In the last moment of light, he took aim at Igor, then threw the lamp with all the force he could muster. He heard the satisfying clunk of lamp hitting flesh, a split second before the four black shadows erupted into the room.

ALISON FINALLY STOPPED CRYING when one of the commandos walked over and slipped her wrists into a pair of handcuffs. "What the *hell* do you think you're doing?" she demanded.

"Arresting you. I have to warn you that anything you say may be taken down and used in evidence at your trial—"

Panic swept over Alison's lovely features. "I don't know what you're thinking of," she said, her voice husky. She looked with desperate appeal toward Dexter, who was talking softly and animatedly to another of the commandos. "Dexter, darling," she called. "Darling, please tell this silly man he's making a dreadful mistake."

Dexter turned slowly, allowing every ounce of his scorn to show. "Why would I do that, Alison? I hope they lock you in jail and throw away the key."

She paled. "A-Alison? Y-you knew I wasn't Liz? All the time?"

"Not all the time. You had me fooled for about five seconds."

"But we're identical!"

Dexter smiled coldly. "You're nothing like Liz. You never have been and you never will be. Liz would no more have sat on that sofa weeping and wailing than she would have flown. Somebody should have told you that silicone implants and a nose job can't change a person's character."

"But you can't let me go to prison!"

"Watch me. You were perfectly willing to have your sister killed. Thank your lucky stars you're in

America, and nobody's going to let me be alone with you in a quiet corner of the jail. Otherwise you'd need another nose job.''

Alison was weeping again. This time her tears might even have been real. A commando entered the living room. ''Ms. Meacham has just arrived, Senator, if you'd like to meet her outside.''

Dexter left the room without a backward glance.

HE SAW LIZ as soon as he stepped out of the front door. Spotlighted in the beam of a police floodlight, her entire face shone with joy as he walked toward her.

''Dex!'' She ran into his arms, and he held her tight, feeling the softness that was Liz, the warmth and the passion that seemed to flow from every pore of her skin. He stroked his hands up and down her spine, trying to reabsorb the essence of her into his soul.

''The KGB are such fools,'' he said, lovingly plucking a dead leaf and a wisp of cobweb from her hair. ''Imagine thinking I wouldn't know the difference between you and Alison.''

She insinuated her fingers underneath his shirt. Wherever she touched, he felt a little explosion of desire. ''How could you possibly tell us apart?'' she asked. ''They made her look just like me.''

''They couldn't capture the magic,'' he said softly, only half teasing. ''When she kissed me, I felt empty. My heart didn't start pounding, and my skin didn't feel as if it was on fire.''

"Is that how you feel when we kiss?" Liz lifted her face, blue-gray eyes dark with wonder. "I thought it was only me who felt like that."

He hadn't realized how much he loved the eloquence of her eyes until he had seen the coldness of Alison's. "I think that's how I feel," he said solemnly. "But Igor had me captive in there so damn long I've almost forgotten. Can we test it and see?"

She raised her mouth eagerly to meet his. Their lips joined in an explosion of need and pent-up anxiety. She tasted warm and passionate, generous and sexy. She tasted of Liz. She tasted of love. His heart started to pound. His skin felt as if it were on fire. He knew that if they remained together for the next sixty years, she would still retain the power to stimulate and entrance him. He wondered why in the world they had wasted so much time apart.

The spotlight mounted on one of the trucks swung around to focus on the squad of commandos escorting Igor, Mikhail, Alison and four other men to the waiting vans. Liz and Dexter didn't even notice.

She put up her hand to touch his cheek. He caught her fingers, and kissed every spot where he could see a cut or a graze. "Did they tell you Amanda is safe?" he asked. "She's been back home with my parents since early this evening."

She nodded. "The commander told me. I'm so glad for you, Dex. My biggest nightmare was that they'd kill her before the Special Forces could get to wherever Mikhail and gang were hiding her."

"We'll fly home tomorrow and see her," he said.

"I'd like that. You won't feel completely secure until you've hugged her."

"Marry me, Liz," he said huskily. "Live with me and be my love. This time we'll get it right, I know we will."

She went very still. She was quiet for so long that he forced a laugh. "I hoped it wouldn't be such a difficult decision."

She looked up, her expression grave. "Dex, you don't have to feel obligated—"

"Obligated? You think I feel obligated? Are you crazy, woman?" He dragged her hard against his body, moving his hips aggressively so that she could feel the potency of his arousal. "Does that feel like a man who's *obligated*? Liz, where in the world did you get such a crazy notion? I love you. I want to marry you."

She looked away. "My twin sister's going to jail for treason," she said. "Sometimes…maybe…love isn't enough."

Dexter felt the relief start to seep into his veins. "Love is always enough," he said quietly. "Answer me one question, Liz. Do you love me?"

"Yes, but—"

"There are no buts. Your sister's choices are her responsibility, not yours. And if you're worried about the damage her actions will do to my career in the Senate, there'll be none. Alison and Mikhail will almost certainly be tried *in camera* and Igor, unfortunately, won't be tried at all. He's already shrieking for his lawyer and claiming diplomatic immunity. The most the State Department will be able to do is get him shipped back to Moscow.''

The commander slammed the door on the second of the navy-blue unmarked vans, then gave the instruction for the small convoy to move out of the driveway. Two rows of faces peered over the bushes on either side of the property, as two sets of neighbors viewed the fascinating goings-on. Liz and Dexter didn't even hear the engines start up, much less notice that the vans were leaving.

''Even if you don't care about Alison and what she's done, there's still the problem of Amanda. She doesn't like me.''

''Darling Liz, I love my daughter to distraction, but that doesn't give her the right to choose my wife.''

''How about the right to choose her stepmother?''

''Liz, you're worrying about phantoms. The week before last, Amanda was all in favor of me getting married. Last week she was opposed. Next week she might be all in favor again. It's not that I'm dismissing the importance of her feelings, but she doesn't know what a stepmother is. I'm confident you can show her that stepmothers are wonderful.''

''I'd like to try,'' Liz whispered. ''I love you so much, Dex. I think maybe I never stopped loving you.''

''I love you, too. Darling Liz, it's so good to have you back.''

Liz was only vaguely aware of the commander of the Special Forces, the driver of the commander's

car, and two rows of fascinated neighbors watching
as Dexter swept her into his arms and demonstrated—with amazing thoroughness—that two human beings can kiss almost indefinitely without any
need to come up for air. Then the outside world
faded from her consciousness, and nothing was left
except Dex: the taste of him in her mouth and the
throb of him in her heart.

She returned to reality when the commander, a
man not normally noted for his overflowing supply
of sentimentality, finally tapped Dexter on the shoulder. "Senator, I'm getting chilly, even if you and
Ms. Meacham seem to be doing a damn fine job of
setting each other on fire. You might be interested
to know that our headquarters contains a most comfortable suite of rooms." He cleared his throat.
"With a king-size bed. We could drive you there
now, if you and Ms. Meacham are ready to leave.
Then you'd be on hand for tomorrow's debriefing."

Dexter grinned. "If your suite has a shower as
well as a bed, it's a deal."

"A king-size shower," the commander replied.
His men would never have believed it, but Liz could
have sworn there was a distinct twinkle in his eye.
"There's also a most accommodating Jacuzzi."

Liz looked up at Dexter, her mouth curving into
a tiny smile. "The possibilities," she said, "seem
almost endless."

Dexter lifted her hands and pressed the tips of her
fingers to his lips. "Yes," he agreed. "They do."

KEEPING SECRETS

B.J. Daniels

This book is dedicated to my aunt Lucille
in memory of her son, Sonny Johnson

CHAPTER ONE

P. T. ALEXANDER GRABBED the Beretta from her shoulder bag and told the taxi driver to keep the pedal to the metal as the cab raced through the dark, sultry streets of New Orleans. Behind them, a black, sleek sports car gave chase, dogging them like a Louisiana bloodhound.

She'd recognized the international jewel thief on the plane thanks to her photographic memory and trained eye for suspicious-looking men.

Darkly mysterious and fabulous-looking with broad, muscled shoulders and slim hips, he was a dead giveaway in jeans that hugged his body like the skin of a banana and made every woman on the plane want to peel that denim.

She'd kept him under surveillance from behind the latest issue of Rosie, but she'd known eventually their eyes would meet across the 757. Still, nothing could have prepared her for the shocking electric blue of his gaze. He took her in like a long, cool drink of water. His look said he knew exactly what to do with a beautiful woman. She didn't doubt it for a moment.

Oh, she'd known men like him. Dozens of them.

All handsome. All dangerous. All expertly skilled in the art of seduction. But this one stripped her bare with a glance, making her skin tingle from her painted toes to the roots of her long, luxurious raven-black hair.

It was a real shame she was going to have to kill him.

The cab jerked to a stop. "Are you sure this is the right place?" the taxi driver asked.

Paige Grayson blinked and glanced around in confusion. She shot a look out the back window of the cab. No sleek, black car. No sexy international jewel thief. No P.T., woman of mystery and adventure. Just plain Paige and her imagination.

Paige dropped back to reality with a thud. A reality that always disappointed her—just as her own reflection in the cab's window did. Instead of long, luxurious raven-black hair and exotic beauty, her hair was chin-length and pale blond, her lightly freckled face cute.

Cute didn't cut it. Not compared to her alter ego P. T. Alexander who Paige fantasized as being everything desirable and exciting—and as far removed from herself as Paige could get.

And right now she would have given anything to be far away from her real life. She stared out the cab window at a less than desirable area of New Orleans.

"This is the address you gave me," the taxi driver said, sounding worried.

She looked through the darkness at the old brick

building. One side was flanked by a narrow, gar-
bage-strewn alley, the other by an abandoned gro-
cery with its broken windows and graffiti-covered
walls.

A dim light over the weathered sign illuminated
the words: Eternal Peace Funeral Home.

She knew she shouldn't have been surprised the
place was a dump. Nor disappointed. But on the
plane she'd dreamed the funeral home would be a
large, stately one, in a beautiful, old New Orleans
mansion with an expansive lawn, stone sculptures
and classic architecture.

Unlike her daydreams, reality wasn't measuring
up to the way she'd imagined.

She checked the address again on the letter, still
holding out hope there was some mistake—and not
just about the address.

Unfortunately, the address at least was right.
"This is the place," she said and looked at it again,
considering telling the taxi driver to take her back
to the hotel, her fear of what was waiting behind
Eternal Peace's door too great.

"You sure it's even open this late?" the driver
asked, no doubt noticing her obvious reluctance to
get out. "Odd time to have a funeral, but this *is* New
Orleans."

Yes. Paige glanced at her watch—11:35 p.m.
While there was only an old hearse parked on the
street in front, she could see a faint light glowing
deep inside the funeral home and she'd been assured
the body would be available for viewing until mid-

night. According to the letter, there would be no funeral service.

She'd come late to avoid running into anyone. Now she wondered if that hadn't been a mistake as she looked around and saw only an occasional car cruise by on the dark, poorly lit street. What pedestrians she saw looked homeless. She could feel the driver watching her in his rearview mirror.

"You want me to wait?" he asked.

"No." She wasn't sure what she'd find inside. Or how long she'd be. But a cab waiting outside the front door would be too conspicuous and she didn't want anyone knowing she was here or had ever been. "I've ordered a cab to pick me up, but thanks." She had fifteen minutes. That would be more than enough time.

She glanced again at the light inside and reached for the door handle, her heart taking off like a racehorse. Last chance to change her mind. She really wished she did have a Beretta in her purse. Not that she would know how to use it. More than anything, she wished she had her imagined P.T.'s courage right now.

The driver hustled out to get the door for her.

The hot, dense, muggy air was smothering as she stepped from the cab. So different from Montana.

"Be careful," the driver said, making her wonder if he didn't have a daughter her age.

Her eyes teared as she thrust a twenty into his hand. "Thank you." She waited for him to leave, needing him to hurry up and go before she changed her mind.

He tipped his hat to her as he got back into the cab. The taillights glowed bright red to the end of the block, and then were gone as the vehicle turned.

She stared down the dark empty street. No cars. No lights in any of the surrounding buildings. Probably most were abandoned. She'd gotten her wish. She was alone.

Hitching up her shoulder bag, she took a deep breath—the smells sickeningly foreign and not just those from the garbage in the alley. She stepped toward the grimy glass-front door with its metal bars and huge open padlock, wondering who'd want to break into a funeral home.

As she tried the knob she almost wished she really did have the wrong viewing times and the place *was* closed. The knob turned in her hand and the door swung open with a soft groan. On wobbly legs, she stepped in and the door whooshed closed behind her with the same soft groan.

The dramatic difference in temperature shocked her as canned, refrigerated air, smelling of stainless steel and chemicals, blew into her face from a large vent overhead. She gagged and covered her mouth, preferring the garbage smell of the alley.

For a moment, she stood motionless. What had she been thinking coming here?

She tried to slow her frantic heartbeat, tried to breathe, fighting the urge to turn and run. But her cab wouldn't be here for at least another ten minutes. The thought of waiting on the street for another cab warred with the thought of what awaited her in one of the viewing rooms.

Something creaked. She jumped, heart clanging against her rib cage, then recognized the sound. The creak of a chair on wheels off to her right. Through a crack between door and jamb she could see what appeared to be an office. A man in a black suit sat with his feet up on a desk, his back to her as he talked on the phone.

She moved past the door soundlessly imagining what her alter ego—the fearless P. T. Alexander would do. P.T. wouldn't even consider turning tail and running.

The dim light she'd seen from outside emanated from a room off the back. The other two viewing rooms were dark and empty as she passed. Only one body tonight.

As she neared the farthest room, she saw that the lamp lit a gold-colored casket, the top half open. Deep red velvet curtains lined three walls of the small, narrow room. Other than the casket and a dozen metal folding chairs, the room was vacant. Next to the open door was a narrow metal plate where the name of the deceased went. It was blank.

Her pulse quickened. Maybe the information in the letter had been wrong after all. Relief swooped over her, but then she would have made this long trip for nothing.

Or had she?

She could still hear the mortician in the office on

the telephone. He appeared to be arguing with whoever was on the other end of the line. Possibly a wife or girlfriend from the wheedling tone and the fact that he wasn't getting to say much.

She stepped into the red velvet viewing room and, with a soft *click,* closed the door behind her. It was quiet except for faint piped-in music—jazz. And dark with only the one lone lamp shining down on the casket. All of the metal folding chairs were perfectly aligned, she noticed as she passed them, making her wonder if anyone else had even been here. How sad that whoever was in the casket had no family, no friends.

Her hand trembled as she clutched the strap of her shoulder bag. She'd never seen a dead body before. But she had to look, had to be sure because of the anonymous letter that had come, informing her mother of the death—and the viewing time.

The irony didn't escape Paige. She would never have seen the letter had her mother still been alive. Grief threatened to overwhelm her. She moved zombielike toward the open casket, terrified of what she'd see, her pulse deafening in her ears, her heart banging against her rib cage like a war drum.

Closer. Closer. Until, she saw him.

She stumbled, startled, tears instantly burning her eyes. There was no mistake. Even through the tears, she could see the resemblance. She felt such a wave of regret she had to grab the edge of the casket to steady herself.

She'd never known how much she looked like her

father and that seemed the most heinous of her mother's omissions.

His blond hair had grayed at the temples, a web of lines etched around his eyes and mouth. Sun lines? Or laugh lines? She'd never know.

Suddenly she felt the full weight of the loss of those twenty-three years she'd spent believing her father was dead. She stared down into his face, trying to see what could have made her mother lie.

He didn't look like a criminal as she'd been led to believe. He wore a dark suit. It appeared expensive. The casket looked expensive as well. And that seemed odd given the funeral home and the fact that no service would be held.

She stared at him, wondering about his life, his death and why he'd never tried to contact her. Was he really a man too dangerous to be around his own daughter? A man so awful her mother hadn't even let him live in Paige's memory through photos of him?

Her mother never spoke of Michael Alexander as if he'd never existed and had been upset when as a little girl, Paige had found his name on some papers and started asking questions about her father.

What had this man done that her mother felt she had to cut him out of their lives? But Paige would never be able to ask her mother. Simone had been killed only a week ago by a hit-and-run driver.

Paige stared down at her father, at a loss to understand. She couldn't help but wonder what he'd looked like as a young man. What he'd been like.

Where he'd been all these years. She looked so much like him, it broke her heart that she hadn't had a chance to know him.

He'd disappeared from her life when she was three, but she thought she remembered him. At least she'd held on to what she believed was a memory of him: a tall, muscular man leaning over her bed in the darkness, tucking the covers up to her chin and kissing her forehead. His cheek warm against hers as he whispered good-night. Or was it good-bye?

She couldn't even be sure it was a true memory because she'd fantasized about her father for so many years. And the man in the memory was faceless. She could have made it up, the way she had a lot of things in her life. At twenty-six, her life was such that she had to fantasize or go crazy.

Except as she looked down into her father's face, she told herself this man had loved her. The memory was real. And for whatever reason, her mother had lied about more than Michael Alexander's death twenty-three years ago.

But the truth was, if her father hadn't been the man she'd hoped he was, she didn't want to know.

Startled, she heard the soft groan of the outer door opening, felt the air pressure change, then heard the door close again as someone came in.

The last thing she wanted to do, if her father really had been a criminal, was to run into any of his *associates.*

The sound of footsteps stopped just outside the

door to the viewing room. The doorknob turned.
Paige dove for the velvet curtains along the right
side of the coffin, not surprised to find the space
behind them an empty additional room. The curtains
could be opened for a larger wake, closed for view-
ings like her father's where few people were expected. Didn't that alone tell her something?

The door opened and over the musty smell of the
velvet drapes, she caught a whiff of perfume, the
pricey, exotic kind. She frowned at the sound of
high heels tapping their way across the worn car-
peting to the coffin, then silence.

Unable not to, Paige peeked through the heavy
velvet, more than curious to see who had come to
pay their respects to her father.

A tall slim woman dressed much like Paige herself, in a dark suit, pale cream colored blouse and
high heels, stood looking down at Michael Alexander. The most striking thing about the woman was
her hair. It was fiery red, long and pulled up in a
chignon. Through the crack in the thick, musty-
smelling drapes, Paige could see the woman's profile. She was young, early thirties, and very attractive. Who was she and what was her relationship to
Michael Alexander?

The woman stood dry-eyed as she stared down at
the dead man, then to Paige's surprise, she reached
into the coffin as if searching for something. Her
movements stopped. She smiled and drew out a
thick newspaper-wrapped bundle. Tearing off a corner of the newsprint, she revealed stacks of money.

The redhead thumbed through the cash, then looked in the casket again. Casually, she tugged one bill from the stack and put it back in the coffin.

"Don't spend it all in one place," she said, her voice sending a shiver through Paige. The rest of the money she dropped into her oversize black purse.

Just when Paige thought nothing else could surprise her, the woman pulled a small white box, about the size of a cell phone, from her purse and slipped it into the coffin. She snapped her purse closed and, crossing herself, turned and left without a backward glance.

Paige was too stunned to move for a few moments. The viewing room door closed, then the outer door. A deadly stillness filled the closed space that not even the jazz music, the mortician's voice on the phone or the pounding of her pulse could drown out.

Paige couldn't help herself. She slipped from behind the velvet and rushed to the casket.

Her gaze fell on her father's hands. Earlier they'd been folded over his chest. Now one of them was turned up, a hundred dollar bill resting in his palm.

But what surprised her wasn't the size of the bill the woman had left, but the calloused hands. What kind of criminal had hands like a laborer? That wasn't all. There appeared to be a dark smudge on the inside of his wrist. No, not a smudge but a small tattoo. The tattoo was obviously old, distorted with age, but it appeared to be a bird of some kind.

Her gaze shifted to his gaping suit pocket and the corner of the white package the woman had hidden there.

With trembling fingers, Paige impulsively slipped out the small box, surprised it was heavier than she'd expected.

The box was neatly wrapped and taped as if the woman had thought Michael Alexander might try to open it in the afterlife? What could be inside? After what Paige had just witnessed, probably not a keepsake from a friend.

Some sort of contraband? That seemed the obvious answer. She stared at the box. She shouldn't have come here.

She'd been trying to get over the shock of her mother's death when the letter about Michael Alexander's funeral had arrived—an anonymous letter addressed to her mother and marked urgent.

Since Paige had believed her father dead for the last twenty-three years, she'd been more than a little shocked to learn he'd only recently died. She'd taken the letter to the lawyer her mother had hired just days before her death, Franklin Cole.

An elderly, obviously conservative man, Franklin had advised her not to attend the funeral. He argued that her mother must have had her reasons for lying about Michael Alexander's premature death. The man must be such that Paige had needed to be protected from him.

"Also," Franklin had pointed out. "You have no idea who sent this letter telling your mother of his death or even if it is true. Suppose the letter writer knew about your mother's death, knew the letter would fall into your hands, had planned it that way and has some sort of ulterior motive?"

"You mean to get me to New Orleans?" she asked, wondering if all lawyers were that paranoid or if it came with advanced age.

Franklin had only lifted one bristly gray brow in answer.

Right now though, holding the mystery package, hefting its weight and imagining every awful thing in the world inside it, Paige realized Franklin might have been right.

If this was a trap, she'd walked right into it.

But how could she not have come? She'd wanted so desperately to believe that her mother had been wrong about her father. And if Simone had been wrong about him being dead, maybe she'd also been wrong about what sort of man he was. Anything was possible with her mother, God rest her soul.

Staring at the small box, all Paige's illusions about her father shattered. Obviously, he'd been involved in something illegal, otherwise why an exchange of money and merchandise via his casket?

She shouldn't have come here. She definitely shouldn't have taken this box from the coffin.

Put it back and get out of here!

The outer door opened with the same soft groan she'd come to recognize. Frantic, she started to put the box back into the coffin, but stopped. Maybe there was something inside that would tell her where he'd been all these years. She needed to know why he'd left her and her mother. Or why her mother had kept her hidden from him all these years.

Maybe whatever was inside would explain all that. Then again, curiosity *did* kill the cat.

The outside door groaned closed. The sound of footsteps grew louder, closer.

As if there had ever been any doubt as to what she'd do, she slipped the package into her suit pocket and dove back behind the drapes as the viewing room door opened once more.

Purposeful, heavy footsteps entered the room, bringing the smells of the street and the more masculine scent of a man.

Paige froze, heart pounding, afraid the visitor might have seen her, seen the movement of the drapes before she'd gotten hidden. She didn't dare peek, feeling trapped and terrible for taking the package out of the coffin. She was no better than a grave robber. What had she been thinking?

Whatever the box contained, it was none of her business. She was probably better off not knowing the truth about her father. She promised herself she'd put the pilfered box back without looking inside and leave. Just as soon as she got the chance.

From the funeral home office, she could hear the mortician still on the phone. Closer, she heard the footsteps halt at the casket, then that awful unknowing silence. She half expected the drapes to fling apart at any moment and to see some heinous man glaring down at her.

Over the drumming of her heart and the jazz, she heard the rustle of fabric. Unable to stand it any longer, she parted the drapes and peered through.

She stifled a gasp. A thirty-something man wearing a brown leather jacket, jeans and biker boots stood next to the casket. He was going through her father's pockets, no doubt looking for the package the woman had left. Even more startling were his dark and dangerous good looks. He was take-your-breath-away handsome in a bad-boy sort of way.

He looked surprised when he didn't find the box. Then angry. He plucked up the hundred dollar bill, balled it in his fist and threw it back into the coffin with a curse.

From the office came the sound of a phone being slammed down. A chair squeaked. Slow, methodical footsteps echoing on the ancient flooring, headed in the room's direction.

Paige watched Dark and Dangerous search the coffin, his movements hurried as the sound of the mortician's footsteps neared the viewing room door.

What was in the box that had him so anxious to find it? And what was that box now doing in her pocket? Had she lost her mind?!

Suddenly, he ceased his search. His gaze moved around the room, halting on the drapes, his dark eyes narrowing.

She quickly ducked to the side. Had he seen her? She held her breath, terrified the drapes would fly open at any moment.

"We're closing," a dull male voice announced

from the direction of the viewing room doorway, the same voice she'd heard on the phone.

Daring to peek through the drapes again, she saw Dark and Dangerous turn to the mortician. "I'm finished." He seemed far from finished, but he walked toward the man.

She imagined him pulling a gun and shooting the undertaker in cold blood. She held her breath, surprised when he just walked on by the man, right out the front door.

Her body sagged in temporary relief before she reminded herself that she was still trapped.

From her hiding place, she watched the mortician step to the coffin and close it. No chance of returning the box now. She said a silent goodbye to her father, adding an apology for the coffin robbing. Well, she *was* her father's daughter. Now there was a thought.

When the mortician reached for the lamp switch over the casket, she quickly tiptoed the length of the drapes, slipped from behind the velvet near the door and quietly let herself out of the funeral home.

Once on the street, she finally released the breath she'd been holding and looked for her taxi, anxious to get out of there.

Unfortunately, the cab she'd ordered wasn't waiting. She glanced at her watch. Maybe it was just running late.

Her relief at having escaped was short-lived. The streets seemed more deserted than they'd been earlier. She felt conspicuous, especially dressed like she was, and exposed, too aware of the package she'd put in her pocket.

From a few blocks away came the sound of traffic, an occasional car horn.

But here there was only a heavy, humid silence that fit with the district's decaying buildings and dank decomposing smells.

Pulling her cell phone from her shoulder bag, she dialed information for the cab company. The light inside Eternal Peace blinked off, making the street that much darker.

Too nervous to stand still, she asked for Bayou Line Taxis as she walked down the block, her short heels echoing on the cracked concrete, and opted to have the number rung for her.

Someone finally answered and Paige asked about her cab.

"Hold on," a female dispatcher said.

Partway down the block, Paige turned at the sound of a door opening. The mortician came out and got into the old hearse without even a glance in her direction. He pulled away, making the street seem even more desolate.

The dispatcher came back on the line. "The driver was there at the time you specified, but some guy at the funeral home paid the fare and sent him away saying he wouldn't be needed."

Her throat tightened. Only one man had come out of the funeral home while she'd been there: Dark and Dangerous. But why would he—

The tiny blond hairs on the back of her neck stood

up as she heard the scuff of a sole on the concrete behind her. She turned. The streetlamp was out so she could see nothing in the darkness at the edge of the buildings, but she sensed someone was there, watching her. That or her imagination was working overtime.

"So do you want me to send another cab or what?" the dispatcher asked, sounding harried and irritated.

"Yes, please," Paige said, voice cracking.

"Twenty minutes minimum," the dispatcher said and sighed as if she had better things to do than send a taxi twice to the same place.

Paige didn't think she could wait twenty minutes. Behind her, she heard the footsteps again. This time when she looked back, she thought she saw movement along the edge of the building.

"No." She disconnected, put the phone in her purse and started walking toward the end of the block again. She would walk over to where she heard all the traffic. It couldn't be that far. She was bound to be able to catch a taxi quicker by doing that than waiting here. As if waiting here was an option. She heard the footfalls again behind her.

She turned, caught a glimpse of a tall man with long, stringy dark hair. She began to run awkwardly in the pencil thin skirt and the strappy, black shoes she'd paid too much for and had never worn before. As she neared the end of the block, she saw a light in one of the buildings. An older woman was working late in an office, operating a vacuum, just across the intersection.

Past the lit office, Paige could see nothing but darkness and deserted streets between her and the busy street a few blocks over. She didn't dare try to get through all that isolated darkness. Dressed the way she was, no way could she outrun whoever was behind her—not that far. But if she could get the cleaning woman's attention, maybe get inside, call for help—

The hurried slap of shoe soles on the sidewalk behind her was so close—

She reached the intersection and leapt from the curb to the street, praying she could reach the woman in the office before—

It was like slamming into a brick wall. Something solid came out of the blackness at the edge of the building. Her body connected with a larger, stronger, more solid body. The impact knocked the breath out of her, but not before she caught a whiff of the now familiar male scent.

In that same instant, a car engine rumbled to life out of the darkness beyond, tires squealing on the pavement as it roared up in a flash of blinding headlights. She thought the car planned to run her down—just as one had run down her mother days before.

But the strong arms that had encircled her on impact now hauled her off her feet. The car screeched to a stop a hairsbreadth from her, the back door flung open and she was thrown unceremoniously into the back seat. Dark and Dangerous dove in on top of her. The car took off, the door slamming as the driver flipped a U-turn in the empty intersection.

Something metallic pinged off the side of the car followed by the sound of soft pops. Dark and Dangerous let out a curse as she tried to free herself and managed to accidentally knee him in the groin. He sucked in a sharp breath and doubled up.

She wiggled free of him and sat up, glancing back. The man with the long stringy hair who'd been following her stood in the middle of the street, the light from the office illuminating the gun in his hand. He raised the weapon. Another *pop* sounded and the car's taillight exploded. The man was shooting at them!

The realization made her noodle-limp. She looked over at Dark and Dangerous, opened her mouth, thinking she should scream or something, but only a tiny squeak came out as the car cornered hard, slamming her against the door.

In the light from the passing streetlamps, she saw him sitting across from her in the back seat, still looking incredibly handsome, but a little pained. He glared at her, his dark eyes hard as obsidian.

She watched in horror as he reached under his leather jacket and pulled out a handgun, his expression making it clear that the idea of shooting her held more than a little appeal right now.

"Well?" he demanded as he pointed the weapon at her. "Where is it?"

CHAPTER TWO

PAIGE SQUEEZED HER EYES SHUT and gripped the edge of the seat as the car took another hard turn.

This wasn't happening. This was just another one of her fantasies. Only this one had gone all wrong and it was time to snap out of it.

All she had to do was open her eyes and she'd be in the back seat of a New Orleans taxi headed for her hotel. When she breathed in again, she would no longer smell the haunting scent of one dark and dangerous male's cologne. Nor would she feel the cold, hard steel of a gun barrel pressed to her ribs.

She opened her eyes and caught her breath, her already accelerated heart reaching Mach II as she met Dark and Dangerous's gaze. Her pulse thrummed in her ears and she thought she might black out, actually hoped she would. If she'd only just left the small white box in her father's coffin, better yet, never have come to the funeral home in the first place—

"Give me the package," he ordered impatiently, using the gun to emphasize his point.

She clung to the door handle, the rational side of her brain noting that leaping from a car moving this fast would be nothing more than painful suicide. She was shaking so hard the door handle rattled in her hand.

Her eyes squeezed shut again. This was only a bad dream. She opened her right eye a slit ready for this to end since she was no P. T. Alexander.

Damn. He was still there, frowning at her, head tilted at an angle as if he was considering something might be wrong with her hearing—or her mind. He had the darkest eyes and lashes she'd ever seen, darker than even his hair, his handsome face so at odds with the malevolent look in those eyes.

Okay, this *was* happening. *Just give him the package. Explain why you foolishly took it. He'll understand. You can blame it on being blond. Men can relate to that.*

She flicked a glance at the driver. Although she could see only part of his face reflected in the rearview mirror, she'd seen faces like his before—on wanted posters at the post office!

Somehow she didn't think giving Dark and Dangerous the package and playing dumb would get her out of this one. Her heart threatened to beat out of her chest as she looked again at the man beside her—and the small black hole of the gun barrel he held pointed at her chest.

He was going to kill her. Dump her body in some swamp to be eaten by alligators. Oh, God.

In her fantasies P. T. Alexander was always amazingly heroic, coming up with brilliant plans to escape—usually with the stolen jewels, the bag of money, the poor kidnapped baby and ultimately the hero.

Paige didn't see that happening given that she couldn't move or speak—could barely breathe. All she could do was think: *Help!*

"Hey!" He snapped his fingers in front of her face with his free hand and leaned in closer to gaze into her eyes. "The package?" He gave her a little jab in the ribs with the barrel of the gun. "Don't make me get ugly."

A crazy thought flashed in her mind: This man could never be ugly.

She was so nervous she was giddy. Perfect.

Don't let his looks fool you. Why do you think the expression is Drop-dead Gorgeous?

Paige opened her mouth, but nothing came out. Not a scream. Not a word. The car seemed to be getting farther and farther from anything—or anyone. What would P.T. do? Certainly not cower in a corner. P.T. never showed fear.

But she wasn't P.T. She was just going to give him the package and take her chances.

Bad idea. Be resourceful.

Easy for P. T. Alexander.

Without warning, he jerked the strap of her purse from her shoulder and dumped the contents onto the back seat as the car sped through the narrow streets of what appeared to be a lightless, abandoned industrial area.

Fortunately she'd left her airline tickets and almost everything else she normally carried in her bag at the hotel, thanks to the advice of an article she'd read recently aimed at women traveling alone.

All that tumbled out of her bag was her cell phone, Chap Stick, a small package of tissues, a roll of spearmint Lifesavers, her generic hotel room card key and her wallet with one credit card and forty dollars in cash.

Dark and Dangerous swore, obviously not pleased with what he'd found.

She realized it wasn't going to take much of a leap for him to jump to the conclusion that the small box he was looking for must be in one of her suit jacket pockets.

"Look, I know you have it," he said in a strained voice that suggested being patient with her was taking its toll on him. "Don't make this more difficult than it has to be. Give me the package and I'll drop you off at the nearest bus stop."

Right. City transit to hell. She might have believed him, wanted to desperately, but unfortunately, she'd caught the driver's expression. Dark and Dangerous had no intention of letting her out at any bus stop.

Fear spiked her heart rate. What was in this box that was so important that one man had shot at her and another had abducted her and was now holding her at gunpoint, threatening to do who-knew-what to her?

Her imagination took off at a dead run—just like her pulse. Maybe inside the box now in her pocket was an assassin's bullet that supplied the name of the hitman for the president or the Pope. Or plans for a terrorist attack. Or strategic military plans encoded on a microchip for an enemy spy.

She felt a surge of patriotism, determined not to give up the box no matter what he did to her.

It lasted only an instant. She realized unless she came up with a plan to save herself and the box quickly, he would just take it off her dead body.

Stall for time until you can come up with a plan. That could take a while.

"If you're finished…" She reached for her purse, then began to pick up the contents from the space on the seat between them, unable to think of anything else to do. Tissues, mints, cell phone, hotel card key, Chap Stick…out of habit, she applied the balm to her lips before dropping it into her purse.

"Who put you up to this?" he demanded, grabbing her arm as she reached for her wallet.

"No one," she snapped in a voice she imagined sounded like P.T.'s. Paige jerked her arm free and reached again for her wallet, which had slid over against his thigh. A very muscular thigh, P.T. noted.

He got to the wallet first, holding it out of her reach as he flipped it open and squinted to read her plastic-encased credit card.

"Paige Teresa Grayson?" he asked, shooting her a look.

It was obvious the name meant nothing to him. For once, she was glad her mother had remarried when she was four, changing Paige's last name as well. At least her captor didn't know she was Michael Alexander's daughter, which had to be good, right?

"My friends call me P.T.," she said, lifting her chin. Why had she said that? She *had* lost her mind. No one had *ever* called her P.T. Except in her fantasies. And this definitely wasn't one of them.

Dark and Dangerous's glance seemed to concur that there was something wrong with her mind. The man was holding a gun on her. She *should* have been cowering in a corner.

Actually, her behavior was just a nervous reaction to realizing she was only moments away from being bodily searched. That and abject horror of what he'd do once he had the box now in her pocket.

His gaze took in her attire, lingering for a breath-stealing moment on the neckline of her thin, gray silk blouse, then dropping to the pocket of her jacket.

Think misdirection!

At a loss, Paige reached again for her wallet.

He jerked it back. Her puny forty dollars in cash fell out. She scooped it up and stuffed the bills into her purse, not looking at him but feeling the heat of his gaze move over her, a heat as disturbing as his eyes, fired with something that sizzled, too hot to touch.

"Take it off."

Her gaze shot up to his.

"Take off your jacket," he said, those blistering jet black eyes locking with hers.

Do something! Anything! Seduce him!

Seduce him?! Hello? If that was her only chance, then she was as good as dead. Would he torture her first? Or just shoot her? She hated to think how little she would be able to stand before she told him everything he wanted to know.

You don't know *anything.*

Good point, P.T.

What would he do, though, once she'd given him what he wanted? She shuddered, her imagination painting too vivid a picture.

Settle down. Use your womanly wiles.

Paige groaned inwardly. If she had wiles, it was news to her. Nor was she a *woman.* Not in the sense P.T. meant, anyway. Her experience was…well, you could say limited. Not even in her wildest imagination could she pull this off.

What have you got to lose?

Let's not go there.

She looked over at Dark and Dangerous. A lock of his dark hair hung over one eye. The scent of his cologne numbed her senses, making her feel weak and helpless. How ironic that her killer would be the most handsome, sexiest man she'd ever met.

She tried to look deep into his dark eyes without flinching and gave him what she hoped was a come hither look, something she'd imagined P.T. doing dozens of times when faced with a dangerous, handsome man and a gun.

He seemed to respond, leaning a little closer.

''Put the piece away,'' she said in P.T.'s imagined silky tone, her voice barely cracking. Holding his gaze was like holding a chunk of smoldering charcoal. Her heart in her throat, she flicked the barrel of the gun aside with her fingertip. "You don't have to hold a gun on me to get me to undress."

She slipped the suit jacket a few inches off one shoulder in what she hoped was a seductive shrug as she tried out one of P.T.'s imagined cat-in-the-cream smiles and let her lashes drop a little.

His gaze burned into hers as he leaned even closer.

It's working!

She was as good as dead.

"Tell me something, P.T.," he whispered so close his breath tickled her cheek.

Her eyes flew open as she realized he had her pinned against the door.

Okay, forget seduction for the time being.

There was always begging.

"Yes?" Paige whispered hoarsely.

He tucked her hair behind her ear and leaned in as if to confide something too intimate for anyone else to hear. She felt herself slide down in the seat. Oh, no.

His lips brushed against the sensitive skin of her ear. She shivered, but it was lost in her already trembling body. She bit her lower lip, her breath held hostage in her chest, her heart a jungle drumbeat. Who was seducing whom here?

She released her lower lip from her teeth as his mouth brushed over hers. The sigh she emitted she swore he stole from her chest as he kissed her.

She was so surprised, her lips might have responded to his. It was over too quickly to be sure. Was that her who groaned?

He drew back a little, his dark eyes igniting with something hot and hazardous. He flashed her a heart-stopping smile revealing a set of deep dimples. Unfortunately, there was absolutely no humor in his smile.

A chill skittered across her skin as he said, ''Are you sure you want to play games with me?'' his voice perilously low.

It must have been a rhetorical question because he didn't give her a chance to answer. He grabbed the front of her blouse in his fist and jerked her upright.

Out of the corner of her eye, she saw a pair of bright red taillights flash in the street ahead as he reached into her suit pocket. He released her as he pulled out the small white box.

He smiled at her, all dimples. ''Now, you're going to tell me who you're working for.''

He never saw it coming. Neither did the driver who was watching the drama unfold in the back seat from his rearview mirror.

She was the only one to see the flash of red taillights as a huge commercial refrigerated truck with FRESH FISH printed on the side backed into the narrow street, blocking both lanes.

The driver heard the growl of the truck's engine. Too late, though. He slammed on the brakes. The car began to skid sideways, headed for the broadside of the truck.

Get the package!

Paige swung her purse. *Thwack.* It smacked Dark and Dangerous upside the head, taking him by surprise. As she flung open her door with one hand, she grabbed the box she'd stolen from the coffin with the other and hurled herself out of the skidding car.

She hit the ground hard, rolled. P.T. had always made it seem easy. And a whole lot less painful. As she stopping rolling, she saw that she'd broken the heel off her shoe.

Forget the shoes. Run!

She kicked off the shoes as she scrambled to her stocking feet, hiked up her skirt to her thighs and ran, aiming for a sliver of space between the front of the fish truck and the garage door that had just closed after it.

She barely squeezed through the narrow gap as Dark and Dangerous grabbed for her. His fingertips brushed the sleeve of her jacket, getting nothing but air.

Their eyes met in that instant. His look stopped her heart. He groped for her, but the space was too small for him to get through.

She heard him curse and what sounded like a fist slam into the side of the truck door then heavy feet clambering over the truck's massive hood after her as she took off running. She glanced back just long enough to see the driver of the truck come out fighting, detaining Dark and Dangerous with a right hook. She stuffed the box into her purse and kept going.

She reached the corner, amazed she could run—and fast. If those snotty girls from high school could see her now! All those years of being pudgy, all the painful physical education classes where invariably she would come in last to the jeers of the other students, all the years of avoiding the mirror... And to think that the only reason she'd taken up exercise this past year was out of boredom.

On the treadmill in the basement of her apartment house, she'd found the perfect place to live vicariously through her imagined P. T. Alexander adventures. No one bothered her or paid the least bit attention to her while she worked out. She could let her imagination run wild.

She knew she'd lost some weight, but what a shock to realize she could run! And she did—in her stockings no less—toward the lights and cars on a busy street ahead.

Halfway down the block, she heard him behind her. She ran as if her life depended on it. It did. And ran right out into the traffic. Brakes squealed. A driver laid on his horn to the screech of rubber, but by then she'd woven her way through the cars to the opposite side of the street and the off-duty taxi sitting at the light.

Behind her, she heard a cacophony of curses.

She jerked open the back door of the cab and

leapt in, hollering, "Please. Get me out of here fast and I'll pay double the fare!"

The light changed. The female taxi driver took one look at her in the rearview mirror and hit the gas, cutting in front of another car.

Paige glanced out her side window and saw Dark and Dangerous. He missed grabbing the cab's back-door handle by a matter of inches.

"Irate boyfriend?" the female cabdriver asked.

"The worst," Paige answered, looking back. He was standing in the middle of the lane, cars going around him, drivers leaning out their windows to yell obscenities at him as if he were a crazy man.

She'd seen his expression. Crazy was one way of describing him. Murderous was another.

With a start she saw that dangling from the fingers of his right hand were her expensive black strappy shoes, one heel missing.

"NICE SHOES," said a familiar voice through the din of the noisy traffic. Jimmy pulled the car up along-side him. "Looks like Cinderella got away, though."

Devon St. Cloud swore as he tossed the high heels onto the front seat and climbed in, slamming the door behind him.

"Want me to try and catch the taxi?" Jimmy asked as he started to drive.

Devon shook his head. The taxi and the blonde were long gone. So was the package. But that wasn't the worst of it.

He let the hot muggy night air blow in the window. It was supposed to have been a simple exchange. Just pick up a parcel from some dead guy's coffin. Morbid and bizarre as hell but no problem.

Except when he'd looked into the coffin, he'd felt his skin crawl. He knew the dead man! Couldn't remember the guy's name, but he knew the face. He never forgot a face. It was something he'd learned from his childhood. Recognizing the difference between an easy mark and an undercover cop. Remembering the faces of those he'd swindled and knowing which ones he had to fear.

And since he remembered the dead man's face, that meant their paths had crossed at some time. Devon just couldn't put his finger on where or why. He had a bad feeling he couldn't shake that wherever he'd seen the man before, it wasn't good—and that he'd better remember—and soon.

He rubbed his jaw where the blonde had hit him, realizing the bad feeling had started the moment he'd looked down into that coffin.

"You dropped this," Jimmy said and tossed him a wallet.

Devon stared down at the slim, red leather billfold he'd taken from the blonde's purse earlier. Well, at least one thing was going right. He went through it in the light from the glove compartment.

Just as he'd thought, it held nothing but a credit card in the name of Paige Teresa Grayson. No ID.

Plus the wallet looked new. He sniffed it. Smelled new. Smelled a little like her, too.

Who the hell was Paige Teresa Grayson? Except her friends call her P.T., he reminded himself. She'd looked so damned innocent, so completely out of her league. Those big baby blues, the chin-length pale blond hair, the line of golden freckles that arced the bridge of her button nose and those lips, so full and lush...

He recalled how she'd trembled at his touch. And her attempt at seduction had been almost laughable. He would swear she was as innocent as she looked.

But she had the package, didn't she? And he was the one who'd gotten kneed in the groin and smacked in the face with a purse. So who was out of his league here? Who'd gotten seduced in the end?

"What the hell was all that about?" Jimmy said after driving for a few minutes. "I thought it was a straight pickup job?" He watched the rearview mirror as if, like Devon, he expected a tail.

"Yeah," Devon said. "So did I." Instead someone had tried to kill them. "Swing back by Eternal Peace."

"You realize the place will be all locked up?"

Devon looked over at Jimmy to see if he was kidding. Breaking and entering was pretty tame stuff considering both of their backgrounds.

"It's just that it's in the middle of the night and it's a...funeral home," Jimmy said. "I've got this thing about dead people."

Devon laughed. No wonder Jimmy had offered to cover the back of the funeral home earlier and let Devon make the pickup. "You can wait in the car. It won't take me long."

Jimmy didn't ask why he wanted to break into the funeral home. Which was just as well. Unlike Jimmy, Devon wanted another look at the dead man.

"Front door or back?" Jimmy asked as he neared Eternal Peace.

"Back."

Jimmy pulled down the alley and popped the trunk.

"Leave it running," Devon told him as he hopped out. "I won't be long." He went to the open trunk and took out the tools he would need, including a flashlight for once he was inside. This was the perfect neighborhood for a B&E. But as he neared the back entrance he realized he wasn't the only one who thought so.

The back door lock had been busted. He set down the tools and, pulling his weapon from his shoulder holster, eased the door open. The silence was almost deafening. So was the old musty closed-up smell.

He snapped on the flashlight and felt a jolt as he noticed that everything was covered with thick undisturbed dust back here. Except on the floor where there were recent shoe prints. This place hadn't been a funeral home in years! The realization sent a sliver of worry through him.

He remembered how the funeral home director

had left right after the blonde as if he'd been in a hurry to get out of the place.

Devon moved cautiously down the hall. He knew before he opened the viewing room door and shone the flashlight inside. The casket and body were gone! Everything had been cleaned out.

He took a breath, his earlier uneasiness now full-blown dread. Someone had gone to a lot of trouble to reopen Eternal Peace Funeral Home for a one-night show.

Why? And who exactly had it been staged for?

CHAPTER THREE

PAIGE DIDN'T BREAK DOWN until she reached her hotel room. It took that long for the horror of what had happened tonight to sink in.

She started shaking on the hotel elevator. By the time she reached her room, she could barely get the little card key into the slot. Once inside, the shaking turned to tears and terror.

She could have been killed! Probably would be dead now if she hadn't gotten out of that car.

What had she been thinking, coming down here? Hadn't Franklin tried to warn her? And she thought the elderly lawyer was just being paranoid. Well, at least she'd gotten to see her father. Right. And now she was involved in his dirty business.

Just remembering her brushes with death made her start shaking all over again. It seemed inconceivable that not only had someone shot at her but abducted her, held her at gunpoint and...kissed her! She shuddered remembering the look in his dark eyes. It had been the prequel to the kiss of death! What would he have done to her if she hadn't gotten out of that car? She hated to think. And all for some package with who knew what—

The package.

She froze, then slowly looked down at her purse, heart pounding.

Cautiously, she withdrew the box, once again surprised by its weight. Maybe the best thing to do would be to throw it away without even opening it.

That idea didn't even survive a second. She *had* to open it, had to know exactly what was inside given that at least one person—probably two—had seemed willing to kill for it. She had to know what she'd gotten herself involved in.

Carefully, she sliced the tape with her fingernail. Heart in her throat, she lifted the lid.

If not an assassin's bullet or terrorist plans or a microchip filled with spy code, she'd at least thought there'd be a slim velvet bag stuffed with stolen diamonds. Or a set of recently pilfered rare coins. Or something priceless that could save the world.

She stared into the box, at first a little disappointed. It was just a key. Oh, it was ornate enough, but it didn't look very old nor valuable. But a key had to open something, right?

She lifted it from the box, thinking there had to be more.

There was.

Hidden under the key was what appeared to be a folded piece of address book paper. She couldn't help herself, she was hoping it would have a treasure map scribbled on it. Or a secret message.

She lifted out the paper and unfolded it, her mind racing with possibilities.

Her heart stopped. She stared down at the handwriting—she'd seen that distinctive script her whole life. No! Tears welled in her eyes. Oh, God. A page from her mother's address book!

Her hand was shaking so hard she could barely read the words: Find Paige. Rare Finds, 3 Prospector, Big Timber, Montana.

DEVON PUT THE TOOLS back into the trunk, slammed the lid and climbed into the car again. "Let's get out of here."

"Find what you were looking for?" Jimmy asked.

"Not exactly," Devon said. "It was just a front. Everything's been cleaned out. Dead body and all."

"You have to be kidding."

Devon shook his head, watching the rearview mirror as Jimmy hit the street, turned right and headed toward the heart of the city.

"Why would someone go to that much trouble?" Jimmy asked.

"That's what I'm wondering, too." He glanced in the side mirror and spotted a car a few vehicles back. It had been with them for several blocks.

He looked over at Jimmy who was also watching the car in his rearview mirror.

"We picked up the tail not far from the funeral home," he said.

"Think you can lose it?"

Jimmy grinned. "Is Flipper a dolphin?" He tromped down on the gas, cutting in between two cars, whipping back in front of the first one to take a right onto a side street. He opened up the engine, braking just enough to make a hard left at the next street, then a quick right, left, right through a residential area until there were no lights behind them.

Jimmy sighed as he slowed down. "What the hell do you think was in that package?"

"I don't know." Devon raked a hand through his hair and looked out at the night. "But I'm going to find out."

"What about the old man?" Jimmy had always called their benefactor the old man. Justice Wyatt Hathaway would have had a stroke if he'd known.

"I'll take care of him," Devon said.

"He won't be happy about this," Jimmy said. "You don't think—"

"That he's behind this?" He couldn't believe Jimmy would even suggest something like that. "We're like sons to him." At least Devon had always felt that way.

Jimmy snorted. "Maybe *you* are. I'm more like a pet project that's gone awry."

"Come on, he saved our lives."

"Yeah, but at what price?" Jimmy said.

Devon looked out at the night. Jimmy had always resented the fact that the great magnanimous Wyatt Hathaway had pulled him out of the gutter as a boy and cleaned him up.

"It wasn't like I asked the old fart to save me," Jimmy would say. "It's his own fault if he couldn't make a silk purse out of a sow's ear." Jimmy believed the genes he'd gotten from a third-rate criminal father and a hooker kept him from ever rising above his birth—and not even the great Wyatt Hathaway could change that.

Devon hadn't known his father and felt fortunate for that. His stepfather had been bad enough. And as for his mother... Well Devon had quit thinking about her a long time ago. Wyatt Hathaway was as close to a father as Devon ever had—and that suited him just fine. He was eternally grateful.

"You love being the black sheep and you know it," Devon said.

"Yeah," he agreed. "But let's face it. If push came to shove, the old man would pick you. He's acting like he doesn't know which of us he'll choose to run his empire when he gets that State Supreme Court seat." Jimmy snorted. "You've always been his favorite."

Devon shook his head. Since the day Wyatt had brought Jimmy home he'd been playing this game. Jimmy had been fourteen, two years older, but he'd always seemed like a little brother. Devon had been protective of Jimmy from the start. Maybe because Devon had been at the judge's for almost six months before Wyatt brought Jimmy to live with them.

Devon wanted to tell Jimmy that he didn't have anything to worry about when it came to getting the lion's share of the Hathaway fortune. Devon was ready to see what he could do on his own. Wyatt had given him so much—maybe too much. Devon didn't like the feeling that his life had already been planned for him. Some time ago he'd decided he would tell Wyatt he didn't want to run the Hathaway empire.

He knew Wyatt wouldn't take it well, but it was time. He planned to tell him right after this job.

"The old man likes me better than you because I'm smarter," Devon said playing the game.

Jimmy laughed. "I think it's because he knows I'm better looking than you and he's compensating."

"He wouldn't jeopardize our lives," Devon said, serious again.

Jimmy shot him a look. "You're right, he would hate to lose his two best employees. Nor could he afford the publicity of our deaths. Might throw a monkey wrench in his career plans. Especially now. But someone was pulling our strings back there."

Devon nodded. "I wouldn't suggest you go back to your place tonight. Nor the office. Stay in the field until I get my hands on that package." *And the blonde.*

"I could disappear for a while," Jimmy agreed, flashing him a smile. "There's this little place in Mexico…serves the best margaritas. And this one senorita—"

"Good. I'll call you if I need you." Devon had spent the past twenty years trying to keep Jimmy out of trouble. It was a role he'd fallen into easily. Jimmy could be a hothead, going off half-cocked sometimes. Devon wanted him out of town until he found out what the hell they'd gotten involved in.

"You think I don't know why you're trying to

get me out of town," Jimmy said. "You're trying to make points with the old man."

"Yeah, that's it."

Jimmy looked over at him again as he drove. "No, I've got it. You're going after the blonde, right, and you just want her for yourself."

"Bingo." He *was* going after the blonde. He wanted to know what was in that package and what she was doing with it. He also wanted to know who'd been in that casket and why it was now missing.

Plus he had a bad feeling whoever had been shooting at them tonight would turn up again. It had been a long time since he'd feared for his life, but he remembered the feeling only too well.

He had Jimmy drop him off at his car where they'd left it earlier. But it wasn't fear Devon felt as he drove toward Justice Wyatt Hathaway's New Orleans estate. There were worse things than dying. Like being betrayed by someone you trusted.

AT THE SOUND OF HER CAR, Justice Wyatt Hathaway poured himself a snifter of twenty-five-year-old bourbon and carried it out on the veranda. He watched her get out of the Mercedes coupe he'd bought her. Aquamarine. The same color as her eyes.

Her perfume drifted up to him, a once erotic scent that now just made him feel weak.

She didn't look up at him as she shook out her long hair but she knew he was watching her, waiting for her. This woman he'd taken into his bed, into his confidence, into his heart. The only woman who had the power to destroy him. Possibly already had.

He looked out through the dark limbs of the live oaks gleaming in the faint moonlight. His. All his. As far as the eye could see this stretch of Louisiana belonged to him, but it was nothing compared to how far the power of the name Wyatt Hathaway stretched.

He was a man who had more than most men could even dream of. He should have been a contented man. He should have been happy.

He heard her come in behind him. The soft rustle of the suit she wore, the scent of her always arriving just an instant before her, warm and lush. Promising.

She moved up behind him and put her arms around him, pressing her cheek against his back.

He closed his eyes. With her arms around him, he didn't feel sixty-eight. He felt like a young buck. She made him want to take on the world. Made him believe he still could. She filled him with a sense of omnipotence.

But he didn't kid himself. That buoyant feeling she afforded him had come at an incredible price. One he wondered if he could still afford.

He turned in her arms to look at her, always surprised by how startlingly beautiful she was, even more astonished by his reaction to her. Sometimes he thought he loved her—loved her as much as he could love anyone.

He cradled his drink in his right hand, touched

her face with the tips of the fingers of his left, cupping her jaw in his palm.

She lowered her eyes, lashes dark against the porcelain of her skin. A true redhead. Only a thin slit of aqua still shone from beneath her lashes, the faint sparkle of her gaze assuring him she was watching him, waiting. Like a cat curled up in a windowsill watching a bird, pretending to be asleep.

"Fiona," he said, the hammer of his heart making his words come out too breathy as if he'd been running. As if he were terrified.

She answered in a soft southern purr that even now had the ability to make him burn with desire. "Have you been waiting long?"

"Not too long." He withdrew his hand from her cheek and saluted her with the snifter, watching her over the rim of the crystal as he took a sip.

She was much too young for him. Too hungry. Too cold and calculating. Too much like he had been at her age.

But that wasn't what he'd seen in her that first time. Then he'd thought she was the daughter of his most dangerous enemy. He'd only wanted her because of who he thought she was. Their lovemaking had been an act of vengeance not passion. He'd spent his life trying to destroy her father. He could have cared less about her.

He'd never meant for it to last between them. Never thought it would.

The bourbon burned his throat, warmed his insides, but nothing could warm the cold that had settled around his heart. He looked into her eyes, expecting to see treachery naked as triumph. The tables had turned. She was now in control. And she had to know it.

But he saw nothing in all that Caribbean blue. No sign that she'd double-crossed him. Betrayed him. Destroyed him. But that didn't mean she hadn't. He knew better than anyone how adept she was at hiding her true feelings. Only recently had he learned just how ruthless she could be.

"How did it go?" he asked.

She smiled. "Piece of cake."

Her and her games. He feared what she might have cost him tonight. What she had cost them both. She didn't know the price of failure. Yet.

THE PIECE OF PAPER slipped from Paige's fingers and fluttered to the floor where the words stared up at her. Her mother had written the note. When? And who had she given it to? It made no sense. Why would her mother give it to anyone?

Paige fought to breathe. To think. Fear paralyzed her. She'd been abducted, threatened, held at gunpoint and shot at. All because she'd taken the box. A box that held a large key and a note her mother had written. How had it ended up in the box? And why had someone been paid a large amount of money for it?

She felt sick. What was in it that everyone wanted so badly? The key and what it opened? Or, she wondered, heart in her throat, was it her name and whereabouts that someone was willing to kill for?

With trembling fingers she picked up the paper from the floor, half expecting the words she'd thought she'd seen there to be gone. Just a figment of her out-of-control imagination.

No such luck.

Just seeing her mother's handwriting made her heart ache. But on closer inspection, she noticed that the words "Find Paige" were not only a different color ink, they could have been written by a different person—or by her mother in a hurry.

She was still reeling from her mother's death. Still trying to understand why her mother had lied about Michael Alexander being alive all these years. And now he too was dead.

She shivered, chilled to the bone. The timing of their deaths scared her. "Find Paige." But how did her mother know she'd be at Rare Finds, the antique store and house her mother had just purchased in Big Timber, Montana?

Paige had been living in San Francisco. She didn't even know about Rare Finds until her mother's death. She knew her mother had moved again because her mother had called to say she was in Big Timber. But that was only a few weeks ago. So how had her mother known Paige could be found at Rare Finds unless—

Unless those words hadn't been written by her mother.

She wished she'd never seen this note, never

come to her father's funeral— A thought struck her. If she hadn't, Dark and Dangerous would have the box right now. He would be the one reading this note.

She shuddered. What would he have done with it? Would he have known the significance of the note? The key? Even if he hadn't, he would know where to find her.

Wait a minute. When he'd read her name off her credit card there'd been no recognition at all, in fact he'd seemed confused by her being at the funeral home at all. She had to believe he wasn't looking for a woman named Paige. At least he hadn't been. Not until he had the box from the coffin.

But he was looking for her now.

She stared at the note. Until that moment, she hadn't even considered that her whereabouts might have been a secret. Was that why she and her mother had moved so often after her father's alleged death? Her mother had always said she hated staying in one place for long, but maybe she'd lied about that the same way she had about Paige's father being dead.

But then who had sent the letter about Michael Alexander's death? They obviously hadn't known about the hit-and-run accident that had taken Simone's life. Or had they?

Paige plopped down on the end of the bed. Her head ached and her eyes felt like sandpaper.

Something made a crinkling sound as she sat. She reached into her jacket pocket and pulled out the letter about her father's funeral from where she'd stuffed it before going into Eternal Peace Funeral Home—the opposite pocket from where she'd hidden the box.

She pulled out the folded envelope and flattened it on her lap, realizing that Dark and Dangerous would have found both the box—and the letter—if he'd searched her. Would he have made the connection? That Michael Alexander was her father? She hated to think what his reaction might have been to that news.

The envelope was white. Typed on the front were the words: Simone Grayson, Rare Finds, 3 Prospector, Big Timber, MT 59011. No return address. It had been postmarked New Orleans, three days ago.

Carefully Paige drew out the single sheet of plain white paper and reread it, thinking she might have missed something.

She hadn't. There was no salutation, no date, no return address. Just simply:

As per your request, this is to notify you that your husband Michael Alexander is now deceased.

A viewing will be held on March 9 from 9:00 p.m. to midnight at Eternal Peace Funeral Home, 1127 Parish Place, New Orleans, Louisiana. There will be no funeral service.

That was all. Typed. No signature.

Your husband? That was odd since the envelope was addressed to Simone Grayson.

Paige frowned as she folded the letter back into the envelope and distractedly tucked it into her pocket again. Shouldn't it have been ex-husband?

"As per your request..." Her mother had asked someone to let her know when Michael Alexander died. That seemed an odd request since her mother had not only lied about his death, but appeared to have forgotten him.

As far as Paige knew, her mother hadn't even kept any photographs of him, no mementos of any kind. Strange behavior considering Michael Alexander had been Paige's biological father. If Paige hadn't seen him tonight for herself, she might suspect he'd never existed. Except for the one memory she had of him. If it was a memory.

Her mother's behavior was a mystery to Paige. Like her mother's latest move. Paige had been shocked when she saw how small Big Timber, Montana, was. She and her mother had always lived in large cities. Her mother liked the anonymity, she'd said.

And why hadn't her mother told her about Rare Finds, the huge old Victorian house and antique business, all four floors filled with antiques and collectibles, some floors filled to the ceiling with only narrow paths through the maze?

It was so unlike her mother to buy an antique shop filled with...stuff. Her mother had always prided herself on the fact that she had managed to collect nothing in her half a century of life. Each time they moved, her mother required little more than two suitcases.

She used to say, "We can always buy what we need when we get there." So what had possessed her mother to suddenly buy a house, a business, collect so much stuff?

A thought struck Paige. If her father had been alive all these years, then what had she and her mother used for money? It had never been clear to Paige how they'd been able to live so comfortably. Her mother had told her that Michael Alexander had left a very large insurance policy that more than took care of them.

Given he only died a few days ago, what had she and her mother *really* been living on? They'd always seemed to have more than enough money, including plenty for Paige's four years of college and a trust fund that kept Paige from feeling the need for a real career.

She never suspected her mother might be lying about anything—let alone *everything*. Had she known her mother at all?

A wave of guilt swept over her. Her mother was all she'd had the last twenty-three years and Paige now regretted that she hadn't seen her in the months before the accident. They'd been close out of necessity when Paige was younger since it had just been the two of them and they'd moved so much. They'd had no other family. No lasting friendships.

But once Paige went away to college, she came home only on holidays, mostly because "home" kept moving. Since graduation, she'd seen even less of her mother.

Then just last week, her mother had called. After they'd discussed Paige's boring job at a cell phone company, her mother said there was something she needed to talk to Paige about.

"Nothing I want to get into on the phone," her mother had said. "I was thinking about coming down for a few days."

"Everything's all right there, isn't it?" Paige had asked, worried. Later, she would think it was odd her mother hadn't invited her to Big Timber since Paige had said she was thinking about quitting her job and going somewhere else.

"Everything's fine. I miss my daughter." She hadn't sounded like herself.

"I miss you, too. When are you coming?"

"I've booked a flight for the day after tomorrow," she'd said, surprising Paige that she'd already bought the ticket and was coming so soon. "Can you pick me up at the airport?"

"Of course." But her mother hadn't made the flight. She'd been killed in a hit-and-run accident in St. Petersburg, Florida, the day before she was to fly to see Paige in San Francisco. No one knew what she'd been doing in Florida, least of all Paige.

It wasn't until Paige reached Big Timber that she'd discovered her mother had hired Franklin Cole to draw up her last will and testament only days before she was killed. It had been Franklin who'd had to tell Paige the news: her mother had been dying of cancer. She had less than six weeks to live.

That's what her mother had been coming to San Francisco to tell her; Paige was certain of it. But why had she gone to Florida first? If only she'd flown to San Francisco first. Paige would have gotten to see her.

Like the trip to Florida, her mother had been doing things that Paige couldn't understand and it scared her. Just like the package with the key and her name and location in it.

Paige got up and moved around the hotel room, too nervous to sit, thinking about the odd instructions her mother had left in her will. Simone had insisted there be no funeral service, no obituary in the paper, no burial of any kind. Her body was to be cremated and put in an urn. Her mother had included a note stating that her daughter Paige would know what to do with her ashes when the time came.

Paige had no idea what her mother might have wanted done with them. And who was taking care of her father's burial, she wondered?

She stopped pacing by the bed to reach for her purse and a tissue— Her heart stopped as she remembered. She snatched her purse up from the bed and dumped the contents onto the spread praying she was wrong.

She wasn't.

Dark and Dangerous still had her wallet! He had her credit card! Could he find her with it? She didn't think so, but she didn't know what resources the man might have and he knew her name, the name she'd registered under at the hotel. Would he call every hotel in New Orleans trying to find her?

She couldn't take the chance since she was staying at the Alamosa Inn at the top of the list in the Yellow Pages. What would P.T. do?

Get out of here and fast.

Hurriedly she threw everything into her suitcase. She hadn't brought much. The clock on the nightstand read 1:30 a.m. Her flight back to Montana left at eight. She only had a few hours before she would leave for the airport.

But she knew she wouldn't get any sleep if she stayed here. Where would she go? And what about at the airport in the morning?

Tears burned her eyes and she bit her lip. If he could track her down tonight, he could find out when she was flying out and what flight number. Her ticket was under the name Paige Grayson.

She tried to calm down.

Definitely get another hotel for the remainder of the night, pay cash and use an assumed name.

She picked up the phone and called down to the main desk for a taxi.

On the way to a motel near the airport, she thought of P.T. and had the driver stop at an all-night drugstore where she purchased a baseball cap with I Love New Orleans stitched on it, a bottle of brunette hair rinse that would last a week and some makeup.

Paige never wore makeup. With her blond, pale

looks and shyness, she blended in to any background. Kind of like a wallflower. But that had always been just fine. She'd always felt conspicuous, especially with the extra weight she'd carried until just recently, so she'd done everything she could not to stand out. If she felt adventurous, she had P.T. to liven things up in the privacy of her mind.

She bought some black mascara, a tube of bright red lipstick Paige Grayson wouldn't have been caught dead in and considered some pale blue eye shadow. But P.T. always wore Wild Passion Purple in Paige's imagination. Grimacing, she went with purple.

She was going back to Montana as P. T. Alexander. Or at least as close as she could get to being P.T. It was crazy, but with a little luck, she might live long enough to get there.

CHAPTER FOUR

THE GUARD WAVED DEVON through the gate to the estate of Justice Wyatt Hathaway. A light was on in the huge house Wyatt had recently built. Devon had grown up in a house smaller but no less opulent.

He pushed the doorbell, thinking of all the jobs Wyatt had given him over the years. None of them had almost gotten him killed. None of them involved a package hidden in a dead man's coffin, either.

But Devon had learned long ago not to question Wyatt Hathaway. Tonight though, he wanted answers and was determined to get them.

He laid on the bell and waited.

Justice Hathaway had no servants who lived in the house. Housing for them was provided down the road on some property he'd bought and on which he had built some moderately sized houses.

The house had better security than Fort Knox and had a security gate and guards. The rest of the time, the old man had Jimmy and Devon. Both carried weapons and knew their job was to protect the judge at all costs.

Not that Wyatt needed much protection. He owned a huge collection of guns and knew how to shoot them. Devon had never known a tougher man. Nor a more powerful one.

The judge turned on the porch light and peered out the window, at first appearing annoyed, then a little surprised, almost worried.

He unlocked the door and swung it open, filling the doorway with his mass.

Wyatt Hathaway was a big man, six-four and wide as a barn. He'd played football in college, made a name for himself both on the field and off because he was as intelligent as he was tough. He prided himself on staying fit, even at sixty-eight.

Under the glare of the porch light, Devon could see that the judge wore a blue terry cloth bathrobe and matching blue slippers. He gripped a .38 in his right hand.

He hadn't been asleep, Devon could tell. What had he been waiting up for? The package?

It seemed to take Wyatt a moment before he put the .38 in his robe pocket and motioned Devon inside, closing and locking the door behind them.

Without a word, the judge headed into the living room, making a beeline for the bar. With his back to Devon, he uprighted two glasses on the bar top. "Anything wrong?"

"Where's Fiona?" Devon asked, looking down the hall toward the bedrooms as he followed the judge into the living room.

"She's not here. Her mother's ill. She went to stay with her."

"I thought her mother was dead."

"Maybe it's her stepmother," Wyatt said irritably as he turned from the bar. "You going to tell me what you're doing here?"

"That little job you asked me and Jimmy to do for you, I thought you'd want to know, it went sour."

The ice in the glasses clinked together. The judge pulled down a bottle of his private stock of twenty-five-year-old bourbon.

"What do you mean went sour?"

"Someone tried to kill us for the package."

The judge's hands shook as he tried to fill the glasses with bourbon. "But you're both all right."

Devon walked over and took the bottle from him and filled the glasses. "What is in the package? Drugs?"

The judge took one of the full glasses, walked to the stone fireplace and switched on the gas. Flames leapt in the fake logs. "Don't be ridiculous," he said, his gaze on the fire.

Devon stared at him, remembering the day Wyatt Hathaway saved his life.

"You did *get* the package?" The judge turned to look at him.

Devon shook his head and watched all color drain from the old man's face. The glass slipped from the judge's fingers and hit the floor. Bourbon splattered like blood on the white carpet.

Devon didn't move, couldn't. The son of a bitch had known how dangerous this job was and hadn't warned them.

The judge dropped into a chair, head down.

Devon stared at him for a moment, felt the rage recede. He walked over, picked up the old man's glass from the floor and took it to the sink at the bar. He filled a clean glass with bourbon. "Here. Drink it."

Wyatt looked up, a flicker of anger in his eyes. He wasn't used to being ordered around. But he took the bourbon, lifting it to his lips. "Where is Jimmy?"

"I told him to lay low until I found out what was going on," Devon said.

"You've always been protective of him." He drank more of the bourbon. It seemed to fortify him a little. "I should have told you the truth."

Devon waited.

He took a breath, sounding as if he'd just run fifty yards. "There is no easy way to say this. I was being blackmailed by the man in the coffin."

"Blackmailed by a dead man?"

The judge's mouth formed a grim line. He sighed. "It happened years ago. I was in the wrong place at the wrong time. A man was killed. A judge. The killer saw me there. In my haste to get away, I dropped a glove."

Devon waited.

"I made the mistake of not going to the police. I had my reasons. At the time, they made sense. The next thing I knew, I got a call from the killer. He had the leather glove, from an expensive pair with my initials on them, but the glove now also had the dead man's blood on it.''

''You paid the blackmail?'' Devon tried to imagine Wyatt Hathaway ever being that young or that foolish.

''I know it was stupid. Especially since I never got the glove back. The blackmailer double-crossed me, took the money and left the country. I later heard he got in a bar brawl in some South American country, killed a man and was sent to prison. I thought that was the end of it.''

''He got out of prison,'' Devon guessed.

''Escaped. I'd completely forgotten about him until I got a call demanding more money. I refused to pay and...I lost my temper. I threatened him.'' The judge shook his head and took another drink of the bourbon. ''He said if anything happened to him, he'd made arrangements for the evidence to come out.''

Devon had a bad feeling he already knew where this was heading.

''He was murdered a couple of days later. I didn't hear about it until I was contacted by a second party who told me they had the so-called evidence.'' The judge looked at Devon. ''I panicked. I wanted nothing to do with this man or his death. I agreed to the deal.''

''Trumped up evidence, years old—''

''There is no statute of limitations on murder but even if I could prove I had nothing to do with it, I can't afford a scandal,'' the old man said. ''I have worked too hard for that seat on the Louisiana Supreme Court. It's finally within my grasp. Do you realize what a man can accomplish on one of the most powerful benches in our country? I couldn't let someone like Michael Alexander take it all away from me—especially from the grave.''

Devon tried to put the name with the face in the casket. Nothing. "The evidence, that's what was in the package, right?''

The judge shook his head. "I'm told there is a key and a note telling me where I can find the *evidence*.''

"And you believe that?''

"I have no other choice. The murder was never solved and the man was a district judge of some affluence. You understand now why I need that package?''

Devon nodded and put down his almost full glass, tired of the required pretense of drinking with the judge. Devon had never acquired the taste for liquor. Not after watching his mother try to drink herself to death. "You have no idea who Michael Alexander gave this evidence to?''

"No, I just received an anonymous note. I was to take the money to the funeral home personally and put it in the coffin before 9:00 p.m. tonight.''

Devon stared at him, trying to imagine the judge going to Eternal Peace, putting a large amount of money into the dead man's coffin. "And you did it?''

He nodded. "I was to have you and Jimmy pick

up the package just before midnight. No sooner. The place was being watched just in case I tried to send you earlier."

"The blackmailer asked for me and Jimmy personally?" He wondered if that had any significance. Unfortunately, Judge Wyatt Hathaway was a well-known public figure and over the years, a variety of national newspaper and magazine stories had been done on the two boys the philanthropist had taken from abused homes to raise as his own.

But Devon still couldn't help but take it personally considering that someone had tried to kill him and Jimmy tonight. Had it been an ambush all along? Or had the blonde been a wild card the new blackmailer hadn't counted on?

That's what he had to find out.

"If anyone can find the package and the person behind this..." The old man's voice broke. "I remember the first time I saw you..." His eyes filled. "There was something about you." He shook his head. "You're my only hope, Devon. A scandal of this magnitude wouldn't just ruin my chances for the Louisiana Supreme Court. It would destroy me and I think you know that better than anyone."

Devon looked away, embarrassed for him. In the twenty years he'd been with Wyatt Hathaway, he'd never seen him show any vulnerability. The judge was known for being tough as nails. He had raised Devon and Jimmy, sent them to the best schools and universities and given them well-paid positions at the top of the Hathaway empire.

But he'd never shown them any love. He'd never shown anyone any love, even his lover, Fiona, who Wyatt seemed to have real affection for. He was a hard man, the judge. And yet he'd been the only father Devon had ever known.

Devon's stepfather Ray had been anything but a father to him. In fact, if the judge hadn't gotten Devon away from Ray when he did, Devon would be dead now.

He met the older man's gaze, feeling the full weight of the debt he owed Wyatt Hathaway. They both knew the judge was finally calling in that debt, both knew the price he was being asked to pay.

"I'll take care of it," Devon said. Then they would be even. He didn't say it. Didn't have to.

PAIGE HAD BARELY fallen asleep when the alarm went off, scaring her awake. At first, she'd thought it had all been a bad dream—until she saw the key and piece of notebook paper on the nightstand.

She leapt from the bed and hurried into the bathroom to shower and apply the dark rinse to her hair. Last night she'd worn a gray suit. Today she put on jeans, a red T-shirt, a jean jacket and sneakers.

She applied the makeup as if she really was P.T, slathering the Wild Passion Purple on her lids and coating her pale lashes in black, then painting her full lips bright red. The effect was startling.

Donning the cap and her sunglasses, she stood back and surveyed herself in the mirror. She felt a catch in her throat as she stared at the slim, trim woman in the mirror. It wasn't just the makeup. She was P. T. Alexander!

THE AIRPORT WAS CROWDED, but she didn't see anyone she recognized. She felt a little silly. In the light of day, it was hard to believe that anyone was after her.

She changed planes twice. Not as an evasive maneuver, but simply because that's what it took to get to and from Montana by air, flying from New Orleans to Houston to Denver and finally Gallatin Field outside of Bozeman, Montana.

In every airport she looked for Dark and Dangerous or his driver or the long-haired gunman or the redhead who'd left the package in the coffin. But none of them suddenly appeared next to her to press a cold, hard steel gun barrel to her ribs and tell her in a hoarse whisper not to do anything stupid.

Too late for that anyway.

Feeling like P.T. she surreptitiously studied the other passengers on the planes and in the airports, seeing people who definitely made her suspicious but none who looked like any she'd run across in New Orleans.

When her plane finally touched down at Gallatin Field, she felt such a wave of relief she wanted to cry. Safe if not sound.

As she came out of Gate One—the airport only had a couple of real gates unless a door and a walk on the tarmac counted as a gate—she spotted Chloe Summers waiting for her.

Chloe, a self-proclaimed former actress, magician's assistant and now full-time garage-saler, was as round and soft as an overstuffed chair. She had a cherub face and bright twinkling blue eyes that disappeared in the flesh of her face when she laughed or smiled.

As she walked toward Chloe, she watched the older woman look past her to other arriving travelers—and Paige realized that Chloe didn't recognize her! The realization thrilled her! Her disguise had worked.

Feeling more like P. T. Alexander than she'd ever imagined possible, she waltzed past Chloe, then turned to tap her on the shoulder.

Chloe turned, squinting, recognition coming with a slowness that satisfied Paige to no end.

She pulled off her cap and shook out her dark hair. "So what do you think?"

Chloe stared, obviously speechless. "What in the…world?" She laughed. "Got tired of your old look, did you?"

"Something like that."

Chloe studied her. "I like it. We could all use a change once in a while." She enveloped Paige in a hug as if they were old friends.

On arriving in Big Timber, Paige had found the robust middle-aged woman sitting on the steps of Rare Finds. Without a word, Chloe had pulled Paige into her ample arms. Paige had never laid eyes on the woman before.

"I knew your mother," Chloe had announced, explaining that she'd recognized Paige from a photograph Simone had showed her. "Simone and I were best friends. I heard you were coming in today to make arrangements. I came by to help."

Paige had never known her mother to have a "best" friend. Actually, Simone had avoided making friends everywhere she and Paige had lived, always saying it was best not to, since she wouldn't be staying anywhere long enough to make real friends.

Chloe had insisted on brewing Paige up a cup of her famous Feel Better tea. The tea had actually helped although Paige could not imagine her mother and this woman being friends—let alone best friends.

"So how are you?" Chloe asked now as they descended the stairs to the baggage carousel.

"Okay." Paige wasn't sure how much she wanted to tell Chloe. As far as Paige could tell her mother hadn't confided much in her "best friend." As a matter of fact, Chloe hadn't said a word about Simone's battle with cancer, something a best friend would be aware of. But then her mother was good at keeping secrets, wasn't she?

While Paige would have loved to confide in someone, she wasn't sure she trusted Chloe enough. Nor was she prepared to talk about it in a crowded airport.

Paige found herself watching the crowd, not that she expected to see Dark and Dangerous or any of the others. Most of the travelers wore ski jackets or the latest in fly fishing attire, carried bags of skis and snowboards or metal tubes with fly fishing rods encased inside. Several large dogs cavorted through the terminal, while shuttle drivers from resorts held up signs with their anticipated guests' names on them.

Paige and Chloe took a spot behind everyone in the corner out of earshot. Nowhere in the throng did Paige see Dark and Dangerous or anyone else she'd crossed paths with in New Orleans. Maybe she really was safe.

"You never said whose funeral it was," Chloe said as they waited.

Paige hadn't told Chloe anything. She'd been leaving for the airport when her mother's friend had stopped by Rare Finds and insisted on giving her a ride. At the time, Paige had been so upset that she'd agreed to let Chloe take her to the airport rather than drive her mother's large four-wheel-drive SUV.

Paige had had such mixed feelings about going to New Orleans, about seeing her father, about her mother lying about his death, she hadn't told anyone where she was going or why, except for her mother's lawyer, Franklin Cole. And of course he'd tried to talk her out of it.

"I went to my father's funeral," Paige told Chloe now.

The older woman looked surprised. "I thought he died last year, right before your mother moved to Big Timber." So her mother had told Chloe that much.

"That was my stepfather." Harry "Gray" Grayson had been a quiet, introverted man who Paige always suspected had greatly regretted his hasty marriage to Simone. Gray had played a non-role in their lives, most often sitting in a chair somewhere reading, forgotten. Her mother had actually seemed relieved at his passing, making Paige wonder why Simone had married him in the first place.

"My mother told me my biological father died twenty-three years ago, when I was three," Paige confided as the baggage carousel began to move. Suitcases thumped out of the plastic curtain and were instantly swarmed on to a dissonance of excited chatter. "But it appears she exaggerated about that."

Chloe let out a snort. "Yeah, a funeral twenty-three years later is kinda like closing the barn door after the cow got out, isn't it? So you saw him?"

Paige nodded.

"That's it?"

She shrugged. "Pretty much."

Chloe was eyeing her again, maybe just trying to read something into the new look.

Paige had to admit she felt different. Every time she caught her reflection, she was taken aback, but pleased. She liked being P. T. Alexander much better than Paige Grayson, although right now she felt more like her old boring self than she wanted to admit.

She spotted her red suitcase come through the plastic blind and start around the carousel. "Be right back,'' she told Chloe. She hadn't taken two steps when a brightly colored ball careened across the carpet in front of her, making her stumble to a stop to avoid it—and the two young children—chasing after it.

Just then a dog came bounding after the ball and the kids, jostling Paige before she could take another step. Chloe picked up the ball and hurriedly threw it down the open hallway toward the rental car agencies before the dog and children reached her.

The dog and the excited yelling kids tore off after the ball to the shrill cry of their mother's protests for them to stop running around like wild animals.

Paige smiled, bemused by the fact that Montanans brought their retrievers into the airport for a romp. She watched the dog, a young chocolate brown Labrador, lope along ahead of the laughing children. She'd never had a dog of her own, but had always desperately wanted one. Unfortunately, it would have been impractical, not to mention cruel, to have a dog cooped up in an apartment in San Francisco all day while she worked.

When she turned back to the baggage carousel, she didn't see her suitcase. At first she thought the conveyor must have been moving more quickly than she'd thought. But when she looked around the stone pillar, no red bag.

The crowd of travelers thinned quickly. Only a couple of suitcases and an army duffel circled on the carousel.

Her bag was gone!

The carousel stopped.

"What's wrong?" Chloe asked as she joined her.

"My bag. I know I saw it come out, but now I can't find it," she said, looking at the departing passengers to see if she could spot the suitcase. "It's bright red so it's hard to miss."

"Airlines are always losing luggage," Chloe said. "It must have been someone else's red bag you saw."

Paige couldn't be sure Chloe wasn't right. But neither could she throw off the fear she'd felt the moment she saw the bag was gone.

"Come on, let's go find out what happened to it," Chloe said. "Probably missed the flight. Don't worry, they'll find it. You're insured, right?"

Her legs suddenly felt like water.

"Are you all right?" Chloe asked, looking concerned. "What was in the suitcase? Nothing you can't replace, I hope."

Paige felt faint realizing how close she'd come to putting the key and note into the suitcase. But at the last minute, she put both in the pocket of her jean jacket, afraid to have them out of her sight until she could find out their significance.

"No, nothing irreplaceable," she managed to say as they walked down the terminal to the airline's ticket counter. She told the clerk what the bag looked like and gave her the baggage claim ticket.

"Did it have any identification on it?" the woman behind the counter inquired.

Paige felt her throat go dry as she remembered.

"It had a tag with my name and address. A large red tag." Anyone who got close to the bag would have seen that it was hers. But maybe someone had been watching her this morning at the airport counter in New Orleans and seen her check the small red luggage. Also watched her remove the key from her jacket pocket at the security check and run it through the metal detector.

She realized that just because she hadn't recognized anyone on the flight, it didn't mean that someone hadn't followed her. Or maybe they'd been here waiting for her.

She left her name, address and phone number with the clerk, all the time fairly certain the airline hadn't lost her luggage. Someone had taken the bag thinking the small box would be inside.

Someone was here in Montana—looking for the key…looking for her. How long would it take before they found her?

CHAPTER FIVE

THE TERMINAL WAS ALMOST EMPTY by the time Paige and Chloe left. Paige looked for anyone carrying a piece of red luggage.

She knew it was futile. If she was right and someone had taken her bag, it was long gone. And by now the thief would know the box wasn't in the suitcase and would be checking out her address.

Fortunately, the tag on her suitcase still had her San Francisco address on it from when she'd flown to Big Timber just days ago.

Unfortunately, her former landlady in San Francisco was a sweet but overly trusting elderly woman who would give out Paige's forwarding address to anyone who asked nicely.

But that would take time.

Which meant Paige was safe. As long as no one followed her back to Rare Finds. Or unless they already knew where she was headed.

She shivered as she and Chloe stepped outside into the growing darkness. The air was cool, the snow-capped mountains etched against the last of the sunset. Lights winked on across the wide valley, the Valley of the Flowers, Chloe had told her, named by the Native Americans who had lived here.

Paige breathed in the smell of spring, fighting tears. She wasn't equipped for whatever was happening in her life. First her mother's death, then her father's and now she had killers after her. The key felt like a weight in her pocket as heavy and deadly as cement shoes in a river, but no more than the piece of paper with her mother's handwriting on it telling someone where to find her.

It was an hour's drive from Gallatin Field to the town of Big Timber. Chloe had brought her garage sale rig, a large bright yellow painted panel van with dozens of bumper stickers. This Vehicle Stops at All Garage Sales. Garage Sale Goddess. Your Trash is My Treasure. I Live to Garage Sale.

The van was nothing if not conspicuous. Following it couldn't be easier unless it had a flashing Follow This Car sign on top.

"Have you decided what you're going to do with Rare Finds?" Chloe asked as they reached the van.

Paige was busy watching the other cars leaving the lot. No one seemed to be paying them any mind as she and Chloe climbed into the front of the van. Paige glanced behind her seat. The rear of the van was filled with used furniture: a bunch of old wooden chairs in the back, a small drop-leaf table, a bureau and a primitive kitchen cabinet.

"I hit a few garage sales today, waiting for you to get back," Chloe said with a smile. "See anything you want?"

Paige shook her head. Chloe seemed to think she

was going to run the antique shop and buy items from her like her mother had supposedly done.

"I was thinking," the older woman said after a few miles. "If you're going to sell the shop, I might be interested."

That surprised Paige. Chloe had given her the impression that she lived on a rather limited income, subsidized by buying and selling stuff she picked up at garage sales and auctions.

"I haven't had a chance to even think about the future," Paige said, realizing how true that was.

"Well, keep me in mind," Chloe said as they drove east. Not far down the old highway, Chloe got on Interstate 90 at Bozeman and headed for the pass through the mountains.

Paige watched the car lights behind them, looking for any car that hung back. None seemed to. She thought of Rare Finds. "Why didn't you buy it from the people who sold it to my mother?"

"The Martins?" Chloe said and glanced over at her. "Your mother already had her foot in the door before I heard it was up for grabs."

It was so unlike her mother to buy a business, let alone one that involved four stories of antiques and collectibles. This from a woman who always liked to travel—and travel light? Had her mother changed that much? Or had Paige just not really known her?

Paige touched the jean jacket pocket, thinking about the key, wondering if it fit something inside the house. If the key went with the note, then it led right to Rare Finds—and her.

"What would you do with the place if you didn't sell it?" Chloe asked as the van slowed for the climb over Bozeman Pass. "I can't see you living in Big Timber. Not after San Francisco."

Chloe was right. While what few people Paige had met so far were friendly, Big Timber was the last place she would have chosen to live. Historically, it was a sheep ranching town. Probably why the high school team was called, what else, the Sheepherders.

The downtown was only about three blocks square with several bars, a hotel, a couple of restaurants, a bowling alley and a theater. The economy appeared to be based on tourism—and sheep ranching.

But Paige also hadn't left anything behind in San Francisco. She'd never felt at home there or any other place. But she especially didn't like the fog and dampness. In truth, she had nowhere she had to be. No plans. No life to get back to. It had been easy to quit her job at the cell phone company, give up her apartment and have what little she'd collected shipped to Big Timber after her mother's death. That was one thing she'd always had in common with her mother: she knew how to travel light.

Unfortunately, she hadn't learned the knack of collecting friends any more than she had collecting belongings.

As they dropped off the pass on the Livingston side, Chloe picked up a little speed, but soon slowed again as Livingston's notorious wind slammed into the van.

Paige watched the cars behind them. One after another passed the bright yellow slower moving van. No one seemed to be following them.

"With the money from the shop, you could take a trip," Chloe said as she drove. "Go somewhere warm and tropical and sip drinks with umbrellas in them and have wild affairs with strange men."

"Whose fantasy is this anyway?" Paige asked with a laugh as she looked over at the woman.

Chloe chuckled, eyes disappearing for a moment, before she sobered. "You're too young to tie yourself down to some musty, old business. You need to kick up your heels, have a little fun, live a little." She glanced over at Paige. "Your mother used to worry about you. She said you were too serious."

As a gust of wind rocked the van, Chloe turned her attention back to the highway, missing Paige's shocked expression as she tried to imagine her mother saying anything remotely like that. In fact, it had always been just the opposite. "Snap out of it. Stop daydreaming. You can't go through life with your head in the clouds. One of these days you're going to walk in front of a bus, if you don't start paying more attention," she'd say.

Paige had always suspected her mother was afraid her daughter would turn out like her. Rootless. Lost. Just drifting through life without goals or ambition or…passion.

"Someday, I hope you'll be able to go anywhere

you want and stay as long as you like," her mother had said to the then tearful thirteen-year-old Paige as they packed for yet another undecided destination. "But I can't. We can't."

"Why?" Paige had demanded angrily.

Simone had touched her daughter's tear-slicked cheek. "It's just not possible. It's just not me. I get...restless."

As Paige stared out the window at the darkness, she wondered if it had been restlessness. Or was it possible her mother had been running from something?

Ahead, she could see the lights of Big Timber. The small town looked so isolated, Paige couldn't help but think about selling the shop and just taking off.

But wasn't that exactly what she was genetically programmed to do? Her father had just taken off, and her mother couldn't stay put for more than a few months. Had her mother still been alive, Paige figured she'd probably have been packing right now. The novelty would have worn off Rare Finds and her mother would be looking for someplace different.

Paige wondered if it had been her mother who'd left Michael instead of the other way around? Was it possible she and her mother had spent those twenty-three years running from him?

She thought of those years. Even though she'd had her mother, she'd been lonely, finding solace in food and daydreaming. When had she begun to live vicariously through her imaginary alter ego P. T. Alexander? It seemed the brave and capable P.T. had always been with her. Of course she'd find fantasy life preferable to real life given whose daughter she was.

"I can't just take off," she said more to herself than to Chloe.

The older woman shot her a look. "Why not?"

"Because not all of us can spend our lives running away from unpleasantness," Paige said suddenly angry with her parents, with herself.

Chloe said nothing as she took the first exit into Big Timber.

Paige didn't know anything about running an antique shop, but she could learn, she thought, then wondered why she'd want to. Owning an antique shop had never been *her* dream. She'd always craved excitement and adventure. She couldn't see finding either in Big Timber, Montana.

Nor could she be sure Rare Finds had been her mother's dream. So why take it on? Just to prove she wasn't like her parents and could stick with something?

Chloe drove the van into town, turned through the downtown and headed south toward McLeod. The old Victorian house stood surrounded by huge old cottonwoods. Behind the house the yard dropped to the Boulder River. It was far enough out of town that there were no close neighbors. Paige was surprised shoppers found the place, but Chloe said Rare

Finds did a fine business, especially during the summer tourist season.

The towering four-story house had once belonged to a rich sheep rancher at the turn of the century, according to Chloe. A single large yard light illuminated the front of the house, the trees casting long shadows across the lawn. The exterior had once been painted white but the paint had grayed. The trim was a variety of colors: pinks, blues, greens, yellows as if the last owners couldn't make up their minds. All of the colors were faded, making the place look a little sad by day, haunted by night.

Tonight it looked downright scary. Too isolated, just like the town, with the snowcapped Crazy Mountains behind it. Wind moaned in the cottonwoods. In the darkness, the Boulder River whispered past on its way to join the Yellowstone on the other side of town.

Paige felt a chill. Why *had* her mother purchased Rare Finds? And would this key she now gripped in her pocket release the secret? Or would it just open something that was better left locked away?

"Let me know if you need any help," Chloe said. "I didn't mean to pressure you about selling. It's just that your mom and I were close and I've always loved the place."

Paige wished Chloe and her mother *had* been close. Chloe might be the only friend her mother ever had. And her last. She thanked Chloe for picking her up at the airport and promised to get back to her about Rare Finds.

On the way through Big Timber, Paige had watched the traffic behind them in her side mirror. They hadn't been followed. She was sure of it.

And yet as she got out of the van and walked to the porch, she felt as if more eyes than Chloe's watched her. She unlocked the door, fumbling a little with the set of keys, her fingers trembling from more than the cold March night air.

Turning on a light, she stepped in and closed the door behind her, locking it and sliding the deadbolt into place. For a moment, she leaned against the door, staring at the lower floor of the house. It was packed with antique furniture, leaving only narrow walkways in between cabinets stuffed with glassware, shelves thick with collectibles and crocks spilling over with anything remotely old. The other two floors above were no better. Fortunately, the fourth floor, where her mother had lived, wasn't as bad.

She headed for the stairs. The house had an elevator, a small, dark old thing that clanked and groaned and frightened Paige out of her wits. She avoided it at all costs, much preferring to take the center stairs up the three flights.

On the fourth floor, she stopped on the wide landing to look back down the circular staircase. It really was a beautiful old house. She wondered when it had been made into an antique shop. It must have been beautiful as a home before all of the living area had been crammed into the top floor.

She opened the door at the end of the landing that closed off the shop from the apartment.

Everything looked just as she'd left it. Her book lay open on the couch in the living room, her coffee cup and saucer on the kitchen counter next to her plate with toast crumbs on it. She'd been too anxious and nervous to even rinse off her dishes before catching the flight.

She looked around the living room, seeing nothing that even needed a key. In the couple of days she'd been here, she'd felt as if she was just visiting, visiting someone she hadn't known well. Still grieving, she hadn't been up to going through her mother's things—or even into her mother's bedroom. It had hurt too much.

She'd slept in the spare room that her mother had obviously furnished for her.

Now though, she realized she would have to search the entire house. It seemed an impossible task, and she felt paralyzed at the thought. Why hadn't she confided in Chloe? She wouldn't have to do this alone.

The phone rang, making her jump. She picked up the receiver, almost afraid of whose voice she'd hear at the other end of the line. "Hello?"

"Ms....Grayson?" Franklin Cole's voice sounded strange, hesitant, as if surprised she'd been the one to answer the phone. Who else did her mother's lawyer expect to answer?

"Yes?" She felt just as hesitant, wondering why Franklin was calling now, this late. How had he even known she was back? Could Chloe have called him? Paige felt her overactive imagination take off, seeing a conspiracy that involved the entire town.

She moved to the window to look out. It was too dark to see much out the back. With Rare Finds at the edge of town and at the end of the road, there was only the one yard light out front, no streetlights, no other house lights. Just the leafless cottonwood trees, limbs etched black against the cold March night sky, and the sheen of the river through the bare branches.

If she really did decide to stay here, she'd get a dog. A big dog. And maybe a state-of-the-art security system. And a Beretta.

Or maybe she'd sell this place to Chloe.

"I'm sorry, for a moment I forgot what number I dialed," the elderly attorney said with a small embarrassed laugh.

Paige moved away from the window. "I've done that," she said kindly and waited for him to tell her why he'd called so late.

"I assume the letter regarding Michael Alexander's funeral proved to be accurate?" he asked.

"Yes," she said, thinking how much she resembled her father. No mistake there.

Franklin cleared his throat. "I discovered something that might be pertinent to your inquires."

She'd ask him to find out whatever he could about her father while she was gone. "What is it?"

"I think it would be best to discuss it in person," he said. "I could be there in ten minutes?"

This seemed so unlike the man she'd come to know in the days she'd been here. She knew she wasn't going to want to hear what he had to tell her and was filled with dread. "That would be fine." She hung up, even more afraid.

Ten minutes later on the dot, she opened the front door for Franklin Cole. It was hard to judge his age. The pink of his skull showed through his thin snow-white hair and his translucent skin appeared lined by the years rather than weather and sun.

He chose to ride the elevator. She took the stairs, both of them reaching the fourth floor at the same time.

Franklin wore his usual: a black suit, crisp white shirt, dark nondescript tie and freshly polished black shoes. In his wrinkled small white hands he clutched the handle of his black leather briefcase.

He could have been an undertaker.

Or the angel of death.

Leave it to P.T. to think of that.

Franklin glanced at her, momentarily taken aback, and she remembered then that she was still a brunette, still wearing Wild Passion Purple eyeshadow, still P.T. Kinda.

He didn't comment on the change in her. He just sat gingerly on the edge of the dark green antique mohair sofa in the room her mother used as a living room, balancing the briefcase on his narrow knees.

Paige took a chair across from him, his grim expression making her knees weak. "You found out something about my father," she prompted.

He nodded solemnly and opened his briefcase. "I employ a private investigator who is very discreet." Was that supposed to make her feel better? "Michael Ramone Alexander died in Billings twenty-three years ago—just as you were led to believe."

She couldn't hide her surprise. "I just saw him in New Orleans."

Franklin cleared his throat. "A Michael Ramone Alexander was murdered in New Orleans four days ago."

Murdered. Four days ago. She felt sick. Her mother's hit-and-run accident had been the same day as his murder.

"The fingerprints of the man in New Orleans matched those of Michael Ramone Alexander who was believed to have died in Billings twenty-three years ago." Franklin tugged at his shirt collar as if his tie was too tight. "It seems Michael Ramone Alexander escaped two weeks ago from a South American prison where he had been incarcerated the last twenty-three years for killing a man."

It could get worse, it seemed. Her father *had* been a criminal. A murderer. No wonder her mother had told her he was dead.

Franklin cleared his throat. He was sweating and the black briefcase jiggled on his knees, his knuckles white as if he were trying to hold it still. "After your father's initial death, your mother disappeared—on paper."

"Disappeared?" Paige asked.

"Yes, until she became Simone Grayson, no middle name, a year later," he said.

"You mean she disappeared until she married Gray? Oh, no, her marriage would have been illegal since my father was still alive, but maybe she didn't know that."

Franklin shook his head. "There is no record of a marriage to Harry 'Gray' Grayson."

Paige stared at him. She'd suspected after reading the letter informing her mother about Michael Alexander's death that her mother and father had never divorced. That would explain why the letter had referred to Michael as her mother's "husband" instead of *ex*-husband.

The attorney appeared even more distressed. "I'm afraid, as far as my investigator was able to ascertain, no person by the name of Harry Grayson ever existed."

She opened her mouth to argue then closed it. "Who was he then?"

Franklin shook his head.

"Then if I'm not Paige Grayson—"

"You are technically Paige Teresa Grayson although your identification was…fabricated as far as we can tell," Franklin said. He looked pained as if he found this kind of thing repugnant. "Like your mother, you ceased to exist for the year after your father's…initial death. Then you were reborn, so to speak, a year later with a false identity as Paige Grayson. You were given a social security number and basically, an existence."

Paige got to her feet and began to pace. "I can't believe this."

"I'm sure it comes as a bit of a shock."

"A bit of a shock? My mother lied to me about everything. *Everything.*" She turned on him. "She never told you any of this?"

He looked mortified at the thought. "I knew nothing of your mother's personal life. I simply drew up her last will and testament for her."

"This can't be right. There has to be some mistake."

He shook his head. "There is no mistake." He snapped the briefcase shut and got to his feet.

Paige felt as if he'd punched her in the stomach. "How is it possible?"

"I suppose with enough money...." Franklin headed for the elevator, obviously anxious to conclude his business and leave.

"Are you saying my mother bought us fake identities—just like that?"

The lawyer shrugged. "I wouldn't know anything about that sort of thing." It was obvious he didn't want to know. She couldn't blame him.

"Thank you for coming over," she said as she saw him to the elevator, then took the stairs down to let him out and lock up behind him.

She watched him leave from the window. The sound of his car engine died off in the distance leaving nothing but the unsettling stillness of the house. She'd always lived in big cities, was used to other people, their sounds, their lights, their movement.

Here she might catch the honk of a flock of geese flying over the river. Or hear an occasional truck shifting down on the highway.

She stared out the window until Franklin's taillights disappeared, trying to make sense out of everything he'd told her. All she could feel was a terrible sense of loss. Her parents were both dead. Her life was a lie. She wasn't even the person she thought she was.

And someone was after her. After her and the key.

She couldn't be sure there wasn't already someone out there, someone who'd found out where she was and was now watching the house, watching her.

Pulling down the shade, she was suddenly aware of just how alone she was. More alone than she'd ever been. There was no one she could call. She thought about calling the police, but even if her name and identity weren't false, she still wouldn't know what to tell them.

That she'd been shot at in New Orleans but hadn't reported it? That her suitcase was missing? That she suspected someone was after her because she'd taken something from a casket? Something a lot of people seemed to want.

Fear swept over her as her fingers closed on the key in her jacket pocket. Her whole life had been a lie and now she feared the key fit a Pandora's box that she would wish she'd never opened.

The problem was, she had a bad feeling the box was already open, had been blown open by her mother's hit-and-run, her father's murder. Maybe she had always been next.

She felt cold to the bone and scared. It was only a matter of time before someone showed up looking for the key—and whatever secrets it unlocked.

That's why you don't have time to stand around feeling sorry for yourself.

Good old P.T.

You have to find out what the key fits. Tonight.

She gave herself a mental shake. As many antiques as were packed into this house, only a few would have keyholes. She could start on the first floor and work her way up.

Just the idea of doing something, made her feel a little better. If any of the answers she desperately sought were in this old house behind a locked door, she'd find them, she thought determinedly.

Taking the flashlight from behind the front counter where she'd seen it the first day, she began her search. She'd expected it to take longer than it did. But she'd been right. Not that many of the antiques had keyholes or locks, especially locks large enough to accommodate a key the size of the one she'd found in the box.

She was tired and dusty by the time she reached the fourth floor apartment. Fortunately her mother had fewer items on this floor since this was where she'd lived. The search took less time, but was just as fruitless.

Standing in the middle of the living room, she realized there was only one room left to look in—

her mother's bedroom. The door was closed, just as Paige had left it. She hadn't been able to look inside, knowing she wasn't ready to face it. What few personal things her mother had kept over the years would be behind that door. Paige still wasn't ready.

But now she had no choice. It was only a matter of time before whoever had stolen her suitcase found Rare Finds—and her. And who knew how many others were after her.

She walked to the closed door, bracing herself for the familiar scents, the wave of memories her mother's things would evoke, the regrets, the sorrow and grief waiting behind that door.

Slowly she turned the knob. The door creaked open.

She reached in and snapped on the light switch. Her breath caught in her throat.

CHAPTER SIX

THIS COULDN'T BE her mother's room. Paige stared in shock and confusion at what was obviously a young girl's room, a stranger's room.

There was a white canopy bed covered in pink eyelet, stuffed animals piled everywhere and a row of pristine dolls on a shelf over the bureau. It looked like a room that a child had just stepped out of and would be back to any moment.

Paige moved deeper into the room. Whose room was this? She stopped, her gaze lighting on a painting hanging over the bed, her heart lodged in her throat.

The painting of the little girl was old, the clothing dated. Paige stepped closer and froze. It was her mother! The little girl in the painting was her mother when Simone was about six.

Paige had never seen any pictures of her mother when Simone was young and was shocked to see that her mother had red hair.

Paige stared, mesmerized. Her mother had always had the complexion of a redhead, now that Paige thought about it. But her mother's hair had been dark brown.

Her mother had dyed her hair! The realization struck her like a slap. Why had her mother done that? To become someone else as Paige had done? Or to hide from something?

Maybe the past, Paige thought as she looked at the painting and wondered why she'd never seen it before. Where had it been all these years?

She turned to look at the room and saw that everything here was old. Her gaze fell on a large fur-worn teddy bear on the bed, one of its plastic eyes worn milky. She picked it up and pressed it to her face, closing her eyes. She'd had a teddy bear when she was little. Boo Bear. The memory came out of nowhere. Whatever had happened to Boo Bear?

This bear had been her mother's. She could smell her scent on it.

She opened her eyes, her heart swelling. Everything in this room had been her mother's when she was a girl! The idea stunned her but she knew it was true. The same way she knew that it had all been hidden away somewhere all these years. How much more of the things in the house had been her mother's? Or her mother's family's?

She touched the painting over the bed. The frame slid over a half inch and she saw the brighter color of the wall beneath it. Her heart jumped.

All of her mother's things hadn't been hidden. They'd been here the whole time—in this house. What had Chloe said about wanting to buy Rare Finds from the Martins, but that Simone had her foot in the door?

Was it possible the Martins had been Paige's grandparents?

The thought made her slump onto the pine bench beside the bed next to the worn stuffed animals. This had been her mother's room. She was sure of it. That meant this had been her mother's house when she was a girl.

The shock left her numb. Franklin had told her that Michael Alexander died in Billings. Not an hour and a half away. Why else would her mother, out of the blue, buy a house in Big Timber, Montana? After twenty-three years of lies and deceptions, her mother had come home.

Come home to die, Paige thought with a shudder.

She wiped her eyes and slowly got to her feet. Everything in this room was from a past Paige hadn't known existed. It was like losing her mother all over again, coming in here, and losing grandparents she had never known.

There was nothing in this room of the mother she'd recognized, either, a restless sad woman who hadn't seemed to value roots or family tradition or human contact other than Paige and even that had been a strain sometimes.

Paige started toward the bureau but stopped as a memory took her. Her mother sitting by the window, Paige coloring on the floor, looking up, shocked to see her mother crying. Her mother never cried. Hardly ever showed any emotion…other than sadness.

"What's wrong, Mommy?"

Her mother had looked startled as if she'd forgotten about Paige. She'd hurriedly dried her eyes, then pulled her little daughter to her, hugging her tightly. "I'm so sorry, so sorry," she whispered into Paige's hair. "I love you but sometimes I'm afraid to love you too much, afraid I'll lose you, too. I wish you were old enough to understand."

"You won't lose me, Mommy," Paige cried. "You won't ever lose me."

She brushed the tears from her cheeks now and opened the top bureau drawer, looking for something of the mother she might recognize here in this room. There was nothing but new lingerie, scarves, nightgowns— Her hand froze. Carefully she picked up the small gold jewelry box at the back. It was one of the few things her mother had always kept with her.

With trembling fingers, Paige opened it to see earrings she remembered her mother wearing. And there was the cheap watch Paige had given her for a birthday years ago. Why had her mother hung on to it after it broke?

She pushed it aside and saw the wedding ring. Not the diamond Gray had given her mother when they married. This wedding ring was a wide plain gold band with something inscribed inside.

Her fingers shook as she plucked it from the nest of earrings. She could barely make out the words. "For Always, Michael."

Paige closed her eyes, closing her hand around the ring. She'd never seen it on her mother's finger.

Never seen it before today. Why had her mother kept the wedding ring hidden along with everything else about Michael Alexander?

She opened her eyes. The diamond ring from Gray was nowhere to be seen. Impulsively, she unhooked the silver spirit bear necklace she wore. Her mother had given it to her for luck. She slipped the ring on the silver chain along with the small bear and put the necklace back on.

A creak of old floorboards floated up from deep within the house making her jump. She hated old houses and all the noises they made. She put the jewelry box back and closed the dresser drawer.

As she passed the window on the way to the closet, she noticed that the wind had kicked up even more. The bare dark branches of the cottonwoods scraped softly against the windowpane.

She opened the closet door, almost afraid of what she'd find. But inside, she saw a dress and a jacket she remembered her mother wearing. She pressed one of the sleeves of the jacket to her cheek, the scent of her mother still alive in the cloth.

Could it be true? Could this be her mother's childhood home? After all the years of refusing to accumulate anything that wouldn't fit in two suitcases and never staying in one place for more than a few months, her mother had come home to this treasure trove of memories.

Because she was dying.

Paige let out a sob and buried her face in the

fabric. Why hadn't her mother told her? About the cancer? About all the rest of it?

Maybe her mother had planned to tell her. That's why she'd called and said she would be flying to San Francisco to see her. Then why fly to Florida first?

Paige let go of the jacket sleeve and started to close the closet door, exhausted. Her head hurt and she was heartsick. The key was still in her jean jacket pocket, weighting her down with worry. She had to find out what it fit, find out why all of this was happening, why her mother had lied for so many years, why her parents were dead and why her name and this address had been in the box she'd taken from the coffin.

Her mother's jacket sleeve got caught in the closet door. She pulled the door open again and started to push the fabric back when she caught sight of something on the floor.

No, not on the floor, but sticking out of the wooden planks—the corner of a black and white photograph.

She stooped down and pried the photo free. At first Paige didn't recognize her own mother. She held the black-and-white snapshot. It was her mother and a man. Her mother was smiling into the camera, her hair obviously lighter even in black and white. Paige had never seen her mother look that happy.

She shifted her gaze to the man and felt that same stab of recognition she'd had at the funeral home. Her father. He'd been so young. The two of them looked heartbreakingly happy. He had his arm around her mother, but instead of looking at the camera, he had his eyes on Simone, the look of love on his face almost more than Paige could stand.

They'd been happy. This photograph proved it. Her mother was leaning into him, contentment in every line of her body and—Paige saw something that stilled her heart. The glint of the gold band on her mother's hand, the hand over her mother's protruding stomach. Her mother had been pregnant!

Paige began to cry again as she got a kitchen knife and pried the wooden planks of the closet floor up, but there were no more photographs. Just a small cardboard box with tiny black corners that had once held other snapshots in an album, the box now empty of all photos.

She glanced around the room, aching for the photos she knew had existed. Why keep everything else, but not the old photographs? Because everything here was from her childhood—not her marriage to Michael Alexander. Nothing in this room tied her to Michael...or Paige.

Why was that? To protect them? Or herself?

Paige realized she'd been right the first time. This was a stranger's room, a woman she'd never known. It was inconceivable how much her mother had kept from her. Why?

Because something happened twenty-three years ago.

She turned out the light, and taking the photo with her, closed her mother's door to go back into the living room. The police in St. Petersburg, Florida, where her mother had been killed by the hit-and-run driver had mailed Paige her mother's purse in a large manila envelope.

Paige had only glanced inside, seen the small tan leather purse, then closed the envelope and put it in the top drawer of an end table near the couch.

Now she retrieved the envelope, sat down on the couch and pulled out the purse.

Somewhere deep in the house something creaked, making Paige jump. Behind her, a bare cottonwood branch scraped against the window. Her nerves felt raw as she opened the purse. It had only one compartment.

Inside it, she found a wallet with over three hundred dollars in cash. No credit cards. No driver's license. How had her mother been able to get on a plane without some sort of identification? Or had someone removed the identification after running her down in the street?

Paige shivered. Outside, the wind whistled through the eaves. Deep in the house, something creaked again.

She tried to ignore the noises. They'd kept her up the first few nights, the old house moaning and groaning, reminding her of an old man. She'd been terrified but finally accepted that it was nothing more than the house settling. That's what old houses did. Tonight though, the house's complaints seemed more ominous.

She dumped the contents of her mother's purse

into her lap. Tissues, mints, address book, airline ticket. The address book opened right to where a page had been torn out. Her mother's ticket to San Francisco was still inside the folder, unused. Several scraps of paper spilled out, fluttering to the floor. As she reached to pick them up, she noticed that one was a crudely torn-out newspaper clipping.

As she unfolded it, she wondered why it had been with her mother's airline ticket. Frowning, she stared down at a grainy color photograph of a circus performance. The shot was from the *Orlando Sentinel*. There was no accompanying story—just a caption.

It was a photo of a woman on an elephant. Behind her someone was performing on the trapeze. A clown juggled balls off to the right. At the center was the ringmaster. The cutline read: Barney Adams's Amazing One-Ring Circus and Carnival comes to the Orange Grove Center for a preseason opener. Ringmaster Antonio Fuentes brings chills and thrills to kids of all ages.

It was dated just days before her mother's death.

Where had her mother gotten this? And why save it?

Paige reached down to pick up the other scrap of paper that had fallen out of the ticket folder. At first she thought it was only the stub from a boarding pass, but saw it was a ticket from a Barney Adams's Circus performance in St. Petersburg, Florida. The same circus company as the one in the newspaper photo.

Her mother had gone to Florida to attend the *circus?*

A floorboard creaked, louder this time.

Paige glanced toward the large window at the back of the house. No moon. No stars. Just the occasional flash of lightning in the distance. A storm was coming. She could feel the electricity in the air even in here.

She reached up to turn on another of the bulbs in the floor lamp beside the couch, hoping to chase away more than the dark. The last thing she needed tonight was this old house and its noises.

She put all of her mother's things back into the purse except for the newspaper clipping someone must have sent her mother and the circus ticket. On impulse, she checked the date her mother had purchased the airline tickets. Simone would have had to have hopped on a plane and flown to Florida right after receiving the newspaper photo in the mail.

Why would her mother do that? Simone had never liked the circus. So what would possess her to go now? Was it possible she knew someone in the photo? Someone she wanted to see before she died?

Not the woman Paige had known. If her mother had friends in the circus, Paige would have been aware of them. Or would she have, given what she'd only recently discovered about her mother?

Paige picked up the photograph of her parents, then the clipping and ticket. A tremor rattled through her as she looked at the performance times on the circus ticket. Her mother had been killed by a hit-and-run driver just minutes after the performance.

Something crashed to the floor far below her. Paige jumped, then froze. Just the wind.

The wind in the house?

A groan, like a door opening. A soft thump. Another thump, this one louder as if someone had bumped into a piece of furniture in the dark.

Her pulse quickened. She strained to hear, holding her breath. The floorboards creaked again and again. Someone *was* in the house!

She couldn't move. Couldn't breathe.

Panicked, she stuffed everything into her purse and grabbed the phone from the end table beside her. She started to dial 9-1-1. No dial tone. The floor lamp went out. The room went black.

She reached for the switch, thinking she must have bumped it. Every cell in her wanted to just sit on the couch and scream for help, as fruitless and stupid as that would have been. The lamp wouldn't come back on.

A flashlight. She'd left the one she'd used to search the dark corners of the house on the end table next to the overstuffed chair.

Slipping off the couch, Paige crept across the room to the end table, stubbing her toe on the chair leg. *Ouch.* She felt around blindly, found the heavy-duty flashlight and thumbed the switch. Watch the batteries be dead.

A sob of relief escaped as the light came on.

That's when she saw the door to the apartment.

It was open! She'd forgotten to close and lock it after Franklin left.

She stared past the doorway to the wide landing at the top of the circular staircase expecting to see someone appear at any moment.

Her first instinct was to scream. Her second to get that door closed and locked. But then she caught her reflection in the window glass and saw P.T. staring back at her.

You close that door and whoever is down there will hear it and know where you are. Anyway, a flimsy door like that won't buy you enough time.

Right now any amount of time sounded wonderful.

Hide the key.

Screw the key.

Once they have the key and you...

Point well taken.

Her heart beat like a trapped bird as she shone the light around, looking for a place to hide the stolen key.

Some place in plain sight.

Such as?

On the lamp cord.

She pulled the key from her pocket, listening to the footsteps far below her as someone moved through the house, her hands shaking. In the flashlight beam, the gold droplet at the end of the lamp cord was almost the same color as the key. Fake gold color.

She clumsily wove the ornate key through the

cord, tying the end with the droplet. Amazing. It looked as if the key had come with the lamp.

Footsteps on the stairs. Help!

Find something you can use as a weapon.

A weapon? It would be so much easier if she owned a Beretta. Better still if she knew how to shoot it.

And could actually pull the trigger if you needed to?

That too.

She shone the flashlight beam around the room filled with mostly Western antiques. No shotgun hanging on the wall. No bow and arrows. No tomahawk. Not even a fire poker, a silver candlestick or a frozen leg of lamb.

Any moment whoever was coming up those stairs would reach her floor and the landing. And P.T. wasn't being very helpful. What did Paige know about weapons?

A stair creaked too close for comfort. The footsteps stopped as if to listen.

Maybe it was Chloe or Franklin or someone her mother had given a key to? Someone worried about her with the phone dead and the electricity out.

On the edge of hysteria, she cried, "Who's there?" still hoping it would be someone she knew.

And how exactly did they open the deadbolt from the outside?

The deadbolt. Damn.

Silence answered. Then the sound of a heavy footfall on the next stair, climbing toward her, moving faster, closing in for the kill.

Great move.

She shone the flashlight around the room again, panicked. The light caught on two bright red...eyes. She tried to scream but when she opened her mouth nothing came out. Her heart was stuck in her throat. And by the time she found her voice, she'd recognized what she was seeing.

A moose head. It hung on the wall of the landing.

A stuffed moose head. *Yuck.*

Unconsciously, she flipped her dark hair back from her face, the same way she'd imagined P.T. doing a thousand times before, as she held the moose in the beam of her flashlight, half expecting him to come to life and attack her. That seemed preferable to her fate if the person climbing the stairs reached her.

She was ready to close and lock the door and take whatever time she had left.

Another stair groaned under weight. Almost to the top.

Going to just give up? Coward.

P.T. was starting to annoy her.

Want to die fighting? Or just make it easy for him?

She didn't want to die at all. But P.T. had a point. Whoever was coming up the stairs had a small flashlight. She could see the tiny beam flash on and off. They couldn't be far from the top of the fourth-floor landing.

She could go out the window. She shone the flashlight out on the steep roof. Then again no reason to make the killer's job easy.

Or she could fight back.

She snapped off the flashlight and clipped it to a

belt loop on her jeans. Her hands trembled as she impulsively rushed to the moose, hoping she would be able to lift it. The mounted head came off the wall, making her stagger.

Whoever was on the stairs had stopped climbing at the sound of her running footfalls. She stumbled to the top of the stairs. She could almost hear him breathing just below her in the dark.

Then suddenly his penlight flicked on. She got only a glimpse of the man on the stairs below her. She heaved the moose at him.

He looked up just an instant before the stuffed moose head hit him, driving him backward. He and the moose and the penlight tumbled noisily down the stairs.

Paige grimaced as she listened to the man and the moose crashing downward. The sound of splintering wooden stair railing was followed moments later by a loud crash, ending in silence.

A little crude, but effective.

After a long moment of petrified silence, Paige unclipped the flashlight from her jeans and shakily shone it over the railing down the center of the staircase, afraid of what she'd see four floors below. In the beam of the light, she saw what looked like a small oak desk. She frowned.

The intruder must have grabbed the desk from the third floor landing as he was falling.

Then where was he?

She shone the light on down the stairway past the splintered hole in the railing at the third floor short landing. Halfway down the next flight she spotted a moose antler sticking out through the railing and something dark behind it.

The silence was heavy as concrete.

Find him.

That was the last thing she wanted to do. But she knew P.T. was right. She shut off the flashlight and leaned over the railing. As her eyes adjusted to the dark, she saw the faint beam of a light shining a few stairs down from the third floor landing. His penlight? It didn't move. Maybe he still held it in his hand.

She turned on her flashlight again and spied a chunk of petrified wood marked fifteen dollars over by the door. She picked it up, holding the weight of it against her chest with one hand, the flashlight in the other. She understood now why murderers used candlesticks and fire pokers. But she didn't have time to find something less heavy or more practical.

She started down the stairs, planning to launch the rock at anything that moved.

She descended the first flight of stairs, then the second before she saw the moose head—and what looked like the sleeve of a plaid jacket beneath it.

You're going to have to get close enough to make sure he isn't going to be coming after you again.

He just fell down two flights of stairs after being hit by a flying moose head.

He could be faking it, just waiting for you to try to go past him before he grabs you!

As if she wasn't scared enough!

She thought she heard the sound of someone on the stairs—moving. She felt spring-loaded, so tense that if he jumped up at her, she would probably leap over the railing to her death.

Suddenly lightning splintered the darkness with a flash of blinding luminance at all the windows. Paige nearly jumped out of her skin. She thought she heard a groan. Then a soft pop like a tree limb snapping. When she looked down the stairs, her heart took off at a sprint. The penlight was gone, the light extinguished.

Don't even think about running back upstairs.

The rock was getting heavy and she didn't think her legs would carry her back up the stairs fast enough anyway. With growing dread, she inched downward.

Snick. That almost sounded like the deadbolt on the front door. A wave of cold air rushed up the stairs, smelling of the river. He'd left.

Right, you really are a dreamer.

Balancing the chunk of petrified wood in her left hand, she shone the flashlight in the other hand on the short third floor landing and the moose head.

A pair of jean-covered legs and one plaid jacket clad arm were sticking out from under it. Maybe he hadn't left.

She moved cautiously forward. Was it the same person who'd taken her suitcase? Or just some burglar? She nudged the man's boot sole. He didn't move.

She shot a quick look around the moose head at the man's face. She didn't think she'd ever seen him before.

Check for a pulse. Not his wrist. He could grab you if he's still alive. Check the artery in his neck.

The last thing she wanted to do was touch him. No, the last thing she wanted was for him to get up and come after her.

Carefully she edged around him to his head, still avoiding looking directly at him. Slowly, she started to lean down— Lightning cracked over her head, making her jump. A burst of light exploded in a flash at the window on the landing next to her, then darkness filled the house again.

She shone the flashlight at him, afraid that the bolt of lightning had brought the man back to life like the Frankenstein monster. Or worse, that she'd look down and the body would be gone.

He hadn't moved. She heard the first raindrops smack the windowpanes. She took a breath, put down the petrified wood on the floor, and reluctantly, she shone the light on his face as she started to reach for the artery in his neck.

She gasped. There was a perfectly round bright red hole between his thick brows.

He'd been shot!

She screamed and stumbled back, trying to get her feet under. Rain pelted the window. Thunder rumbled overhead. Closer, a floorboard creaked.

Someone's behind you!

She swung the flashlight, but it was knocked from her hand. It clamored to the floor next to the body. A hand clamped over her mouth as an arm circled her chest, pinning her arms to her sides. The barrel of a gun bit into her temple.

"P.T.," Dark and Dangerous whispered next to her ear. "We finally meet again."

CHAPTER SEVEN

DEVON ST. CLOUD didn't think the blonde could surprise him. Her past was as squeaky clean as she looked. Paige Teresa Grayson's life as innocent as her kiss.

The only thing he hadn't figured out was what she'd been doing in New Orleans at Eternal Peace Funeral Home or why she'd taken the package. That had seemed completely out of character based on what he'd dug up on her.

Or so he'd thought. But now as he looked past her to the body on the floor with a bullet hole between the eyes and a stuffed moose head on its chest he wondered.

"Nice shot." Damn, she'd plugged him right between the eyes! Who was he kidding? Everything about this woman surprised him. And it appeared she was a hell of a lot more cold-blooded than she looked.

She mumbled something he didn't catch against his palm covering her mouth. He tightened his grip on her, his arm over her breasts pinning her arms to her side. Her back felt warm against his chest, her breasts full.

The problem was: he had to take his hand from her mouth to search for the gun she'd used unless he wanted to feel the bite of a bullet himself.

"I didn't shoot him!" she cried the moment her mouth was free.

"Right."

"Hey, what do you think you're doing?" she demanded.

"Searching you for the gun you used." His hand skimmed along her back, around to her ribs. Nothing in the waistband of her jeans. He ran a hand down each leg, trying hard not to notice her body, trying to keep it purely professional. She had a great body.

"I told you I didn't shoot him."

"Uh-huh." No gun. But she did have a weapon— a body that was slim and yet deceivingly womanly. But from what he'd seen of her, he didn't think she'd figured out how to use it to her advantage yet. When she did, she'd be deadly.

Nor did he see a weapon on the third-floor landing other than the chunk of petrified wood next to the body. What had she planned to do with that? He hated to think.

"I suppose you didn't have anything to do with the moose head on him, either," he said, pulling her down with him while he searched the dead man. No weapon. No ID. No big surprise. "Or the package at the funeral home."

No comment. He felt her breathing change, though, the rise and fall of her breasts under his forearm, the sound of each breath through her lips.

He didn't have to see her face to know if she was lying. He could feel it. Just as he could feel the strength of her will, as powerful as the heat of her body. It was a damned shame she'd gotten involved in this, whatever the reason.

But right now he had a bigger problem than P.T.

"If you didn't shoot him, then who did?" he asked close to her ear as he drew her to her feet, picking up her flashlight from the floor as he did. Cautiously, he moved to the railing and shined the light over the side.

"How do I know *you* didn't shoot him?" she asked, her voice breaking.

"If I shot him I wouldn't be worried about why your front door was standing open," he whispered against her hair, which was dark, almost black.

She'd dyed it. Did she think she wouldn't be recognized? He smiled at the thought. He'd know that body of hers anywhere, even kneeling over a dead man in dim light.

He snapped off the flashlight, afraid it made them both too easy a target. Her hair smelled of peaches. "You pulled the deadbolt earlier, right?"

She must have seen the door ajar because she opened her mouth to scream as if she thought there might be someone outside who would come to her rescue. Not even remotely likely. There were no houses close by and if there was anyone out there, he wouldn't be coming to her rescue. Quite the opposite.

"Shhh," he whispered next to her ear as he

cupped his hand over her mouth again before she could get out a sound. She struggled against him.

He tightened his hold on her, listening. He'd come in the same way as the dead guy and no doubt the killer—through a back basement window with a rusty, now broken latch. Maybe the killer had left when he heard the woman descending the stairs, not knowing she only had a rock for a weapon. Or maybe the gunman had gone out the front when he'd heard Devon moving in from the back. Or maybe the killer just wanted him to believe that.

"Whoever shot your moose man is still in the house," he whispered into her hair. "Want to take your chances with him or me?"

She stopped struggling.

"Smart woman."

A floorboard creaked below them. She went rigid in his arms. Lightning ripped a tear in the dark beyond the window, throwing a ghostly light on the body at their feet for an instant.

He waited until the thunder rumbled loudly, then he started pulling her up the stairs, hiding the sound in the storm. She had the sense to not fight him.

From the darkness below them came the quick flicker of a flashlight, then blackness. A stair far below them groaned under the weight of a step.

They definitely weren't alone.

He'd wondered if she still had the package she'd taken from the coffin. The dead man on the landing and the footsteps on the stairs below them made him think that she did.

Now all he had to do was get it from her. Unfortunately, he couldn't just leave her here. He'd have to get them both out of the house alive. Neither seemed promising at the moment, but at least now he could feel P.T.'s fear and it didn't appear to be all directed at him.

At the top of the steps was another landing. His eyes had adjusted enough to the dark to see that the top floor was an apartment. Rain drummed on the roof overhead.

Below them, footfalls moved cautiously upward under the creak and groan of the stairs. He heard a second set of footsteps behind the first. Damn.

He was going to need her help to get them out of here. And given their earlier encounter in New Orleans…

He pulled her into the apartment, waited for the next crack of lightning before he closed the door and locked it.

"To get us out of here alive, I'm going to need your cooperation," he said. "Do you understand?"

Paige understood she was in deep doo-doo.

"I'm trying to keep us from both getting killed," he said in a hoarse whisper. "Are you going to help me?"

She nodded slowly.

"Is there an outside stairs off this floor?"

She shook her head.

He dragged her over to the window. Raindrops ricocheted off the roof and ran down the glass. "There has to be a fire escape of some sort." He shone the light across the expanse of jagged roof-lines. "Over there. See it?"

Her blood turned to ice. Piled on the roof was what appeared to be a rope.

"Be quiet," he warned, his breath tickling her cheek. Slowly, he took his hand away from her mouth and turned her to face him. "Get the package."

Don't scream!

She wasn't that dumb, was she? "I hid it."

"Is there time to get it?"

She shook her head.

He eyed her as if he didn't believe her. Imagine that. "Is there any chance they'll find it?"

"I don't think so," she whispered.

More footfalls on the stairs. Something crashed below them. It sounded like the moose head tumbling down the stairs. Whoever was coming up must have bumped it. That meant they had reached the third floor landing just below them.

With a low curse, he raised the window. Rain splashed on the sill, the spray cold. Lightning zig-zagged across the darkness, followed quickly by a teeth-rattling rumble of thunder. "You'll have to cross the roof to the rope."

Was he crazy?

"I'll try to hold them off long enough for you to get away."

She looked at him and saw that he hated like hell to let her go. Especially since he still didn't have the contents of the package and in a few minutes, he wouldn't have her, either.

"Get out of here before I change my mind," he said, gently pushing her toward the open window.

Tell me I'm not crazy for doing this—

She rushed to the lamp, quickly untied the key and stuffed it into her shoulder bag. She heard the sound of footsteps on the stairs.

"Hurry!" he whispered.

She dropped the shoulder bag strap over her head and stepped to the window and looked out again. He might as well just shoot her. She couldn't do this.

"Stay high on the roof," he whispered. He sounded like he was giving directions to the Mini Mart down the street not sending her out in a suicidal dash across a rain-slick roof, over the peak of the roof to what appeared to be nothing more than a pile of rope.

Even if she made it across the roof, which was doubtful, what were the chances she could make it down four stories on a rope? She bit her lip.

Don't you dare cry.

Given her current situation, crying seemed like the only thing she could do well.

There are killers coming up those stairs!

Exactly.

If they get up here before you get away, you're a goner.

She was a goner.

"You can do it," he said next to her.

She looked over at him. Tears filled her eyes. She could dye her hair, wear purple eye shadow and kid herself all she wanted. But as much as she wanted and needed to be P. T. Alexander right now, she was just plain old wimpy Paige and she saw that he knew it.

He leaned toward her, his dark eyes bottomless. She felt as if she were already falling. "You can do it." He kissed her.

It happened in an instant. Like a bolt of lightning. A rumble of thunder. Raising a storm inside her, making her ache for his touch as if they were lovers and only he could liberate the passion kept locked inside her.

"I don't even know your name," she said.

"Devon." He smiled, all dimples. "Go. I'll catch up with you."

Fired by the kiss, she actually hoped he would.

"Go!" He gave her a gentle push and she stepped through the window and out onto the roof. The rain stung her face and hands.

"Just don't look down," he whispered as he handed her the flashlight and closed the window.

At least the fall would get it over with quickly...

A series of boards had been tacked on the roof in a ladderlike design. She stepped from one to the next, shining the light ahead of her, trying to move quickly.

At the steepled part of the roof, she realized she would have to walk across a two-inch strip of copper. If she slipped—

Just don't slip.

She stepped up onto it and looked down as lightning splintered the sky above the dark limbs of the cottonwoods. Her heart dropped. She began to sway.

Come on. It's this or be tortured and killed by whoever is in the house.

Leave it to P.T. to always put things into perspective.

Why didn't she just leap off the roof now?

She brushed a lock of soaking wet hair from her eyes, the rain beating her, and started across, shining the light ahead of her only as far as her next step, desperately trying not to look down, not to think.

One step, then another, then another. She thought about the kiss, about Devon. About anything but falling. Suddenly she was across to another roof. A series of boards had been tacked down the side to the edge. She scrambled down them, the storm too loud to hear what was happening in the house.

At the edge of the roof, she squatted down in the drenching rain to shine the light on the pile of rope. It was a ladder with rungs. Her relief was short-lived however. Metal rungs in a thunderstorm?

Assuring herself the ladder was securely attached to the roof, she dropped it over the side. One of the metal rungs pinged against the side of the house. She couldn't see over the side and just had to trust that the rope went all the way to the ground.

Needing both hands, she clipped the flashlight to her jean loop again. She was operating on a lot of faith, she thought, as she turned, and clinging to one of the boards tacked to the roof, lowered her legs over the side, trying hard not to think about the four-stories of air between her and the ground. Her sneaker toe found a slippery metal rung and she let out a sigh of relief that sounded a lot like a sob.

As she began the swaying, suspended descent, thankful for the darkness, she thought how ironic it would be to reach the ground and have Devon and several of his goons waiting for her.

The sound of a gunshot or thunder made her quicken her pace. She clambered down as if the hounds of hell were after her. As far as she knew, they were. She moved so swiftly that the ground came up much faster than she'd expected. Her left foot hit earth. She stumbled backward, losing her grip on the ladder, and then there was nothing but air and hard ground as she tumbled.

She fell, belatedly remembering how the ground sloped toward the river. She tumbled backward in the dark, head over heels, once, twice. Her shoulder scraped the bark of a big cottonwood, an exposed root gouging into her back, then her feet came down with a splash and cold water rushed into her sneakers, but she was no longer falling. She grabbed hold of a limb. No longer moving.

The icy cold water was swiftly up to her knees, but she didn't think she was hurt, other than a few scrapes and scratches and she still had her purse and the flashlight, and she'd gotten away. She'd gotten away.

She let out a soft, painful sigh. Overhead, lightning splintered the sky, exposing her, followed quickly by a teeth-rattling boom of thunder. Behind her, she heard one of the metal rungs of the ladder clink against the eave. Just the wind? Or was someone coming down the ladder?

A little early to start celebrating.

The front door slammed and footfalls drummed on the concrete walk beside the house.

It was too dark to make a run for it on land, even

if she could climb back up the hill fast enough. Nor was plunging into the icy river an option.

As her eyes adjusted to the blackness, she saw that the limb she'd grabbed was connected to a large, old cottonwood tree so close to the river that the water had washed the earth out from under it, leaving a web of roots like arthritic fingers, the tips embedded in the gravelly river bottom.

The beam of a flashlight flickered over her head. She ducked, squeezing through the roots. It was dry against the bank, smelling of damp soil and dried leaves.

She crouched down, hidden in the palm of the root system, hit with a fleeting feeling of déjà vu. She peered out at the river through the thick growth and waited, listening, trying to hear over the pounding of her heart and the approaching storm. Was she hidden enough? How long would it be before they found her?

"Did you see her?"

The closeness of the female voice startled Paige. She caught a whiff of exotic perfume, a scent she now associated with the package she'd taken from the coffin and the redhead who'd hidden it there.

"No," said a male voice she didn't recognize. "She's gone. So is Devon."

"Find them."

CHAPTER EIGHT

PAIGE DIDN'T KNOW how long she stayed huddled in the dark tangle of tree roots. At one point, she thought she might have dozed off because she was startled awake by a bad dream where she was hiding, someone was calling her name and then there was blood everywhere and she was screaming.

It was the wind that screamed, though. It whipped the bare branches over her head, whistling and moaning as the rain fell in sheets, and lightning and thunder cracked and rumbled in the distance.

From her hiding place she watched the rain. Hard drops plunked into the river, dimpling the surface and sending up a cold spray.

She huddled under the tree, afraid to move, afraid to fall asleep again, haunted by the dream. The scream had sounded so much like her own.

Finally she heard the sound of two separate vehicles driving away. Going back to the house was out. She couldn't be sure someone hadn't stayed behind, waiting for her return. Nor was there anyone in this town to turn to. At least no one she felt she could trust, not even her mother's supposedly "best" friend Chloe. She wondered where Devon was, how he'd gotten away.

When she finally crawled out of the knot of roots, the rain had slowed and the storm moved on a little to the east where lightning shimmered in the sky to the distant rumble of thunder.

She waded through the dense darkness along the edge of the river and climbed the slope a good distance from the house. She was shivering from the cold, the wetness, fear's exhausting grip on her and her ever-present grief.

Afraid to use the flashlight, she stumbled through the tall grass of a field, holding tight to her purse with the key inside, expecting someone to jump out from every tree or bush. For some reason whoever was after her didn't just want the key. They wanted her. Needed her. And that was why her name had been inside the box.

She was almost to the interstate when she sensed rather than heard someone behind her. Her throat went dry as she turned. A large shadowy figure came out of the darkness and was on her before she could scream or run. Devon grabbed her and kissed her into silence. In her surprise, she found herself kissing him back.

Try to keep in mind that you're kissing the enemy.

It was difficult.

He drew back, his face so close she could see the shine of his eyes, feel his warm breath against her cheek. Behind him she saw something in the trees. A vehicle.

"Come on." He took her hand, trying to lead her

toward what appeared to be a minivan parked in the trees not far away.

"Wait." She dug her heels in, pulling free of him.

He turned to look at her. "We have to get out of here."

She couldn't argue that. She just wasn't sure going with him was the smartest thing she could do. She stared at the dark shape of the minivan, wondering if there was someone waiting in the car for her.

You think he's working with the other two back at Rare Finds?

Was she crazy? Hadn't he just saved her life?

"I'm alone, if that's what you're worried about," he said, holding his palms open in surrender. "I'll take you anywhere you want to go. Let's just get out of here before we get caught out in the open. All right?"

She shivered and licked her lips, still tasting him, still feeling the thrum of her heart beneath the wet jean jacket from just being in his arms. She really needed to get out more.

He waited. Not pushing, not moving. Just waited.

She could hear a car on a road nearby. Could feel the clock ticking. The redhead and the man would be looking for her, for them. Unless of course they were waiting in the minivan.

Call her a fool, but she was going with him.

Fool.

She started toward him. He took her hand and they ran to the van. It was empty, just like he'd said.

She climbed into the passenger seat, glad to be out of the rain, but not so sure she just hadn't jumped from the frying pan into the fire.

Once behind the wheel, he started the engine and headed down the narrow dirt road through the pasture without turning on his headlights.

"Where to?" he asked, looking over at her.

"Billings," she said as if she'd known all along that that was where she was headed. Billings and the truth about her father. She caught her reflection in the passenger side window and wasn't the least bit surprised to see P.T. looking back at her, this time with approval. "Take the interstate east."

He nodded, casting her a glance. "Are you all right?"

She shivered, unconsciously gripping the strap of her purse. The expression in his eyes held compassion, a look that could prove her undoing unless she remembered that this man was after only one thing: the package.

Without a word, Devon reached over and kicked up the heat. A few moments later, he took the interstate on-ramp, headed for Billings.

Paige wondered where he'd gotten the van as she glanced around the inside, noticing the fast-food containers in the back and children's toys. She looked over at him in surprise.

He'd been watching her. He now grinned. "The keys were in it."

He stole it. She was going to end up in jail. Or

worse, prison. Why didn't that scare her more than it did?

Probably because you'll be lucky to get out of this alive.

There were worse things than death, she thought, as the highway followed the Yellowstone River, the headlights picking up sandstone bluffs and ponderosa pines from out of the night. Like what she might learn about her father in Billings.

DEVON SAW that she was still a little pale, but she looked great, even soaked like a drowned rat.

She nervously tucked a lock of hair behind one ear as if she felt his gaze on her, but was ignoring him. She looked so different with dark hair. Why she'd dyed it, though, was still a mystery to him. He'd never understand women. Didn't she realize that half the world would kill for natural blond hair like hers?

But there was something else about her....

He squinted, trying to put a finger on what was different. Not just the hair and makeup. There was a sexy self-confidence about her that had even more appeal because the innocence was still there, just under the purple eye shadow.

"What?" she demanded, swinging her gaze on him.

"I'm trying to figure you out," he answered truthfully. "I keep telling myself there's a good reason you were in New Orleans at Eternal Peace Funeral Home—other than to pick up that package."

"The package," she said with a sigh as if bored with the subject. She leaned back in her seat and closed her eyes. She looked disgusted with him and he wished he hadn't brought up the damned package. Not yet, anyway.

"I didn't go to New Orleans for the package," she said impatiently. "I didn't even know it existed."

He had a hard time believing that, even though part of him wanted to believe whatever she told him. But that part of him could get him killed and he knew it.

She looked away, her gaze going to the darkness outside. He felt a sudden stab of regret, wishing they could have met under different circumstances. Just as he wished he could forget about the damned package. But he couldn't. And after what had happened back at Rare Finds, he knew she couldn't, either. She wouldn't be safe until he had that package—and the evidence against the judge was found and destroyed.

"How many more times am I going to have to save your skin before you trust me?" he asked quietly as he drove.

Out of the corner of his eye, he saw her catch her lower lip in her teeth, her blue eyes wide with emotions he could only guess at as she turned to look at him again. "I was there to see if the deceased man at the funeral home was my father. He was."

Paige had wondered what Devon's reaction would be when he learned who she was. She'd thought he might already know. He seemed to have unlimited resources when it came to finding her.

But he took the news like a blow. "Your father? Michael Alexander was your father?" He sounded shocked, upset. He raked a hand through his hair, his dark eyes stealing glances at her, as he steered the minivan down the highway. "You're Michael Alexander's *daughter?*"

"Why are you so surprised?"

"You don't look like—" He shrugged, glanced away. "It's just that—" His gaze came back to her. "I just wouldn't have expected that."

"You sound like you knew my father." Not the best of references.

He seemed to hesitate. "No, I didn't. That is…I know the name."

"Don't you mean you know his reputation?"

He dodged that like a bullet. "You said you went to the funeral home to see if the man was your father. You didn't know? I don't understand."

He wasn't the only one who didn't understand. She sighed and leaned back into the seat. Devon had saved her life tonight. Maybe the night at the funeral home as well. But the truth was, whether or not she was making the biggest mistake of her life, she desperately needed to confide in someone and the thought of finding an ally had such appeal, her heart ached at the thought. She'd felt so alone for so long and now with killers after her—

Easy girl. You don't know anything about this guy.

She knew he'd saved her life. At the very least he'd gotten her out of the rain back there.

Believe me, he didn't do it out of the goodness of his heart. He wants the key—and the note.

Even if that was all he wanted, at least she wouldn't be alone in trying to find out what the key fit.

Just watch your back...and your lips.

"I took the package thinking there might be something in it that would tell me where my father had been the last twenty-three years, why he left us..." She shook her head. "I just needed to know something about him. For all those years I believed he was dead."

Devon frowned.

"My mother told me he'd died, which as it turns out is kind of true. It seems he might have faked his death in Billings years ago."

"That's why you're going to Billings?"

She nodded. "All I know is that everything I was told by my mother seems to have been a lie. I need to find out the truth." She looked over at him. "Since we're being honest, why don't you tell me what your involvement is in all this? Why do you want the package so badly?"

He didn't answer at first, just drove. When he finally looked over at her, his dark eyes seemed to soften. "It's bad enough to speak ill of the dead. On top of that, the man's your father."

"I have to know." The words sounded so brave,

but her heart raced. She knew she didn't want to hear what he was going to tell her.

"Your father...sold the package to my employer."

She felt her eyes widen in alarm. "Blackmail?" So Devon worked for a...crook? What did that make *him?*

"It's a long story, but it seems your father framed my employer with some trumped-up evidence," Devon said quickly. "There was supposed to be a key in the package at the funeral home and a note telling him where to find the false evidence."

She felt the blood rush from her head. She leaned against the passenger side window and took deep breaths.

"I told you you didn't want to hear this."

She shouldn't have been surprised. Hadn't she known it would be something like this?

"I'm sorry." He actually sounded like he meant it.

"This employer is...?"

He seemed to hesitate. "Judge Wyatt Hathaway."

She blinked. "The judge who's in line for the Louisiana Supreme Court."

"That's the one."

She'd seen Judge Hathaway in the news for weeks. A man with an impeccable reputation—unlike her father. She wanted to argue that there must be some kind of mistake, but she couldn't. She'd witnessed the money exchange in her father's coffin herself—and she had the contents of the package and Devon knew it. She felt sick.

"I'm surprised you didn't think I was working with my father," she said, looking over at Devon.

He gave her a deep-dimpled grin. "I did. But you didn't have the money on you—just the package."

Good point.

"You understand now why I have to find that package. Judge Hathaway is on his way to the Supreme Court—unless something prevents his appointment," Devon said. "Like a scandal for a crime he didn't commit. I can't let an innocent man's life be ruined by this. I have to find what that key opens before his enemies do."

Hadn't she known when she'd taken the package she'd also taken some high moral ground? If she could help Devon find the trumped-up evidence, she would have taken a step toward making things right. It was a small step, but one she had to take. "I'll help you."

His gaze held hers for one heart-pounding moment. "I know you must have been hiding behind the drapes at the funeral home, you must have seen the person who took the money and left the package."

She nodded. "It was the same woman who was at Rare Finds tonight. She and some man were looking for the two of us."

He stared at her. "A woman? What did she look like?"

"Tall, slim, about thirty with red hair and—"

"Red red?" he interrupted.

"Fire-engine."

He let out a low oath.

"You know her?"

He rubbed his stubbled jaw. He looked tired. "Let's just say I've seen her around, if it's the same woman. I just can't believe Fiona would—" He waved a hand through the air. "You're sure it was her again tonight at the house?"

"I recognized her voice and smelled the scent of her perfume," Paige said. "There was a man with her."

"Did you get a look at him?"

She shook her head. "I didn't recognize his voice, either. But he mentioned you by name."

Devon didn't seem surprised by that. "You know they won't stop looking for you and the package."

She watched the night blur past for a moment, then looked over at his tanned, strong fingers holding the wheel in the glow of the dash lights. Didn't a man's hands tell a lot about him?

Yeah, right.

Well, his obvious loyalty to his employer did. And the sweet way he'd kissed her back at Rare Finds to get her to go out the window.

Sucker.

She opened her purse and pulled out the key and the note in her mother's handwriting on the address book paper. She held both out to him. "That's what was in the package."

He pulled over to the side of the road and flipped

on the dome light. His gaze went from the key and note to her. "That's all? No other note telling you what the key went to?"

She shook her head. "Judge Hathaway has no idea?"

"No."

"The note is in my mother's handwriting, at least I think it all is. It was torn from her address book."

"Why would your name be in the package?"

"I have no idea," she said. "I hadn't been to Rare Finds before my mother's death. I didn't even know it existed. When I searched the house and the apartment and shop, I couldn't find anything that the key fit."

"Had you seen the key before?"

She shrugged. "I don't think so, but I was three when my father disappeared from our lives. I thought for sure it would fit something at Rare Finds."

"That does seem the most likely place, doesn't it," he said. "So why are we headed for Billings?"

"I found out earlier tonight that Billings was where my father died—the first time," she said. "It seemed like the place to look for answers."

He studied her for a moment. "I'll help you."

Wasn't that exactly what she'd been hoping for?

"That is if you'll let me." He handed both the note and key back to her.

Her fingers trembled as she took them and returned them to her purse.

I told you I could trust him.

Uh-huh.

And maybe there was a good reason her father had disappeared from her life twenty-three years ago. When she'd seen him, she'd sensed his love. She'd believed she would find a good reason why he had disappeared. As foolish as it seemed, she was still holding on to that hope. There must have been some good in her father at one time. She prayed she would find it. But she'd been wrong about so much—she just hoped she wasn't wrong about Devon, she thought looking over at him.

Her heart lurched a little at the sight of him. She wasn't wrong—hearts don't lie.

"I want to tell you about my mother. I have a feeling she and I might have been running from something," Paige confided in the semidarkness of the van, needing to tell him everything if he was going to be able to help her. And Devon was a captive, willing audience.

You realize there is no going back after this.

Yes. She told him about her life with her mother, all the moving, her shock to find that her mother had suddenly settled down, then the news about the cancer.

Paige even told him what Franklin had found out, how she and her mother had disappeared a year after her father had faked his death, then resurfaced with new identities under the name Grayson. She told him about Gray, the mystery man who'd lived in their shadow all those years.

Devon listened attentively. "Your mother would have needed help to disappear like that."

"Yes." But Paige had no idea who her mother had turned to. Maybe her family, the family Paige hadn't known existed. She closed her eyes, holding on to the hope that they would find out the truth in Billings as she drifted off into an exhausted sleep.

The next thing she knew, Devon was gently nudging her awake. She opened her eyes to sunshine and the outline of buildings etched against the big sky and the rimrock cliffs.

Her heart caught in her throat. Whatever had happened that destroyed her family twenty-three years ago, it had happened here.

But what did it have to do with the key and note in her purse? Maybe nothing. Maybe everything.

CHAPTER NINE

DEVON WATCHED P.T. stare down at the black-and-white photo she'd taken from her purse. "Your parents?" he guessed.

She nodded and handed him the photo across the table in the booth where they sat, the sounds of the noisy, busy truck stop café comforting after the rainy night on the road.

Devon had led P.T. to a table at the back and ordered them both the Trucker's Special: biscuits and sausage gravy, two eggs, hashbrowns, ham and a side of pancakes.

"I'll never be able to eat all of that," she'd cried, her blue eyes wide with surprise.

"I've been listening to your stomach growl for the last fifty miles," he'd told her.

She'd laughed and eyed him as if he might be lying.

He'd laughed with her, loving the sound, loving even more the sight of her smiling. Her whole face seemed to light up and he wished he could make her smile all the time. Better yet, make her laugh. It was damned dangerous thinking and he knew it.

Last night he'd pulled over on a ranch road off

the interstate and slept until the sun came up. Then
he'd sat watching P.T. sleep. She made him think
of houses with white picket fences and picnics,
cheesy things like that, fairy-tale endings he didn't
believe in.

Finally, he'd gotten back on the interstate and
driven to Billings. P.T. had slept the sleep of the
dead until he'd awakened her just before the truck
stop.

"They look happy, don't they," she said as he
studied the photograph in his hand.

"Very."

"That's the part I don't understand. Why would
my father leave us? You can see in the snapshot that
my mother is pregnant with me."

He nodded and handed the photo back, not having
any more answers than she did. This morning she'd
insisted on calling the police, telling them about the
break-in at Rare Finds, the dead man on the stairs.

The sheriff said a woman named Chloe had called
saying the front door was standing open. Further investigation turned up evidence of a break-in, but no
dead body. Not even any blood.

Devon had watched P.T. convince herself the man
on the stairs must not have been dead. Right. Just
like he hadn't bled from that shot between the eyes.
Obviously some people had disposed of the body
and all evidence—just like they'd taken any trace of
Michael Alexander from the funeral home.

But damned if Devon knew why. It worried him.
He felt like someone was pulling his strings, making

him dance to their tune and he wasn't doing one blamed thing about it.

He watched P.T. put the picture back into her purse next to the key as the waitress slid a huge plate piled high with food in front of each of them. "Devon, you can't be serious about this."

He smiled at her. "I'm betting you can make a real dent in that. Unless you're one of those women who eats like a girl," he challenged, pretty sure he knew what they were going to find out today. P.T. was going to need her strength.

She picked up her fork, taking the challenge just as he knew she would.

They ate companionably for a while without talking, then she said, "I thought we could start at the library. There should be some record of my father's alleged death."

He nodded.

"Something happened here twenty-three years ago," she said, glancing out at the city. "Whatever it was, I just have this bad feeling that it got both of my parents killed and will get me too, if I don't find out."

He reached across the table to take her hand as tears welled in all that blue. "I won't let that happen."

She smiled through her tears as if she didn't have much faith in his ability to keep her safe.

She was right. But damn if he didn't want to move heaven and earth to try. He reminded himself what he was here to do as she took her hand back and worked on the plate of food again. He just hoped to hell he wouldn't ever have to choose between saving the judge or saving P.T. He pushed his plate away. Suddenly, he'd lost his appetite.

FULL AND STRANGELY CONTENT, Paige wished she could forget why they were in Billings. She watched in her side mirror for a tail as Devon drove the rental car to the public library downtown. He'd left the minivan in a lot and rented them a car.

She didn't see anyone following them. But she couldn't be sure. She saw Devon glance in his rearview mirror a couple of times and frown. Was he worried that they'd somehow been followed?

She knew there was reason to be concerned as she and Devon entered the large brick library building. The redhead Devon thought might be a woman named Fiona had found her at Rare Finds. Had the man Paige hit with the moose head also been working with Fiona? Or were a lot of people after the key—and the note? For all Paige knew everyone might still be one step ahead of her and Devon.

At the library's front desk, P.T. asked about old phone directories from twenty-three years ago and local newspapers from the same time, figuring she would have to go through a lot of microfilmed papers to find her father's obituary.

"The phone directories are back here." The elderly librarian got to her feet. The nameplate on the desk said her name was Lucy Fraser. Lucy had a pencil stuck in her gray bun and wore sensible shoes with a shapeless print dress. She led Paige to a musty corner at the back of the first floor while Devon walked to the front of the building and stood staring out at the street. He *was* worried that they'd been followed.

Paige pulled out a phone book from the year before her father had supposedly died and was amazed to find that Michael and Simone Alexander had been listed. She checked two other years and found the same listing. 2114 Crestview. That's where she'd lived for the first three years of her life.

She put the phone directories back.

"Find what you needed?"

Paige started. "Yes." She'd been so distracted, she hadn't realized that Lucy hadn't left. The woman had been standing behind her all this time. Paige hadn't even noticed.

"Then I'll show you to our morgue," Lucy said. "What did you say you were looking for?"

"An obituary. It would have been twenty-three years ago."

"We now have the last twenty-five years of local newspapers computerized," Lucy said as she walked, the soles of her sensible shoes making no sound on the linoleum. "Come this way." She led Paige to the elevator. Devon fell into step beside Paige. Was it just her imagination or did he look worried?

Lucy pushed the fourth-floor button and the elevator doors closed. "Quite the storm last night, wasn't it." She didn't look at Paige. Nor did she wait for a comment. "But we really needed the rain. Snowfall was down again this year."

The elevator stopped, the door opened and Lucy led the way. Paige and Devon followed her through the stacks, turning here and there until the elderly librarian stopped at a glassed room at the back of the stacks. Inside it was a long table with three computers and three chairs.

"What's the name of the deceased?" Lucy asked, plopping down at the first computer.

Paige hesitated, glancing over at Devon. He seemed distracted. She said, "Michael Ramone Alexander."

The librarian typed it in. A half dozen references came up on the screen. Lucy stood up. "There you go. Just click on the articles you want. Printed copies are a dime each. All you have to do is call up the article, deposit a dime and hit the print button." She left.

Paige sat down at the computer. Devon was watching Lucy retreat down through the stacks.

The elevator door opened and closed, followed by an eerie silence. The library wasn't busy this early in the morning. In fact, Paige hadn't seen another soul.

She looked at the computer screen. Her heart pounded as she clicked on the first Michael Ramone Alexander reference, then stared in shock as her father's face appeared, much younger than the last time she saw him in New Orleans.

Paige heard Devon let out a gasp behind her.

"Your father was a *cop?*"

She stared at her father dressed in a police uniform. The headline read: Local Police Officer Receives Commendation For Bravery.

Michael Alexander had been a *cop!*

She quickly read the glowing story about her father, including his love for his wife Simone and their daughter Paige Teresa. She fought tears as she read. How could this man have ever become a criminal? Hearing about his dedication, it seemed impossible.

Devon looked as surprised as she was as he read over her shoulder. Obviously something had happened to change what appeared to be not only a great career—but a good, honest, happy life.

She skipped down the list and clicked on another reference. A headline flashed on the screen: Decorated Cop Facing Charges Of Misconduct. The article was dated a year later.

Devon let out a low whistle as she clicked on the next article: Days Before Facing Misconduct Charges Respected Police Officer Commits Suicide. She felt his hand on her back, comforting as she read the story.

She was stunned to read that her father had allegedly driven his car off the rimrocks at a spot called Suicide Cliff east of the city, killing himself after recent bouts of depression and pending alleged misconduct charges.

Fellow officers reported noticing a recent change in Alexander. He had seemed distracted and down, according to his partner, Buford Wright.

The car had crashed in the rocks below the rims, bursting into flame with Alexander's body trapped inside the burning vehicle.

Her father had faked his death. Just as she'd suspected. She felt sick, claustrophobic and only wanted to get out of the room. Hurriedly, she dug out what dimes she had and fed them into the printer to make copies of all the stories, including his obituary that said he was survived by a wife and three-year-old daughter. Neither was named. Also no mention of parents on either side of the family. Why? Even if they were deceased it was common to list them. But then this wasn't a normal obituary. The deceased wasn't dead.

What had made her father fake his death, leave his wife and child? The article hadn't said exactly what the misconduct charges were. And whose body had really been in the car that went off the rims that night if not Michael Alexander's?

An even bigger question: had her mother been in on it from the start?

She was printing each of the articles when one of the photos caught her eye: a shot of the burned wreckage of her father's car. Next to it on page one was a story about the opening of a new mini mall, the murder of a local district judge and a fire in the police station evidence room.

Devon made a sound. A short intake of breath and suddenly she knew.

"You never said what crime my father was blackmailing Judge Hathaway for," she said, realizing she hadn't wanted to know.

Silence. Then, "The murder of a judge."

She stared at the story about the judge who was killed in Billings twenty-three years ago on the same day her father had faked his suicide. "Judge George Tripp?"

"Wyatt didn't tell me his name, but I'm betting that would be the one."

A BAD FEELING settled in his chest as Devon read the story about the murdered judge and the fire at the police station. Suddenly, he felt uneasy, worried on more levels than he wanted to admit.

But one worry was pressing. He'd seen the librarian go straight to a phone at the end of the stacks before returning to her desk on the first floor.

He hadn't thought anything of it at the time. But now it worried him. Worried him just like the newspaper articles from around the time of Michael Alexander's faked suicide. Alexander had been a cop. He hadn't expected that.

"I'll be right back," he said to P.T. and moved toward the front of the library.

He watched the street, not even sure what he was looking for. Until the cop car pulled up and a big man in uniform climbed out and hurried toward the library entrance. Devon swore. The cop hadn't just stopped by to check out the latest Tom Clancy release.

As Devon started to turn away from the window, now anxious to find P.T. and get the two of them out of here, he saw another car pull up. Even from this distance he recognized the redhead behind the wheel. The passenger side seat was empty. Where was the man P.T. said had been with Fiona last night at Rare Finds?

Fiona seemed to hesitate just long enough to let the cop get inside the library, then she climbed out of the rental car, holding her purse as if it were heavy, as if there was a gun inside, and headed toward the library.

PAIGE REREAD THE STORY about her father's alleged suicide still on the computer screen while the other articles printed. She now knew what he'd been doing up on the rims, parked at the edge of the rimrocks overlooking the city in the wee hours of the morning. Had he killed Judge George Tripp? Is that why he had to fake his death?

It was bad enough believing her father was a blackmailer, but a murderer? He'd been a highly respected police officer with a young family until the misconduct charges. It still didn't make any sense.

Worse, had her mother been in on it from the beginning? If not, she had definitely found out at some point that Michael Alexander wasn't dead. Why else would she have requested that she be notified when he "really" died?

Maybe Simone had planned to disappear with him. Maybe something had gone wrong.

Paige's head ached. She couldn't imagine how her mother had gotten false identities for herself and Paige. And who was Gray? Had they lived on her father's fraudulently claimed insurance policy? Paige leaned over the computer monitor and closed her eyes, the lies and deceptions too much on top of the weight of losing both parents.

"Are you all right?" a male voice asked behind her.

Not Devon. Startled, she spun around to see a man in a police uniform framed in the doorway. He was in his early fifties, short brown hair, a massive man, both tall and muscular. Her gaze fell on his name tag. Buford Wright. Her heart leapt to her throat and for a moment she couldn't speak. Her father's former partner?

"Are you ill?" he asked, looking down at the printer and the newspaper article lying in the tray.

She shook her head. Ill didn't even cover it. "I was just resting." She got awkwardly to her feet, scooping up the printed copies. Where was Devon?

"Sorry, I didn't mean to rush you." Buford Wright smiled the kind of smile he'd give a little kid. But his gaze went to the computer screen where she still had up one of the stories about her father's suicide.

She quickly returned the screen to the main menu, telling herself it was just a coincidence that the man who'd been her father's partner at the police department would show up at the public library now.

Are you nuts? The librarian must have tipped him off.

Paige tried hard not to appear as if she were hurrying as she folded the copies into her purse, her back to the door. Her hands were shaking, fear crushing her lungs making it hard to breathe.

A man would need help to fake his own death. Who better than his partner?

She took a ragged breath. How far would Buford Wright go to keep the past dead and buried?

He's not going to kill you. Not until he finds out why you're snooping into his former partner's death.

An encouraging thought.

She turned, ready to scream. Maybe the scream would carry to wherever Devon had gone off to. Or maybe Devon was in no shape to hear her. Maybe someone would hear her.

Buford Wright wasn't standing in the doorway. Her gaze swung to the stacks. No sign of him.

She clutched her purse. She had to get out of the building, but if the librarian at the front desk had warned Buford that someone was looking at old newspaper stories about his partner—

There has to be a back door, an emergency exit.

She started down through the stacks, intent only on getting out of the building, getting help. The shelves rose to the ceiling, filled with musty-smelling books. She couldn't hear over the pounding of her pulse in her ears. Buford could be just on the other side of the stack of books. Or he could be behind her.

She couldn't stand it. She looked back. The aisle between the stacks was empty. It was all she could do not to run. She looked for an exit sign. Fear made her mind go blank and knees weak. She couldn't remember the route the librarian had taken to lead her back to the computers. She felt as if she was going in circles. He could be anywhere... Just waiting for her.

DEVON HURRIED BACK to the computer room, only to find it empty. P.T. was gone! She wouldn't just leave. Not unless something had happened. Damn.

He heard the *clank* of the elevator and hurried through the stacks toward the sound. The cop was in the building and by now so was Fiona. He watched the numbers flash over the elevator door. It was going down to the first floor again.

At a run, Devon headed for the door to the stairs, his heart in his throat. What if one of them had P.T.? They wouldn't hurt her, he told himself. Not in the library. Not until they had a key.

How had Fiona found them so quickly? It didn't make any sense. He knew he and P.T. hadn't been followed last night. But Fiona hadn't followed them to the library— She'd followed the cop!

Devon slammed open the door to the stairs, stepped into the stairwell and heard the door start to close behind him before he realized he wasn't alone.

The blow took him by surprise since the cop couldn't have had time to reach this floor. Neither could Fiona. That only left the man P.T. said had been with Fiona last night at Rare Finds.

But the realization did him little good. He saw nothing but the floor coming up at him. Then there was darkness.

PAIGE HEARD THE ELEVATOR and started toward it.

Don't be a fool. You'd be a sitting duck.

Buford would have her trapped. He might already. She wanted to call out for Devon. But she had a bad feeling he wouldn't be able to hear her. She listened. Heard nothing, only the grind of the elevator as it started back up from the first floor.

She looked around, panicked. Her heart ached from the fear, from everything that had happened, from all the lies and the losses. And her worry over Devon. Where was he?

She felt overwhelmed by it all and just wanted to give up. The pain, the grief, the bone-deep hurt of what she'd learned paralyzed her.

And let them win? No way, sister. You're a whole lot tougher than you think! You can do this.

Funny. It wasn't P.T. she heard, but Devon. She spotted what appeared to be a back stairs. On the door was printed emergency use only.

She pushed open the door and looked down the stairs. They were narrow and steep. She started down the steps, half running. Just let Devon be all right, she chanted in her mind as she ran.

When she reached the ground floor, she was faced with two doors. One back into the library. The other to the alley.

The sign on the door to the alley warned that an alarm would sound. She'd have to move fast.

She charged the door, practically throwing herself against it. The door slammed open. She was running when her feet hit the pavement outside. She'd anticipated the shrill cry of the alarm, the sound that would bring Buford Wright racing after her. She'd taken several running steps before she realized the alarm hadn't sounded.

But it wasn't until the arm looped around her neck, a hand closing over her mouth, that she realized why. Buford Wright had turned it off.

CHAPTER TEN

"DON'T FIGHT ME," the cop whispered fiercely.

She tried, but it was futile. He was too large for her, too strong. He dragged her down the alley away from the library's back door to a small alcove set back in another older brick building behind some Dumpsters and gave her a shove.

She stumbled, catching herself before she hit the side of the brick wall. He was going to kill her just as she'd suspected. No one would be able to see them back in here. No one would find her body for days.

Turning, she came face-to-face with the business end of a police revolver.

"Give me your purse, slowly," he ordered.

She knew it would be useless to scream even if the alley hadn't been empty. Even if the sound would carry far enough out of this isolated spot. The man was a cop. No one was going to come to her aid. Her heart threatened to burst from her chest. He was going to kill her! Maybe had already killed Devon.

She slipped the strap from her shoulder and handed the purse to him, watching as he took the new wallet she'd bought at the Houston airport from her purse, all the time still holding the gun on her. He glanced at her driver's license and frowned.

"Paige?" His eyes seemed to widen as he took a good look at her. "Mike's daughter?"

From down the alley came the sound of a car. He glanced that way. Was he waiting for someone?

Paige felt her skin crawl, her terror escalating, as he holstered his weapon and pushed her back where they both couldn't be seen. The car drove slowly down the alley toward them.

Don't let him get you into that car.

She jerked free of his hold and darted for the opening between him and the brick wall, not sure where she was going to run, just knowing she had to try. If she could get down the alley and away, she could call for help. Someone might hear her. Someone had to.

He grabbed her before she could get a foot, his hand covering her mouth as he pulled her back into the shadows of the building behind some wooden pallets.

"Quiet," he ordered.

She heard the murmur of the engine grow closer and closer, the crunch of gravel beneath the tires. The car, a medium-size sedan, drove past. Behind the wheel was the redhead who'd been at Rare Finds last night! She didn't look their way. The car stopped behind the library, the motor running as if she was waiting for someone.

"She was in the library looking for you," Buford whispered.

Paige felt her heart drop.

"A friend of yours?"

She shook her head, no longer fighting his hold on her.

"There was a man with her. He must still be in the library." Buford still had his hand on her mouth, was still holding her against the rough brick wall. "Does this have anything to do with your father?"

She closed her eyes, feeling the tears leak from her lashes and nodded.

"You're in trouble, aren't you."

She nodded.

The back door of the library opened. Paige couldn't make out the words nor see who'd come out, but she recognized the man's voice. It was the same man who'd been by the river last night behind Rare Finds with the redhead Devon called Fiona. Fiona and the man seemed to be discussing whether to search the area for her. She heard the car door open, close and the car begin to move again.

Buford Wright swore under his breath as he reached into his shirt pocket with his free hand. "The last thing I need to do is get involved in this again." He pulled out a business card and dropped it into her purse. "I must be out of my mind— Call me on my cell phone number," he whispered. "Use your cell phone so it can't be traced easily." His gaze softened. "You look like your dad." He returned her purse. "That man you came into the library with, you can't trust—"

She opened her mouth to warn him, but was too late. Devon struck the cop with the butt of his weapon.

Buford went down like a sack of rocks.

Devon grabbed her hand and took off down the alley with her racing to keep up. She glanced back, remembering Buford's last words, and saw that the cop had gotten to a sitting position and was watching the two of them. She would have sworn he mouthed the words *Call me*.

She and Devon rounded the alley and she couldn't see the cop any longer. What had Buford been going to say? That she couldn't trust Devon?

Devon opened the passenger side of the rental car and practically shoved her in, closing the door behind her before he raced around to the other side and hopped in.

"Did he hurt you?" Devon asked, the tension in his voice surprising her.

"No. He was my father's partner."

"I gathered that." Devon looked over at her. "You realize the librarian tipped him off. My bet is that Buford Wright is the one who helped your father fake his death, the last person on this earth who wants that coming out."

She thought about the business card Buford had put in her purse with his cell phone number. What was it Buford wanted to tell her? Something. Something about Devon.

"Oh, my God, what happened to you?" she cried, noticing the caked blood on Devon's temple. "Are you all right?"

"I'm fine. Someone blindsided me in the stairwell. I woke up in the janitor's closet."

"Buford?"

"I think it was the man you said was with Fiona last night at Rare Finds." He shot her a glance. "Fiona was at the library. I'm pretty sure she followed the cop so she must know he was your father's partner."

Paige stared at him. "Then she really is one step ahead of us."

"Or more," Devon said as he stopped at a red light. "Where to now?"

She had no idea. She still felt shaky from her encounter with Buford back at the library...worse from the seed of doubt he'd planted. Could she trust her father's partner, a man who'd probably helped fake a man's death. She wondered again whose body had been burned up in her father's car.

She looked over at Devon, warmth spreading through her at the sight of him. But did she trust him? "2114 Crestview."

He nodded solemnly as if he knew she needed to go back to where it had begun.

She opened the glove compartment, took out the city map they'd gotten at the rental car agency and directed him on how to get there.

Devon took a circuitous route, then drove east toward the river, watching all the while for a tail—

and not seeing one. They left a commercial district, driving through an older residential area. As they neared their destination, the streets became more narrow, the houses older, farther apart.

He stopped next to what had one time been a park along the river. In the huge cottonwoods and tall grass there was a broken wooden teeter-totter and the rusted framework of a swing set. Through the bare limbs of the trees Paige could see the Yellowstone River. Just outside her window, she saw something lying in the tall weeds. A rotten sign. Riverside Park. The name sounded so familiar—

She blinked, struck by a flash of memory? Blood. Her father running with her in his arms away from the park. She was crying, screaming.

Paige blinked, the memory, if that's what it had been, gone as quickly as it had come.

"Are you all right?" Devon asked. "You look like you just saw a ghost. You've been here before?"

She nodded. "With my father." She glanced off to the right and spotted the older small cottage-style house set back in the trees. The numbers beside the door read 2114 Crestview.

Trembling, she got out and walked away from the park to stop in front of the little stucco house. There was a big willow out front and tulips poking up through the weeds in beds along the side. She heard Devon get out of the car and follow her. At one time, this had been a nice house in a nice neighborhood, she could see that.

Her eyes blurred with tears as she stared at the home where she'd lived until the age of three. She thought of the flash of memory when she'd seen the park down the street. Of course her father would have taken her there. Maybe she'd fallen off the merry-go-round and bloodied her nose.

She tried to recapture anything that felt like a memory of father and daughter at the park before the imagined accident, but couldn't.

Just as she couldn't recall her life in this house with the mother and father from the photo in her purse. But she felt they'd been happy here. But maybe she was deluding herself, the same way she had about her father.

A loving father didn't fake his death and disappear for twenty-three years. Didn't destroy their family. Leave his wife and child. Didn't blackmail a judge. Didn't possibly kill someone.

"Who knows what makes people do what they do," Devon said beside her as if he could read her mind. He was staring at the house, frowning.

"I have to know what happened," she said. "My father was a good man at one time. What made him change?"

Devon shook his head and followed her back to the car.

Her father had hidden evidence against Judge Wyatt Hathaway. Evidence in a murder of another judge. Trumped up evidence. And the key was in her purse. And in the past, she thought. So how did she find what the key opened and get to the so-called evidence before whoever else was after it?

She was out of her league, completely inexperienced and there were killers after her, but she'd gotten this far, hadn't she?

But what choice did she have? She didn't know who she could trust. She couldn't return to Rare Finds. Nor would she be safe until she learned the truth. What did that leave?

She could feel Devon sitting behind the wheel, waiting. She hadn't thought past Billings, past finding out about her father's first death twenty-three years ago. She'd found out more than she'd expected, but was still no closer to understanding what had happened or if it had anything to do with the key...and her.

As she glanced down at her purse clutched in her hands, she thought of the circus ticket stub and the newspaper clipping she'd found in her mother's bag.

No way did Simone fly to Florida for the day to see the circus elephants and a ride on a Ferris wheel. There had to be another reason for the sudden trip and whatever it was, Paige feared it had gotten her mother killed. Plus, it was Paige's only lead. Her last lead.

She wondered how quickly she would be able to get a flight to Florida and smiled to herself. Maybe she was starting to get the hang of this.

"I need to go to the airport," she told Devon.

He raised a brow, but didn't question her as he put the car into gear. "I'm going with you."

How had she known that? She looked at the map again. Billings International Airport was located on top of the rimrocks. How appropriate.

While Devon got rid of the rental car, she called Barney Adams's Amazing One-Ring Circus and Carnival to find out where the nearest show was and was told the troupe would be performing tonight near Tampa, Florida. There was a flight leaving for Minneapolis with connections to Tampa in about an hour.

She realized she would have to fly as Paige Grayson since a photo ID was required to get on the plane. She would be leaving a trail anyone could follow, but she had no choice. Not that it seemed to matter. The people after her seemed to know what she was going to do almost before she did. Almost as if they'd planned it that way.

The thought sent a chill through her.

She got in line at the ticket counter and bought two one-way tickets to Tampa, Florida, unsure when they would be coming back. If they would be coming back.

She had no plan, no idea what she was going to do once she got to the circus other than ask around about her mother. All she had was the clipping and ticket stub. But maybe someone in the photograph would know something since the newspaper photo seemed to have initiated her mother's flight to Florida.

Fortunately, there were plenty of seats available on the flight. By the time she got into the security line, Devon had joined her sans the gun he'd been carrying earlier. They were going to the circus!

She moved to the back of the mostly empty plane. She took her seat by the window, having already checked out the other coach passengers on the flight. There wasn't anyone she knew. Or anyone who paid her or Devon any mind that she noticed.

As Devon sat down beside her, she opened her purse. The key was still there. If only she knew what it opened. And what it had to do with her.

She thought about the redhead who wore the exotic perfume and the man who'd been with her last night at Rare Finds and again at the library. Was he the same one who'd shot at Paige in New Orleans? It seemed likely.

The flight attendants closed the plane door. The engines revved and the plane began to taxi.

She closed her eyes, telling herself that she was safe—for the moment. But she'd noticed something. The people after her seemed to have a great deal of resources. And so did Devon.

Was that why she hadn't mentioned Buford Wright's cell phone number to Devon?

She closed her purse and shoved it under the seat in front of her as Devon plopped down next to her and snapped on his seat belt.

"Don't you think it's time you told me where we're going?" he asked.

She looked over at him, telling herself she hadn't made a terrible mistake by trusting him. "Florida."

"Florida?!"

His startled upset reaction surprised her. And worried her. "Any reason you wouldn't want to go to Florida?" she asked.

Florida? Oh, yeah, Devon could think of a half dozen reasons he didn't want to go anywhere near Florida. He let out a silent oath. Florida. The last place on earth he ever wanted to go. But he was committed to following this woman anywhere— even to hell, and Florida would definitely be his own private hell.

"You seem upset," she said.

He gave her his best smile, but he could see her studying him, suspicion in her gaze. Damn. He'd gotten her to trust him, making some headway with her. Until earlier in the alley. What had that cop told her? Something. P.T. had been acting differently toward him.

He'd let the cop get her in the alley. He had only himself to blame if she'd started mistrusting him.

"I spent some time in Florida when I was a kid," he said. "They weren't exactly Kodak moments."

"I'm sorry," she said quickly. "I've told you so much about me. I don't know anything about you."

Yeah. Hadn't he been afraid she'd start asking him a bunch of questions about his past? Years ago he'd come up with a pat story about a *Leave It to Beaver* family. He'd found that was what women wanted to hear. They needed that two-story house in a small suburb, a big brother who teased him but fought battles for him, a best friend who skipped school with him to go fishing, a father who was strict but fair and a mother who baked.

But Devon couldn't bring himself to tell her those

lies. Nor could he tell her the truth. "I don't like talking about my childhood. What do you hope to find in Florida?"

P.T. tensed as the plane began to roll toward the runway.

"I told you my mother was killed in a hit-and-run accident last week," she reminded him.

"You didn't mention where."

The plane turned, stopped, engines roared.

"Near Orlando. She'd gone to—"

The plane took off down the runway, driving them back in their seats.

The hit-and-run had been in Florida?

P.T. closed her big blue eyes and gripped the edge of the seat, her face pale, freckles popping out like gold flakes.

He reached over and pried one of her hands free to cradle it in his own. "Don't worry. Flying is safer than driving." How easy it would be to get in the habit of saving this woman—a woman he didn't even know. So why did he feel the way he did? Because of a couple of kisses? Maybe.

The plane left the ground, bobbed a little, then began to climb. She didn't open her eyes, holding on to his hand as if her grip alone kept the plane aloft. Her teeth worried at her lower lip, making him remember the times he'd kissed her. He wanted to kiss her now. Wondered if it would take her mind off flying.

Bad idea. He closed his eyes, thankful to be out of Billings. The guy in the alley had been a cop and, unless he was mistaken, had recognized him. But why did they have to be going to Florida? His gut instinct told him it was a mistake for him to go back there. Especially with this woman.

The captain announced that they were at thirty thousand feet and that he'd turned off the seat-belt sign. Devon opened his eyes and saw P.T. looking at him. The depth of all that blue always startled him.

"Better?" he asked.

She nodded and looked down at her hand clenched with his. "Thanks."

"My pleasure," he said, opening his palm and letting her go free. He was making a habit of saving her—and letting her go. Except he had her now. No other passengers were sitting close by.

"Don't like flying, huh?" He studied her openly. He just kept learning more and more about her. He'd always considered himself a pretty good judge of character. It went back to that early training as a kid con artist. And yet he couldn't get a line on her. Maybe that was why she intrigued the hell out of him.

"Motion sickness and all that G-force stuff," she said. "I'm not afraid of flying."

He nodded. She was still a little pale, but she looked great. Outside, white fluffy clouds floated past. He wished what was happening in the world below them didn't matter. But it did. He tried not to think about Florida. It was impossible not to think about P.T.

THE CAPTAIN ANNOUNCED they would be landing soon, and Paige was surprised how quickly the time had gone. She and Devon had talked about all kinds of things—as if they'd known each other forever and had always been friends. She hadn't even noticed that she was flying.

It was motion sickness. That's why she hated flying, she thought. Last night on the roof proved she didn't have a fear of heights. Halfway across the ridge of the roof she'd realized she was on some kind of adrenaline high.

She had felt lighter than air. Scared for her life because there were killers after her, yes, but strangely exhilarated walking on that roof in a downpour with lightning cracking all around her. She couldn't explain it.

Maybe it had been her mother who had a fear of heights. Her mother who couldn't stand to watch tightrope walkers or trapeze artists even on television.

Paige felt the tears and squeezed her eyes shut tighter, fighting the grief. Her mother wouldn't have gone to a circus performance to see the show. She had to have gone there to see someone.

As the plane landed, Devon took her hand again, cradling it in his palm.

Once they were on the ground and taxiing toward the gate, he asked, "So where exactly are we going in Florida?"

"To the circus."

Was it just her imagination or did he flinch?

"Which one?"

"Barney Adams's Amazing One-Ring Circus and Carnival. There's a preseason show today in Gibsonton."

It hadn't been her imagination. When she'd told

him they were going to Florida he'd looked upset. But now at the mention of Adams's Amazing One-Ring Circus and Carnival, he paled, dark eyes narrowing as if in pain.

"Is something wrong?"

He shook his head and flashed her his dimples. But the smile never reached his dark eyes. "Just a little headache." He picked up her purse from the floor, holding it while he helped her into her jean jacket as the other passengers began to unload.

Paige felt as if a weight had been lifted from her shoulders as she led the way off the plane with Devon behind her. She was no longer alone in this.

She glanced at her watch as she came out of the gate to a crowd of people waiting for the next flight. With luck, she and Devon could rent a car and still get to the circus performance in time to talk to someone before it packed up and moved to another town.

She turned to tell him that, but she didn't see him.

That was funny. She thought he'd been right behind her. She looked around for him and thought maybe he was still on the plane, but as she walked toward the gate, the airline clerk told her that all the passengers had disembarked.

Paige stood in the middle of the noisy, busy terminal telling herself he was here somewhere. They'd just gotten separated. He was probably looking for her, too.

But ten minutes later, after the crowd had thinned, she quit kidding herself.

Look in your purse.

Her heart thumped against her ribs as she reached into her shoulder bag. The key was gone! And so was Devon.

CHAPTER ELEVEN

PAIGE WAS SHAKING when she filled out the forms for the rental car. She had searched her purse, praying she was wrong. But the key wasn't there. And only one person could have taken it.

She remembered the way Devon had helped her up out of the airplane window seat, taking her purse from her and helping her with her jean jacket before he handed the pocketbook back to her.

That must have been when he'd taken the key—and after that show of giving it back to her, letting her think she could trust him. What a laugh!

Is this what Buford Wright had been trying to warn her about? She dialed the number he'd given her on her cell phone. No answer. She left her number and a message for him to call.

By the time she was in the rental car and headed south on Highway 41, she was still shaking but with anger. Damn Devon. Letting her pour out her soul to him. Getting her to trust him. Damn him.

What did she care if he had the key? Let him find the evidence and destroy it. Maybe now everyone would leave her alone.

Except she had a bad feeling it wouldn't be that easy.

Did Devon really think he could figure out what the key opened without her?

I think you'll be seeing him again.

A tiny shiver of anticipation escaped her before she could squelch it.

She tried to think of a good reason why he would have taken the key and disappeared, but couldn't.

Well, she'd come to Florida to find out the truth and that was what she was going to do. The more she'd thought about it, the more convinced she was that her mother had come here to meet someone. Michael Alexander?

Was it possible? She didn't know, but she was bound and determined to find out.

Florida. The note from the address book. The key. It all ties together.

Maybe.

Ahead, she saw the sign: Gibsonton. Twenty miles.

Her cell phone rang making her jump. She pulled it out of her purse, surprised Devon hadn't taken it, too. For just an instant, she thought it might be him calling. Then she remembered he didn't have her number. But Buford Wright did.

"Are you alone?" he asked.

"Yes." Very alone. Again.

"Are you all right?"

"Yes." Not really.

"Why are those people after you?"

"I don't know," she said. "I think it has something to do with my father and the reason he faked his death," she said. "I assume you helped him. Do you know why he did it?"

Silence.

"Please. I need your help. My mother is dead and now my father."

"Mike is dead?"

"He was murdered and I have reason to believe that I'm next. They want something from me. Do you have any idea what it is?"

The cop let out a low oath. "You don't realize how dangerous this is."

"Oh, I think I do. What does all of this have to do with Judge Tripp's murder, my father and Judge Wyatt Hathaway?"

Buford swore. "Enough to get us both killed."

"Then it's true that my father was blackmailing Judge Hathaway?"

"Mike? Blackmail?" Buford swore again. "If anyone was being blackmailed, it was your father."

"I have to know the truth. Now."

He paused before he asked, "Where are you?"

"Florida." No reason not to tell him at this point.

"Florida?"

"What happened twenty-three years ago that changed my father's life?"

Silence, then a sigh. "Mike chased down a drunk hit-and-run driver one night in Billings. Unfortunately, there were two judges in the car in town for some district judge conference."

Paige caught her breath. "Wyatt Hathaway and George Tripp."

"Yeah. Hathaway talked Mike out of hauling them both in. Hathaway was a big shot judge and he promised to show up the next morning in court. When Mike stopped them, Tripp was driving, but he was so drunk, Mike suspected Hathaway had been behind the wheel at the time of the accident. The next morning Mike found out that a homeless person had been killed in the hit-and-run. Before he could find the judges to arrest them, Hathaway called, set up a meeting in the park, said there were extenuating circumstances Mike needed to be aware of, that there was a third person in the car that night."

"So they met at the park, Riverside Park, by my house."

"You remember?"

She felt a chill. *"Remember?"*

"What happened in the park that day. You were there."

She gripped the phone, her throat suddenly dry as sand. "You must be mistaken." She couldn't have been there. Her father wouldn't have taken a three-year-old with him, would he?

"You were with Mike. That was one reason he was so freaked. He kept saying you'd seen it all."

She hit the brakes and pulled over, the cars behind her honking furiously as they went around her. The memory. Her father running... Her screaming... Blood. "Oh God."

"Are you all right?"

She couldn't believe this. "My father took me with him?"

"Hell no. You were home with your mother, but you must have slipped out and followed your father. You used to hide in the base of some old tree that had burned out. You were in there when Judge Wyatt Hathaway pulled your father's gun and blew away Judge George Tripp to keep him from testifying that Hathaway was driving the night of the hit-and-run. Hathaway killed that homeless man and just kept right on going, Tripp told your father."

Her hand holding the cell phone began to shake. "But it was my father's word against Judge Hathaway."

"It gets worse. Mike struggled for the gun. Hathaway was wounded, but got away—with you. You'd come out of your hiding place and were covered in Judge Tripp's and Hathaway's blood. Hathaway used the distraction to knock your father out, grab you and take off."

It hadn't been her father running with her?

"Mike made a deal with Hathaway. Mike would confess to the murder. Hathaway would give you back."

"That's why he faked his death."

Buford let out a sigh. "Mike was my partner, but he was also my best friend. I helped him because I knew him, knew the kind of man he was. He said he had to disappear, permanently. So we faked his death using a John Doe from the morgue."

"No one suspected?"

"While the Tripp murder went unsolved, everyone pretty much thought Mike had killed Tripp. Tripp was the judge who'd brought up the misconduct charge against your father over a speeding ticket Mike wrote his daughter. Dirty business, politics and justice."

"But you're still a cop," she pointed out.

"Still a street cop. No chance of ever being anything more with the department. Not with everyone suspecting I helped Mike fake his death," Buford said.

She felt sick. "If what you're saying is the truth—"

"It's true, kid. If your father hid evidence against Judge Wyatt Hathaway, then it's the real stuff. That's probably why Hathaway sent the perfect person to find it. That guy who hit me in the alley, the one who hauled you out of there."

"Devon?"

"Yeah, Devon St. Cloud. You realize who he is, don't you?"

"I know he works for Judge Hathaway, but the judge told him that the evidence is trumped up, that my father murdered Tripp and blackmailed Judge Hathaway."

"Devon St. Cloud does Hathaway's dirty work all right, but Hathaway also raised him and my sources told me that Devon is slick, smart and totally dedicated to seeing that Hathaway gets that State

Supreme Court seat. You understand what I'm telling you?''

She felt tears flood her eyes. ''Yes.'' She understood perfectly.

THE SUN HAD SUNK into Tampa Bay and a cool dusk settled in the orange orchards as Paige crossed the Alafia River into Gibsonton, Florida. The sweet scent of the orange blossoms wafted in through her open window, at first pleasant, then overwhelming and nauseating.

The town was small and the circus and carnival easy to find. The lights of the Ferris wheel glittered against the twilit sky as she parked her car and walked through the mild spring evening toward the excited sounds. Music played and children screamed as the rides whirled. A large red-and-white striped tent had been erected in the big field at the edge of town. Flags blew gently in the breeze and she caught the smell of corn dogs and cotton candy. It was later than she'd planned to be here.

She tried not to think about Devon. Or the key or how stupid she'd been to trust him. But she couldn't help but wonder where he was. Had he beaten her here? Why would he do that unless he knew something about the key? Or about her mother's hit-and-run?

Paige thought of the look on his face when she'd told him where they were headed, especially which circus.

He'd looked scared. Because he'd had something to do with her mother's death? She couldn't believe it. Refused to. Maybe she'd been wrong to trust him, but Devon St. Cloud wasn't a killer. Not the man who'd held her hand on the plane. He couldn't be.

Yeah, the guy's a real hero.

Okay, she'd been a fool, losing the key, losing herself in his dark eyes. One look at Devon and she'd known he was anything but a hero. Unfortunately, his lips had said something completely different.

One kiss and you're taken in.

It was two kisses, but who was counting? And what was more intimate than a kiss?

She felt a tightening in her stomach as she watched a tilt-a-whirl go round and round in a flash of color and screams. As she neared the circus tent, she saw that the performance was over and men were taking down the rigging. Maybe she was too late.

She had put all of her hopes on a circus ticket stub and a grainy newspaper photograph. But now that she was here she wondered what she'd hoped to find out. Maybe she didn't want to know why her mother had come here. She'd learned more than enough to last a lifetime.

Buck up. So the bum dumped you and stole your key. You going to let him win?

This wasn't a contest.

Oh, really. What if Buford's right? What if there is evidence that proves Judge Wyatt Hathaway is a murderer? You going to let Devon find it and give it to the judge?

She stopped walking. If she'd really been at that

park that day... She thought about what Buford had told her. About Judge Hathaway's story. How could she believe her father's partner, the man who'd helped him fake his death, over that of a judge on his way to the State Supreme Court? And yet she did. Or maybe she just wanted so desperately to believe her father had been a victim rather than a criminal.

But then how did she explain the blackmail? She'd seen money exchanged in her father's coffin. And now she had a key that if she could figure out what it opened, would lead her to proof of who was lying?

She couldn't believe a man like Judge Wyatt Hathaway would lie, though.

Hello? Why does anyone lie? To save his neck. But isn't it more likely that Devon just didn't tell you the part you played in all this?

There was a thought. If Devon knew she'd been there that day, maybe he was just hoping she would remember so she'd know what the key went to. Is that why her name had been in the package?

But she'd only been three and the memory, if it was even real and the same day as the murder, was too vague. And, if that was Devon's plan, then where was he? Why had he skipped out on her?

The answer has to be here at the circus.

Or had she been lured here just as her mother might have?

The air was warm and damp as a swamp as she walked around to the back of the tent where all the trucks and trailers were parked. She would at least talk to the ringmaster from the photograph.

Her throat went dry as she neared an old truck, the hood up, two men leaning into the engine.

Behind her in the midway, carnival music and the shrill cries of children filled the air.

"This area is closed," said one of the men when he saw her.

"I'm looking for the ringmaster?"

The man stepped away from the truck and walked over to her. He gave her the once-over. "What's it about?" He was intimidating enough with his thick ham-size arms and grease up to his shoulders from working on the truck engine, but there was a huge spider tattooed on his neck, one of the spider's legs coming around to his cheek like a sideburn.

"It's personal," she said, trying to hide the fact that he unsettled her.

"Mr. Fuentes don't see people without an appointment," the man said.

"He'll want to see *me*," she bluffed.

The man's eyes narrowed. "You with one of them animal groups? 'Cuz if you are—"

"I'm not with any group. I told you, it's personal." She felt nauseous, the smell of frying corn dogs thick in the air. Somewhere nearby, one of the rides clanked loudly over the shriek of the riders. "I'd appreciate it, if you'd tell Mr. Fuentes I'm here."

That didn't prove necessary. The ringmaster from

the photograph came out of the big tent. He stopped when he saw her.

For a moment, she wondered if he could have recognized her, but how was that possible? "Mr. Fuentes? I'm Paige…Alexander. I need to talk to you." She thought he recoiled. From the name? Or was it her outstretched hand. He moved toward a small trailer. "It will only take a moment of your time. I will make it worth your while," she added to his back.

He stopped walking, glanced over his shoulder at her, then at the men who'd been working on the truck, but were now watching her and their boss with interest. "Get back to work!" he barked, motioning for Paige to follow him.

The trailer was round and small, almost comical like something a dozen clowns would come pouring out of. He opened the door and went in first, ducking his head. She did the same.

Once inside, he went to the cabinet over the miniature sink and pulled down some paper cups and a bottle of whiskey. "You want some?"

She shook her head and watched as he poured himself a paper cup half full and downed it. Was he drinking because of her? Or was this a nightly ritual?

He let out an "Ahhhh," then put the bottle back, along with the unused cups and closed the cabinet door. "So?" he asked, turning to look at her with obvious suspicion.

Now she wasn't so sure he'd recognized her or

the name. He probably treated everyone like this. "I'm looking for someone."

He seemed to stiffen.

She took the photo from her purse and held it out to him. "She came to your St. Petersburg show last week."

He let out a laugh and didn't reach for the photo she held out to him. He almost looked relieved as if he'd thought she might be looking for someone else, other than a woman who'd attended one of his shows last week.

"You can't be serious," he said. "Do you have any idea how many people I see in a night? In a week? In a year?"

"I'm quite serious," she said and pushed the photo at him. "What would it hurt to take a look?"

He seemed to hesitate, eyes hooded. He took the photo, glanced at it and tried to hand it back.

She didn't take it. "She's much younger in the snapshot. She would have been in her mid-fifties when she came to see your show." She waited for him to take a good look. She wasn't leaving until he did.

He must have realized that. With obvious reluctance, he looked again at the photograph.

She watched his face.

He studied the snapshot of her mother. Then his gaze shifted to the man in the picture. It was so subtle she wouldn't have been able to swear she saw the change in his expression. He handed the photo back. "If she was at one of my shows, I don't remember her. I'm sorry."

This time she took the snapshot of her parents from him when he held it out. "You recognized the man."

"What?" He looked startled.

"You recognized the man in the photo."

His face darkened. "I don't know what you're talking about. Look, I tried to help you. I couldn't. I have a show to tear down." He moved toward her, but she was blocking the door.

"The woman came to your show a week ago. If she didn't come here to talk to you, then maybe it was to meet the man in the photograph. I need to know," she said, hearing the pleading in her voice.

"Why don't you ask *her* instead of bothering me with it?" he demanded impatiently.

"Because she's dead. She was killed by a hit-and-run driver just minutes after she left your performance."

He hadn't known. She could see it in his expression. He moved her aside and opened the trailer door. "I'm sorry, but I really can't help you." He sounded concerned.

She stepped out into the warm, wet Florida air. The carnival lights and music throbbed against the sounds of shrieks and cries. The big top was already down. By tomorrow, this would just be an empty lot again, all signs of the circus and carnival gone. Almost as if it had never been here.

Fuentes closed the trailer door behind him and

started toward the truck where the tattooed man was still under the hood.

"The woman in the photo was my mother," she said to his retreating back, her voice cracking with emotion. "The man was my father. His name was Michael Alexander. He was murdered last week."

Fuentes stopped, shoulders hunching, his chin dropping to his chest. He didn't turn to look at her. "I'm sorry. But I still can't help you. You'd be smart to leave now."

She watched him walk away. He'd recognized her father in the photograph. He'd been surprised and upset to hear Michael Alexander was dead. He'd known her father.

Behind her, Paige heard the sound of an elephant roar followed by voices and the heavy thump of a large animal's feet on a metal floor. Through a narrow alley between two of the semi trucks and trailers, she caught a glimpse of several people trying to load an elephant into a stock trailer. One of them was small, female and barking out orders to the two others. The animal trainer from the newspaper photograph?

Paige wound her way through the house trailers and campers toward the back of the huge lot where the larger semis and trailers had been parked in a line, just a few feet apart. She lost sight of the stock truck and elephant as she cut between two trucks, the sides like canyon walls towering up to the slit of sky overhead.

Outside the tunneled blackness between the trucks

and attached trailers came screams, canned music and the clank of metal as a nearby carnival ride spun a kaleidoscope of colors into the sky overhead like fireworks.

The carnival noises masked the footsteps behind her. Paige didn't realize she'd been followed into the darkness between the trucks until she felt the first blow.

Something hit her from in back. She stumbled but didn't fall, her scream more startled than frightened. As she turned, a gloved hand smacked her hard in the face. She cried out. The sound echoed down the tunnel between the trucks, lost in the noise of the midway.

She didn't see her attacker before the next blow struck. She was trying to get her feet under her, trying to get her legs moving. The blow knocked the air from her lungs. She caught just a glimpse of a dark form standing over her before she hit the ground.

CHAPTER TWELVE

DEVON LEANED OVER P.T. She was still breathing. He checked her pulse. Strong. Just like her. The depth of his relief almost buckled his knees. Just as the breadth of his anger did. He'd seen a lot of violence in his early life and thought he'd become immune to it. But seeing her on the ground and that goon standing over—

He scooped her up from the dust and carried her through the row of trucks to the hole in the fence he'd come through earlier.

Any moment now the others would be coming. He was in as much danger here as she was. More. He'd sworn nothing could get him back to this place. Certainly not some key and what it opened. Not even an old debt he owed.

He'd come here for her, knowing that following her could get them both killed. As soon as he was able, he'd tried to catch up with her, but there'd been a wreck, traffic backed up for miles. He'd gotten off the highway and taken back roads to get here. Just not quick enough.

And here he was in Gibsonton, Florida. 'Gibtown' as the carnies called it. The town where the carnivals wintered and the carnies called home. The home of his nightmare childhood.

He looked down at the woman in his arms. He'd never had any strong spiritual beliefs, but this had to be some sort of retribution for his sins.

Hadn't he known that one day he'd have to face the past? Did he really think he'd shaken it off like dust from his shoes? He'd pretended for so long that those first twelve years of his life hadn't existed.

He should have known he couldn't erase who he'd been any more than he could who he'd become. But damned if he didn't feel like there was something cosmic going on. It felt as if he'd been destined to be drawn back here, though not by revenge as he had often planned. Quite the opposite. The irony didn't escape him.

He looked down at P.T.'s face as he headed toward his car parked at the edge of the field, feeling like the heel he was. He'd taken the key, telling himself he was protecting her. All these years, he'd only been kidding himself. He wasn't that much different from the boy he'd been, the one who had earned his keep by lying, cheating and stealing. He just wore fancier clothes now.

Every cell in him just wanted out of this town. But he knew it wouldn't be that easy. He'd thought he would just find the evidence, destroy it, finish this. Simple enough.

He hadn't anticipated meeting someone like P.T., nor the feelings she evoked in him. He didn't want to see her hurt anymore. She'd already been through so much. And it felt far from over.

She stirred. She was light as a feather, her soft supple body warm against his chest, her dark hair brushing his arm and he felt an unbearable ache at just the sight of her.

He figured she would be anything but happy to see him. Under the circumstances, he couldn't blame her. She'd be angry and hurt that he'd taken the key. The last thing he wanted her doing was opening her eyes and screaming bloody murder. Not now.

Behind him, he could hear a commotion between the trucks. The other roustabouts had found one of their own, bruised and bloody, beneath a truck trailer. There would be hell to pay.

Devon reached his rental car, opened the door and slid P.T. into the passenger seat. As he ran around to the driver's side, he saw the first carny come through the fence. The man had a tire iron clenched in his fist.

Devon leapt into the car, fumbled the key into the ignition and hit the automatic door lock, locking all four doors.

P.T. was coming to. He figured she'd come awake fighting mad. Just what he needed. He wouldn't be able to fight her—and the carnies. And right now he needed to get her away from the mob coming through that fence.

Her eyes came open an instant before he turned the key in the ignition. Several more carnies came through the fence, all running, the one with the tire iron almost to the car.

"You!" P.T. cried, the look in her eyes killing him. Did she think he was the one who'd attacked and beaten her? Or was she just mad about him deserting her and taking the key? "You bastard!" She grabbed for the door handle.

In that instant, the car engine roared to life. He hit the gas, popped the clutch and grabbed her to keep her from getting out. The tires squealed on the pavement as the car took off. P.T.'s door swung open. The carny with the tire iron threw himself onto the hood, clinging to the wiper blades as he brought the tire iron down on the windshield. P.T.'s side of the windshield fractured into a white web.

Devon cranked the wheel in the opposite direction, sending the car into a spin. P.T.'s door slammed shut. The carny's eyes widened. One wiper blade broke, then the other. The thug went flying off the hood, crashing into several of his buddies. One of them managed to grab the door handle on the driver's side, but he didn't hang on long as Devon straightened the car out and floored the gas, leaving the mob in the dust and darkness.

Devon didn't look back. He took roads he thought he'd forgotten. He knew the carnies would give chase. He also knew he and P.T. would be lucky to get away with their lives.

"You bastard!" P.T. cried again and began to wail on him with her fists.

"I just saved your life," he said, holding up an arm to ward her off. "Again."

"Saved my life?!" She was crying, her lower lip split and bleeding, the skin around her right eye discolored, soon to be black, and there was a cut on her cheek.

Devon looked at her and wished he'd killed the man who'd done this to her instead of just knocked him out.

"I pulled some guy off of you, a carny with a bad attitude and some kind of huge ugly tattoo on his neck and face," he said. "I took care of him."

She stopped pummeling him and sat back. But her eyes were on him, her gaze scorching. "Violence seems to come as easily to you as lying and stealing," she said, her voice tight.

"Only when it's necessary," he said without looking at her as he zigzagged his way through the back lanes of Gibtown. He caught the occasional glimpse of carnival trucks and rides, cotton candy and corn dog wagons parked in the trees, illuminated by a yard light. This was where circus and carnival people had wintered since 1937 when the Giant and his wife, Half Woman, opened the Giant's Camp.

"Where are we going?" she asked, glancing out at the passing darkness, looking worried.

He told himself he hadn't even thought about where to go, but as he glanced down the road, he realized he'd been headed in this direction the whole time. "I should be taking you to the hospital, but it's not safe." He would take her to the next best place.

"I'm fine. I don't need a hospital."

He might have argued the point, but her injuries didn't seem to be life threatening, just painful.

"So where are you taking me?" she demanded.

"Some place safe." At least he hoped it was still safe.

"You didn't have to take the key." She sounded more hurt than angry and he hated himself for deceiving her. "I would have given it to you."

He could feel her gaze on him. He wanted to tell her that he took the key to keep her safe, but he didn't bother, knowing she wouldn't believe him. He wasn't sure he believed it himself.

"So why did you come back?" With her sleeve, she dried her tears, wincing at the pain.

He shook his head, watching the rearview mirror. "I didn't abandon you. There were cops waiting for me at the gate. Some old warrants. Judge Hathaway took care of it." One phone call to Wyatt and Devon was free again. Wasn't that the way it had always worked? If he ever thought he didn't need the judge's protection, he quickly learned that he did.

So the judge had cleared things with the cops. Then Devon had given him the bad news about Fiona. "She was the one who picked up the blackmail money at the funeral home. I think she's also behind trying to kill me and Jimmy. She isn't working alone. There's a man with her."

"What man?"

"I don't know yet."

The judge had answered with a long, tired sigh and, "I'll take care of it. Any luck on the other?"

"Not yet."

"I have some bad news of my own," the judge had said.

"Something else happened," P.T. said now, her anger quickly turning to concern. "What is it?"

"When I called the judge—" Jimmy. My God. The pain was unbearable. "I wasn't the only kid Wyatt Hathaway took under his wing years ago. He brought home this skinny short kid a few months after me. Jimmy. He was like a kid brother."

"The guy driving the car the night at the funeral home?" she asked quietly.

"He was murdered last night in New Orleans. His place was torn apart. It looks like he was killed for the package."

"Oh, my God, no. Oh, Devon, I'm so sorry."

He nodded. Why hadn't Jimmy gone to Mexico like he said he would? He felt the weight of Jimmy's death on him as well as his obligations to the judge. Another debt that demanded payment.

"I tried to catch up to you." He looked over at her, sick that he hadn't gotten to her in time.

She nodded, tears shimmering in her eyes.

He felt his chest tighten at the sight of her pain. "This isn't your fault," he said quickly. He knew what taking on guilt could do to a person. It made him a prisoner. Guilt. And gratitude. He didn't want that for P.T.

He slowed to turn onto a lane that wound down to the Alafia River. As a shack of a place came into view, he saw that nothing had changed. It was exactly as it had been in his memory.

He stopped the car, turned out the lights and sat for a moment just looking at the weathered wood. A single light shone inside. He opened his door. "Wait here a minute, okay?"

"Devon—"

"I'll be right back." He stepped out, closed the door, extinguishing the interior light and pitching himself and the shack in darkness. He heard P.T. roll down her window to listen, surprised she'd actually done what he'd asked her given how he'd deceived her earlier.

For an instant, he feared he'd been wrong, that everything had changed in the years he'd been gone. Then he heard a familiar sound come out of the dark—the click of a double barrel shotgun being snapped closed.

"You best have a real good reason for being on my property," said a scratchy, aged female voice from the blackness.

His throat tightened, his voice breaking as he said: "Mae, you're just as mean as I remember. I guess some things *don't* change."

He could hear the palm fronds rustling in the breeze coming up from the river. A flashlight came on, blinding him. A soft curse rose from behind the light. "Bless my stars." The light flicked past him to the car and P.T., then to the ground where it seemed to vibrate as if the hand holding it were trembling.

Devon moved to the old woman, taking the shotgun from her hand and pulling her into his arms. She was thin as a rail and just as steely.

Mae Drummond hugged him tightly, still strong. Then she leaned back to look at him, a trembling smile turning up her lips as her eyes filled with tears. "I never thought I'd ever see you again."

He shook his head, still convinced he shouldn't be here. And for very good reasons none of which had to do with the warrants out on him.

"Get that girl in here. You can hide the car behind that old trailer over there," she said, pointing off to the side.

"Thanks, Mae."

She brushed off his gratitude, her gaze acknowledging that she knew the only reason he was here now was because he was in some sort of serious trouble.

P.T. having heard Mae, had opened the car door, quickly closed it and was moving toward them.

"I'm Mae, honey. Get yourself inside." She motioned for Devon to shake a leg as she took one look at Paige and ushered her into the house.

He hid the car and went back to the shack. The place didn't look like much from the outside, but was warm and cozy inside. It had once been a trailer years ago, but Mae had built over it, adding a wooden porch from which she fished the river and a long dock that stretched out into the water.

P.T. looked up as he came in. She was sitting at the small kitchen table, a cup of coffee the color of mud in front of her, both hands cradling the steaming brew. One blue eye was wide, demanding answers. The other was swollen shut.

"Put this on your eye," Mae ordered, handing P.T. a bag of frozen peas from the small fridge-freezer and shooting Devon a look, half-question, half-accusation.

P.T. did as she was told, her one good eye not leaving his face.

"Okay, let's hear it," Mae said, filling two jelly glasses with iced tea. She handed one to Devon and raised the other. "What are you doing back in Gibtown?"

BACK IN GIBTOWN? Paige stared at him with her good eye. No wonder he'd seemed to know how to get away from the men after her. At first she'd thought he was just driving, not knowing where he was going. Until he'd pulled off into this place and she'd realized he'd been here before.

"What *am* I doing here," he said and glanced toward Paige. "I wish I knew."

She lowered the icy bag of peas for a moment to glare at him. "You used to live here?"

"Back in my so-called childhood. My stepfather was a carny. With Barney Adams's Amazing Circus and Carnival." He smiled at her surprise. "The last thing I ever wanted to do was come back here."

But he had, following her. To protect her? Or only

because he needed the key—and her to get what he wanted?

She took a sip of the coffee. It actually tasted good. She tried to remember the last time she'd eaten as her stomach growled.

Mae glanced at her. "You look starved." The older woman didn't wait for an answer. She whipped up some sandwiches even though Devon said he wasn't hungry. "Eat," she ordered. He did.

Paige ate hers gingerly because of her cut lip, and the frozen peas on her eye made her head ache. When she'd finished, she looked up to see Devon watching her.

"Do you still keep a first aid kit around?" he asked Mae.

She opened a cabinet door, handed him a small box then glanced at the window at the sound of a vehicle passing by. "Does anyone know you're back?"

He shook his head. "But someone's looking for us. She asked too many questions tonight after the show just up the road."

Mae nodded. "What does this have to do with you?"

"Nothing," he said. And possibly everything. "I had a talk with the guy who beat her up."

Mae sighed. "He didn't recognize you?"

Devon shook his head. "I don't think so."

"Good." Mae downed her drink and placed the glass on the kitchen counter. "I'll make up the spare room for your friend." A look passed between the elderly woman and Devon just before she turned and disappeared to the back of the trailer.

He opened the first aid kit and slid his chair closer to her. She started to protest, but he silenced her with a look that he wasn't going to brook any arguments. She wasn't up to a fight anyway.

He took the peas from her. His fingers were gentle as he cleaned the cut over her eye, on her cheek, on her lip.

"This is going to burn a little," he said as he swabbed each cut with a disinfectant.

Her eyes blurred with tears, but she refused to make a sound. Or maybe she was just too tired to.

He met her gaze and smiled. "You're something, P.T., you know that?"

Something good? Or just something? The way he was looking at her—it was something amazing. She shook her head, hating it when he was kind to her. All it did was confuse her.

She liked the way he called her P.T. and she realized somewhere along the line she'd become her imagined alter ego P. T. Alexander, that she'd always had the potential and that she wasn't the same person she'd been before this had all started.

It made her a little sad. But for what she'd lost— her naïveté—she'd gained even more. She was stronger now, more confident, more sure of her own capabilities. And she didn't need anyone to remind her that she should be careful where Devon St. Cloud was concerned.

He carefully smoothed a bandage over the cut on her cheek, his touch amazingly soft.

Her hand went up to cover his. He stopped in midmotion. She opened her mouth to thank him, but no words came out. She squeezed his hand, unable to put her gratitude into words. Whatever his motives, he'd saved her life tonight.

She let go and he gently brushed his fingers across her cheek, his expression so tender... She looked into his eyes and thought for a moment she saw—

He dragged his gaze away as if afraid of what she might see. What secrets did he keep hidden in all that darkness? If they weren't a pair. Both with so many childhood scars. She closed her eyes to the thought.

A moment later, he surprised her by placing the key in the palm of her hand. She opened her eyes, except he had already turned his back and was busy putting away the first aid kit.

Unconsciously, she rubbed her fingers along the worn surface of the key as she watched him, her body aching for him to take her in his arms.

"We'll stay the night," he said quietly, his back to her. "In the morning, I'll try to get you out of this town and far away from here."

"I can't leave. I'm pretty sure my mother came down here to see my father. The ringmaster knew my father."

"He told you that?"

"No," she admitted, "but when I showed him the photograph of my parents, he recognized my father. I'm sure of it and he seemed upset when I told him that Michael Alexander had been murdered.''

"That's probably what got you beaten up,'' Devon said softly.

"I don't believe that,'' she said stubbornly. "I know if I talk to him again—''

"Forget it,'' Devon snapped, shaking his head. "All you'll accomplish is getting yourself killed. He isn't going to talk to you. No one will. You don't know these people. They're a family, close-knit, and the one thing they distrust is strangers. Especially those who come in asking questions.''

She wanted to argue, but she didn't have the energy. Worse, she suspected he was right. But she had no other plan.

"You're not going to stop looking for the evidence, are you,'' she said.

His smoldering gaze came up to meet hers. What desires fired such a look? More than gratitude. More than revenge. "I have to keep looking for it.''

She nodded, remembering what Buford had told her. "You would do anything for Judge Hathaway, wouldn't you?''

He seemed surprised, then wary of her question. "I owe him my life.''

She nodded. "Would you kill for him?'' She already knew that Devon would steal for him.

His dark gaze hardened. "There is only so much you can owe another person.''

It wasn't the answer she'd hoped for. Devon had risked his life for Wyatt Hathaway. Risked his life to save her in order to save his benefactor—and find the evidence. And now Devon had Jimmy's death to vindicate.

She looked down at the key in her hand. She'd been rubbing the worn metal with her thumb and could feel what at one time had been some kind of design imprinted on the key. She stared at it, but couldn't make anything out. Maybe it was just an imperfection. Life was certainly full of those.

"I talked to Buford Wright," she said with obvious antagonism. She was spoiling for a fight, she realized. Angry with Devon, but for reasons that had more to do with the way he made her feel than anything he'd done.

A flicker of worry flashed in his gaze.

"He told me a story that is far different from the one you said Judge Hathaway told you," she said.

He visibly stiffened. "What did he tell you?"

She repeated Buford Wright's account of the events that had led up to her father's faked suicide.

"Do you believe him?" Devon asked.

She had expected him to adamantly deny Buford's claim, to point out that the cop had been part of a criminal cover-up, that Buford's credibility couldn't compare to Judge Hathaway's, that Buford had every reason to lie. And she'd been ready to fight to the death for Buford's story. But Devon's answer had taken all the fight out of her. "I don't know."

He shook his head, his smile sad. "Neither do I."

"I want to believe it." Tears filled her eyes.

He came over and sat down next to her, taking her free hand just as he had on the plane. "I don't know what to believe. That's why we have to find whatever that key unlocks," he said softly. "That's the only way we'll ever know the truth."

We. She liked the sound of that. She nodded, the key clutched in one hand, the other gripping Devon's hand.

"You should get some rest," he said after a moment. "We can talk in the morning. I'll be sleeping just outside in the cabana if you need me."

She needed him now. Was that why he seemed so anxious to get away from her? "Will you even be here in the morning?"

He gave her a hurt smile. "Yes, you have my word on it. For what that's worth."

"Yes, for what that's worth," she repeated.

"Can't you see she's exhausted and in pain?" Mae said coming into the room. She turned to Paige. "Don't worry, Devon will be here." The older woman shot him a warning look that said he damned well better be here.

Mae led her down the hallway to a small bedroom.

"I put out a cotton gown for you," Mae said, fluffing one of the pillows on the bed. "You want a bath or a shower?"

"Shower, thank you." She couldn't stay awake long enough for a bath. She hadn't realized how exhausted she was. The window was open and the night breeze smelled sweet with flowering orange trees mellowed by the scent of the river. A breeze stirred the white curtains. The bed was turned down, the pale blue sheets looked cool and inviting. "It looks heavenly."

Mae smiled and helped her out of the jean jacket, then went to hang the jacket in the closet. "Enjoy your shower. There's plenty of towels. Holler if you need anything."

"You look beautiful," Mae said, smiling at her when she came out of the bathroom in the wonderfully worn white cotton gown. Tears welled in the older woman's eyes as she moved to Paige and took her hand in both of hers.

"Thank you for every—" The rest of what Paige was going to say died on her lips. She stared down at Mae's wrist, heart in her throat. "That tattoo. You have the same tattoo as my father." The same stylized bird.

Mae's smile widened as she sat down on the edge of the bed and patted a spot next to her for Paige. "It is a symbol of flight. All of the Alexandros wore it, even the small children."

Paige sat, knees too weak to hold her any longer. She felt light-headed and faint. "Alexandros?"

"You resemble your father," Mae said, still smiling.

"You knew my father?" She didn't know why that surprised her. Not after seeing the tattoo.

"He was my grandnephew."

Paige stared at her, wondering if the knock on her head was making her hallucinate.

"And you," Mae said, taking her hand again, "are my great-grandniece."

Paige shook her head. "How can that be?"

The older woman's hands felt cool, the thin skin smooth, the fingers surprisingly strong. "Your father left his family years ago. I'm sure he never told you about us."

"He didn't tell me much of anything. He... disappeared when I was three," she managed to say.

"We were the Alexandros, once a great family of trapeze artists." She smiled. "Your father loved the trapeze and he was very good, even at a young age."

"My father? We are talking about Michael Alexander?"

Mae nodded. "He changed his name after he left. You see he saw his mother fall to her death when he was sixteen. There was no net. He was devastated and could no longer fly. He quarreled with his father, wanting someone to blame. He left and was not heard from again."

"Then how did you know I—"

"He came to me in a dream."

Paige felt her heart drop. The woman was loony. Paige should have known this couldn't be true.

"I have something for you," Mae said and got up. She went to a drawer. "I put it here after I had the dream." She came back with an eight-by-ten framed publicity photograph.

Paige took it, her eyes widening. A banner ran across the top with a circus wagon on it and the words: The Alexandros. Below were a troupe of trapeze artists. The photograph was obviously old. And on the side of the circus wagon was the stylized bird like the tattoo she'd seen on the inside of her father's and Mae's wrist.

"That is your father," Mae said pointing to a boy in costume. "And that was his mother, your grandmother, my sister. Yes, she looks like you."

Paige felt her good eye blur with tears. She looked so much like her grandmother— She looked again at her father. "It's true, isn't it."

"Of course it is true." Mae sat down again on the bed. "In my dream your father told me of his imprisonment far from here, of all that he had lost in his life, of you. It was you he worried about. He had heard that a very powerful man was about to take an even more powerful position. He said that man might hurt you to get what he wanted." She shrugged. "Ah, dreams. Sometimes they are so clear and other times— Does this make any sense to you?"

Paige felt a chill. It did if that powerful man was Judge Wyatt Hathaway, and what Buford Wright had told her was true.

"I see that you understand. Good. Your father had many heartaches. He ached to be with you but it wasn't safe. He said Simone was with him now and that he would find peace as soon as you were safe."

Simone was with him? Paige felt goose bumps prickle her skin. "When did you have this dream?"

Mae smiled sadly. "The night after he was murdered."

Paige was trying hard not to put too much store into Mae's dream, but she still felt a chill. How could Mae have known about Simone? About the rest of it?

"When I woke, it felt as if he'd been here," the older woman said and smiled. "Maybe he had." Her smile faded as a sadness came into her eyes. "He ran away to escape the tragedy of his mother's death only to find more tragedy." She shook her head as if life were a mystery she could never decipher, then she brightened. "Your father asked me to help you when you arrived."

"You knew I was coming here?" Paige asked, the room suddenly feeling cold.

"Not until your father told me in the dream. I didn't know Devon would be coming with you, though." She shrugged again. "God works in mysterious ways, yes?"

"Yes." Paige looked at the photograph again, studying a younger Mae before she turned to the older woman and gave her a hug. Whether Mae had seen her father in a dream or not, Paige was thankful for the peace Mae had given her. "Thank you."

"You are family," Mae said, hugging her tightly. "Now get some rest."

"How do you know Devon?" she asked as Mae was leaving.

"He lived up the road and he would come down to visit me when his stepfather was in a mean mood and his mother was drunk.'' She shrugged. ''He had a very hard life. But is his life so easy now?''

''Can I trust him?'' Paige asked suddenly, needing desperately to know.

''Only you can know that.'' Mae tapped the spot over her heart with her arthritic fingers, smiled and with a wink, closed the door.

DEVON STOOD ON THE PORCH, staring out at the river and listening to the once familiar sounds of the Florida night. He knew he wouldn't be able to sleep. He'd sprawled on the couch in the cabana attached to the trailer, praying for the oblivion of sleep, but ended up only staring up at the watermarked ceiling, unable to shut down his mind.

All he could think about was P.T. He'd let her get hurt. He could never forgive himself for that. But he also couldn't have waltzed into that carnival with her. As far as he knew, his stepfather still worked for Barney Adams and the carnival had a memory that went back much farther than two decades when Judge Wyatt Hathaway had had Ray thrown into jail and sobered up Devon's mother Lisa long enough to sign her son over to him.

Being here, in his town, was like reliving his stepfather's cruelty, his mother's indifference, the constant struggle of his childhood to just survive. If it hadn't been for Mae—and later Wyatt—Devon knew he would be buried here.

But he'd gotten out. Thanks to Judge Wyatt Hathaway. He could never forget that. Just as he could never forget Jimmy. Both debts hung over him, heavy as the hot spring night air.

"You know who she is, don't you?" Devon said as Mae joined him out on the porch. The river moved silently past, the moon full and bright through the palm fronds.

"She's Michael's girl," Mae said.

Devon nodded. He knew he'd seen Michael Alexander before when he'd seen the body in the casket at the funeral home. It just hadn't clicked until tonight. Alexander. Alexandros. It still surprised him sometimes how small the world was. Especially his. And the center had always been Gibtown.

"What are you doing with her?" Mae asked.

"I'm trying to save her."

"Oh?" she asked, lifting a brow. "I thought you were trying to save your judge."

"It's all the same thing."

"Is it?" Mae asked.

"I never thought I'd be back here," he said, staring again at the river, not wanting to deal with the issues Mae was determined to stir inside him.

"Maybe you needed to come back and face some of those old ghosts," she said, not letting him off the hook.

"I'm not that kid who left here."

"That's too bad," she said, turning to go back into the trailer. "I liked that kid." Over her shoulder she added, "You know your mother left you something before she died. Ray's been keeping it for you."

CHAPTER THIRTEEN

THE LAST THING Devon wanted to do was see his stepfather. Ray had been nothing but mean to him as far back as he could remember. He had only bad memories.

But he knew he couldn't leave without whatever his mother had left him. One way or the other.

He walked through the darkness down the narrow lane before stopping outside a chain-link fence, memories drowning him as he looked at the place where he'd spent the first twelve years of his life. No wonder he'd never looked back.

He could see the old trailer through the trees, a light on inside. Several broken-down carnival trucks and rides rusted off to the side of the lot.

A dog barked in the neighbor's yard. The gate was large and unlocked. Bracing himself, he pushed it open and walked toward the trailer. The dog next door started growling and jumping on the adjoining fence, raising a racket.

A dim porch light came on at Ray's trailer. Devon slowed as the door opened and someone stepped out onto the porch.

"Who's there?" The voice sounded old and male.

Devon stepped closer, stopping short of the porch steps and his stepfather. He couldn't hide his shock. The past two decades had not been kind to Ray. His hair was white, his shoulders stooped, his skin hung from his large frame. As a boy, Devon used to pray for the day that he would be a man and could take Ray on.

Now he couldn't imagine raising a hand to this old man.

"Well, I'll be damned," Ray said in his old man voice. "Look what the cat dragged in."

Devon thought maybe Ray had mellowed with the years. But as he moved up the porch steps, he saw that same cruelty he remembered in Ray's eyes. That meanness.

"Mae told me my mother left something for me," he said as he mounted the steps.

"Yeah, she wrote you a letter on her deathbed. Knew she'd seen the last of you while she was alive." Ray had the good sense to step back. He seemed surprised to find Devon towering over him as if he'd always thought he would be the larger, stronger and meaner of the two. One out of three wasn't bad.

"Where is the letter?"

"I'm surprised you had the guts to come back here," Ray said as he lowered himself into a worn lawn chair at the end of the porch. "Your mother always said that some day that highfalutin father of yours would show up and take you off my hands."

He wagged his head. "Took the son of a bitch long enough though, don't you think?"

"He wasn't my father," Devon said.

Ray laughed, a sound that cut like a sharp blade. "So he never owned up to it? That doesn't surprise me."

"The letter."

It was clear Ray had been drinking and didn't know what he was talking about. "Just inside where your mother kept her pretty things," he said, his voice hardening.

The trailer door was standing open. Devon stepped in and looked on the shelf next to the door where his mother had kept her menagerie of tiny glass figures. There had only been a half dozen, all in different colors, all stylized different animals. When he was little, she'd let him hold one if he was good.

She'd once told him his real father had bought them for her, but she'd been drunk at the time. Even if it were true, the figures were just cheap glass, probably something his father had picked up at one of the carnival stands. But she'd loved them as if they were solid gold.

He picked up the letter from the shelf where the animals had always sat. The envelope was thin and flat. His mother must not have had much to say to him.

"I didn't open it," Ray said from the chair out on the porch. "Don't expect you to believe me, though."

The letter was sealed, but any fool could have opened it and resealed it.

"What happened to her glass animals?" Devon asked as he came back out.

"Broke 'em to smithereens the day she died," Ray said from the dark end of the porch. "Should have done it sooner."

Devon couldn't see Ray's face in the darkness. He'd hated this man as far back as he could remember and always thought that some day he would tell him what he thought. But now as he looked at the heap of a man at the end of the porch, he could think of nothing to say.

With the envelope in his hand, he stepped off the porch and started toward the gate.

"She drank herself to death, you know," Ray called after him. "All because of your father. The son of a bitch broke her heart, left her with a kid she couldn't support. If she hadn't written him to come get you..."

Devon reached the gate, his heart pounding. He stepped through, fighting the urge to run. It wasn't true. None of it was true. He gripped the letter as he started down the dark lane, not looking back, not at the trailer or Ray or his childhood.

PAIGE DIDN'T KNOW what had awakened her. She stayed perfectly still, listening, then rose from the bed and, opening the door, looked out.

A faint light burned out in the cabana. She opened the trailer door and went out onto the porch.

Through the screen to the small cabana, she could see that the couch was empty. Her heart lurched. Then she spotted Devon's shoes on the floor by the couch. He wouldn't leave without his shoes.

She moved quietly across the porch, worrying about him. Obviously, he couldn't sleep any more than she could. She knew this place must hold horrible memories for him.

Through the palm trees she saw the river, the surface silver coated, and Devon and the dock he stood on bathed in moonlight.

She followed the path barefooted to the dock, stepped onto the warm, smooth wooden boards and walked soundlessly toward him, afraid she was the last person he wanted to see. He had his back to her, his gaze on the river as if his thoughts were miles away. Or maybe just up the road.

She stopped just inches from him. He still hadn't heard her. He had something in his hands...a sheet of paper. His head was bent close to the paper as he was reading the words in the light of the moon.

Suddenly, he let out a sound like a sob, balled the paper in his fist and threw it into the water. She stared at his broad back as he watched the paper float away on the river.

Her heart filled to bursting as she stared at him standing there, seeing the pain in the slump of his shoulders, feeling it as if it permeated the air around him.

She reached for him, a thought piercing her heart like an arrow: I love this man.

The simple proclamation caught her off guard. She knew absolutely nothing about loving a man. But she was ready to learn with Devon. Her heart told her to trust the goodness in Devon St. Cloud and in that moment, standing in the moonlight, she went with her heart.

DEVON DIDN'T HEAR her approach, didn't know she was behind him until he felt the warmth of her palm on his back. He closed his eyes, unable to contain the sigh that escaped his lips. Her touch was like a balm to his soul and yet he fought it.

"I don't want your pity."

"Is that what you think I feel for you?"

Desire sliced through him at her words. Her hands began to massage his shoulders as if she thought she could rub away those years. Her fingers were magic and much stronger than he'd thought they would be. But then she continued to surprise him, didn't she?

"I grew up hearing about the family Alexandros," he said quietly, not wanting her to stop. "But I had no idea that the youngest son who'd left the act years ago was your father."

"Why didn't you mention that this had been your home when I told you on the plane?" she asked.

"I don't tell anyone," he said, closing his eyes as he remembered the wobbly words on the paper he'd just thrown in the river. "Wyatt Hathaway saved my life the day he got me the hell out of here."

"I just didn't realize you meant literally." Her

hands continued to work at the knot of tension in his neck and shoulders.

"If he hadn't come by that day when he did and seen Ray beating me, I would be dead now. My stepfather is a mean man who used his fists to make a point. My mother…"

"What about your mother?"

He'd never told anyone about his…family. But he remembered the things Paige had told him the night on the way to Billings, the way she'd opened up to him.

"My mother was too drunk to notice I was gone," he said, surprised by the bitterness in his voice. "You thought your family was…dysfunctional." He let out a laugh that held no humor.

"What about your father?" she asked quietly.

He shook his head. "Some guy she'd known before Ray. I guess there was a time when my mother didn't hide in a bottle. I've seen pictures of her when she was younger. She was beautiful." The pain was unbearable. If it wasn't for P.T.'s hands—

"I'm sure she was beautiful. Look how handsome you are."

He laughed at that and turned, opening his eyes. She was so close he didn't have to reach far. She looked like a ghost standing there in the long white nightgown. The moonlight cut through the thin cotton silhouetting her lush body beneath. He took her hands and pulled her to him.

"You are the one who is beautiful," he whispered.

She shook her head, dropping her lashes. "Sure with this black eye and my face all—"

He silenced her with a finger to her mouth, careful not to hurt her cut lip. "Everything about you is beautiful."

He took her hand, circling his thumb in the smooth warm skin of her palm, then moved up her wrist to feel the steady beat of her pulse. His gaze locked with hers in the light from the river's surface. Her pulse quickened beneath his thumb.

He had never wanted to kiss anyone more than he did her. The other kisses had been hurried. He wanted to take his time, to feel her lips beneath his, to trace the fullness with his tongue, explore her mouth. "Tell me if I hurt you," he said and leaned down to gently kiss her lips.

He felt he could kiss her the rest of his life and always be surprised by her wonderful mouth. He pulled her closer. Her eyes widened as their bodies touched, as if she'd only just realized what she was doing to him.

"Are you surprised I want to make love to you?" he whispered.

She bit her lower lip, her eyes full, but shook her head. "Would it surprise you to hear I want you to?"

He smiled and cupped the back of her neck as he drew her closer until their lips touched again. He brushed his mouth over hers. He felt her tremble as he touched his tongue to her lips, following the full contour of her mouth, entranced by the taste of her.

His hand curved down around her slim throat to the top of the gown. He slipped the gown off one shoulder, then the other exposing the lightly freckled skin to the moonlight.

Her nipples were dark and hard against the thin white fabric. He cupped one breast with his hand and she gasped, arching against his hand, her lips parting, her head thrown back. He thumbed the rigid rosy tips of her breasts and dropped his mouth to hers again, invading the warm wetness inside with his tongue. When he pulled back to look at her, what he saw in her eyes threatened to drop him to his knees.

PAIGE HAD NEVER KNOWN that the right man's touch would bring such pleasure. He freed her breasts, the gown falling to her bare feet. He moaned and ran his hands across the tops of her bare shoulders, then down to lift the weight of her breasts in his hands.

''Oh, Paige,'' he groaned as he pulled her down to the warm, worn wood of the deck. He took the tip of one breast in his mouth. She could feel his tongue doing amazing things to her nipple. She let out a gasp of pleasure and surprise as he bit down gently.

He released the nipple, his eyes dark as he met her gaze. His mouth dropped to the other breast. She arched her back, pressing her breast hard to his mouth.

"Devon, please," she pleaded, needing a release before she exploded. "Please don't stop."

His warm hand moved from her breast down her ribs to her belly and farther. She let out a cry as his light touch sent a jolt arcing through her. He pulled her all the way down until he was lying next to her. He held her gaze as his fingers gently touched the warm wet notch between her legs. She thought she would die from the pleasure of it.

He took her higher and higher, his gaze holding hers until she felt the sky around them explode in a burst of bright light, felt his lips on hers as he took her into his arms. His hand cupped one breast, teasing the already hard bud until her body quivered.

Only then did he roll her over onto her back and gaze down at her as he gently entered her. She let out a moan of pain and pleasure. His eyes widened. "Paige," he whispered, then shook his head. "Oh, Paige."

She wrapped her arms around his neck and pulled him down to her kiss. He began to move inside her, a slow, steady building like waves coming harder and harder against a smooth beach. Like a storm building and building until the night exploded in a flash of brilliant light.

He let out a cry, his arms wrapped around her back, hers about his neck. She loved the weight of him on her. The warmth as her body quieted into a pleasured, peaceful calm. She now knew euphoria. She was finally a woman.

The warm, orange-scented breeze cooled their

bodies as they lay bathed in the moonlight, sheltered
by the trees and the sweep of the river, holding each
other.

PAIGE FELT the warm blood on her face and arms
and fought to surface. Running. Screaming. The
thump of her father's heart against her cheek as he
ran with her toward the house, the sound of a voice
raised in anger echoing in her ears.

But they never reached the house. The car she'd
heard before appeared, and the bad man was hurting
her daddy. The bad men were putting something
over her face as they took her away from her
daddy— She wanted Boo Bear. Boo Bear!

Paige woke screaming and reached for Devon,
needing to feel his arms around her. He wasn't next
to her. Nor was she on the dock.

Devon burst into the trailer bedroom. He looked
as if he'd been asleep. He wore nothing but jeans,
just as he had on the dock earlier. She stared at his
bare chest, remembering the feel of it against her
breasts. Or had that just been a dream too?

She pushed herself up to a sitting position against
the headboard in the bed where Mae had left her
earlier, her eyes starting to adjust to the light, the
nightmare still with her.

"It's okay, baby," he said, pulling her into
his arms.

She breathed him in. It hadn't been a dream. This
close to him, she could remember the feel of his
body on hers, the pressure, the pain, the pleasure.

He must have carried her back to bed after they made love.

"Devon," she cried, shaking from the nightmare that was now slipping away, leaving only a residue of horror.

"She just had a bad dream," Mae said from the doorway. "I'll make her some warm milk."

Paige closed her eyes, hugging Devon to her, never wanting to let him go. "It was so awful."

"You're awake now," he said, holding her tightly. "You're safe."

Yes. Safe. The nightmare hunkered at the edge of her memory, echoing what Buford Wright had told her.

"Who is Boo Bear?" Mae asked as she came into the room with a glass of warm milk.

Paige pulled back from Devon in surprise.

"What is it?" Devon asked, looking scared.

Not half as scared as Paige.

Mae pressed the glass into her hand.

Paige wrapped her fingers around the warmth, needing it desperately. "How do you know about Boo Bear?"

"You were crying out for Boo Bear, begging someone to go back for him," Mae said.

"My father." Paige froze, her heart a hammer trying to beat its way out of her chest. "Oh, God."

"Don't try to—" Devon started to say.

"Leave her be," Mae ordered.

Paige stared, unseeing, at the warm milk in her hands. "I *was* there. In the park that day. They didn't see me. I was in my little hiding place under the tree.'' She remembered the hollow beneath it. Like the tree she'd hidden in the night at Rare Finds. ''I heard the men arguing. I climbed out. There was a loud sound, then another. I was in my father's arms. He was running. There was blood everywhere. Only—'' She dragged a breath from her chest. ''Boo Bear. I'd dropped Boo Bear.''

She looked up, her eyes slowly focusing on Devon. ''I was there when Judge Tripp was murdered.''

CHAPTER FOURTEEN

DEVON STARED AT PAIGE, the ramifications of what she was saying scaring him. He tried to tell himself it was just a dream. Probably brought on by what that cop, Buford, had told her. Of course she couldn't have been there. And a man like Wyatt Hathaway wouldn't have kidnapped a three-year-old child.

"I was hiding in the base of an old tree. I heard men arguing, then my father was running with me in his arms," she said. "But just before we reached the house, someone attacked him and took me."

"Took you where?" he asked.

She shook her head and looked close to tears. "That's all I know."

Devon looked up to see Mae standing in the bedroom doorway. "She just had a bad dream," he said, unable to get P.T.'s bloodcurdling scream out of his head. Nor the look on her face when he'd come into the bedroom. She'd been terrified. Was it possible she really had been there, really had seen the murder and been what...? Kidnapped by someone? Just not Wyatt Hathaway?

Mae nodded and gave him a look that said there

was no such thing as just a bad dream. She looked worried and afraid for P.T. He knew the feeling well. "It's almost daylight. I'll make some coffee."

Devon turned his attention back to P.T. He noticed she held the key in her hand, her thumb rubbing the surface as if the rest of the story was in the cool slick metal. "P.T.—"

"That's not really my name. It's Paige. Paige... Alexander."

"Okay. Paige." He took an extra blanket from a nearby chair and wrapped it around her shoulders. Her hair was blond again, almost back to its brilliant shade. She looked like the woman he'd met that first night in New Orleans, but he knew she wasn't. This woman was stronger, more confident, all the more captivating.

"You don't believe me, do you?" she whispered.

"I told you, I don't know what to believe. But it's obvious the dream was very real for you."

She nodded, her thumb pad rubbing at the key.

He picked up the photograph next to the bed of the Alexandros flying trapeze family. "When I saw your father at the funeral home, I knew I'd seen him somewhere before." He shook his head. No wonder he had a bad feeling about where. Gibtown.

Suddenly Paige's fingers stilled. She stared down at the key as if surprised to see it in her hand and let out a small cry.

"What is it?" he cried in alarm.

"Do you see it?" she asked excitedly as she held out the key. "It's faint, worn down so much that I didn't realize what I was feeling. The Alexandros flying symbol. Like the bird tattoos. Like on the side of the circus wagon in the photo.''

He took the key and ran his thumb over the faint ridges on the key. "P.T.—Paige, I don't feel—"

"It is the key to the wagon," Mae said from the doorway, her voice breaking as she stepped into the room and held out her hand for it.

Devon laid the key into her small palm and her gnarled fingers closed over it as if it were a priceless jewel that had long been lost.

"Where did you get this?" Mae asked, tears welling in her eyes.

Paige told Mae the story over coffee in the trailer living room. The older woman listened quietly, glancing at Devon periodically, worry in her aged eyes.

When Paige finished, Mae said, "The bird was a symbol of flight, a symbol of the flying family, Alexandros. Your great grandfather had this key made along with our circus wagon many, many years ago.''

"Where is this wagon now?" Devon asked.

She shook her head. "It was lost years ago."

"No," Paige said getting to her feet. "It has to be at Rare Finds. Why else would a key like this and my name and the Big Timber address have been in the package?" She looked to Mae.

Mae smiled. "It would be a wonderful thing if the wagon had survived." She sounded as skeptical as Devon felt.

"You searched the antique shop," he said to Paige. "A circus wagon isn't something you would have missed. And how would it have gotten to Montana in the first place?" He shook his head. "I think we have to accept that we might never find what this key opens."

"That would be very unfortunate," Mae said, meeting his gaze. "How else will you ever know the truth?"

What was she trying to tell him? That he wouldn't like what they found? He didn't like any of this especially, even the chance that Paige's dream might actually be true.

He didn't need to tell them that whoever was after him and Paige and this damned key weren't going to stop. But what if Paige had been there that day? What if she was starting to remember and her father really hadn't been the killer? Her life would be in even more danger if the killer found out.

"I'm going to find out what this key opens," Paige said. "I'm going back to Rare Finds."

He knew that determined angle of her chin, just as he knew each curve and hollow of her body, knew the feel of her against him, the scent of her, the sound of her. He could never forget their lovemaking earlier on the dock. Nor did he have any intention of leaving her side until the evidence was found. After that— He didn't dare think about it.

"Looks like we're going back to Montana," he said, suddenly afraid of what they *would* find.

Paige rushed to him and kissed him, making him

ache with an unbearable need for her. He knew their
fates were now hanging on finding an old circus
wagon and what might be hidden inside. *If* the
wagon still existed.

"We will see each other again," Mae promised
her grandniece as Paige hugged her goodbye and
thanked her for her help.

ON THE PLANE TRIP back to Montana, Devon held
Paige's hand, her head on his shoulder as she slept.
He wished he could drift off, find oblivion. Instead
he couldn't shake the bad feeling that they'd gotten
out of Florida too easily. He told himself that the
judge had taken care of Fiona and whoever the man
was who was working with her, that's why he and
Paige weren't being tailed. They were home free, so
to speak.

So how did he explain the bad feeling in his gut?
He told himself it was because he knew they weren't
going to find a circus wagon back at Rare Finds.
Paige had this crazy idea that the house had secret
rooms.

"I remember seeing a roll of blueprints behind
the counter on the first floor," she'd said on the way
to the airport. "The wagon is in that house. I just
feel it."

He hadn't wanted to dampen her spirits. He loved
seeing her excited, hopeful, happy. He'd seen her
happy only once. That night on the dock. Happy and
content in his arms. He desperately wanted both
again.

As the plane landed at Gallatin Field outside of Bozeman, Devon watched for a tail. Maybe he was just being paranoid. Maybe he had nothing to worry about. Except for what Michael Alexander had hidden, he thought, as Paige opened her eyes when the plane's wheels touched down.

He knew how badly she wanted to believe she might have seen something that would prove her father was innocent. He hated to see her get her hopes up.

He kissed her, aching to do a whole lot more. When this was over—

She pulled back from the kiss and smiled at him, her fingers toying with the ring on her necklace. She'd told him it was her mother's wedding ring. It was hardly worn and there was something terribly sad about that.

"I'm right about a secret room," she said. "I know what's in it. My life."

PAIGE DIDN'T KNOW why she hadn't realized it before.

As soon as they landed, she called Franklin on her cell phone to confirm her theory.

It took a little badgering, but he finally gave her a number of one of the old-timers in town, Myrtle Westfield.

"I'm doing some genealogy on my family and I need to know about the Martins who lived just outside of town on the road to McLeod. They owned

Rare Finds, the antique place,'' Paige said when an
elderly woman answered the phone.

"The Martins? Bill and Tess Martin. I knew them
well.''

"Did they have a daughter?'' Paige asked and
held her breath.

"Why, yes, Simone. A beautiful girl. I heard she
moved back after her parents died and reopened the
antique shop, but then was killed. A hit-and-run accident, I think. So tragic.''

"Yes, thank you,'' Paige said. "That's all I
needed to know.'' She disconnected and looked at
Devon. "I was right. It was my mother's family's
house.'' She headed for the rental car agency.

"You already suspected that,'' he said, catching
up to her.

"Yes, but don't you see? There is nothing of me
or my father in that house—except for this wedding
ring.'' She clutched the gold band in her fingers.
"My mother must have been wearing it, took it off
and put it in the jewelry box before she flew to Florida.''

He nodded, obviously not seeing where she was
headed with this as they got their car and headed
toward Big Timber.

"I found the one photograph and the box that the
others had been in,'' she said. "So I know she saved
the things from our lives together and she kept them
at her parents' house in Big Timber. So where are
they? She hid them. Must have thought she had to.
I'm telling you, they're in that house somewhere.''

He looked skeptical.

"Chloe told me that the house was built by a wealthy sheep rancher back in the days when the sheep and cattle ranchers were at war over the range and still vulnerable to Indian attacks," she said. "Some of those old houses have hidden rooms or passages to get the family out and safe."

He looked over at her as he took the interstate east. "Who's Chloe?"

"A woman who says she was my mother's best friend."

"You don't believe her?"

"I don't know. I never knew my mother to have a friend," she said as he drove. "I've been thinking. How did the blackmailer get the page from my mother's address book? She had just moved to Big Timber so that hadn't been her address for long. The page had been ripped from the small address book I found in her purse, so she had it with her the day she was killed."

"You think she ripped it out and gave it to someone," he said.

"Yes, my father. How else did the blackmailer get it?"

"Good point," he said as he frowned at the highway ahead.

"What if my mother gave him the key as well?"

He shot Paige a look. "You think she had the evidence hidden all these years?"

"Only, I don't think she knew it. If I'm right, my mother would have taken it to the authorities."

"Unless keeping it hidden was the only way she could protect you and her husband," he said.

Paige nodded. "There's a chance, isn't there, that the evidence proves my father didn't kill Judge Tripp?"

He looked over at her, reached out and took her hand and squeezed it. "I wish there was some way we both could be right about the men we thought of as our fathers."

Yes, but that wasn't possible, was it.

Paige wanted to believe her mother had given her father the address from her book, planned to fly to San Francisco the next day to tell Paige everything, and then the two of them were going to meet her father back in Big Timber at Rare Finds. If something happened to Simone, Michael Alexander could find Paige in Big Timber.

But what about the evidence? What if it didn't even exist? What if this had been for nothing?

She looked over at Devon. He was frowning again and looking worried.

"If your theory is even partially right," he said, "then the person who killed your father took the note and key from him and put it into a box. Why didn't that person just get the evidence?"

"Because he or she didn't know where it was?"

He shot her a look that sent a chill through her. "They needed you to find it."

"*Us* to find it."

The valley opened up, tall grass running to foothills to mountains. Big Timber sat at the center of it alongside the blue-green sweep of the Yellowstone River, the snowcapped Crazy Mountains in the distance, the afternoon sun making them gleam. And for a moment, it took her breath away. She'd been so filled with grief, she hadn't noticed just how beautiful this country was.

It seemed different now that she knew for sure this had been where her mother was raised. Even the old house set against the cottonwoods and the Boulder River seemed more inviting.

She stared at it as Devon parked out front. *The answer is in that house,* she thought with a chill. Dear God, she was finally going to know the truth.

Devon locked and bolted the door behind them as they entered the house.

"You get the blueprints," he said. "I want to make sure we're alone."

The house seemed eerily quiet. Whoever had taken the body the sheriff couldn't find, had left no trace that a man had been killed here. Someone had cleaned up well. Just as they had cleaned up at the Eternal Peace Funeral Home.

Why go to so much trouble? Devon knew it was just as Paige had guessed. Whoever had found the key and note hadn't located what they were looking for. They'd needed Paige to find it for them. But what part was Devon to play in it?

He had a bad feeling he already knew.

"I have the blueprints," she called up.

He checked the apartment, then came back down. They seemed to have the house to themselves. He hurried back downstairs to her, anxious to see the blueprints. If there was a secret room, he wanted to find it quickly. The sooner the evidence was found, the sooner Paige would be out of danger— She handed him the blueprints.

He spread the paper across an old oak table priced at four hundred and fifty dollars. "You'd better have a look at these since you know the house better than I do."

She leaned over his shoulder, filling him with the scent of her. Damned distracting, this desire that plagued him whenever she was near.

He thumbed through the blueprints floor by floor.

"Wait a minute," she said. "There on the first floor. It shows a stairway going down, but there isn't one."

He looked up at her. "Isn't there?"

They moved to the spot on the blueprints where there was supposed to be a stairway. They found a wall instead.

"Maybe they changed their mind," he said. "Since according to the blueprints the basement doesn't extend that far over."

She shook her head. "It must have a secret panel you have to open."

"Uh-huh." He looked over at her.

"Trust me."

He did trust her, but he hated to see her get her hopes up. Worse, it was catching.

She helped him move the furniture away from the wall. He tapped on the plaster. "It's definitely hollow," he said. Was it possible she was right?

He began pressing here and there on the wall. No secret panel opened.

Paige had gone farther down the wall and was

looking at an old wall light. He watched her flip the switch. Nothing happened.

"I wonder if the bulb is burned out or—" As she turned the lamp to inspect the bulb, a panel in the wall popped open.

Devon swore. "You're good at this stuff."

She grinned. "How about that."

He pried the door open while she found a flashlight. He took the light from her and shone it down the steps. "Maybe you should wait here."

"Right."

"At least let me lead the way," he said. "Let's put something in the door to make sure it doesn't close while we're down there."

"Good thinking." She pulled a wooden bench over to prop the door open.

"Come on," he whispered and started down the steps. It was dark and dank. He shone the light on the stairs. There were footprints in the dust.

He saw Paige shiver and knew it wasn't the cold that had raised goose bumps on her skin. He had no idea what they'd find, but he didn't think it would be a circus wagon. There was no way Michael Alexander could have gotten a wagon in here. Not in one piece.

He could hear Paige right behind him, felt her hand on his back as he reached the ground and she joined him. He shone the light around the room. It was small with floor-to-ceiling shelves filled with jars of canned goods on the three open walls. Just a root cellar separate from the basement. No circus wagon.

Paige looked as disappointed as he felt. They had

looked everywhere. Now he was wondering if there had ever been any evidence or if it had all been a ruse, nothing more than a bluff to get money from Wyatt Hathaway.

"Devon," she said, touching his arm. She motioned to the wall.

Behind the shelves on the back wall facing the stairs was a circus poster. He moved closer, focusing the beam on the picture. At the center was a circus wagon—the Alexandros wagon.

He shone the light on the floor, noticing the scrape marks on the concrete. "Stand back." He pulled on the shelving. The wall of shelves swung toward him a few feet. He shone the light into the space behind it. The light picked up something brightly colored. He let out an oath. And heard Paige's sharp intake of breath.

"There it is," she said and squeezed through with him into the room.

The circus wagon had obviously been brought down here in pieces and put back together. A labor of love, he thought. The walls were lined with circus memorabilia from the Alexandros family circus days.

"My father couldn't have collected all of this. He was in prison," Paige said, turning to look at him. "My mother must have done this for him."

"Or for you," he said. "You look so much like your grandmother." He saw that she was crying. Just as she'd thought, her life was in marked boxes along the walls. Paige's first Christmas. Paige's dolls. Paige's artwork.

He pulled her into his arms, buried his face in her

hair, breathing her in, suddenly afraid of losing her. As if he had her to lose.

She pulled back, dried her tears and reached into her purse. She handed him the key.

The wagon was beautifully painted, the symbol of flight on the door with the stars and moon above the stylized bird. Over the door was painted the name: Alexandros.

They let out a collective sigh as the key fit perfectly.

Feeling like there was a two-ton weight on his chest, Devon turned the key and pulled. The door swung open. He looked over at Paige for a moment. He could see she was holding her breath. He shone the light inside the wagon.

For a moment he thought it was empty. Then the light caught on something in the corner. A plastic bag with— He heard Paige gasp. "It's Boo Bear!"

He pulled the bag toward him. Through the plastic the teddy bear stared out at him. As he started to remove it from the bag, he noticed the dark stains on the fur—and a man's leather glove, the initials visible through the plastic: W.I.H. Wyatt Ivan Hathaway.

He jerked his hand back. Boo Bear was covered in dried blood. Just like in Paige's dream. So was the glove.

"I'll take that," said a female voice behind them.

CHAPTER FIFTEEN

PAIGE TURNED at the familiar voice.

Chloe Summers stood in the narrow opening, a gun in her hand. "FBI," she said, flashing her ID with her free hand. "I'll take that."

At first Paige was too stunned to move. "FBI? You were just waiting for me to find this?"

"A lot of people have been waiting," Chloe said. She motioned for Devon to toss her the bag.

Devon reached as if to hand it to her, but at the last minute, swung the bag, knocking the weapon the agent held aside. The next thing Paige knew, Devon was gone through the space and the shelving wall was closing behind him, trapping her and Chloe. He had taken the evidence. His last words ringing in her ears. "I'm sorry, Paige, but some things are more important than justice," he yelled through the wall.

Chloe swore as she tried to push the wall open. "He put something against it."

"He took the evidence," Paige said, still shocked that Devon had done that.

Chloe nodded solemnly. "Proof of who killed Judge George Tripp twenty-three years ago."

"It wasn't my father," Paige said.

"I believe you, but without that evidence." She looked around the room. "We might as well make ourselves comfortable. I called for backup before I came down here, but who knows how long it will take them to find us. I'm sure he closed the hidden panel upstairs."

"I can't believe he would do this," Paige said, near tears. "He believes he owes Judge Hathaway his life." He was determined to pay that debt no matter what. Even if it meant betraying her. She looked over at Chloe. "So you never even probably knew my mother."

"Your mother and I were best friends, just like I told you," Chloe said. "We grew up together here in Big Timber. It's one of the reasons I was put on the case when your mother came back to town after she was diagnosed with cancer."

"You knew about the cancer?"

Chloe nodded and moved to put her arms around Paige. "I tried to get her to let me help her, but she was too afraid for you. I knew she was in trouble. She just disappeared with you all those years ago after Michael died. When she came back to Big Timber, she told me about the cancer and that Michael was alive and coming back. She said he had hidden evidence to prove his innocence and nail the person who really did kill Judge George Tripp twenty-three years ago."

JUDGE WYATT HATHAWAY opened the door, his gaze going to the plastic bag Devon held. He smiled and stood aside. "I knew you wouldn't let me down. Come in. Here, let me take your coat."

Devon slipped out of his leather jacket, but held on to the plastic bag with the bear and glove inside.

The judge hung the jacket by the front door. "I was just going to make myself a drink," he said, leading the way into the living room. "Join me."

Devon thought for once that he really could use a drink. A good reason not to have one. But he said nothing, just followed the judge into the living room, glancing around as he did, wondering if the judge had really taken care of Fiona.

Wyatt turned from the bar with a glass of bourbon in each hand. He looked pleased with himself. With Devon.

Devon took one of the bourbons.

"To the future," the old man said and lifted his glass.

"To the future." Devon took a sip of the strong liquor. He'd never developed a taste for it and to-night it turned his stomach. He put down his almost full glass and handed the plastic bag with the teddy bear and glove in it to the judge.

"So this is it," Wyatt said, glancing through the plastic to see the glove. He closed his eyes, his hands clutching the top of the bag as he let out a sigh. Opening his eyes, he stared at the contents. "A teddy bear?"

"Seems Michael Alexander's little girl was there with her teddy bear," Devon said.

The judge shook his head. "All these years and all because of a glove and a teddy bear."

"It's a little more than that," Devon said. "The dark spots on the bear's fur and the lining underneath appear to be bloodstains—just like on the glove."

Wyatt shrugged. "There wasn't anything else?"

"No. This was it."

The judge let out a breath. "Then it's finally over."

"You know, when Alexander saved that bear twenty-three years ago, DNA testing wasn't what it is now," Devon said. "Nowadays I'll bet a lab could get enough DNA from that blood-soaked fabric. If the killer was wounded and some of his blood and Judge George Tripp's is on that bear it would be damned incriminating."

"I suppose it is well preserved enough that a lab could get DNA from it." The judge studied him. "What makes you think the killer was wounded? Is that what his daughter said?"

"She doesn't remember anything about that day."

Wyatt lifted a brow. "That's probably just as well. She wouldn't want to remember seeing her father murder a man." He set the plastic bag on the coffee table and went to refill his glass.

"But I would think after being blackmailed by this man all these years that you would want some kind of justice. Even revenge. I know I would."

The judge turned to watch Devon pick up the plastic bag and walk to the fireplace.

"What would be the point?" Wyatt asked. "There isn't anyone who can hurt me further. Michael Alexander is dead and I have the...evidence he manufactured to frame me."

"You're not worried about the daughter, then," Devon said, turning on the gas. Flames licked at the logs.

"Why should I be? She has nothing against me, right?"

Devon shook his head. "Like you said, it's all over."

"Yes."

Devon opened the glass doors and in one swift movement, tossed the plastic bag with the glove and teddy bear into the flames. The plastic bag caught fire first, disappearing in a burst of heat. The bear burned more slowly, plastic eyes melting as the once golden fur curled and charred black.

The judge watched it burn until a small pile of stuffing lay smoking on the logs.

Devon closed the glass doors and looked at the old man. "That's it."

"You did a good job," Wyatt said. "You'll be rewarded. In fact, name anything you'd like and if it's in my power, it's yours." He smiled, assured no doubt, that there was little that wasn't in his power.

"There is something I would like," Devon said as he glanced at the still smoldering stuffing in the fireplace, then at Wyatt again. "I'd like the truth."

The old man looked taken aback for a moment.

"The evidence is destroyed. It's just you and me. What really happened the day Judge Tripp died?" Devon asked.

"I already told you."

Devon shook his head. "You said anything I wanted. Is the truth that hard for you?"

The judge's eyes narrowed. "I think you'd better go. Neither of us wants to say something we'll regret." He turned his back on Devon and walked to the fireplace to stare down into the flames. "I think you'll see things clearer once you get the Alexander woman out of your system—"

"Why me?"

"I beg your pardon?" Wyatt turned with his bourbon to frown at him.

"That day in Gibtown, why did you stop your car and take me with you?"

"I would think it was obvious. Your stepfather would have killed you. If not that day, then another." He took a sip of his drink, watching Devon over the rim of the glass. "You don't owe me anything, if that's what you're worried about."

Devon laughed. "That's not what worries me right now. What worries me is what you were doing in Gibsonton that day."

Wyatt waved the glass, waving off the question. "What does it matter?"

"It matters. After my stepfather would beat me and my mother would sober up, she would cry and promise me that my father was Somebody and that someday he'd come and take me away with him."

The judge took another drink. "Why don't you take some time off. Take the private jet you had in Montana. Fly wherever you want. You can go anywhere in the world. It's all yours. When you get back we can talk about you taking over my enterprises after I become a Louisiana Supreme Court Justice."

Devon smiled as the old man dangled the bribe in front of him. He thought about all the years that he'd looked the other way, always weighing what the judge had done for him against any improprieties he might have witnessed. Proving again and again that he could be bought.

"Yes, the Louisiana Supreme Court," Devon said. "You know my mother left me a letter before she died."

"I wouldn't believe anything your mother had to tell you," the old man said. "She was a drunk who gave up her only child."

"Yes," Devon agreed. "At least she admitted to being my mother. But then you wouldn't look as magnanimous if you had taken in your own son from an affair with a woman from a carny family, right? Was Jimmy another one of your affairs? Or was he just cover so you could keep me with you, someone you could use to your advantage when the time came? Were you ever going to tell me the truth?"

"Take that trip. It will clear your head," the judge said.

Devon walked to the door, grabbed his leather jacket on his way to the foyer. "I won't be needing the private jet. I won't be needing anything else from you because when I walk out that door, I don't plan on ever seeing you again."

"You'll be back," the judge said confidently as Devon opened the door and took one last look at Judge Wyatt Hathaway and the evidence smoldering in the fireplace, then he turned and walked out, closing the door behind him.

He was almost to the rental car when he heard someone behind him. He turned, telling himself the old man wouldn't try to stop him. He saw the gun first, then the person holding it and thought for a moment he was seeing a ghost.

PAIGE CLOSED HER EYES, the pain too intense. Had Devon known all along? How else did she explain him taking the evidence and leaving her and Chloe down here?

So much for trusting your heart.

She felt heartsick.

"Your mother had been living in fear the past twenty-three years. But now that she knew she was dying, it freed her to come home," Chloe said. "She wanted to nail Hathaway. She just had to be sure that you would be safe especially after the kidnapping."

She really had been kidnapped?

"I guess your father made a deal with him to get you back. But he knew there was no way Hathaway was going to let him stay alive—or you."

"That's why he faked his death."

"And helped you and your mother disappear. Then they were going to meet up. Only your father never made it," Chloe said. "Your mother really did believe he was dead."

Paige understood now her mother's sadness all those years.

"We assume Hathaway couldn't have another murder on his hands, especially Michael Alexander's so he shipped him to South America and saw that he was imprisoned there. Last week, your father escaped. He didn't know what had happened to the proof he had that Hathaway had killed Tripp."

"My mother had it, but she was afraid to use it." Because she'd feared for Paige's life. And maybe Michael's? "And the photo from the Florida newspaper about a circus?"

"I would imagine it was their signal," Chloe said. "We had a tail on her but she lost us. Did you know your father comes from a family of circus performers? Trapeze."

"Yes, I just found that out."

Chloe stilled. "Sounds like my backup is here." She got to her feet. "You realize I have to go after Devon."

"Why should I care?"

Chloe smiled sadly. "I think you lost more than the evidence to Devon St. Cloud."

More than Chloe knew. Paige heard the sound of the panel door opening.

"You know he's going to take the evidence straight to Hathaway," Paige said.

Chloe nodded. "Once the judge has what is in that bag, he'll be home free. Except for you. And Devon."

Paige stared at Chloe, her heart in her throat. "You think he'll kill him?"

"If we don't get there first," the FBI agent said.

Devon was walking into a trap. A trap he'd set for himself.

The wall of shelves began to move. Chloe stepped toward the opening to greet the cops.

Paige caught a whiff of perfume an instant too late to warn Chloe.

The redhead hit the FBI agent with the butt of the gun in her hand. The blow caught Chloe before she could pull her weapon. She dropped to her knees and looked up at the redhead. "Fiona Fuentes." Then Chloe hit the concrete floor.

Paige jerked her gaze from Chloe to the redhead. "Fuentes?"

The redhead smiled. "I heard you met my father at the circus." She laughed and pointed the gun in her hand at Paige's head. "Come on. There's someone who is dying to meet you."

CHAPTER SIXTEEN

PAIGE TRIED to catch her breath but it felt as if the roof had fallen in on her. Fiona Fuentes had a private jet standing by at an airfield outside of Big Timber, a similar one, Fiona said, to the one that had taken Devon to Louisiana. Within minutes, they were in the air. Paige was too upset to be airsick.

She should have been scared. Should have been plotting an escape plan. All she could think about was Devon. About his betrayal.

But that wasn't all. She thought about the way he'd held her, the way he'd made love to her last night on the dock, the way he'd protected her. She knew in her heart that it hadn't all been about the evidence to him. She'd seen it in his eyes that last moment, when he'd looked back at her in the secret room. Regret. And what had his parting words been?

Some things are more important than justice?

How could he say that? What could possibly be more important?

"You know he thought I was you," Fiona said smiling, then added at Paige's confused look, "Wyatt Hathaway. I became his lover because he thought I was Michael Alexander's daughter. Politics really does make strange bedfellows."

There were some things Paige didn't want to know. She closed her eyes and tried to come up with a plan to get herself out of this. She should have been more afraid. Instead, anger and hurt overwhelmed even her fear.

She couldn't believe Devon had taken the evidence to Wyatt Hathaway and yet that's what he said he was going to do from the start, wasn't it. At least he never lied about that.

But he had to know that Wyatt would destroy the evidence. Had to know that Wyatt was the murderer. Had to have planned it this way from the beginning.

So why couldn't she get herself to believe it? Because she was in love with him. Last night on the dock, she'd known it. And it was true. She loved Devon St. Cloud and she wanted to believe he'd been taken in by the judge. Misplaced loyalty. No way would Devon protect a killer. Not the Devon she knew.

"You realize you can't get away with this," Paige said, opening her eyes to look at Fiona. At least she hoped that was true. "That was an FBI agent back there. Once her backup gets there—"

"By the time they find her and come after me, I will have a new identity and be living in another country," Fiona said and smiled. "Did I mention that I'll be rich?"

"Wyatt Hathaway can't get away that easily."

Fiona laughed. "Wyatt Hathaway can get away with anything. Even murder."

So it appeared, and the evidence was no doubt

gone by now. Paige felt sick. If Chloe was right, all Wyatt had to do now was get rid of her and Devon. Unless Devon was so dedicated to the judge that he was safe. She almost wished that were the case.

"Won't be long and you'll be seeing Devon again," Fiona said as if reading her thoughts.

DEVON WOKE, head aching, to voices.

"You shouldn't have hit him so hard." Wyatt Hathaway's voice.

"He's got a hard head, he'll be all right."

Devon opened his eyes at the sound of Jimmy's voice and stared at him, shocked. "You're alive."

Jimmy laughed. "See, I told you he had a hard head."

Devon tried to get up from the couch where he lay. The room swam. He managed to push himself into a sitting position and saw where he was. In the living room of Wyatt Hathaway's house. It all looked so normal. Him and Jimmy and the old man together here.

He could almost kid himself that none of the rest of it had happened, all just a bad dream. Except for the ache in his heart that was Paige.

"You told me Jimmy was dead."

Wyatt nodded. "I was afraid that getting the evidence for me wouldn't be enough incentive. But I knew how you felt about Jimmy. If you thought he'd been killed because of this—" Wyatt waved his bourbon glass in the air. "Obviously, my little deception did the trick."

Devon swore under his breath. "So, you've been in on it all along," he said to Jimmy.

"It was all Jimmy's idea," the old man said, sounding proud.

"Surprised? You always underestimated me, Devon," Jimmy said. "Always treated me like some kid brother you had to protect."

Devon rubbed his head. It hurt. "That man who shot at us at the funeral home—"

"A hired gun," Jimmy said. "Although he came a little too close for my comfort, but he was damned convincing, wasn't he? Too bad he had to be dispatched after that awful fall he took in that junk shop in Montana. What the hell was that on him?"

"A moose head," Devon said. His head ached but he couldn't tell how much of it was from the blow Jimmy had dealt him or from betrayal. "I don't get it. You already had the package. Why have Fiona put it in the coffin for me to find?" Where was Fiona? He felt sick with worry about Paige. He'd left her with an FBI agent. How much safer could she be? And yet he worried. The only place he would have felt she was safe was in his arms— and that wasn't the place to be right now.

"Unfortunately, Jimmy got a little carried away and killed Michael Alexander prematurely. A key and a piece of address book paper weren't very helpful," Wyatt said.

"But I had this plan," Jimmy said, sitting down on the coffee table in front of Devon, brandishing the weapon as he talked. "How about set it up where Devon finds the key and the address and name we already had from when we knocked off Simone Alexander?''

The anonymous letter that Paige had gotten. ''You got Paige to New Orleans.''

''You're there, man!'' Jimmy cried. ''I figured if anyone could find out what the key opened, it was you. But you might need a little help.''

''Paige.''

''We couldn't figure out why her name was with the key. She had to be the...key, so to speak.'' Jimmy laughed. ''I thought if we got you two together you just might be able to find the evidence, as bright as you are—and you did.''

''I played right into your hands,'' Devon said, looking past Jimmy to the judge. ''Gave you the evidence, even destroyed it for you. So what do you want from me now?''

Jimmy shot him a pitying look.

Devon heard a car door slam and his anxiety kicked up. He looked over his shoulder as the front door swung open. The last person on earth he wanted to see walked into the room.

PAIGE FELT A WAVE of relief at the sight of Devon sitting on the couch, followed quickly by fury.

He started to get up from the couch, but a man she recognized as the driver from the night at the funeral home, shoved him back down, ordering him to sit.

Jimmy? But Devon had said he was dead.

Devon looked like hell, she realized as Fiona shoved her down on the couch next to him. And Jimmy was holding a gun on them both. It was just like Chloe had figured. The judge couldn't let either of them live.

She met Devon's gaze. Any question she had about his loyalties was right there in his eyes. If only it wasn't too late—

"Paige Alexander."

She dragged her gaze from Devon to the gray-haired distinguished-looking man standing at the bar, who'd just spoken.

"Judge Wyatt Hathaway."

He saluted her with his drink. "I do wish we'd met under better circumstances. You are quite lovely."

Anger bubbled up, pushing aside the sheer terror she'd felt an instant before. "And you're a murderer."

He pretended her words were like a shot to his heart. Anger flickered in his gaze. "You may have destroyed my chances for the Louisiana Supreme Court, young woman. Something I've dreamed of my whole life."

She doubted he believed that. "Oh, you did that to yourself when you killed Judge George Tripp and tried to frame my father."

Wyatt shook his head. "You don't just look like your father. Let's get this over with," he said to Jimmy.

"The evidence is gone, let her go. She can't hurt

you," Devon said. He tried to get up from the couch, but Jimmy pushed him back down, waving the weapon at them both.

"She has already hurt me," the judge said. "And there is always the possibility that she will remember what happened that day in the park. True, she was so young.... But I prefer not to take the chance. I've spent the last twenty-three years looking for her and her mother. If Simone hadn't tried to see her husband one more time...."

Rage overtook her. Paige flew up off the couch before Jimmy could react. She launched herself at Hathaway. He was unprepared for her attack. She slammed him into the bar, and all the expensive bottles of bourbon came crashing down on his head. Blood mixed with bourbon as he slid down the wall to the floor, stunned but not out.

Fiona was on her in an instant, wrestling her up against the bar, fumbling for her weapon.

Wyatt was yelling, "Kill them! Kill them both!" and holding his bleeding head.

"You're going to kill me? Your own son," Devon asked, sounding too calm in all this chaos.

In that instant before all hell broke loose, Paige looked over at Devon.

Jimmy had the gun to Devon's head, but all of his attention was on Wyatt. "Your *son*?"

Even Fiona was distracted for a moment by that news.

Paige connected with Devon's dark gaze, his look jump-starting her heart. She grabbed up one of the bottles of bourbon from the bar and flung it at the distracted Jimmy. Fiona was still fumbling for her gun.

Grimacing even as she did it, Paige swept up another bottle and swung it at Fiona's red head. Whack.

Fiona dropped like a rock. Behind her, Paige could hear Jimmy and Devon struggling. She didn't bother to look, she scooped up Fiona's gun that had fallen to the floor when she collapsed and turned it on Wyatt who was struggling to get up, struggling to get a weapon from the cabinet behind the bar.

"Move and I will shoot you deader than hell," she swore. Deader than hell. She almost smiled, realizing just how much P. T. Alexander she had in her. "Tell Jimmy to let him go! Now!"

Behind her, she heard a gunshot then a horrible groan. Her heart leapt into her throat. Not Devon. Please, don't let it be Devon who's been shot.

DEVON STARED at Jimmy for a moment as they still struggled for the gun in the aftermath of the shot. Jimmy met his gaze and smiled, his fingers slowly letting go of the weapon.

"See ya, big bro," he said and slumped to the floor.

Devon closed his eyes for an instant, the loss of the man he'd loved as a brother no less now, even knowing that Jimmy had managed to live up to his genes—with Judge Wyatt Hathaway's help.

He turned to see Paige holding a gun on the judge

who was bleeding profusely on the floor and not going anywhere.

When he met Paige's gaze he saw the relief in her eyes.

"You took the evidence," she said, her lower lip trembling and her blue eyes filling with tears.

He nodded. "But I didn't give it to Wyatt." He'd purposely burned the teddy bear and glove before Wyatt had a good look at either. The real bear and glove were hidden at Rare Finds. And he had no doubt now that it would clear her father's name— and destroy Judge Wyatt Hathaway.

"You said some things were more important than justice," she said.

He moved to her. "They are. Like love," he said as he took the gun from her trembling hands and pulled her into his arms. This time Justice Wyatt Hathaway would not get away.

"Love?" Paige whispered.

"Yes, love."

"You damned fool," Wyatt spat. "You could have had everything."

"I do have everything," Devon said as he looked at Paige.

EPILOGUE

"You look beautiful."

Paige glanced past her reflection in the mirror in the church wedding room to Chloe standing behind her.

"I'm so glad you're here today," Paige said.

"Now don't go crying and ruining your makeup," Chloe warned her.

"She's right," Mae said as she straightened Paige's train. "Let us do all the crying. Are you ready?"

Paige looked into the mirror and saw a stranger in a wedding gown staring back at her. She was blond with blue eyes and a row of freckles across her nose. Paige Alexander.

She smiled at herself, liking what she saw. A lot had happened to her, but for the first time, she really liked who she was.

She felt free of the past. Wyatt Hathaway had been arrested. Her father had been exonerated.

Fiona would also be facing criminal charges, although Devon thought she might get a lighter sentence thanks to Paige asking the court for leniency in her case. Paige remembered Fiona's father that day at the circus, his reaction to her father's death. She had suspected then that he'd helped bring her parents together one last time. She felt she owed Antonio Fuentes. And like Devon, she liked to pay her debts.

Over the weeks after Wyatt's arrest, a lot of the story had come out. Harry "Gray" Grayson had been a former cop, a friend of Paige's father. He'd insisted on taking on the job of protecting Simone and Paige. His wife and son had died in a car accident and he'd quit the force, his life over. Protecting Simone and Paige had kept him alive all those years.

After his death, Simone had refused any more protection. She found out she had cancer and that Michael was still alive, but in prison in South America. She started doing everything she could to get him out—and financed his escape from prison.

Paige touched her mother's wedding ring, still on the chain around her neck. She had something old, something new, something borrowed from Mae and something blue from Chloe. She just wished her mother and father could have been here.

Looking past her own reflection, she met Mae's gaze in the mirror.

"She's here, honey," Mae said and winked. "She and your daddy, too."

Tears filled Paige's eyes as she reached for her great-aunt's hand.

"Your mother wanted you to have this place,

these roots that she had denied you all those years, and to find happiness here,'' Chloe said.

And that was exactly what Paige and Devon planned to do. They would keep the antique shop, but add a private investigations business. That way they both could work out of Rare Finds. Devon wanted a garden and a dog and children. He wanted her.

"Ready?" Mae asked.

Paige nodded. She couldn't wait to become Devon's wife.

"We'd better take our seats," Mae said to Chloe.

Franklin was waiting for Mae outside the door, looking handsome in his black suit, to take her to her seat.

"I can't believe Franklin," Chloe said with a grin. "Your aunt has put life back into that man!" She kissed Paige on the cheek. "Break a leg!"

Paige glanced once more at the mirror, smiled at the blonde looking at her and thought she caught a glimpse of P.T. grinning back at her.

You go, girl!

The door opened behind her and she turned as Buford Wright stuck his head in. He'd been moved to tears when she'd asked him to walk her down the aisle.

"There is nothing I'd like better," he'd said. "I always wanted a daughter." Buford had three grown sons.

He offered his arm and a smile. She took it as the music swelled.

As she and Buford started down the aisle in the same church her parents had been married in twenty-eight years ago, Paige could feel her parents with her. She saw them reflected in the faces packing the church, people who had known her mother and father so long ago.

Then she saw Devon. He couldn't have been more handsome in his tux. Her heart somersaulted in her chest and she had to fight for her next breath.

He smiled that killer all-dimples smile of his as she joined him. She felt herself begin to melt under his mesmerizing dark gaze as he promised to love her until death did they part.

"I love you, Paige St. Cloud," he said.

She smiled up at him, tears welling in her eyes.

"You may kiss your bride," the pastor said.

Devon took her in his arms and kissed her like she'd never been kissed before and she knew she'd finally come home.

Later, when she and Devon were alone and in each other's arms, snug in their new bed, he asked, "Are you sure you won't miss it?"

"Miss what?" she murmured as she snuggled against him.

"The adventure, the danger, the excitement."

"Oh, I think you'll provide plenty of excitement," she said and grinned over at him.

"You can always help me with investigative work if you feel the need for a little adventure," he said.

"Not me," Paige said adamantly.

We'll see about that, P.T. whispered with a grin. We'll just see about that.

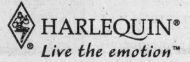

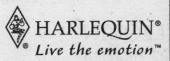

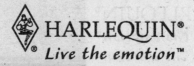

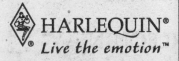

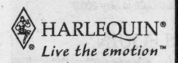

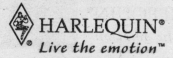